Life as a Teenage VAMPIRE

by Amanda Meuwissen

Life as a Teenage Vampire

Editor - Willow Wood

Cover design - Alexandra Ishchenko

Book layout - Mario Hernandez

Author Photo - Kyle Olson

ISBN-13: 978-1-943619-32-0
ISBN-10: 1-943619-32-8

First U. S. Edition: October 2016
Printed in the United States of America

For **Kaitlin** and **Anjali**

Possibly my biggest fans. Thank you.

Life as a Teenage VAMPIRE

by Amanda Meuwissen

CHAPTER 1

We watched in anticipation, expecting the teddy bear to explode, but it didn't rise up into the air so much as hop slightly and then fizzle as it caught on fire.

"Shit!" Connor cried.

I scrambled for the hose. "I thought you got the recipe from your dad!"

"I did! Do you know how many things *he's* set on fire?"

Connor ran to turn the hose on as I aimed it, holding steady once the first burst of pressure poured through. At least we'd been prepared—mostly.

"Connor? Emery? What are you two doing out there?" Connor's mom called from inside the house. "You're going to be late for school!"

"Coming, Mom!" Connor turned panicked eyes on me, which looked more honey-colored than brown whenever they went that wide, but he soon choked out a laugh. He turned the hose off again. "That bear never looked better. Maybe if you'd blown it up *before* giving it to Liz, she wouldn't have dumped you."

I rolled my eyes as I let the hose drop back to the grass. The overlarge teddy bear's now blackened fur was only slightly smoldering. Plus, it looked like rain soon. We'd just finished Easter Break, so having no snow on the ground this time of year was a blessing in Minnesota. Of course, the change in weather also meant I was due for another sinus infection. I sniffled miserably.

"I think Liz did me a favor," I said. "We were never right for each other." I was just tired of starting over—especially with only a couple months left of senior year.

"Ah, so blowing up the bear finally made you realize that, huh? I'm a genius." Connor came over and gave my shoulder a firm smack with his left hand. The dark teal prosthetic was one of the lighter designs he'd come up with recently.

"I'll never doubt your methods again, man," I muttered.

We shared a meaningful grin.

Connor always knew how to make me feel better after a break up. Usually it involved building something, like a new prototype for his robotics course, or a new design for his left arm that his mom would never actually let him wear to school, but today's break up remedy had been chemistry. Connor wasn't nearly as adept at chemistry.

"What are we going to do with that?" I pointed at the charred bear. We'd planned to rake up the blown up bits of fluff and toss them into the garbage before we left for school. Not as good of an idea when the bear was smoking.

Connor scratched his buzzed, dark blond head a moment, then grabbed the empty recycling bin from next to his family's garbage can and carefully set it on top of the bear. It didn't completely cover it—it was a large bear. I'd won it at the indoor carnival for Liz only a few weeks back, but she'd told me to hang onto it for her. I should have taken the hint then.

"It'll be fine 'til after school," Connor said. "Not hot enough to melt the bin—I don't think. I'll take care of it later."

"Thanks. I have work after class."

"Mr. Leonard is making you go?" Connor gaped at me as we grabbed our bags and headed out the back gate to his car.

His mom waved at us as she pulled out of the driveway in her Subaru. Georgia Daniels had the same dark blonde hair as her son, the same small dusting of freckles over her cheeks, but with pale blue eyes behind bronze-framed glasses.

"Arm?" she called out her open window.

Connor held up his prosthetic.

She nodded and headed off down the street.

"Geesh, they raise me on Japanese video games and wonder why I want a gun arm someday. She keeps threatening to homeschool me if I wear the Rocket-Punch one out of the house."

We climbed into Connor's hand-me-down white Thunderbird, which was in fairly good shape for its age, having belonged to his sister first, despite the one headlight that didn't pop up. He was a better driver than me even when he wasn't wearing his arm.

Connor was born without his left arm from just below the elbow. He and his dad had been building their own prosthetics for years, though Connor had surpassed his dad's skill level at about age twelve.

I groaned as I checked my phone for any last minute messages from my folks and saw that the battery was already at two-thirds life. "I hate this thing. It'll be dead by practice at this rate."

"You seriously need a new phone, Em."

"It's happening! Dad finally caved to buy me one. He promised it doesn't have to count as a graduation present."

"Lucky."

"Anyway, Mom said I should go to the Leonards, if you don't mind dropping me off later. If I wasn't coming from school, she'd probably send me with a casserole or something."

"What, no hot dish and bars?" Connor snickered in his best approximation of a terribly over the top Minnesotan accent.

"Mr. Leonard's a nice guy; I *want* to go. I can't imagine staying in that big house alone."

"Especially after someone was murdered in it," Connor said. We both shuddered.

Mrs. Leonard's murder was big news for such a small town. I'd worked for the Leonards since I was fifteen. They were both good people, and paid me way too much for the little yard work and landscaping I did. It was still hard to believe that Mr. Leonard had found his wife with a hole in her chest only a few days ago. Not even a bullet hole—bigger.

"Maybe it was gardening sheers," Connor said as we headed toward the school.

"Huh?"

"The murder weapon."

"I hope not, or they might look at me as a suspect." I'd meant it as a joke, but the possibility of that happening bottomed out my stomach. "No," I shook my head, "I heard it was rounder than that."

"From who? Did Tim say something?"

I tossed Connor my best 'are you shitting me' expression. Connor and I lived next door to each other. Tim Ashby—*Chief of Police*—lived across the street. And while he was friends with both of our parents, he never let anything official slip. Ever.

"Point taken," Connor said.

"I just heard a few rumors, but who knows what's true. And before you even ask," I hurried on when I saw Connor take a deep breath, "there is no way I am pushing Mr. Leonard for details. If he brings anything up, I'll listen, otherwise I'm planning on keeping him on happier topics. I don't think he's left the house all week other than for trips to the police station."

Connor shuddered again and gripped the steering wheel tighter, the geometric shapes of his teal fingers curling as closely around the rubber as his flesh and blood ones.

We pulled into the high school parking lot a few minutes later, and I immediately groaned. Almost 1000 kids in our high school and over 200 in our graduating class, and somehow we'd arrived at the same time as Liz. I watched her get out of her blue Corolla across from us, then averted my eyes before she could catch me staring.

"You could always switch teams," Connor said as he shifted into PARK. "But then you'd have to join me in lamenting the absolute travesty of how few viable males we have at our school, and we'd end up torching the place before graduation. I swear I am one conspirator away…"

"What about Nick?" I said. We'd waited an appropriate amount of time for Liz to get ahead of us without looking suspicious, and finally made for the school. "You guys have been spending a lot of time together lately."

"Well, yeah, because we're both doing backstage for the play. But…meh," Connor said dismissively. "He's not a bad guy. Good looking, sure. Totally my bro. But date him? No thanks. It's not that all the guys here suck, okay, I'm just not interested in anyone." He stared straight ahead, not even passing me a sideways glance. He always got touchy when his love life came up, but as much as I wanted to pry, his tight shoulders told me to lay off.

"We'll just have to wallow in singleness together then," I said. "Again."

The truth was, Connor wasn't wrong. There were plenty of cool people at our school. Our class was small enough that everyone knew each other but still big enough that we weren't all friends. And yet, when I considered dating someone new, it felt like there were no options left.

"Hey, Mavus! *Excuse* me, Mister Sped Out of the Auditorium the Second Practice Was Over Last Night."

I whirled around to discover Aurora Frank hot on my heels with a piece of paper outstretched in her hand. Aurora was stage manager for the spring play—actually, she'd been stage manager for the fall musical and the one-act play for as long as I could remember—which basically meant she owned my soul for several months out of the year, ever since I'd ditched football halfway through Sophomore season to do theater instead.

The play was probably the best we could have hoped for during senior year—*Noises Off* by Michael Frayn. The rotating set had Aurora a little on edge.

I reached for the paper she was offering only for her to press it hard into my chest. "New schedule for tonight, Mavus. Mark wants you there at 6:30 during the dinner break to practice the glue scene with Tyler again. I hope you're wearing boxers with buttons today." She grinned prettily as she left the paper—and me scrambling to keep it from falling to the ground—while flipping her long auburn hair over her shoulder. It swished all the way down her back. Her almond eyes were intensely dark, and scared the hell out of me when narrowed my direction.

Somehow, Connor always took her in stride. "Slave driver," he said, and stuck out his tongue.

I spent a large portion of the play with my pants around my ankles, so having boxers on with an actual firm closure was a necessity. I'd forgotten a few times and had to do the scene only pretending to drop my pants for decency's sake, which was apparently getting more on Aurora's nerves than our director's.

I clutched the now crumpled paper and searched my brain. What shorts *had* I put on that morning? "Totally the right boxers this time, promise. And I didn't speed out on purpose last night, I'm fighting a bad cold! But I can do 6:30. I'll just be half dead come Saturday morning..." I grumbled.

"You better," she warned me.

"What, show up half-dead?" Connor said.

She glared at him. Then at me. "Be on time."

"Unnnng." A groan sounded, followed by the full form of Jules Miller half-collapsing with her forehead into Aurora's shoulder. A muffled, "Too much *Warcraft*," followed after.

Aurora resisted the urge to flip her hair again, and patted Jules' shoulder mechanically.

"We got out of play practice at 10:30 last night," Connor said.

"You played?"

"Only a couple hours to unwind," Jules mumbled, rolling her head toward us and blinking pale blue eyes. Her blond hair contrasted starkly next to Aurora's auburn.

Jules lived in skirts most days, many of which she had made herself. She could bake better than any of our mothers and her own combined, and she was the best first-person shooter and *World of Warcraft* player I knew. She had the role of blonde bombshell Brooke in the play and totally killed it every practice, no matter how tired she was. She just had a tendency to not sleep—ever. She also spent most of the show in a nightie.

We were so lucky they'd let us do this play.

"Come, ladies, we have Jazz Band to attend to." Connor pushed in between the pair, grabbing each of their arms and dragging them toward the doors with a wistful grin thrown my way. "See you later, Em!"

Both girls followed along without resistance.

"6:30, *Emery*!" Aurora called back at me. She definitely meant business. Connor called me 'Em' but everyone else at school always used my last name.

I sighed and followed after them to head to Honor Choir. So much for having some time to myself between visiting Mr. Leonard and play practice. After the charred bear incident and nearly running into Liz in the parking lot, the day was off to a winning start.

~

Connor

Connor pulled up to William Leonard's large home just outside of town to drop Emery off for work. Or maybe it was more charity or a therapy session, since Connor doubted Emery would be doing much *work* today.

"Let me know if you need a ride to practice later," he said as Emery hopped out of the back. Aurora had claimed the front seat.

"Shoot," Emery said when his phone gave a telling beep and he fished it out of the front pocket of his backpack. He looked at Connor imploringly through the rolled down window. "I'll call from the house phone if I need you. This stupid battery is on its last legs."

"Good thing you're getting a new one," Connor said.

"Yeah, two-day shipping. Although, nine times out of ten I'm just next door at your place anyway." He glanced at the house as if nervous to approach it. "Well…later, guys."

"See you at practice," Aurora said. "Six—"

"6:30, I got it. If I'm not there, I'm either home nursing another sinus infection, or dead." Emery grinned crookedly at her persistence.

Connor's heart seized at the sight. He swallowed back the all too familiar thickness in his throat, and managed to wave as Emery headed for the double doors, framed between two pristine white pillars on the front porch. He didn't try to hide from Aurora how he followed his best friend's retreating form.

At six foot even, with perfectly gelled, dark brown hair and bronze skin from the Middle Eastern roots on his dad's side, and warm hazel green eyes from his mostly Irish mom, Emery had a glow about him that Connor had been in love with since his first rush of hormones—which had sucked, considering they'd been friends since they were in diapers. Even the ever so subtle pudge Emery had developed after quitting football made Connor's face flush. Not that dance practice when the musical came around wasn't slimming.

"You are the worst stereotype in the world," Aurora said when they finally pulled back onto the road.

"Last I checked, my wardrobe is too lame for me to be a stereotype," Connor said.

"You know what I mean. High school. Unrequited love for your best friend. Pining and sighing and all that crap."

"Ung," Connor agreed.

"Break the stereotype, Mr. Daniels," Aurora said with a twist of her full lips, which were painted bright red, "confess already. Wasn't that your New Year's Resolution for, like…the third year in a row?"

It was.

"No," Connor said defensively.

"We have two months of school left."

"He—"

"Just broke up with his girlfriend," Aurora reminded him.

"But he—"

"Has never actually expressed that guys are totally out of the equation, so the least you can do is admit the truth before graduation."

Connor sighed into the steering wheel. "I just want one week where something insane doesn't happen. No strange murders, no idiot freshman writing bomb threats in the girl's bathroom, no distractions. Just one week…and I'll tell him."

Aurora huffed. "Good luck with that." She pulled out her school planner, which still had two months left to fill, but as she finished a month, she proceeded to cover the used pages in scans of *Sailor Moon* manga art. It was now five times as thick as it had been at the start of the year.

"What are you doing?" Connor asked as she took a pen and began filling out something for next month.

"Documenting the next time I'm scheduled to bug you about this when you inevitably don't follow through."

If Connor didn't know how right she was, he would have protested.

He pulled into the middle school parking lot, across town from the high school, but where the large auditorium was housed for plays and music concerts—despite the fact that the high school used it far more than the middle school did. He sat staring forward a moment after shutting off the Thunderbird.

"Come on, Con-Man," Aurora said playfully, accompanied by a swift kiss on the cheek to catch him off guard and prompt a smile. "We have to find the right spot on the stage to turn the set between acts so we don't hit the wall with one end or let the other fall into the pit." She winked when Connor turned and caught her gaze. "That would *so* spoil opening night."

CHAPTER 2

Mr. Leonard's house is the kind of place that one really cool, young aunt of yours might have: half modern, half antiques, the occasional comic book, and always super tidy. I liked the way the grandfather clock in the entrance hall made the place feel like some Victorian palace, but the spiral wooden staircase without any railings was my favorite modern touch. I'd never actually gone up it, since I was pretty sure I would fall to my death.

The walls throughout the house were covered in paintings Mrs. Leonard had done. My favorite hung in the living room; a rendition of Marvel's Cloak and Dagger. The rest were mostly abstract or landscapes, so a painting of two comic book superheroes definitely stood out.

Hanging beside the grandfather clock was the one actual photo, something the Leonards had taken before they moved here, both of them styled in an old-timey, 1800s look. It was really authentic, and Mrs. Leonard was beautiful in the corseted gown with her long, curly black hair, and eyes even greener than my mom's.

A sour feeling filled my stomach as I looked at the photo, and I tried not to think about where her body might have been found.

"Mr. Leonard!" I called as I stepped farther into the entryway. They'd always insisted I come right in without knocking, but it felt different today. I heeled off my shoes, and set them and my backpack by the door like usual, but I wasn't sure where to go. Normally, one of the Leonards was right there to meet me, and even with all the lights on, the place was too quiet.

I remembered the first time I'd been over to mow their lawn. The house had smelled like fresh baked cookies, and when I commented about it, Mr. Leonard said, "See, Mallory, I told you. Everyone loves a home that smells like cookies."

Mrs. Leonard had turned to me with a wide smile. "You can see why I married him. Would you like a cookie, Emery?"

Today the house smelled like ammonia.

"Mr. Leonard?" I called again, walking cautiously toward the living room.

"Here, Emery."

I found him standing in front of the fireplace, staring at the large flames. It wasn't cold enough outside to warrant a fire, but he seemed transfixed, even though he had called my name.

Are you okay? flashed through my mind, but that seemed so inadequate. Of course he wasn't okay. His wife was dead.

"I know there isn't much yard work to be done right now, Mr. Leonard, but I thought I'd come around anyway, see if there was anything else you might need help with around the house. I don't mind. I have a couple hours before play practice, and…" I trailed off as he turned away from the fireplace to look at me.

He was about my height, with light brown hair that was usually styled to perfection, but today it was askew as if he'd run his hands through it several times. His pale eyes looked molten in the light of the fire. His cheeks weren't wet, but his eyes were red-rimmed like he'd only just stopped crying. His clothes were rumpled too; dark blue button-down and jeans with his sleeves rolled up—he never had his sleeves rolled up. He was usually more put together like a sharp businessman, even though no one was really sure what he'd done for work to be able to retire out here at thirty.

"Is there…anything I can do?" I asked again.

He tried to smile, but somehow the expression made him look even sadder. "I appreciate you coming today, Emery, but you don't need to work. Maybe…" His eyes unfocused a moment before softening as they centered on me again. "Would you sit with me a moment?"

That was the least I could do. Though I was pretty sure I'd be calling Connor to pick me up later. Mr. Leonard usually dropped me off on his way into town for errands, but I didn't feel right asking for that today.

We sat on the micro-suede sofa in front of the fireplace. It was too hot for me, so I tried to casually unzip my hoodie without calling too much attention. I didn't want to be any trouble, but Mr. Leonard didn't seem to notice. When he talked, he stared into the fire.

"I bet you can't even guess how long we were together."

I stiffened. "More than a decade?"

"More…" he said. "Growing old with the right person is easy, Emery, but facing the unknown alone, knowing so many years stretch on without them, it's…"

"I'm so sorry, Mr. Leonard."

That's always the mantra that comes to mind, right? *I'm sorry for your loss.* But I've never lost anyone close to me. I couldn't possibly understand. So it felt hollow, and I wished there were better words.

Empathy sucks, because feeling bad for other people's sake doesn't mean you get it, doesn't mean you know what to say to make it better, just means you feel a little of their awful with them without any of the good.

I had good memories of Mrs. Leonard, but that wasn't enough either.

Mr. Leonard stood, jolting me out of my thoughts, and walked behind me where the Cloak and Dagger painting hung on the wall.

"It's the contrast, she used to say," Mr. Leonard said when I rose to join him, "that's why she liked them, why she painted them. Shadow and light. Masculine and feminine. Have you ever heard the quote about how these two characters came to their creator after he visited Ellis Island? They aren't as old as most of the heroes you're familiar with."

I shook my head. I had my fair share of comics, but Connor was the expert. I'd always liked Cloak and Dagger's designs though; Dagger all white light like a blond warrior fairy, and Cloak dark and mysterious controlling the shadows from beneath his hood. The painting depicted them side by side, leaping into action.

"The creator said…'They came in the night, when all was silent and my mind was blank. They came completely conceived as to their powers and attributes, their origin and motivation. They embodied between them all that fear and misery, hunger and longing that had haunted me on Ellis Island'. I think that's how it always is when two halves come together. Fear and misery, hunger and longing. Somehow, together, and only together, it subsides, it's bearable. But when that other half is gone..."

I felt silly for thinking I could have distracted Mr. Leonard with happier topics. But if this was what he needed, I didn't mind listening. I thought of how my mom always found a way to put her hand on someone's arm or shoulder, her complete attention on them when they discussed something painful or important. I reached to touch Mr. Leonard's shoulder and he turned to me with that same mournful smile.

"I was relieved the police were finally done with me today."

"I'm sure it's been really hard on you."

"Yes, but it isn't over yet."

"The killer's still out there," I said, then bit my lip, wishing I'd said something else.

"I'm thankful they never suspected me—the police, though I'm sure the town has been talking. I don't think I could have handled that on top of everything else…being accused of…" He clenched his eyes shut before returning his gaze to the painting. "But they're still out there, as you said. Now that there are no more police around the property…they'll come for me."

"What?" I pulled my hand back as if I'd placed it in the fire. "Did someone threaten you? Have you told the police? Tim—"

"Chief Ashby has been very helpful and understanding, all of the officers have been, but they can't help me with this, Emery," he said, sounding weirdly detached now, resigned.

"What do you mean?"

I'd been so used to Mr. Leonard's eyes looking away from me or through me that when they focused on me again, I flinched. His eyes really did look like they were glowing, almost white-blue with flicks of orange from the fire. But the fire was behind him now…

He began a sudden, steady trek toward me, and with every new step, I took a step back to match him. That nervous feeling in my gut curdled into something else. Mr. Leonard was menacing in a way I'd never seen before, larger somehow too, like a predator. But his blank expression was what scared me.

"If I had contacted him the moment Mallory died, he might have made it in time, but he won't arrive before the hunters do. He told me not to do anything foolish, but if I do nothing, I'll die, the hunters will leave, and the trail will run cold. Mallory will never get justice."

His voice floated around me like an echo, his eyes too bright. "He told me to run if they came, but that is something I cannot do. I know you can't help me fight them, Emery, but you can give them a reason to stay, give Alec time to discover the truth."

"Alec?" My back hit the wall and I gasped. He had me cornered.

"My Maker, my friend. He can ensure they pay for their crimes. But if I don't give them a reason to stay in town, he'll be too late."

I had no idea what he was talking about. If he had more emotion in his voice I'd worry he was delirious, but he sounded so even, so certain. The twist in my gut nearly doubled me over, and I held out a hand to keep him from getting closer. "Mr. Leonard—"

"Hush, Emery."

I made to push him away, but in that same moment, the fear that had crept under my skin feeling like it might burst out my pores, lessened. Everything about Mr. Leonard seemed different. He didn't move. His expression didn't change. It was the air around him, the atoms buzzing, something intangible that shifted. His eyes were mesmerizing, and as I returned his stare, all the anxiety in my stomach washed away. I felt warm, but not uncomfortably so, more like I was snuggling up for an afternoon nap.

My hand dropped.

"I am so sorry, Emery. I have no other choice."

I didn't see him move. He was there, standing in front of me, and then he wasn't. Instead, the curve of his shoulder was in front of my face, and a sharp pain in my neck tore the air from my lungs, like he'd struck me with a knife or a needle. But the pain faded almost instantly, and the tight pressure felt almost soothing.

I sagged against the wall, seeing only the dark blue of Mr. Leonard's shoulder, the hazy background of the sofa and fireplace fading in color until there was nothing but calming darkness.

~

Something warm and tangy lingered on my tongue. I licked my lips to get another taste, feeling starved. My vision was blurry around the edges as I blinked awake, but I could see movement above me, the ceiling moving quickly past my head. Mr. Leonard must have been carrying me, but I felt like I was floating.

A distant crash of glass sounded, and Mr. Leonard cursed—at least I think it was a curse from his tone, but it wasn't a word I recognized.

"They're earlier than I expected. I have to hide you," he said.

I must have fallen asleep, I told myself. It was the fire. It had been so warm…

I licked my lips again; whatever this was, I wanted more of it.

Mr. Leonard tried to lean me against a wall, but I was too tired; I slid down it and sat, eager to lie down. There were shouts now; more things breaking.

"I pray they don't find you, Emery, but Alec will. Wait for him. He'll explain everything. I hope both of you can forgive me someday."

I opened my mouth. I wanted to tell Mr. Leonard that it was okay; I felt fine. Everything would be fine. But then he was tucking me in, soft, fluffy warmth all around me, covering my face, and what little light remained went out at the sound of a door clicking shut. A nap sounded fantastic.

I licked my lips one last time, catching the last traces of that strange, sweet…what was it? Then I felt myself slip back to sleep, not even bothered by the sound of Mr. Leonard arguing with someone outside the door.

~

"Mr. Leonard!"

All my grogginess gone, I bolted upright, the coats that had been tossed over me falling from around my face and upper body. I was in a closet, the door closed, with very little light creeping in. I held my breath, listening for sounds outside the door and checking myself for wounds at the same time.

My hand flew to my neck where I remembered that sharp pain, but there was nothing, just smooth skin, not even sticky traces of blood. I looked down my shirt, but even there, not a single drop. I wondered if I'd imagined it all, but then…why was I in the closet?

No sound came from the other side of the door, though my senses seemed a little foggy, like I couldn't quite focus on what I saw, or heard, or smelled, even though my head felt clear and I didn't feel hurt anywhere.

I hoisted myself to my feet and tried the door. I opened it slowly, peering out. Bright light filled the living room from the windows, but that didn't make sense. It should have been getting darker.

"Mr. Leonard?" I called. The closet was near the doorway that led into the living room from the entryway. I could see the sofa and fireplace ahead of me—the fire was still burning but it was down to embers.

Then I noticed the side table by the back wall had been toppled. Papers were strewn about from somewhere. A lamp lay sideways on the floor. The far window was shattered. I remembered hearing the glass break…

I'd been out all night, the clock on the wall confirmed that, but where was Mr. Leonard? My memories of him attacking me couldn't be right. He wouldn't do something like that, and even so, I didn't have any wounds. This struggle hadn't been us.

I knew I had to be remembering things wrong. There was only one explanation—the murderer had come back to finish the job.

I wasn't usually a realist—life was real enough—but as I came to the edge of the sofa and saw the shattered glass coffee table, in pieces like the window, and the body splayed over the carpet in front of the fire, I knew I was right.

Mr. Leonard was dead, with the same gaping hole in his chest that had killed his wife.

CHAPTER 3

Connor

Connor tapped his hard, plastic pointer finger on the bench by his front door, tapping his feet along with it as he sat there waiting. He'd grabbed his Terminator arm without thinking—it was Emery's favorite; he'd dubbed it that since it was silver colored and had bony looking fingers that gripped better than any of Connor's other prosthetics.

He stopped the motion of his finger with his other hand as he caught sight of the sliding glass doors leading out to the backyard. He'd forgotten about the giant, singed teddy bear. It was still under the recycling bin, its blackened, furry feet sticking out the bottom.

"We're just waiting for John to bring the car around, hon, okay? We'll ride with them, and your dad will follow in the Subaru," Connor's mom said as she hurried around the corner, grabbing her coat and habitually checking her purse to make sure she had everything she needed. Her purse was literally a pharmacy, since she was an RN, and tended to house a few dozen random other things that might be needed in a clinch.

Connor gripped his plastic hand harder to stop it from shaking but couldn't prevent his feet from tapping out a constant rhythm. He looked at his mother blankly. She was in her coral scrubs, ready to head to work as soon as they finished at the Leonards.

Mr. Leonard…

"Paul, Kay and John are going to be here any second!" Georgia called over her shoulder.

"I'd hope so, they live next door," Paul Daniels said with a faint smirk as he appeared. He looked perfectly at ease, as if they weren't about to follow the police to the Leonards' house to look for Emery, who they weren't even sure was still there.

Connor was just glad they hadn't been made to wait a full twenty-four hours, not with Mr. Leonard part of an ongoing murder investigation—and the last person who'd seen Emery.

When Emery never showed up at practice, Connor had assumed his friend's cold had gotten the better of him. He'd even been the one to give that excuse to Mark and Aurora, since he knew Emery's phone had been about to die when he dropped him off.

Emery's parents assumed he was at practice and, since it was a Friday night, that their well-behaved nearly-adult son had stayed over at Connor's afterwards. It was only when Connor went to check on Emery in the morning that they realized he was missing. They called the police right away when Connor reported he'd last seen Emery at what had so recently been a crime scene. Well, they called Tim directly. It paid to be friends with the Chief.

"I'm sure he's there, kiddo, and just fine," Paul said, rubbing a hand over Connor's short cropped hair that only somewhat mirrored his own fully shaved head. "And if we don't get an answer this time, Tim can burst right through that door and pull a John McClane on Leonard's ass."

Georgia snorted.

Connor attempted a weak smile.

"Terminator today?" Paul said, seeing the prosthetic. "Well, then, we won't even need the cops if things get hairy."

"Paul," Georgia admonished, though her tone was playful.

The sound of an engine had Connor jumping to his feet. "They're here," he said, and dashed out the door before his parents could reply.

As soon as he climbed into the back of the Mavus' Tahoe, John Mavus gave him a reassuring smile from the driver's seat.

"Calm down, T-1000, I'm sure everything's fine," he said, only betraying his concern in the crinkle of his dark eyes. His brunette beard was getting fuller again, though not really long the way his wife implied when she called him Grizzly Adams.

Kay Mavus peeked her head around the seats as Connor's mother climbed in after him. Kay's hair was like a sunset, offset by her bright green eyes. "Tim just called to say they see movement inside the house. They're going to check it out now before we get there. They have an ambulance on site, just in case." She opened her mouth to say more but stopped, eyeing Georgia with sudden, unspoken panic.

Connor had felt that same panic all morning.

"Go ahead, John. Paul's right behind us," Georgia said, then placed a hand on Kay's seat. "It'll be fine."

Everyone kept saying that; it was really getting on Connor's nerves.

~

I had to get to my phone.

I turned from Mr. Leonard's body and raced for the front doors where I'd left my backpack. Once I saw the flashing red and blue lights outside, I froze. I could see Tim's face through the glass. I don't know what my expression betrayed of the situation, but as soon as our eyes met, he charged in through the unlocked door.

"Emery, where is Mr. Leonard?" he asked, approaching me slowly, two officers at his back with their hands on their guns, ready to draw them.

My eyes felt hot. My hand shook as I pointed back to the living room.

Tim motioned to the other officers and they hurried around me, making me flinch at their close proximity. I looked at Tim and…erupted.

"He said they'd come for him, and they did. I heard glass breaking, and yelling, but I couldn't wake up. He put me in the closet. I passed out or something, and I…I couldn't wake *up*."

"Emery." Tim's hands came down on my shoulders. He had blond hair and kind brown eyes, his uniform just the smallest bit too tight from holiday weight he hadn't been able to work off yet, or so he'd said, laughing to my parents about it only a couple weeks ago. Laughing…

"Chief," one of the other officers said from the living room entrance.

"He's dead," I said before the officer could. "I was right here and…I didn't even…I *couldn't*…"

"Emery, it's okay. I know you had nothing to do with this," Tim assured me. I hadn't even thought about them considering me a suspect. "We're going to have to bring you in for questioning, just to get the details, but you're not in trouble. You've had your parents pretty worried. Right now I'm going to have Officer Rogers take you out to the ambulance to make sure you're okay. All right?"

I nodded. I couldn't look Tim in the eyes. I kept staring at his uniform, the way the buttons pulled…

Officer Rogers came up to lead me outside while Tim went to join the other officer in the living room. I put on my shoes, grabbed my backpack, but I was numb until we hit the open air. The brightness of the sun made my eyes burn. I'd been in the closet too long, because it felt like it took the entire walk to the ambulance before I could see clearly past the brightness. My skin felt hot, too hot when it was early morning and colder than yesterday, but the sun felt like it was trying to beat me into the pavement.

I knew the EMT. I'd seen him at St. Mary's Hospital while visiting Connor's mom. He was huge, like a Viking. They used him when they needed to lift heavier patients. He had full lips that smiled wide as he flashed a light in my eyes. It didn't burn the way the sun did, but at least now I was in the shade, sitting in the back of the ambulance with my feet dangling out onto the driveway.

"I think I have a concussion. I was unconscious all night, but I don't remember why. And it's so hot. Should I feel hot?"

"Don't get ahead of yourself now, son," he said in slow, soothing tones. "You look alert to me, and your skin feels pretty chilled. Maybe just disoriented and a little in shock from what happened last night. I'm Doug."

I nodded. "Emery."

I answered his questions, stuck my tongue out, let him take my pulse. My blood pressure was low, but nothing to be alarmed about. Everything was normal.

Everything was normal…

I heard the sound of our Tahoe like it must have been right in front of me, but it was another minute before I saw my dad pull up. Everything felt too sharp or too dull—not normal at all. I told Doug, but he just smiled, said it would be okay. I didn't believe him until I saw my parents get out of the car. And Georgia. And *Connor*.

I jumped to my feet, but Doug asked me to stay where I was; my family could come to me. The direct sunlight made my eyes sting, so I obeyed and sat back down.

My mom had me in a hug a second later.

"You didn't curl your hair today," I said, "or straighten it." She never went out with her natural wave.

"Well excuse me for having something else on my mind," she said with a short laugh.

"Sorry…"

"Don't you dare be, honey, we're just glad you're okay."

Then Dad was there, his burly arms engulfing me as he kissed my cheek like grandma always did, and squeezed too tightly to let me know how worried he'd been even though he was smiling and said he hadn't worried at all. Mom punched him in the arm for that.

Georgia was talking to Doug, getting the low-down on me. She looked satisfied with his answers, but my attention shifted to Connor.

"You look awful," he said as my parents parted to let him through, half his mouth twitching like he was trying so hard to mean that as a joke, to not look scared.

This wasn't the kind of scared I was used to when we played a horror game or watched a scary movie; he'd always have a smile on his face then, even when he was hiding his head behind a pillow or clutching my arm until it hurt.

No. This was the same kind of shaky fear I was feeling.

"That bad, huh?"

"Nah," he said, forcing a smile, though it didn't reach his eyes. "Just a little pale like you might throw up all over my shoes.

What…" He stopped, his smile dropping as soon as he thought of his next sentence. "What did he do to you?"

"Nothing. He's dead. Whoever murdered his wife, they…" I looked at Mom and Dad. "He didn't…"

…*a sharp pain in my neck tore the air from my lungs, like he'd struck me with a knife or a needle.*

I shook my head. That hadn't really happened. I didn't have any marks, there wasn't any…blood.

I licked my lips. They were dry now, cracked.

"Let me see if Tim will let us take you home for now, honey, and bring you to the station later after you've had some rest," my mom's voice phased into my hearing like an echo. "I'm sure they'll have their hands full here."

I must have zoned out, because I jumped when Connor touched my arm. He was sitting beside me now—when had that happened? My eyes felt hot again when I turned to him.

"Dude, don't look at me like that," he said, a catch in his voice that made it harder to keep the warm tears from sliding down my face.

I hugged him so hard when he put his arms around me, I heard him grunt for air, but he didn't push me away; he hugged just as fiercely back. The feel of his prosthetic grounded me.

I was safe. I was okay.

"You should go to practice," I said when we pulled apart. I didn't know what time it was, but it had to still be early enough for Saturday morning play practice.

"You kidding?" He raised an eyebrow at me, which finally resembled a normal expression.

"You can tell everyone I'm okay. I'm probably going to crash when I get home anyway. I must have slept all night, but I feel so tired. I just…" I looked past him at the house. It all felt like a dream, like I was delirious or about to be sick. Maybe it was shock.

"Okay," Connor said, "but I'm coming over as soon as we're done. You promise you'll tell me everything that happened?"

"I don't really remember anything," I said. Not anything that made sense.

"I'll bring Swedish Fish and the original *Mortal Kombat* movie," he offered hopefully.

His smile touched his eyes this time, as I turned my attention back to him. They looked gold this close. I could see flecks of brown, and bronze, and what honestly looked like gold all detailed in his eyes like I was seeing them under a microscope. I pulled back, thinking I must be zoning out again, but when I did, Connor was the one who looked dazed.

"Okay, boys, we're going to get going," Mom said. She and Dad had gone to talk to Tim with Connor's dad, but now all four parents stood in front of us, with Doug hanging back behind them. I looked at Connor again, who blinked like he'd been somewhere else.

"Huh? Oh yeah. Let's get out of here, Em." He grinned at me as he stood and held out his silver hand to help me up. He knew Terminator was my favorite; definitely the most badass—besides the Rocket-Punch one.

"Yeah," I said. Even though the sun still burned my eyes and made me feel beaten by the heat I knew couldn't really be there, the only thing I wanted was to get away from the ambulance, away from that house, and crawl into bed.

~

Wendy

Police swarmed the property. It was too late to get any information now, at least until they left, and then Wendy would have to be careful.

Her dark brown eyes surveyed the commotion in front of William and Mallory Leonard's now ownerless home from a safe distance. She brought the kickstand up on her black Ducati and adjusted the zoom she had equipped in her specially made motorcycle helmet. It had night vision, infrared, but she'd seen all she needed to for today.

Wendy knew she was right about the boy who'd come out of the house. It was the only explanation for how he was still alive.

As she drove off, leaving the house—and the boy—in her rearview mirror for now, she couldn't help thinking that things were about to get much more complicated.

CHAPTER 4

Connor

Connor rushed upstairs to his room. After getting home from play practice, he had discretely snuck outside to take care of the charred bear in the backyard, thankful his parents hadn't noticed it yet. It was now safely jammed inside a garbage bag with the rest of the trash.

He had wanted to go straight to Emery's after practice—being in charge of several plates of fake sardines was trying his sanity even without a couple murders and a traumatized best friend to distract him—but his dad had insisted he wait a few more hours so Emery could rest, and to call first instead of just walking in uninvited like he usually did. Connor decided he'd obey halfway and call over their walkie talkies.

The walkies were from Walmart, nothing special; black, thirty-five-mile range. He and Emery had gotten them when they were thirteen, since they hadn't been allowed cell phones until they were sixteen.

"You don't need a cell phone until you can you drive," their parents had agreed.

Emery didn't drive much anyway since his family only had the Tahoe. His mom had never gotten a license, and Emery had decided he'd rather save up a couple extra years for a nicer car after graduation. Connor certainly didn't mind lending out his car on occasion, or playing chauffer, though he had been deeply disappointed when he learned that his prosthetics meant he couldn't get handicap plates for better parking.

They had cell phones now, of course, but Emery's was constantly dying, which had played no small part in last night's events. And besides, there was something intimate about the walkies, just the two of them, connected across their lawns. They'd spent countless nights talking on them when they should have been sleeping. Emery's voice was a smooth baritone that sounded lyrical to Connor even just talking. Connor loved falling asleep to Emery's voice.

"Auntie Em, Auntie Em," Connor whispered into his walkie. He kept it charged next to his bed. Their rooms weren't in the right locations to see into each other's windows.

Static replied. Emery might have his turned off, turned down, or not charged at the moment, but Connor still had to try.

"Dude, are you awake? Dad won't let me come over unless you give the okay."

Static.

"Em, come on. You are going to be bombarded Monday if the way everyone grilled me was any indication. People are freaked. Mark even said he was worried we should postpone the play if there's really some serial killer on the loose striking at young, defenseless suburbanites. Well, he didn't word it quite like that…"

Still nothing.

Connor huffed and clutched the walkie to his chest. They hadn't spent more than a night's sleep away from each other since they were toddlers, even if one of them was sick—which usually didn't matter anyway, since what one of them got, the other caught quickly as well, excluding Emery's chronic sinus infections.

It left a dry thickness in Connor's throat not knowing what had happened to his friend. He'd been able to dismiss his concerns last night, but he'd spent all morning worrying that Emery was dead in Mr. Leonard's basement.

"I never would have forgiven you if you'd died on me, you know," Connor tried one last time. When static replied, he flopped down onto his bed, holding the walkie close in case Emery woke up.

~

I was freezing, but my body wouldn't shiver. That's how you get warm, isn't it? By shivering? It was as if I was a statue; I couldn't move, but everything felt cold, even though the sun outside had been too hot.

I was back in the Leonards' house. Everywhere I could see there were shadows, but the fire was burning in the fireplace, casting light on Mr. Leonard lying on the carpet. I wanted to turn away, but I was rooted to the spot, my neck stiff and eyes directed at where Cloak hovered over Mr. Leonard's head, ominous in his giant black cape and hood, while Dagger held him down and stabbed one of her psionic light daggers into his chest.

Something like a rush of hot water poured over me from the neck down. I still couldn't move my head, but my hand twitched at my side. Whatever covered me felt sticky and thick, and I just wanted to get out of there. I tried to scream, but no sound came out. I tried so hard to move, even just an inch.

Then Cloak and Dagger turned to me. They didn't look like heroes anymore.

I jolted awake feeling like my pulse was vibrating, but when I touched a hand to my throat it felt steady, almost weirdly slow. There was nothing sticky on me, not even a little drool, but the cold part had been true. I'd slept on top of the covers and felt like I was freezing deep down to my core.

"I never would have forgiven you if you'd died on me, you know," Connor's voice said quietly from somewhere in the room.

I sat up to look for him before I realized the fuzziness of his voice was because it had come through my walkie. It was plugged in on my computer desk, blinking at me that it was now fully charged.

Rubbing my hands up and down my arms to warm them, I scooted to the end of the bed. When I stood, I caught sight of myself in the long mirror on the inside of my closed door. I really did look awful. I couldn't remember the last time I'd been so pale. My skin isn't quite as dark as my dad's, but still dark enough that pale just looks weird on me, like someone did me up in bad zombie makeup. I guess nothing else seemed off, maybe a little darkness around my eyes like I needed more sleep, though my eyes also seemed sort of…bright.

And I was cold. And starving.

I hadn't eaten anything since lunch the day before. When Mom asked if I wanted anything before heading up to bed, nothing she'd mentioned sounded appetizing.

The alarm clock on my dresser told me it was 12:30—Connor must have just gotten back from practice. "If you're the reason I woke up from that nightmare," I spoke into the walkie as I unplugged it from the charger, "thank you. What's up?"

"Em!" Connor called, louder than before. "Do you want company yet? Dad is being way too paranoid about you needing rest."

"Same here. Mom said she didn't want me out of the room until I'd gotten some real sleep. They're probably going to have me on a short leash for a while."

"Damn. Well…I could climb the trellis again?" I heard the smirk in Connor's voice as he suggested this.

The lights were off, and I'd shut the blinds earlier to keep the sun out. Now it seemed too dark, with shadows everywhere making me think of my dream. I moved to the switch on the wall to fill the room with light again; I didn't care if it was silly and childish to not want to be in the dark.

"Company," I said. "I definitely would prefer that. Just don't get hurt this time, okay?"

"Please, that was just a scratch."

"And eight stitches."

"I wear the scar proudly. Be right there," Connor said.

As static filled the walkie, I moved to open the window the trellis led to. I'd convinced Mom it was a cool look for the house and that it was *most* fitting on the wall outside my room; the trellis couldn't be blamed if it made it easier for Connor to sneak over. He'd only done it a couple times though. Usually we didn't need to be covert.

The sun was almost directly overhead now, but still aligned just right to shoot into my window, making me squint. Even if I didn't have a concussion, I guess I could have a migraine, but my head didn't really hurt and I wasn't nauseous. Besides, my room was pretty bright with the light on; it didn't make sense for only the sunlight to bother me.

I decided to change into fresh clothes while I waited for Connor. I'd napped in the same ones from yesterday and was probably covered in dust from that closet. Plus, I didn't care what temperature it was outside, I wanted a sweater.

I was still only in my jeans, deciding that my light grey sweater with the high collar was probably the warmest, when Connor climbed in through the window.

"Sweet, free show." He winked at me.

"Ha. Ha." I pulled the sweater over my head. "I can't seem to get warm. Can you close the window?"

He did so but left the blinds open. "You feeling better otherwise?"

When I looked at him, I half expected my stomach to emit a loud growl—for some reason I felt ten times hungrier now that he was here. "Mostly. Are you sure the whole thing wasn't just a bad dream?" I offered a smile I hoped wasn't as weak as it felt.

"'Fraid so. You ready to tell me what actually happened last night? Because if it's too soon or whatever, I can totally be patient."

I raised an eyebrow at him as we sat on my bed. I felt clearer now, at least, like my senses that had seemed dulled earlier were back to equilibrium. I could even smell the familiar, musty scent of the stage curtains on Connor.

"I can be patient," he insisted. "I'd always rather not be, but I *can*."

"It's okay. I probably should try and work things out anyway, if I'm going to have to give a statement to Tim later. I just keep thinking about finding Mr. Leonard like that, and wondering what it must have been like when he found his wife. I only looked for a few seconds before I bolted for my phone, and then Tim was there, and…" I took a breath. "Not gruesome or anything, just…too real, or something? Does that make sense?"

"It's someone you see every week, almost every day, and some psycho murdered him while you were in the house. It doesn't get realer than that. How did they not find you?"

I told him about being in the closet all night, and was impressed he didn't make any cracks about that. He just listened. When he asked how things had led up to that, considering I didn't think the killer—or killers—had gotten inside the house until after I was in the closet, I didn't know what to say at first. I knew I couldn't tell Tim the truth; what I remembered was fuzzy and sounded crazy without evidence, but I needed someone to know.

"So it felt like he cut you?"

"I couldn't really see; he was too close to me."

"Maybe he bit you."

"But I don't have any marks. See, it's crazy. I must have imagined it."

"Wait." Connor got up from the bed and started pacing in front of me. "So first it was like he was getting real intense, had you worried he was losing it, but looking in his eyes made you stop trying to get away?"

"Sort of. Like it didn't matter anymore. Almost like I was—"

"Hypnotized?"

"Yeah."

"And then he bit you—"

"Maybe—"

"And you blacked out. And the next thing you remember is tasting something, like he'd given you something to *drink*." He wasn't asking questions anymore, so I didn't feel the need to answer. I'd told him everything I remembered, even how the sun stung my eyes.

Connor stopped pacing and stared at me, this blank look on his face while his eyes went wide, making me feel like some awful blow was about to strike.

"Dude, what? I must have been delirious, okay? Maybe I hit my head, or he told me something that scared me so much I passed out. There's no way all of that happened the way I remember. What would it even mean if it had?"

"I know exactly what it would mean," Connor said evenly. "The Leonards were vampires."

I barked a laugh. "Real funny." Connor had set me up good on that one.

"Only I'm not joking."

He grabbed my arm and hauled me off the bed, jerking me toward the window before I could laugh a second time. He pushed me directly into the sunlight's rays. I squinted at the brightness and backpedaled out of its path.

"Mr. Leonard turned you into a vampire!" Connor declared.

"That's insane." I rubbed my eyes before shooting him a glare. "It's not like I'm bursting into flames, it just irritates me. And I have a reflection. See?" I gestured back at my mirror, feeling ridiculous that I even had to defend this idea. "Vampires don't exist, Connor. It's just a lot of weirdness adding up to something that doesn't make sense yet."

"But it does make sense if you're a vampire. Not having a reflection's stupid anyway," he added in a matter-of-fact tone. "No one actually believes that part of the lore is real."

"But vampires existing at all is?!"

Connor held out his hands, pleading with me to be patient while he explained the stupidest thing he had ever tried to convince me of. The window was between us now, the sunlight creating a transparent barrier, with the corner of my room at Connor's back. I didn't get how he could look so serious while he insisted I was a vampire, of all things.

"Think of how the Leonards were both found," Connor said. "Holes in their chests too big to be bullets—stakes through the heart! And that Alec guy you said he mentioned, what did he call him?"

"His…maker, but—"

"Of course you don't have any wounds, Em. You already healed them. And there wasn't any blood on you, because real vampires wouldn't be messy like they make them in the movies. Mr. Leonard turned you so that the hunters who killed him and his wife would stay in town long enough—"

"Just stop!"

Connor flinched, eyes wide again, but this time in fear—of *me*. I hadn't meant to roar like that. I knew when he was joking, and the fact that he honestly thought this was real was not helping. The sun, the cold, the murders; not to mention how hungry and frustrated I felt, like the pressure of it all was building low in my stomach, and I couldn't see straight through the ache.

I took a step toward Connor into the path of the sun. It was bright and hot, worse every time, and the sudden pain of it made me surge forward back into the cold. On the other side of the window there wasn't much space, just Connor backed into the corner and me right in front of him.

"I'm not a vampire. Vampires don't exist."

"Em…"

Connor was so close, all I could focus on was his smell, like dust, and plywood, and paint from the set, with something salty and rich and fragrant beneath it—what *was* that? I thought of the taste on my lips last night with Mr. Leonard, and swiped out my tongue. The taste wasn't there anymore, but it was close.

I looked at Connor but couldn't see him as a whole. He was under a microscope again, his eyes brown, and bronze, and gold, every little fleck perfectly detailed. I could see the movement of each breath he took, the way the tendons in his neck moved, twitched, shifted with the pulse of the veins underneath…

Em! Emery!

My stomach lurched with a twist of pain—the worst hunger I'd ever felt. My hands were on either side of Connor's head against the wall and I didn't even remember putting them there. The smell, the taste, I knew it was right there beneath the skin, and when I leaned forward and parted my lips to press them to Connor's neck, that rich, wonderful flavor flowed over my tongue with no effort at all.

CHAPTER 5

Connor

Connor had dismissed the way Emery's eyes flashed in the ambulance—making him lose time and sense of self—as just getting caught up in being that close to his friend after fearing he'd lost him. He couldn't dismiss it this time.

Emery's hazel eyes glowed with a shimmer like a cat caught in the light. Connor had tried calling his friend's name but the words turned thick in his mouth until they trailed away. He couldn't speak, couldn't move. Emery's hands came up so fast to press into the wall on either side of his head, he didn't register the movement; they were just there. When Emery's lips parted, Connor could see the fangs, long and sharp from his eyeteeth like right out of a monster movie.

It was a trick. Emery had made it all up, knowing that the details would lead Connor to vampires. These were just Halloween fangs. Connor wasn't really hypnotized into submission; he was just stunned, believing his own crazy imagination. He'd longed for years to have Emery this close, after all, crowding him into a corner, lips descending. He'd just imagined them descending a little closer to his mouth, though his neck wouldn't be so bad…

…if not for the sharp sting, the breaking of the skin and rush of blood sucked out of him so fast he felt dizzy, and then—*wow*.

It didn't hurt at all. It felt like Emery was tucked into his shoulder intimately, fully aware of the pleasant buzzing he caused in Connor's gut every time they touched. Connor had dreamed of this, imagined it just like this, and felt lulled by Emery's body being so close, and the way he shivered feeling those lips on his skin. He almost thought he heard Emery's soothing voice whispering affirmations he'd always wanted to hear.

"Em…" Connor breathed out, barely audible.

The room was dimming, but he felt cozy where he was. His arms were limp and heavy as he lifted them to pull Emery closer, feeling the soft fabric of the sweater against his somewhat numb right palm. He pulled tighter, twisting flesh and plastic fingers alike in the fabric, pulling…with the faint sense that he should be pushing instead.

"*Em…*" he choked out like a whimper, like he was crying. Why was he crying? This was everything he'd ever wanted…

Reality snapped back into painful, terrible focus when Emery released him, his fangs pulling from the tender skin of Connor's neck, the brief feeling of a tongue licking over the wound, and then Emery jerked away from Connor with a harsh intake of breath.

Emery's hands had moved at some point from the wall to Connor's shoulders, and the second he removed them, Connor dropped straight to the carpet.

"Connor!"

Even blinking felt sluggish, like the world was moving in slow motion. Connor felt drugged and weak, still hazy, but the pain wasn't dulled anymore; he felt that distinctly, and said with clear accusation when Emery's face swam into view, "Ow."

"Oh god, Connor, I'm so sorry! I didn't mean to. I couldn't *stop.*" Emery ranted on and on a series of apologies and assurances that he hadn't meant to do that—as if Connor would ever think otherwise.

Connor waved his right hand ineffectually until his friend grasped it. It was the hypnotism, the glamour, whatever it was called, not the blood loss. It couldn't have been that much blood. He just needed a minute for his head to clear.

He slurred out something that he hoped conveyed that, and leaned against the wall at his back. At least he hadn't crumbled completely. He was in a sitting position, with Emery crouched, soon sitting in front of him, still holding his hand. Connor figured he could enjoy that longer than usual given the situation.

He stared ahead at Emery, waiting for the image to stop swirling, and as soon as he saw Emery's eyes give an extended blink, squeezing tight to stay tears, the spell broke. Connor coughed and shook his head. His head throbbed, the wound—*bite*—on his neck stung, and his rear was a little sore from falling, but he only felt mildly dizzy, like after giving blood to the Red Cross.

Connor squeezed Emery's hand as tight as he could to show he was okay, he just didn't feel like moving yet. "That actually didn't suck as much as you think," he said, though he had no plans to elaborate on how *good* some of it had felt. "Believe me now?"

A bitter, huff of a laugh escaped Emery's lips. "Nah, you're clearly out of your mind."

Connor laughed, which turned into a slight coughing fit, then eventually back into laughter. "Ass."

Emery offered a weary smile. He released Connor's hand, which would have been a disappointment, but he moved to Connor's other side to sit between him and the nightstand—close, hip to hip. "I think I almost killed you."

That monotone did not befit Emery at all. "Listen to my complete sentences, Em. I'm just a little winded. I've never fainted after a blood drive. That was you, remember?"

Emery lurched away from the wall as if he might leap to his feet. "You need like…orange juice and something to eat."

Connor clamped a hand down on Emery's thigh before he could go anywhere. "Five minutes and I'll go downstairs with you."

"But—"

"Your parents are both home, right?"

Horror filled Emery's face.

"So take a minute, and then we can face them together. You're less likely to suddenly confess vampirism if I'm with you. Plus, if you went alone you'd have to either admit I was hiding in the room, or try and lie, and then your mom would probably keep you down there talking for an hour while I wither away up here alone. Listen to my superior common sense, Em." Connor stretched his grin, willing himself to stay alert. He really didn't feel that bad, not like he'd pass out. Though orange juice and a cookie sounded amazing.

A new throb of pain pulsed from his bite, and Connor brought his hand up to it without thinking. Since the bite was on the left side, when he gasped from the sting and brought his hand down again, a smear of red gleamed at him from his silver Terminator fingertips.

"Shit, better find a way to hide this," he murmured.

"Emery?" Kay's voice called from the doorway. Connor hadn't even heard her open it, and by the way Emery jumped, he hadn't either.

"Here!" Connor raised his right hand so she would see that they were hidden by the bed.

Emery turned to him with an extra helping of that horrified expression.

"We can't hide, Em," Connor whispered. "It'll be okay. We'll figure this out."

Kay came around the side of the bed, a drawn, sympathetic look on her face. Connor tried to think of some way to hide his wound, but Kay's eyes went straight to the contrast of red on silver, then up to the bite mark.

Emery tensed.

"You boys," Kay said with a sigh. "Let me grab you a Band-Aid, Connor. You know climbing that trellis is dangerous. How did you even manage to cut yourself there?" She turned without waiting for a response, probably taking their slouched positions on the floor as her having interrupted some hushed conversation about the previous night's events.

"Leave it to your mom to give me an alibi," Connor said.

Emery stared forward. "What are we gonna do?"

"Well, for starters, I figured we'd grab some food for me, come back to the room, and stay in here figuring out the specifics of real-life vampires until you go talk to Tim."

"Oh god," Emery pulled his knees to his chest and burrowed his face in his jeans, "what do I say to Tim? I can't tell him the truth. But what lie makes sense? I don't want to say Mr. Leonard knocked me out. He was just desperate. He wasn't thinking straight."

"So say he pushed you into the closet to hide you when he heard people coming, and you accidentally hit your head and got knocked out."

"I don't have a single mark on me."

"Then…you had a panic attack and *passed* out."

"Maybe…"

"You're one of the best actors I know, Em. *Act* your way through this. It's Tim. He'll believe you."

Emery didn't look convinced, even as he nodded into his knees.

Kay returned with a box of Band-Aids, and Connor kept his silver hand up near his wound in case closer inspection revealed that it was punctures instead of a scratch. He accepted the box gratefully as he and Emery stood.

"Thanks. And sorry. I was just worried," Connor said.

"I know, I'm not really upset. I'm just glad to see you talking about what happened, honey," she turned to Emery, "because we still need to bring you to the station later. Do you think you're up for that?"

Connor feared Emery would lose it, fail to hide his anxiety and confess the truth, but like the amazing actor Connor knew his friend to be, Emery smiled.

"Just a couple more hours, Mom. Maybe we could meet Tim at three?"

Kay's face lit up at Emery's easy disposition. "I'll let him know. Do you two want some lunch in the meantime?" she asked, passing her gaze between them.

"Please," Connor said. "Can we bring it up here?"

"Of course." She reached a hand to the back of Emery's head, digging her small, white fingers into his dark hair, and pulled him down toward her to kiss his forehead. "Whatever you need, honey." She looked back to Connor. "Now get yourself patched up, mister. And when you leave later, do it through the front door."

"Yes, Ma'am."

The bite wasn't bleeding freely, but enough red smeared Connor's skin and hand that he wanted to get cleaned up. Once Kay left, Emery followed Connor into the bathroom across the hall and insisted that he help.

He proceeded to sit Connor down on the toilet seat so he could get a better vantage point. He wet a rag in the sink with warm water and carefully wiped the skin clean, leaving behind what Connor could only assume were two very prominent puncture marks by the way Emery scowled.

It felt nice though, Emery's warm fingers brushing his skin after the washcloth, and the tender way he used a towel to dry the area before securing an antiseptic-covered bandage. When he was done, he looked on with creased eyebrows as Connor washed off his silver fingers in the sink.

"Stop that, I'm fine," Connor said.

"I *ate* you," Emery droned.

A smile quirked at the corner of Connor's mouth.

"No wisecracks, Connor, this is serious," Emery hissed. His expression softened as he said more hushed, "I'm dangerous."

Connor leaned back against the sink. "You just helped clean my wound. Did you feel like biting me again?"

Emery's mouth opened, closed, and opened again before he spoke. "No. I don't feel hungry at all anymore. I feel good—great. But that just makes it worse. How often am I going to need to do that? What if I can't control it next time either?"

"What 'either'? You stopped yourself this time, and you didn't even take that much." Connor stood up straighter only to feel the room tilt. He leaned back on the sink again as Emery shot him a pointed look. "Whatever, I just need lunch, and I'll be fine. We'll take this all one step, one day at a time, figure out all your vampire kinks and quirks—"

"What if that Alec guy shows up?"

"Then he'll probably want to help take care of the hunters."

"Oh god, there are vampire hunters after me." Emery turned to the wall and pressed his forehead against the marbled tiles. "I have fangs, a statement to give to the police, vampire hunters probably already looking for me, and a test in Psych on Monday. How is this anyone's life?"

"Currently it's *your* life." When Emery grumbled in response, Connor reached out with his Terminator hand to squeeze his friend's shoulder. "We'll figure it out, Em."

"How? I can't even go in the sun."

Connor thought a moment, then turned his gentle presence on Emery's shoulder into a tight grip on his arm. He whirled him around and yanked him out of the bathroom, back across the hallway. He refused to be slowed down by his lurching stomach or the dizziness clawing at his vision, and didn't stop, despite a few harried protests from Emery, until they were back in front of the window where he thrust his friend into the sunlight as before.

Emery shot up his hands, looking ready to stumble away, only to slowly lower them and blink blearily into the light.

"It's not as bad," he said, amazed. "But it was awful that last time. I felt like I was on fire. It's not even as bad as this morning." He leaned cautiously closer to the glass, as if expecting all of that to change at a moment's notice.

"I figured," Connor said, arms crossed in victory. "You just needed to feed."

"*Please* don't use that word." Emery looked at him with a grimace.

"Okay. You just needed to *eat me*, then."

"Let's stick with feed."

Connor grinned, and when their eyes met, they tumbled into laughter.

"Come on," Connor said, reaching to squeeze Emery's shoulder once more.

He hated that Emery had gone through something so terrible, hated that there would likely be worse to wade through in the future, but he also kind of liked that it gave him an excuse to touch Emery more. He knew that was pathetic, but he enjoyed every moment of it anyway.

"I'm starving."

CHAPTER 6

I was a vampire. I had been one for twenty-four hours, and I still didn't believe it.

When I went to the police station that afternoon, the lie that I'd had a panic attack when the killers showed up, and then passed out when Mr. Leonard put me in the closet, fooled Tim just as Connor had predicted. No, I hadn't gotten a look at any of them. If I had, they would have seen me go in the closet; they would have found me.

I wondered how long it would take 'them' to find me now.

No one was going to put my name in the papers, but there had been a statement that a 'local teen' was found alive. That was probably all it would take for the hunters to stick around and start looking, and enough people knew it was me—probably everyone at school—that it might only be a matter of days before they figured out where I lived. I really hoped Mr. Leonard wasn't wrong about his friend Alec coming here—his maker. Which meant Mr. Leonard was *my* maker. Or had been…

Connor and I figured out quite a few things about what I could do, though none of it made me feel better. I could eat, and everything tasted like I remembered it, I just didn't feel full by any of it. I could probably eat and eat forever; my body just seemed to absorb it. Connor made a big deal over the fact that I hadn't used the bathroom since we left school the day before, and we realized that I really must be using everything for energy, so I guess that was a weird plus.

Silver had no effect.

"That's werewolves anyway," Connor had said. "I don't know who started the idea of it working on vampires."

The jar of garlic he made me smell was potent, but the sting it left in my nose only seemed to be caused by enhanced-senses, not an aversion to the plant. We didn't test having me eat any though, just in case. We didn't bother with some of the sillier myths either, like crossing running water, needing to sleep in the earth or a coffin. I'd already slept plenty.

We also knew I could—like Mr. Leonard had done to me—glamour someone to let me bite them. At least that's the word Connor used. I hated that part, because it had made me, and now Connor, stop fighting. It scared me even more than I'd admitted to him that I might have killed my best friend if I hadn't snapped to my senses.

Connor's parents made him stay home after I got back from the police station, since I needed my rest, apparently, though I think it was more that Mom and Dad wanted some time alone with me. We watched one of my dad's favorite movies, *Murder by Death*, which we all agreed was the exact right kind of inappropriate, and I laughed like always at the ridiculous whodunit plotline, at ease if only because not once did I feel like biting either of them.

Connor and I talked into the night over our walkies, planning to spend Sunday figuring out more of my abilities. The thought of going back to school on Monday terrified me, but when my parents offered to let me stay home for as long as I needed, that sounded worse.

"Hungry yet?" were the first words out of Connor's mouth when we met in my backyard Sunday morning. It was brisk out, but I didn't feel cold anymore. And direct light from the sun didn't make me feel hot, though the glare did bother me a little.

"Not hungry. So at least I don't need to feed every day…so far."

We'd decided on my yard because first, my parents were still a little over-protective, even about me going next door, and second, our yard had a higher fence with very low risk of anyone seeing what we were doing.

I frowned at Connor as he proceeded to drop his baseball bag on the damp, cold ground, and pulled out his catcher's gear. There had been some weird regulations argument about whether it was okay for his mitt to actually be attached to his arm—because of course he'd made a prosthetic for that purpose—but he'd bowed out before his parents could raise any fuss. He preferred robotics and backstage to sports anyway, but he still kept his gear for fun.

"What's that for?" I asked.

"I figured we should start with strength, speed, and agility today," Connor said with the same professor voice he used when doing experiments on a new arm. "This is the best gear I have for extra padding."

"I'm not going to hit you," I said, watching him put the gear on regardless of my protests.

"What else are you gonna hit? I think your folks would notice a dent in the fence."

I stared down at my hands. "I can't be that strong."

"We'll start simple and find out." He grinned at me, moving to the center of the backyard.

Mom was out judging one of the high school Speech meets today, which she always volunteered for, and I'd insisted that she not cancel. I'd have joined my school team again if senior year hadn't been so busy. Anyway, I knew how much she loved it—having been in Speech herself in high school—and I think she needed a distraction from all this even more than I did.

Dad was inside cleaning the house, though there was a new tactics role-playing game he wanted to show me, so as long as he was either cleaning or playing that, he shouldn't look in the backyard until we went in. I hoped.

"What happened to bringing me Swedish Fish and *Mortal Kombat*?" I scowled.

"I figured the fish would be in poor taste since you don't need to eat anymore, but *Mortal Kombat*…" he pointed to the side pocket of his bag, "is your reward once we're done."

I looked around for any possible sign of peeping eyes as I squared off in front of Connor, and he—in full catcher's gear, sans mask and mitt—got in a ready stance like a Sumo wrestler.

"What are you expecting me to do, exactly?"

"Come at me as fast as you can," he said. "Don't think about hitting or anything, just charge me."

He was enjoying this a little too much. I looked from his grin to his bright red prosthetic. It was the most resilient one he had, as indestructible as he could make it, but that just made me think, "What if I break your arm? Or your *other* arm? Or any other bones, for that matter?"

Connor stood up straight as if he hadn't considered actual injury, but then settled into his ready position again. "Okay, maybe not as fast as you can. Don't try to break me. And if you do, well…I am due for a broken bone. Rynn broke her arm before she was two."

"Your sister is not an example I want you to follow." Rynn was pursuing a theater major in college, but actually wanted to get into stunt driving. She was a tall, gorgeous, blonde beast.

"Then go easy," Connor said.

He must have forgotten how many years I'd been Defensive Tackle for the football team. I squared my shoulders, aimed for the center of his chest, and charged. The next moment, I was standing where Connor had been, and he was halfway to the fence flat on his back.

"Sweet!" He jumped up before I could call out in concern, and rushed forward to meet me. "Dude, I barely even saw you move. You were like The Flash—for *real*. And…ow," he rubbed his chest protector as if that would sooth the bruises forming beneath, "that was going easy for you? I wonder what going full pelt would be like…"

I stumbled back a step. "I knocked you like fifteen feet without trying. I am not doing that again."

"I didn't say we *would*." He gripped my shoulder with his gloved right hand. He'd been doing that a lot lately, which I assumed was to make me think he wasn't afraid, though I couldn't understand how that was true. I'd bitten him, hurt him…

I shook his hand away. "I don't think we should do this anymore."

"Em." He followed every step I took backward, a glower darkening his honey eyes. "Would you rather not know what you're capable of and accidentally tear a door off its hinges at school? When you know your limits, you know how to pull back from them." He stopped advancing on me and held out his gloved hand. "Shake it, just like you would normally."

"What?"

"This is the control—you doing something with normal, average strength. When you see that you can do that without going too far, then you'll feel better about trying things that go past the control. It's science, dude. Sort of."

I stared at the offered hand. I'd done normal physical activities last night. Helped Mom make dinner, helped Dad with the dishes, taken a shower, kissed Mom and Dad goodnight. None of those actions had seemed out of my control. But now I was scared of crushing Connor's fingers. We'd crushed one of his prosthetic hands testing the resistance once. These he would feel.

"You're not going to hurt me," he said, and advanced another step.

I took a breath, took his hand, squeezed with the normal pressure I was used to giving, and we shook.

"No different than usual," Connor said.

"Because we shake hands so often," I muttered.

He smacked me in the chest with the hand I'd just shaken, and I could feel that he did so pretty hard, but it didn't even slightly push me back. His eyes widened. "Whoa, maybe we should practice me trying to charge you next. You're like a concrete wall."

He pressed his palm flat to my chest and pushed as hard as he could—I could tell by the strain on his face. I hadn't really been trying to remain immobile when he first smacked me, but now I gave it some effort. It was actually kind of funny how much it looked like he was struggling to move me.

"Must be all that Aikido paying off," I said.

Connor laughed. He gave up pushing and smacked me again. "See, knew you could still joke about this. Come on, let's try something else." He danced excitedly over to his bag. "I want to see how good your reflexes are."

After successfully catching every ball he threw at me, including several he purposefully threw out of range, he got this gleam in his eyes as he wound up; said, "Now try *this*," and turned 180 degrees to chuck the ball at the fence.

It was as if my body knew how fast to go, how far to travel, just from my desired outcome. I just thought, *catch*, and I felt the ground move beneath my feet, the air whip around me like a strong wind, this wonderful zing in my chest, and suddenly I stood with the ball Connor had thrown at the fence easily caught in my fist. Somehow, I'd zipped around behind him like a speedster and caught the ball in half a second—effortless. It made me want to take off down the street, see how fast I could really go, if I could race to the end of town and back again without feeling winded, and how fast my time would be while doing it. Connor was rubbing off on me.

Then I thought of how many ways this power could hurt him.

"No, no, don't you dare drop that smile, Emery Mavus," Connor chided me as he approached. "This is fun. Of course it's fun. You're a freaking superpower."

I dropped the ball. "I'm a vampire, Connor. A mon—"

"Don't say monster." His face was blank when I looked up, too serious as he poked me in the chest with his red plastic finger. "People can be monsters, Em. But what you are doesn't make you one automatically. Mr. and Mrs. Leonard weren't. You don't really think they were, do you?"

I guess I didn't. If they had been killers, there would be evidence of that, but I'd never heard of any weird deaths in our town, or any surrounding towns. Somehow they'd managed to feed without anyone finding out, without hurting anyone.

"And *you're* not," Connor stressed. "Not unless you choose to be. Don't make me force that old book on you," he said with a renewed gleam in his eyes.

"What old book?" I squinted at him.

"You remember." And rather than explain, he started in on the chorus to "O Holy Night," and I instantly knew what book he meant—*The Vampire Who Came For Christmas*.

The villain was brought to tears by that song at the end of the story. We read it in Elementary school. It had been Connor's, which he'd let me borrow, but when he handed it off to another friend, that person moved before he got it back—lost forever. I got a copy for him as a Christmas gift last year, which he'd gotten endless amusement out of. If only I'd known I was predicating our future.

"Please stop singing," I said before he could butcher any more notes, though I couldn't help grinning at his antics. There was a reason he was in band and not choir.

"Is there some kind of satanic ritual going on back here?" came Tim's voice from the back door as he stepped outside to join us, "because that has got to be torture I'm hearing."

He was off duty judging by the civilian clothes, but his presence made me flinch. Dad came out behind him.

Connor spun on his heels to face them without missing a beat at his interrupted wailing. "What's up? Catch those killers yet, Chief?"

"Not yet, but we're taking bets on what day this week we'll have them in the back of a cruiser. Just like we did when Officer Larson had her twins." Tim winked at Connor, his more common joking nature undeterred. He'd tried to ease my nerves at the station yesterday with humor, but it hadn't helped much.

"Do you need something from me, Tim?" I asked. "I'm sorry I don't remember more."

"You're fine, son, just wanted to check in on you. All of the evidence is keeping you in the clear as a suspect—not that there was ever any doubt—but I figured you'd want to know we can say it officially now. We noticed some motorcycle tracks out by the house that we're looking into, and have some other leads I can't discuss, but I also wanted you to be aware of a bit of a babysitter we'll be assigning you."

"Babysitter?" Connor repeated.

"Just a single patrol to keep an eye on things for a while," my dad spoke up. "If it had been just Mallory, it would be different, but after the killers returned for Will, the police want to be sure you aren't under any additional threat. Just think of it as having a secret admirer for a few days; following closely in an unmarked car with an armed officer inside." He smirked, trying to make light of this, but his anxiety always showed in his eyes, a telling crinkle of the skin. He was really freaked out.

"So, like, watching the house? Following me to school?" I asked.

"And play practice," Tim said. "But besides that we'd like you to try and stay close to home for a few days. It's much more likely that the Leonards were the target, and with both of them gone now, you're in the clear, but seeing as how everyone knows everything about everybody in this town…"

I nodded. I'd put that together myself, but now it felt even realer, the thought that these hunters—who had taken out two experienced vampires easily—were coming for me next, and some lone cop probably wouldn't be enough to protect me.

I struggled to smile but saw the way Dad's expression fell. He could read me as well as I read him, and my eyes probably looked three shades of panicked.

"It's fine," I said. "It's a good thing, right? Just a precaution. Probably won't even matter."

I zoned out for whatever else was said before Tim waved goodbye and headed back across the street to his house. Somewhere nearby, some cop would be watching me from now on, so practicing any abilities in the backyard was out for the foreseeable future.

Dad's large brown hand came down on my shoulder. "Why don't we head inside so I can show you boys that new RPG, huh? We can order hot wings for lunch."

A little of my terror abated, but only a little. My dad was a big guy, solidly built, stockier than me by quite a bit, and the strongest person I knew—well, before I'd grown superpowers. He'd stop at nothing to protect me and Mom if something bad happened. If the hunters came for me, I wasn't the only one at risk, and that made me feel like I might throw up.

I wondered if it would look like blood.

"Did I hear something about a video game, coz I'm pretty sure someone promised me *Mortal Kombat*." Jules' blonde head peeked over the fence, and someone else's much more tanned hand waved by her ear. I knew it could only be Aurora—she was too short to see over the fence.

I looked to Connor as the girls came around to the gate. He shrugged with a not at all innocent smirk on his face.

Jules held the latest *Mortal Kombat* video game in her hands and waved it at my dad. "Connor brought the movie, Mr. Mavus, and there is no way we are watching it without me first schooling you with Sub-Zero. Finish him!" she announced in a hilariously accurate approximation of the game's iconic announcer. The pink sundress she was wearing in no way lessened the affect.

"You're on, Miller." My dad pointed at Jules with a dramatic flourish. When he dropped his arm, he turned to Aurora. "And you, young lady, need to inform your mother that she is way overdue for hosting our next block party. I wouldn't think she'd be so slow to plan something that gives her Korean fortitude the chance to drink me under the table again."

Aurora flipped her hair with one hand, the other clutching a large, button-covered tote bag slung over her shoulder. "I'll tell her, if it means the parents are at my house while we get yours for the night."

Dad laughed. "Remind me not to vote for you when you run for office."

There was a great rustling of activity as he ushered the girls inside, who each shot me a smile—without asking about yesterday or if I was okay or any other telling, grating questions—and Connor gathered up his baseball bag and removed his gear.

I just stood there a moment, awed by everyone, but especially by Connor, who'd obviously orchestrated this. The feeling of normal was small, and probably wouldn't last, but it was better than feeling the panic creep up again.

I nudged Connor's shoulder as we headed inside.

"I know," he said, "you love me."

"I really, really do."

CHAPTER 7

Connor

Connor grinned at Emery as his friend climbed into the Thunderbird next to him, toting his brand new cell phone that hopefully wouldn't die as easily as the last one. Without even a 'good morning', Connor passed Emery a small oval case.

"What's this?"

"So you don't have to keep squinting all the time."

Emery opened the case to discover a pair of dark aviator sunglasses that Connor had snatched from the props of their freshman school play—*Who Dunit... and to Whom?* "But you love these. And I already have sunglasses."

"Not that cool, you don't."

"True…"

"And you need them more than me." Connor nodded definitively and pulled out of the driveway as Emery donned the aviators.

"Thanks," he said.

The smile that graced Emery's tan face, and the small sigh of relief he offered once the bright light from the sun was blocked, made Connor's stomach flutter.

Tan. Emery was naturally darker skinned, though he'd looked sickly pale up until he fed from Connor the other night. This thought successfully distracted Connor from his dreamy musings and launched him into a diatribe on vampires and white skin that lasted all the way to school.

"But dead skin still tans," Emery said as they walked inside. "Someone brought it up in Biology once."

"I did." Connor rolled his eyes. "Do you actually think of your skin as dead?"

Emery stuttered over his feet, nearly shouldering into the lockers they passed. "I...don't know."

"Well I'm going with 'no'. And besides, there's an obvious reason why vampires wouldn't be tan anyway."

"Who's talking about tan vampires?" Nick McPherson joined them as they neared the music alcove that split off into the band and choir rooms.

Nick played percussion in Jazz Band. He was broader than Emery and easily could have been on the football team, but he preferred access to power tools over blunt trauma. He had a sort of quiet intensity that everyone agreed could easily turn to nefarious purposes if not given direction, which was why they always made sure he helped with backstage for the plays. His tightly coiled black hair stayed perfectly still a she bobbed his head to the last refrains of the music he'd been listening to, before pulling out his remaining earbud.

Emery widened his eyes at Connor, but since he was still wearing the aviators, it just looked like his eyebrows arched.

"Back me up, Nick," Connor said, taking the interruption in stride. "Why would vampires be pale even if it's been proven that dead skin tans in the sun?"

"Why would a vampire go out in the sun?" Nick frowned. "If it bugs 'em, even if it didn't burn 'em, like, go up in flames, wouldn't it make sense they'd avoid it? Normal people who stay indoors most the time are still pale."

Emery stopped at the choir room door. "Oh. Right. Okay, I concede, that was a stupid idea. Even someone with darker skin would naturally get paler over time."

"Thank you," Connor smirked.

"They still wouldn't turn porcelain if they started out mocha." He pointed subtly at himself. Nick nodded, since his skin tone was more like coffee, no cream.

"Point," Connor conceded.

"What brought this on?" Nick asked.

"*Once Bitten* was on last night," Connor said, unperturbed. He watched Emery flinch and then relax out of his tension.

"What's that one about?"

"Vampire queen turns virgins into vampires to keep herself young, and Jim Carrey is the only older virgin left. So, you know, *you'd* be safe if that lore was true." Connor patted Nick's shoulder with his left hand, wearing his teal prosthetic again since it was the best for playing the piano and they'd been warned about starting a new song today.

"Nice," Nick said with a glare, "so you wanna give me the play by play of *your* last—"

"Bye, Em!" Connor shoved Nick toward the band room.

Emery choked out a laugh, "See you guys after," and waved goodbye as he slipped into the choir room with a look of decided resignation.

Connor didn't envy him the array of questions he would most likely face from his fellow choir kids—there had already been quite a few curious looks from passing students on their way inside that Connor had done his best to distract Emery from.

He and Nick headed for Jazz Band across the alcove, Nick shooting Connor a sly smirk before they parted inside—Aurora wasn't the only one who knew about Connor's crush on Emery, the bastard.

Most of the other students were already in their chairs, warming up their instruments or chatting, including Aurora with her clarinet and Jules on alto sax. Aurora had her Sailor Moon planner out, as always, and Connor flashed her a smile as he sat down at the piano. His mom had taught him, ensuring he could play his scales even before his first prosthetic.

Five minutes later, Mr. Nellis, the band director, was just starting to introduce their new piece of music when the intercom went off, preceded by a sharp beeping noise.

"Attention students. I'm afraid that due to the presence of a new bomb threat this morning, we are going to have to evacuate for a full sweep. Please file out of your rooms and follow your instructors as we've gone over in the rehearsal protocol."

The principal's voice sounded tired, as sick of this nonsense as the students were, punctuated by the loud groan that filled the resonant band room as soon as the intercom went silent—after another annoying beep. This led into persistent beeps every ten seconds to indicate they were in a state of RED ALERT, as Connor called it.

"You heard him," Mr. Nellis said with a deep sigh. "Instruments away but left in their places, and lineup at the door."

"If they add a single day after graduation because of all this time we're missing," Jules grumbled as Connor joined Nick and the girls in line, "screw it, I am done. I mean, we'll have already walked. What are they gonna do?"

"We don't actually get our diplomas when we walk," Aurora said in a bored tone, still half buried in her planner, "it's empty. They mail it to us later. So they could still refuse to mail yours."

Jules wailed dramatically.

They paraded out of the room, meeting up with the students from Honor Choir. Emery shuffled in line when he saw them so he could walk parallel.

"Do you think it was in that bathroom again?" he asked as they passed the girls room just outside the music alcove.

"Probably," Nick shrugged.

"Urg, what is the point?" Jules snarled.

"Time out of class, duh," Connor said. "Which is stupid if they force us to make up the time later. This is how we know it's a freshman. No bigger picture mentality."

"It's not like there's a real bomb," Aurora said, at last tucking her planner into her shoulder bag—she'd never had a normal backpack for as long as Connor had known her. "And that would be the smart thing if you really wanted to take out students—make a bomb threat but then don't actually have it be a bomb."

"What do you mean?" Emery asked with a scowl. He still had the aviators on, which wasn't completely unheard of given Jazz Band and Honor Choir were Zero Hour classes that started at 7:30, so a few students sleepwalked their way through the first couple songs.

Almost the entire school was in attendance by this time, just not all of them were in classrooms. Those who had been in the commons area, waiting for normal classes to start at 8:15, were lined up and led outside by the assistant principal.

From there, the entire school trekked across the street to nearby Trinity Lutheran Church where they smushed into the sanctuary and basement depending on grade level. All of this without being able to go back to their lockers if they'd left their coats in there, which was most of them. Connor hadn't brought a coat, so he was grateful he'd chosen a warmer sweatshirt today since it wasn't supposed to get above forty degrees.

"I get it," Connor said, addressing the group. "Think of how many times we've practiced this evacuation protocol, and how many times we've done it for real since the threats started. If you actually wanted to cause trouble, you could turn a bomb threat into a school shooting and be way more successful."

"How do you figure that?" Jules asked with an elegantly raised, blonde eyebrow.

"Yeah?" Nick's expression mirrored hers, though not quite as regally, since his eyes always looked a little twitchy.

"Everyone knows the path we're taking to get to Trinity," Aurora said. "All anyone would have to do is write the threat and then setup shop on the roof. Then once the majority of the school is outside heading across the street...open fire."

"Genius, really. We'd walk right into a trap." Connor looked back up at the roof as they exited the building, which prompted the others, and a couple students who were close enough to overhear, to do the same.

"Are you two seriously plotting how to successfully pull off a school shooting?" Emery hissed at them. His sunglasses looked perfectly in place now, as several other students pulled on theirs for the walk.

Connor and Aurora looked at each other.

"Good point," Connor said. "If anyone in authority overheard the two kids in school who actually have regular access to firearms having this conversation, we might be in trouble."

"Academic discussion does not constitute condoning something...but agreed," Aurora gave in. "And speaking of guns," she flipped her hair as if unbothered by that dose of reality, "for Jules' birthday this summer, I was thinking we could take her to the range. Let her try your dad's .22 and my mom's Glock."

"Really?" Jules' eyes lit up. She had been angling for an outing at the shooting range ever since the first of them turned eighteen. She was the baby of their entire class and didn't turn eighteen until July.

"The rifle or the handgun?" Connor asked. "Because the handgun is Mom's."

Jules' face split into an even wider grin. "Both. Definitely both."

"Do you think you'll have that prototype gun arm ready in time, Con-Man?" Aurora asked. "You keep making promises and not delivering."

"Yeah...Mom's been putting the veto on that pretty hard, but Dad's wearing her down. Right, Em?" When Connor didn't receive any answer, he turned to look at his friend. They were almost across the street to the church, but Emery's attention had drifted. "Hey, you okay?"

"Sinuses still bugging you, Mavus?" Aurora asked.

Emery's attention snapped back to them. "Huh? No, I...I'm fine, I just...felt like someone was watching me for a moment."

"Well someone probably is, remember?" Connor said. "Police babysitter?"

"Right," Emery said, but his frown indicated he thought otherwise.

"You have police following you, Mavus?" Nick said.

"Just to be safe." Emery's shoulders tensed at this opening for further questions about what had happened Friday night. The kids in line with Emery all conspicuously tilted their heads to hear more. "I'm, uhh...not allowed to talk about anything while they're still investigating," he said, using the rehearsed lines Connor had given him. Tim hadn't actually told them that.

Connor elbowed Nick in the side with a pointed raise of his eyebrows and a hinting chin-jut at Emery.

"Cheer up, man," Nick said as he caught on, his voice a low but encouraging rumble. "It's a shame about the Leonards. They were cool. But at least we get to spend the next hour playing Egyptian Ratscrew. You got the goods, Aurora?"

Aurora shot him a triumphant smirk as they shuffled into the church and down the basement stairs. She pulled a deck of cards from her bag. "Don't I always?"

~

Today the game had quickly gone down from our group and two others to just me, Connor, and Aurora. She had sharp nails and was lightning fast—a ringer if there were ever any newbies to the game. Nick sat with his hand poised, ready to slap back in if any doubles appeared. Anyone who came over hoping to pry me for details about Friday night was drowned out by the game.

Egyptian Ratscrew, Egyptian War, ERF—whatever name someone gave it, it was the best card game in history, if a little dangerous at times. The main fun came when there were doubles and it became an evil Slapjack—best reflexes won.

I was focusing half of my attention on the game and half on making sure that when I did slap doubles, I didn't break any bones if there were hands beneath mine. No one had grimaced more than usual so far.

What I was having a harder time controlling was how fast I was. I told myself to hold back with a lighter touch, but once the speed around the circle got going and doubles appeared, I was nearly impossible to beat today. Connor kept shooting me little half-smirks, the only one who knew why I had an edge.

The rest of my senses were sharpened too, something we'd discovered right away over the weekend. I remembered how well I could smell Connor when we were alone in my room. That was still true. It took him three weeks to grow peach fuzz, so he rarely smelled like aftershave, but he used mint-scented shampoo. I'd never noticed it the way I could now.

I let my nose drift around the circle while we played. Jules had this green tea perfume she'd mentioned, but it didn't smell like green tea to me, more like fresh and earthy. Aurora smelled like strawberries, probably from her body wash. Nick—I coughed and missed a passing pair of doubles. Nick needed new deodorant. Though I was probably the only one who could pick up on the subtleties; it's not as if Nick straight-out smelled bad.

I drifted back to Connor's mint. I really liked that smell, though I think I liked it even better the way it had been Saturday morning, mixed with sawdust and smells from the stage. He smelled like that after a day in his workshop, too; the renovated side of their garage where he and his dad made prosthetics.

I missed another pair of doubles and shook my head. Daydreaming about how Connor smelled was definitely on my 'too weird to share with him later' list. I must have been distracted after what happened outside.

For a moment I'd had that feeling like someone was watching me, that eerie prickling in my periphery, and when I looked, I could have sworn I saw someone duck out of view around the school. I was pretty sure my babysitter was remaining in a vehicle, not stalking around school grounds. Whoever was supposed to be watching me had probably been called in to help with the school sweep anyway.

But then, who had been outside? Even with my new eyesight, whoever it was had been fast enough that all I caught was a blur of black leather.

"Head in the game, Mavus," Aurora chided me as I missed a pair of Jacks this time.

But it was too late. Even as a superhuman—which Connor kept reminding me I was now—I lost a few turns later as my failed slapping revealed that the rest of my hand was a whole lot of nothing.

CHAPTER 8

Connor

"I'm just saying, it's awesome to do a play with equal parts men and women, but hard to be a hundred percent happy about it when one of the female characters runs around in lingerie the whole time as the proverbial dumb blonde bimbo," Aurora said without looking at Connor. Her eyes were trained on the stage beyond the curtains, her headset securely in place as stage manager, and her long hair rolled into a perfect bun at the back of her head.

"I think that's a bit of an exaggeration," Connor said. "You could interpret the character as all about sexual empowerment."

"Is it still empowerment if it's exploitative for the sake of others?" Aurora asked, watching Jules saunter across set in a slinky turquoise nighty that accentuated her ample figure. Aurora glanced aside, down Connor's body none too subtly, then back up to his face. "Present company excluded, of course."

Connor's voice rose to something a little louder than an acceptable stage whisper. "Wait, am I not allowed to like boobs? Who decided that? I'll have you know that there is a proud tradition of gay men appreciating boobs. It was the one reprieve my dad got when I came out."

Aurora snorted, returning her attention to the scene. "Mandy needs that extra set of sardines prepped, Con-Man. And I suppose *someone* needs to go prep Mavus' pants. I hope he's wearing appropriate boxers today."

"Ha. Ha. Who's being exploitative now?" Connor pouted.

Mandy Lakin was the prop master. She made sure that all props were ready and in their appropriate locations, usually on the prop table for the actors to grab without anything getting misplaced. Connor was in charge of preparing extra sardines, however, since his mother had been the one to create the sludge they used to simulate the real thing. The sardines themselves were grey Styrofoam marked with black sharpies for eyes, but the goo was Chemistry genius. Why Connor hadn't inherited his mother's prowess for the subject, he had no idea.

"And okay, fine, so Brooke is meant to be a dumb blonde, but you can't tell me some girls don't look at Jules playing the pants off of that part and find it empowering. You start telling people what they are and aren't allowed to be empowered by and you totally miss the point."

"I'm not saying it shouldn't be allowed," Aurora said. "Just sad this kind of thing is so expected."

"Fair, but this play was originally written in like, what, the 70s? Isn't it bad enough we have to change all the 'damns' to 'darns'? If we trade book burning for torching plays—or bonfires made out of TV show boxsets and video games—I will not consider that a victory." He paused as he was about to walk further into the depths of backstage. "Crazy, huh? I think maybe our grandparents were fighting for the opposite of what so much of our generation is fighting for now."

"Crazy?" Aurora said with a smirk tossed over her shoulder. "Sounds more like history."

Half the time, Connor wasn't sure which side of an argument Aurora was on, or if she just liked to see where a discussion might lead. There was good reason he considered her one of his best friends—after Emery.

As Connor finished preparing the plate of sardines, which needed to have tape on the bottom to stick to Emery's hand for his next entrance—while Mandy peered over his shoulder, listening for where they were in the script the entire time—Nick walked up and whispered, "Funny, right? The whole play within a play thing? The characters are confused about how many plates of sardines there are and where and when they go on stage. And so are we." He offered a crooked smirk.

Connor and Mandy turned to him at the same time, with the same glare.

"Hilarious," she deadpanned.

She and Emery had dated sophomore year, so try as he might, Connor never could get himself to like her. For this, though, he could share a moment of camaraderie.

Nick held his hands up in defense and lumbered along toward the other side of backstage, passing Emery as he came over to get his plate of sardines. It was one of the few spots in the show when Emery had enough time to collect his own prop. He grinned, holding out his hand for Connor to tape it.

Their director and school counselor, Mark Olson, had pulled Emery aside when they first arrived at practice; Connor assumed to have a quick talk about recent events and make sure Emery was still good to perform. They had almost a month until opening night, but every practice counted, especially with a show as complicated as this one. Connor knew Emery wanted the distraction more than anything else, and since Mark hadn't said anything to the cast before practice started, he must have understood that too.

Connor let his flesh and blood hand linger on Emery's wrist maybe a moment too long as he finished taping the plate for the next scene, where Emery's character was meant to have accidentally glued it to his hand. But, despite Emery's grin, he seemed distracted and didn't notice the tender caress.

"How'd the test in Psych go?" Connor whispered before Emery could dash away.

Emery shrugged. "I'll know tomorrow. Sucks having Liz in the same class, but I think some of my studying managed to sink in." He flashed another almost believable smile, and his hazel eyes shimmered green in the dim lighting.

Connor reminded himself that it would be way too obvious if he swooned.

He wanted to ask if Emery was hungry, or feeling weird at all, or anything else vampire related, but he could only pretend they were talking fiction so many times before someone started asking real questions, especially with Mandy right there and other stagehands about.

It was quite a few pages later in the script when Emery needed to drop his pants on stage—well, for Act I; it was a recurring theme later too. And someone did need to prep his pants. Emery had the plate of sardines taped to one hand and would have a piece of paper taped to the other, so he wasn't capable of undoing his slacks himself at that point. When Aurora originally volunteered to do it, Emery had politely asked for Connor instead.

"It's at least slightly less awkward if you do it," Emery had said.

Connor hadn't the courage to explain to him how it so, so wasn't.

Emery with his pants down totally made up for Jules' cleavage, though—Connor would have to remember to tell Aurora that later.

"Gotta go. Don't forget to help on my next exit," Emery said with an exaggerated wink that he had no idea made Connor weak in the knees, and headed back to his stage mark for his next cue. He had the taped up piece of paper hidden behind the set. All he had to do was stick his hand to it before he went on.

During the next scene, Connor finished putting aside the sardine supplies so no one would accidentally step in or knock over any goo, then made his way across set to Emery's door. After Emery exited, they had a few pages before his pants needed to be mostly undone so that it was easier to drop them when his character realized the poison he was using to eat through the glue on his hands was eating through his pants as well. Connor moved to assist his friend immediately, so no one would be caught with, well…their pants *not* down.

Emery's stomach tensed as Connor's cold hands—the plastic of his left hand probably colder than his skin—brushed the slight pudge there while undoing his slacks. The pudge was soft, with just the slightest bit of dark hair trailing downward, and Connor used all of his will power not to let his thoughts stray.

This was his best friend. He felt low as dirt sometimes for the fantasies he had about Emery, without his friend even knowing how he felt.

"Connor?" Emery whispered, his brow knit when Connor looked up and realized he hadn't moved away yet.

"Still ticklish, huh, even as a vampire," Connor said, poking the favored bit of pudge with his finger.

Emery tensed again at the obvious tickle, then stifled a laugh—then frowned.

"Feeling okay?" Connor asked, as someone breezed by behind them and he remembered he was supposed to avoid using the word 'vampire'.

"Yeah, it's nothing like...*that*," Emery said. "It's just everything. Wanna come over for a bit after practice? I know it'll be late, but—"

"Of course."

Emery's shoulders sagged in relief. "Thanks. I really don't know how I'd get through this without you." He mustered a renewed smile, but just as their eyes met and lingered, his attention was taken by a familiar line, signaling it was almost time for him to go back on stage.

Connor gave a small wave and left his friend to it, moving swiftly to find the spot he always went to for this scene—the one with the best view of Emery when his pants dropped. He told himself it wasn't for the partial nudity but for the humor and how perfectly Emery played the role of bumbling, adorable idiot.

A mimbo. Totally fair play to Brooke's bimbo.

"You are seriously disturbed," Aurora said as she slipped up behind him, where he was somewhat hidden between the side curtains and flats.

Connor didn't bother turning around. "Yep."

"It is a nice view though."

"Sexist."

Aurora laughed.

Connor felt more like crying, watching for that magical moment when Emery playing the character of Frederick who in turn was playing the character of Philip stretched out his hands, one with sardines and the other a stuck tax return, losing the hold he had on his pants so that they dropped straight to the floor.

Cue laugh. Cue Connor's never-ending downward spiral at the sight of those strong dark legs and Emery's green and purple plaid boxer shorts.

~

Mom and Dad were curled up together on the sofa watching an episode of *Mystery Science Theater 3000* when Connor and I got home. Having had another bomb threat at school meant they were more agreeable about Connor staying over for an hour—at max—before we parted and went to bed. Connor had already gotten permission from his folks, but I suspected the cheesy humor of the "Space Mutiny" episode was what helped sway mine. It was hard being strict while watching a Canadian Space Opera.

We assured my parents that the bomb threats had nothing to do with anything other than freshmen antics, and headed upstairs with a swiped bag of potato chips for Connor to snack on. I hadn't decided yet if my lack of an appetite was something to mourn over. At least I *could* eat, like at lunch so no one questioned me, but it was weird that I didn't really miss it when I skipped a meal.

"Truth?" I said as we neared my room. We hadn't had much opportunity to talk alone all day. "I can't stop thinking about that person I saw during evacuation. What if the hunters already know who I am?"

"They'd have to question people for your name first, since it wasn't in the papers," Connor said smoothly, "or have some reason to suspect you after watching everyone. Just don't do anything too vampirey out in the open." He gave my shoulder a playful nudge.

"Like wearing sunglasses all day?" I nudged him back. I really liked those sunglasses. I still couldn't believe he'd given them to me.

"You took them off in class, right? And tons of people had shades on during the walk to Trinity."

"I guess."

I pushed my door open without really thinking about it, distracted enough that I didn't register how weird it was for the door to have been mostly closed…until I walked in on a stranger lying casually on my bed with my *Captain America: Man and Wolf* comic propped up on his knees.

My arm shot out on instinct to keep Connor behind me.

The stranger had somewhat smoothed back, curly brown hair, and a neatly trimmed, reddish brown mustache and beard. He wore dark jeans, a black blazer, blue Converse sneakers, and what I was pretty sure was a navy blue T-shirt with the TARDIS from *Doctor Who*. Like some goth hipster.

"Why is there a goth hipster on your bed?" Connor hissed, and my panic was momentarily quelled by how in synch we were.

The stranger looked up at that. His eyes were such a pale blue they looked silver, his skin fitting of a goth since it was almost white, and he had this smoothness about him that made it impossible to guess his age, though I wanted to say around thirty.

Like Mr. Leonard…

"Alec?"

His neutral expression flipped into an immediate, wide smile as he nodded toward the comic. "Cap Wolf? I preferred *Forever Avengers*, personally, but I suppose there's no accounting for taste."

CHAPTER 9

So Alec was who I'd seen by the school. I wanted to feel relief, but this was still a stranger, someone I knew to be a vampire, kicked back on my bed—with Connor behind me and my parents both downstairs.

Then it struck me just how much I could *tell* he was a vampire. It came in a rush, like getting hit with a strong scent, only it was more like an invisible shockwave. He had a scent, but it was too clean, like he never perspired, which I suddenly realized might be true. He was a sterile, sleek predator, and I was not nearly as high up on the food chain. The hair on my arms prickled, my vision sharpened, and I noticed for the first time that I could hear Connor's heartbeat like a metronome doing double time, because Alec's pulse was slow and steady.

"How lovely to realize that despite being under duress—which William obviously was to justify his actions—at least he turned someone interesting," Alec said, with a sharp British accent that sounded like it held another accent underneath, like he'd learned how to speak English in the UK but was originally from somewhere else.

Alec spun on the bed to drop his feet to the floor and stand in one flawless twirl. As he tossed the comic aside, Connor pushed me the rest of the way into the room and closed the door behind us.

"I can see why William liked you, trusted you," Alec said, glancing around my room with a look of satisfaction, maybe approval. "He'd never have hired you to be so close around his grounds if he didn't. He mentioned you once, I think; his gardener, is it? You'd think I'd know, wouldn't you, but children these days, not calling home as often as their parents would like. Don't you dare do that when you go off to university, young man," he pointed a slender finger my way, "it breaks the heart."

"Uhh…" I was sure there was an eloquent sentence in me somewhere, but I was too floored. Sure, I was a vampire, but I'd never met another one before—at least not knowingly. He was probably hundreds of years old.

"Do you think I could borrow that, actually," he said, gesturing back at the comic on the bed. "I didn't get to finish it, and I missed that run."

Okay, maybe he was a newer vampire? But Mr. and Mrs. Leonard had always seemed wise beyond their years—more so now when I thought back on it—and Alec was their maker; he had to be older than them. Their love of comics and pop culture had probably come from him. He certainly didn't conjure up any dark, broody images of Dracula or the vampire Lestat.

"I thought you said you preferred when Cap was a vampire in *Forever Avengers*," Connor said, moving around me toward Alec, which had felt like certain doom a moment ago, but I didn't get the impression he needed my protection anymore. "Which is seriously cliché, dude. Branch out beyond your species, why doncha?"

"Well. At least someone's paying attention," Alec said with an appraising look at Connor, the same way he'd appraised my bedroom. "And I am branching out. Why do you think I want to finish the werewolf story? As my young protégé said, I'm Alec. And you are…?" He held out a hand, and when they shook, I marveled at how Alec's skin was whiter than Connor's.

"Connor," he introduced himself. "I'm this sorry excuse for a vampire's best friend."

"Ah. I take it William didn't get to give any lessons on discretion, then."

"He didn't get to any lessons period, way I heard it."

They turned to me as their hands dropped, and I realized I should probably join in on the conversation. "He didn't tell me anything. He turned me, shoved me into a closet, and died." I winced at how blunt I'd just been, or maybe it was because I saw Alec wince, ever so slightly, like an eye twitch.

"Yes…" Alec said, his recently wide-smiling face reset to neutral. "When he called, I knew he'd do something foolish. I didn't think he'd actually turn someone, but I smelled you the moment I set foot in their house. Didn't take me long to track you here. It's…"

He trailed and for the briefest moment he looked ancient, like a thousand lifetimes were replaying behind his eyes, before he perked back up and stretched a Joker-like grin at me.

"It's your lucky day!" He tapped a finger to his lips and his eyes lit up like he'd just remembered he had a package coming in the mail. "My, I haven't trained a newly turned vampire since William and Mallory, and that was ages ago. A pity they aren't here to share all of their embarrassing stories about me, but you'll just have to use your imagination. Shall we get started on any basics you're curious about?" He rubbed his palms together, then glanced at Connor and winked. "Revealing your secret to a mortal would normally cost you a demerit, but given you had a few days without proper instruction, I suppose I can let him live."

I wanted to be horrified, but Connor huffed like he thought it was a joke.

Was it a joke?

"Wait, you're here to train me?" I asked, fully aware that Alec's glowing impression of me was probably being overshadowed by reality. "What about the hunters?"

Alec waved a dismissive hand. "Oh, we'll have to deal with them as well. I very much intend to discover why they thought it necessary to slaughter my children without probable cause." A swift edge of darkness clouded his expression before his smile once again returned. "But! All in good time. I can't very well have you running about unchecked and drawing attention to yourself. I'm a professional."

"A professional what?" Connor snorted. Apparently, he wasn't taking this—or Alec—very seriously, and it made me a little annoyed because I was still pretty freaked.

"The hunters—"

"Have no idea where you are," Alec interrupted me. "If they did, I would have noticed disturbances around your home. Actually, if they did, you'd probably be dead," he said thoughtfully—

thoughtfully, like it was fascinating instead of horrifying. "They're good, whoever they are. Barely any traces of them left behind at the house, nothing concrete to follow. It's likely they're still in town because of you, but it could be days, weeks before they show their hand or leave me a good enough trail to follow. We'll just have to be patient."

Connor crossed his arms with a scowl. "That's it? Can't you just, like, sense them?"

"I need a starting point, dear boy, I'm not psychic." Alec turned back to him with a matching incredulous stare, and seemed to notice Connor's prosthetic for the first time; teal plastic clashing against the light grey of his sweatshirt. He raised his eyebrows at it before looking Connor in the eyes. "We can be a bit like bloodhounds, admittedly, but I need something to track. Understand?"

That seemed to satisfy Connor. I wasn't sure I was satisfied by anything. I'd expected, I don't know, someone more like Mr. Leonard. This guy was much more scatterbrained and—what was the polite way my mother put it?—eccentric.

"You've already fed, it seems, though quite poorly." Alec squinted at Connor, at the Band-Aid on his neck peeking out of the sweatshirt, and reached without warning to rip it from his skin.

"Ow!" Connor's teal hand flew up to the red and angry puncture wounds.

"Don't be a baby," Alec chided him, "I'm just going to show our fledgling here—so sorry, dear boy," his gaze snapped to me, "but I haven't actually gotten your name yet." He folded up Connor's Band-Aid and tossed it at my waste basket. At least he didn't miss.

I had to tell him if only to stop him from calling either me or Connor 'dear boy' again. "Emery. And you're going to show me what?"

"How to heal your good work, of course." Alec grinned at Connor in a somehow equally playful and predatory manner. "Now move that lovely contraption of yours aside and let me demonstrate."

Connor backed up a step. "What are you—"

"Don't be difficult," Alec said and caught Connor in a fierce stare. A stare that moments later had Connor's arm dropping back to his side while a blank look washed over his face.

"Hey!" I hissed before Alec could take a single step closer to Connor. "You can't just glamour him!"

Alec frowned at me like I was the one being unreasonable. "I think I just did."

"I mean you don't...have permission. I won't let you." It dawned on me as I said this that Connor and I had forgotten one of the major vampire tropes to test out—needing permission to enter someone's home. Obviously, Alec hadn't needed permission to sneak into my room. Or did it not count since I lived here and was also a vampire? But I didn't own the house, it belonged to my parents; or did that not matter either?

I pushed these questions aside for now and pointed to Connor, who stood there staring forward like a wax statue, which was really disturbing. "Let him go!"

Alec rolled his eyes and, without any seeming effort, broke the spell. Connor blinked awareness and continued right on as if he hadn't lost any time.

"—planning to do, because you need to at least explain whatever it is before you do it."

"We could go over some glamouring basics as well," Alec ignored him, "since you seem to be under the impression it's dangerous or some rubbish. Clearly, he isn't hurt. You merely need to get better at enthralling people and then releasing them when you're done."

"Fine, but no more glamouring Connor without permission," I said.

"Wait, he did what?" Connor shot Alec a glare.

"See, he doesn't even realize anything happened. What's it matter?"

"Because it *matters*."

We engaged in maybe a ten second staring match before Alec yielded, his manic smile coming back in full force as he laughed.

"My, you are fun," he said. "Well done, Emery. I would have worried about William's common sense after all if you were flippant about consent. Obviously, occasions might arise where it is unavoidable and you must glamour someone and feed from them to survive. A retainer is preferable, of course, but we aren't all that lucky." He glanced again at Connor.

"Retainer?" Connor thrust a finger back at Alec. "Is that some fancy way of calling me a juice box, *Fright Night*, because I am not an open bar." His frown gave a telling twitch that meant he was actually joking, but the whole thing just made me feel nauseous.

Alec laughed again. "Come, let me demonstrate. If I may be allowed." He looked at me first, then at Connor for permission.

Connor's shoulders tensed as his joking demeanor fell away, the tendons in his neck shifting in nervousness the way I remembered from when I bit him the other day. I didn't want to watch Alec do that to him. I didn't want anyone to do that to him.

"Goodness me, I'm just going to heal the wound. No need to steal a taste." Alec held up his hands in surrender, as if he'd read both our minds. "Retainers—much more personal than a juice box," he said to Connor with a smirk, "are regular sources of blood, certainly, but it's quite intimate, not something every vampire has. If you're willing, however, Emery could feed from you about a pint a week and be satiated indefinitely. Well, for as long as you're around, of course." He lowered his arms and looked at Connor expectantly. "May I?"

Connor sucked in a sharp breath but nodded, tugging on his sweatshirt to reveal the fullness of his wound. I wanted to intervene, but I was also insanely curious to see what Alec would do if he wasn't going to bite Connor.

"Just so you are both aware, I *am* going to glamour you, Connor, as a courtesy. Enthralling ensures that the person we're feeding from feels no pain, and while I'm not going to feed from you now, it's good practice."

Connor's eyes instantly unfocused, going blank again, while the rest of him held still. Alec moved into his body, close, and gently grasped the back of his neck. Then he looked over at me, and his silvery eyes were brighter, like they were glowing. When he talked, I saw the sharpness of his eyeteeth.

"Our blood has healing properties, but don't take that to mean you can cure bullet wounds or broken limbs. A small wound, a cut like this, can be healed without consequence. Something larger would require more blood, and that would likely make the person ill, possibly kill them. Drain them enough first, and then feed them from you…and you turn them. Don't get those details confused."

He was serious now, all business as he deliberately bit down on his tongue with his fangs, drawing blood. I watched him bend his head toward Connor's wound, my heartbeat hammering against my ribs as he licked the skin slowly to spread the small traces of his blood along the marks.

Connor's eyes fluttered within his daze, his right hand coming up to grip Alec's arm. The sight made me swallow low in my throat, like it was something private I shouldn't be watching. The way Connor trembled. And flushed. And almost imperceptibly whimpered.

Had he been like that with me?

"No," I said aloud.

Alec, thinking I was talking to him, pulled away from Connor. "Nearly done," he said, and licked once more to clean the wound of any remaining traces of blood—only there was no wound, only smooth skin. "There. Then you simply release the person from glamour, and if you choose, they can forget what occurred—and you—entirely. Of course with a willing retainer, you needn't use such subterfuge."

Connor blinked awake, and the way his cheeks reddened further told me he remembered every moment of what had just happened. He brought his right hand over to where the bite marks had been, and his eyes widened in amazement at the feel of healed skin. His prosthetic hung at his side, and while he was distracted, Alec reached for it, taking the teal plastic fingers in his own.

"Marvelous," he said. "Did you work out the mechanics for this yourself?"

"Uhh…yeah."

"You're a regular da Vinci."

"Nah," Connor said, smiling in the humble way I was used to whenever someone praised his robotics. "I have a ton of 'em. It's an easier design than other working prosthetics since I have my elbow."

"Oh?"

"Sure. A lot of the control we have with arm movement comes from that joint. It would require extensive extra engineering for a prosthetic elbow to do all that work. I just need my fingers to move." Connor wiggled them to prove his point, and Alec marveled at them, letting the hand go but keeping his own hovering like he wanted to snatch the prosthetic up again.

People asked about Connor's arm all the time. He had the layman's terms explanation down pat.

"So," Alec said once he finally looked Connor in the eyes again, "do you think you can allow your sorry excuse for a vampire best friend to do what I just did to you once a week? Plus the feeding part, of course."

The smile dropped from Connor's face as he was reminded of what had just happened, and probably of when I'd bitten him earlier. I could tell he purposely avoided looking at me while he considered Alec's question, and I wondered if the answer was no, but that he was too good of a friend to say so. It *was* private, and intimate, and not something friends should have to do for each other.

But instead of answering, Connor said, "I thought you needed eight weeks to replenish from donating blood."

"Four to six, really, eight is just a precaution, but he shouldn't need to take a full pint each time, and getting a little of our blood in your system when he heals the wound should help you replenish faster." Alec sounded like a doctor giving a diagnosis now. "If you feel like you're becoming sluggish over time, best for him to feed from someone else for a bit."

Resolve settled over Connor's features. "Okay. Yeah. I can do that."

"Good."

I opened my mouth to put an end to all this—they were making a serious life decision for me *without* me—but they turned to me at the same time again and I froze.

"Glamouring effectively is all about will and intention, Emery, nothing else to it," Alec said. "Shall we continue?"

I looked to Connor, desperate to drudge up those fading feelings of dissent, because this was asking too much of him. But when our eyes met, I knew there was nothing I could say to change his mind.

He wasn't blushing anymore, or stammering, or nervous. That steady resolve had taken over his entire stance, and even though Alec was a couple inches taller than him, they stood like twin sentinels staring me down, daring me to rail against them—even while Alec gave me that frenzied grin again, and Connor quirked his mouth into a smirk.

I sighed. Clearly, I had been outvoted. I did have a lot of questions for Alec and only so long before my parents came up to see Connor home.

"Okay," I relented, focusing my attention on Alec, "what's next?"

CHAPTER 10

Connor

Alec had been a pleasant if also bizarre surprise, considering Connor had initially feared for his life when they'd discovered the vampire on Emery's bed. In hindsight, he knew it was silly to have worried—the Leonards had always been cool, and Connor had been the one to remind Emery of that fact. He was just thankful Alec hadn't turned out to be one of the hunters.

When Alec finally left, saying he could sense that Emery's parents were shuffling around downstairs and would probably be up soon, he jotted his cell phone number down on a purple post-it and stuck it to the computer desk. If there was ever an emergency, Emery could call him, but in the meantime Alec was going to dive into investigating the murders. He hoped to find the hunters before they found Emery. Once that was taken care of, he promised he'd be at Emery's beck and call for further training and advice.

He also plucked the Cap Wolf comic from Emery's bed on his way out.

During their practice session, Alec had confirmed everything they'd already discovered about Emery's abilities and weaknesses, and also added a few more. No, vampires did not need permission to enter someone's home; that was just old folklore to make people feel safer. And if Emery noticed animals acting weird around him, that was normal. They'd be drawn to him, and once he honed the skill, he might even be able to control and summon animals at will.

Connor's first question had been, "Do you think it would work on any animal?"

"Please don't make me mojo a squirrel," Emery groaned.

Alec just laughed.

Connor had gone straight upstairs to bed once he was home safe. He'd considered bugging Emery on their walkies for a while, but he was more flustered than he'd let on. Alec whammying him like that had felt nearly identical to when Emery did it—he'd gone limp and heavy, cozy, like everything was right with the world. He couldn't fight what was happening, he didn't want to, and when he felt Alec's tongue swiping languidly over his skin, all he could think about was how it would be Emery doing it next time. Once a week.

How Connor was supposed to survive letting Emery do that to him once a week, he had no idea. He'd been so obvious the first time Emery bit him, even more of a blubbering mess with Alec, which probably had Emery thinking he had a thing for the guy or something and…ew. Alec was cool, and charmingly weird, and had this angular look about him that really worked, even with the sometimes psycho smile, but Connor wasn't into older guys. Usually, he was only into Emery.

At least Emery was adjusting better now to being a vampire. Having finally met his mentor and getting a little actual mentoring seemed to have rejuvenated him. He got into Connor's car the next morning with his sunglasses already in place and a bright smile he hadn't greeted Connor with for days.

The smile promptly vanished when they arrived at school and didn't realize they were walking parallel with Liz until both she and Emery reached for the doors at the same time and their hands nearly touched.

"Oh!"

"Sorry, I—"

"No, you go ahead."

Connor tried not to glare. Liz was captain of the volleyball team—which had won State more times than their championship football team—an Honor Roll student, popular. The perfect girl-next-door full package. The worst part was that she was actually really nice, too, to everyone, not only those in her clique. When she and Emery had still been dating, Connor had been certain he could never compete with the girl destined to be Prom Queen.

She wasn't a blond bombshell like Jules, or a gorgeous dark spitfire like Aurora, but she had this presence of sweet and caring that made her mousy brown hair and eyes glow with attractiveness someone else might have been without. Plus, with her volleyball arms, she could probably beat the crap out of Connor if she wanted; he was pretty sure she'd out-benched several guys during weight lifting class.

Even now she didn't narrow her eyes at Emery, or flaunt that she had dumped him. She smiled genuinely apologetic, and said "Sorry" once again before hurrying inside.

Emery let his forehead rest on the glass after she'd gone, rather than follow her. "That could have gone worse, right?" His breath made a little cloud in its wake. When he pulled away, Connor drew a smiley face in the aftermath before the glass cleared.

"If you'd been dating someone else, probably. But for Miss Perfect? That was as bad as it gets. Good thing you're not missing her or anything..." Connor didn't mean to sound as leading with that statement as it came out.

But Emery grinned, looked for a moment like all he needed was to be reminded of that fact, and nodded back at him. "The awkwardness will pass, the rest is golden. You're right. Thanks, man." He grabbed the handle unabashedly and headed into the school.

Connor followed, feeling a little of the tightness in his stomach alleviate—

"Hey, gimp!"

—then stuttered mid-step and nearly tripped. "Urg, god, not today. What?" he snarled as he whipped around to see Michael Fergus, quarterback and captain of the football team, almost upon him.

Michael stopped short when he reached Connor, every perfect Ken doll part of him. If Liz was the stereotypical Prom Queen then Michael was the male version on crack. His dimpled smile fell. "What's your deal? I just wondered if you had time for a tune-up today."

"Why, what did you do to it?" Connor got right in Michael's face. They were nearly the same height, so it wasn't difficult.

"Nothing!" Michael said, but the guilty look on his face begged to differ.

"Go on without me," Connor called over his shoulder at Emery, who had paused in the hallway, smirking at them. "Guess I'm skipping Jazz Band today."

With that, Connor grabbed Michael roughly be the shoulder and manhandled him toward the gym. Once inside the locker room, he pushed Michael toward a bench and crouched in front of him on his knees.

"Jeans off," he ordered.

Michael was used to this treatment by now and kicked off his shoes, socks, and shimmied out of his jeans before sitting on the bench and extending his left leg closer to Connor. Michael was missing the leg from just above his knee, which had prompted a sense of camaraderie between them ever since Michael lost the leg three years prior. He was lucky the tractor accident on his family farm hadn't taken more of his leg—or his life.

Connor had offered to make him a prosthetic as soon as he'd discovered that Michael's family couldn't afford one. Everything had snowballed from there as Michael never seemed to upkeep the leg or its replacements to Connor's satisfaction, but it had helped him expand his knowledge base. A prosthetic leg was completely different from his arm models.

Michael's tastes were less flashy than his, which Connor would have found boring if the design itself wasn't so interesting. Printing a fairly realistic looking foot had been fun, and the rest was all in silver and bronze colors. The joint for Michael's knee had been the tricky part, and still required tweaks now and again, but it hadn't slowed him down on the field, even when he ran the ball.

Connor noticed quickly that the balance was all off, causing the joint to wear more heavily where it connected. "How long has it been like this?" he asked as he took his tool kit out of his backpack. He always had the tools with him in case he needed to tinker with something on himself, but it had been used far more often to help Michael.

"I don't know, a week or two?"

"Dude! You know you have to come to me with these issues right away. You can mess up your skin, the leg itself, strain other muscles—"

"I know, geez."

"Then why do you torment me, Fergus? You're lucky I always find out about these things before your parents or your doctor." Connor shifted Michael's plastic foot to rest more comfortably on his thigh as he set to work on the joint. "Now pay attention to what I'm doing so you can do this sort of thing yourself occasionally. I will gladly make you legs into old age, man, at a discount, every time, but you'd save us both a lot of trouble if you could just upkeep better."

They had done this so many times, there was no anxiety over the intimate position, not like it would have been if Connor was doing something like this for Emery. On his knees with Michael's prosthetic foot in his lap was like being a mechanic under a car. Michael snorted in only mild affront whenever Connor mentioned that out loud.

Not that Michael wasn't good looking. His blond hair was only slightly longer and lighter than Connor's own, his blue-green eyes deep-set and focused, a quirk to his almost always smiling lips. So many people would be jealous of Connor's current position if they caught them—and a few people had in the past, which was why they tried to find a discreet corner of the locker room—especially since Michael was single at the moment. Connor had actually enjoyed most of the sharp looks he got from people walking in on them, and Michael did make a pretty backdrop while he worked.

"So…I heard Mavus and Liz broke up."

Connor tensed, nearly dropping his screwdriver. "Yeah…?"

"You gonna do something about it?"

The screwdriver clattered to the floor. Connor waved it threateningly in Michael's face once he snatched it up again. "Stop distracting me!"

Michael held up his hands. "Just saying. I mean, how has no one asked you out before? Or do you turn everyone down, waiting for Mavus to catch wise?"

Connor gauged Michael's smirking face and the casual way he sat back on his hands, wiggling his leg for Connor to continue.

"You better not be hitting on me," Connor grumbled as he got back to work. "You're enough of a chore as it is."

Michael laughed. "Seriously, everyone—and I mean *everyone*—knows you have a hard-on for Mavus except Mavus. Probably because he's the only one who can't see how you look at him when he's not paying attention."

"I think it might be considered a superpower if he *could*."

Michael wiggled his leg again.

"Stop that!"

"Prom is like a month away, Connor, and as Prom *King*—"

"You know we haven't actually voted yet, right?"

"—it is my duty to make sure everyone goes. No senior is missing out just because they don't have a date. Go as friends if you're too chicken, but I expect you and Mavus to be there."

Connor remained silent the next few minutes while he finished up with his tweaks to Michael's leg. When he was done, he looked up to find blue-green eyes staring at him intensely, the smirk gone. Connor assumed it was Michael's Student Council President side that made him so charmingly intimidating, not the quarterback part, though the combination was highly unfair.

"Why does everyone care so much about my love life?" Connor asked the air more than Michael directly as he stood and offered a hand to his friend. Michael tried out his leg with a few steps, a jump or two, an extra wiggle, and looked satisfied. He started to pull on his jeans.

"Our own lives are tragic enough, Connor—we're teenagers. Personally, I don't enjoy watching the suffering of others."

"Pity," Connor scoffed. "Everyone's trying to play match-maker for me out of pity."

"Nah, I just owe Mavus one for quitting football. He'd steal all my thunder if he was still on the team. He deserves you." Michael winked as he finished doing up his jeans and patted Connor on the shoulder. "Thanks, gimp, you're the best."

Connor wasn't sure if he should be amused or annoyed. "We've discussed that your loving pet name for me has more than one meaning, right?"

"Why do you think I keep using it?" Michael winked again. How he did that without looking cheesy, Connor would never know.

They left the locker room to the sound of the late bell—or rather, sequence of beeps. Connor could still make it to Jazz Band, and probably wouldn't get into too much trouble for being tardy.

"Consider my advice, will ya? One way or another, I expect you both at Prom," Michael said as they parted. "Thanks again, gimp!"

"Later, cripple!" Connor called back.

A freshman at a nearby table in the lunch room shot them a glare until she realized who the two seniors were. Connor made a point to wave at her with his left hand.

~

"I can't believe you aced that Psych test," Connor said.

"I can't either."

I really couldn't. I'd studied, but I'd been more distracted during this one than for any other test I can remember, even one I had right after Liz and I broke up. It helped that the Milgram experiment on obedience to authority was disturbingly interesting. People will—and often do—willingly go against their personal beliefs and morality as long as someone who is perceived to be in power tells them to do so. Creepy.

We crossed the parking lot toward Connor's Thunderbird so we could head to the middle school for play practice. The test was a minor win, all things considered, but after learning so much from Alec last night, it really pushed me over the edge with feeling better about things. Maybe I wasn't doomed. Living a normal life despite being a creature of the night might actually be possible.

Alec still made me feel…awkward, I guess was the right word. Maybe because I didn't know him well enough yet. He was nice, and not as scary as I'd first thought, and while his teaching methods were unconventional, for the most part they were direct. He genuinely wanted to help.

Well, he mostly wanted to find the hunters to avenge Mr. and Mrs. Leonard, but that protected me from them too. Although we hadn't actually discussed what he planned to do once he found them. I had a nauseated feeling he didn't mean to just turn them over to Tim and the police.

Connor was rambling on about other disturbing psychological experiments that in no way would be legal if conducted today, and I got a little lost in the words, just listening to the sound of his voice—sharp, and quick, and even toned. It was so much easier to tune out everything around us and focus only on him with my new senses, the same way I could look at him and notice the pale freckles along his cheek bones, or focus on the smell of mint and cedar that lingered around him.

I'd been trying to do similar things with others whenever I had a spare moment, singling out one person and focusing on what my heightened senses could pick up about them, but it was easier with Connor, even listening to the most ambient sounds. The sort of halting skip of his walk, the faint creak of plastic as his prosthetic fingers curled around the strap of his backpack, the way his heartbeat tripped and beat faster when he caught me staring...

I frowned as he darted his eyes away. Was he scared of me? He was trying so hard to hide it, but I'd noticed several other telling signs ever since I'd bitten him. I'd hoped I was misreading things— he certainly kept insisting he wasn't afraid—but after learning I'd need to feed from him regularly, maybe it was starting to get to him.

I opened my mouth to say something, not exactly sure how I wanted to ask if my best friend was really okay with me drinking his blood once a week, when static in the air—as if something just wasn't right—made me stumble.

Someone was watching us. I scanned our surroundings but saw no sign of anyone darting out of sight this time.

"What's wrong?" Connor asked.

"Someone's here..."

He came around to stand in front of me. We were nearly at the car. There were other students all around us getting ready to leave for the day. "It might be the cop Tim assigned you. I mean, obviously Alec knows how to get around the guy, and maybe the hunters do too, so he's probably useless, but it could be him. Or maybe just Alec himself checking up between leads."

I started to nod but shook my head instead. "If it was Alec, why would he hide? Maybe he wasn't the one watching me the other day. I never actually asked him. Why didn't I ask him?" I grit my teeth and tried to be nonchalant as I made another pass around the parking lot.

"Calm down, Em, you don't know it's not—"

"But I do know. I know what Alec feels like. Now that I've met him, I have this sense of him, and whoever I just felt…" The feeling started to subside, but I had this awful gnawing twist in my gut. "Let's get in the car."

Once we were safely inside and Connor started to pull out of the parking lot, I considered calling Alec, but what could I tell him other than that he might already be too late?

I looked at Connor, and his eyes darted to meet mine, just as panicked as I felt. "I think the hunters know who I am."

CHAPTER 11

.

Connor

Connor mourned the loss of his brief reprieve with Emery, who had been back to his old, jovial self. His assurance that someone—likely one of the hunters—had been watching them in the parking lot had sent his upward swing swooping back the other direction.

Emery was off all throughout play practice. Forgetting lines, missing cues, distant and flat with his delivery. By the time Mark called it a night and gave notes for everyone to review before the next night's practice, Emery's face was ashen and he only gave one word replies or grunts to Connor's inquiries.

The steering wheel felt cold under Connor's flesh and blood fingers, the air colder tonight too, the sun long set as they headed home. He found himself tapping both flesh and plastic fingers at every stop light, anxious and unsure what he could say to sooth his friend. "It'll be okay," could never be the right words, not with this, not when he couldn't say that with any truth behind it. They were dealing in monsters and fairytales now.

They were just passing the park, barely any other cars on the road in their small town in this particular neighborhood at night, when Connor decided the silence was going to choke him.

"Em..."

"Stop the car." The order was abrupt, Emery's voice far lower than usual.

"What? Why?" Connor asked, even as he did as he was told.

"Call Alec."

But before Connor could fully turn toward his friend to ask what he meant, the passenger door hung open as Emery dashed from the vehicle and across the street into the trees.

Connor dived for Emery's cell phone left on the vacated seat, somehow managing to kill the engine and start to dial Alec's number at the same time. Emery hadn't said anything about Connor waiting in the car. Even if he had, Connor wouldn't have listened. He darted into the trees after Emery with the phone at his ear as it rang.

Connor hated this part of the park. All trees, more like woods than the edges of a proper park, with barely any trails, so if you weren't careful, you could end up right in the lake. If Emery had seen someone watching them from the trees, why the hell had he decided to follow?

As Connor stumbled a few yards more into the dark park, the other line finally picked up.

"Emery?"

"It's me!" Connor said, not thinking to state his name for the elder vampire. "Em just bolted from my car into the park after someone. It's on the edge of town near the lake, between the middle and high school. Do you know—?"

"I'll be right there." He hung up.

Connor growled in frustration, sorely tempted to hurl Emery's phone into the trees…when he nearly ran into his friend's back. "Em! What the—?" but he didn't get to finish.

Emery wasn't alone. He stood on guard, monument still, across from a woman in black. She didn't appear to be armed, but her leather jacket could easily be hiding a gun, or a blade, or a… stake.

"I saw her watching us from the trees. She waved me in," Emery said, eyes trained forward.

"And you thought it would be a good idea to have a chit chat?" Connor hissed. He pressed Emery's cell phone into his friend's palm, trying to keep it hidden so the woman wouldn't see it and expect the backup that was coming.

She had an edge and strength about her that Connor found gorgeous, like she could kill you with a look. She wore no makeup except a touch of black eyeliner, with dark skin from seemingly

Indian heritage, and long wavy brunette hair hanging past her shoulders. She stood about eye to eye with both of them in her combat boots. "I figured someone who wanted to kill me wouldn't try to get my attention," Emery said.

"I have no intention of killing you, Emery." The woman had a raspy, jazz singer voice with a much more proper English accent than the amalgamation Alec used. She brought her hands up slowly, presumably to reiterate the unarmed point, but her gloved hands unnerved Connor. "Or you, Mr. Daniels," she shifted her sharp gaze to him. "Unless, of course, either of you is feeling particularly homicidal."

Connor cringed at being called 'Mr. Daniels'. How come Emery got first name treatment? "It's Connor," he said, "and we're not the ones committing homicide around here. From what we can tell it was you and your hunter buddies who offed the Leonards. You really that much of a stereotype, *Buffy*," he challenged her, since he was still partially hidden behind his vampire best friend, "going around killing people for being different even when they didn't do anything wrong?"

"'Fraid not, love," she said, as she lowered her arms with a faint smile. "Hunters aren't like that at all actually."

"Oh." Connor had been so sure he had this pegged. He glanced at Emery, but his friend was keeping his eyes on her, tense and alert like an animal poised to attack.

"You were the one watching me at the school," he said.

"I was. But don't fool yourself into thinking I'm the only one. The actual killers of your sire and his wife are still in town, looking for you. You're lucky I found you first. For now, I can't find any evidence to suggest you've done anything wrong. Even if the Leonards had, you'd be exempt from any punishment they earned. The problem is, I can't find any evidence that they did anything either. So it begs the question…why are my contemporaries here, and why did they kill two seemingly innocent prey, and are at this very moment hunting you?"

"So glad to see we're on the same page with that," Alec's voice interjected as the vampire stepped out of the trees on the woman's right. He seemed unhurried, despite having managed to find them in barely a minute's time from wherever he had been when Connor called.

The woman, to her credit, straightened but didn't flinch. She looked aside at Alec slowly then back at Emery, perhaps wondering if she'd been the one led into a trap. When her eyes went back to Alec, they widened as if she recognized him.

"And who are you?" Alec asked. He smiled his wide grin, wearing similar dark jeans as before and his black jacket, but in a different T-shirt with a picture of DC's Constantine. The guy did have good taste.

"Wendy," she said. She didn't seem glamoured, merely offered her name willingly.

Connor snorted. English accent. *Wendy*. There had to be an opportune moment to mention green tights…

"And you're Alec, aren't you?" she said, following his path with her eyes as he moved to stand next to Emery.

"Always a pleasure to meet a fan." Alec brightened in that creepy, excitable way of his. "Well then, darling, do share with the class what you've discovered if we're going to be doing show and tell tonight. I'm on a bit of a tight schedule." He tapped his wrist that definitely did not bear a watch.

"You know her?" Connor couldn't help asking, because that would have been useful information.

"I know of her."

"Just like she knows of you?" Emery said, finally turning his gaze away from her to look at Alec. At last, Connor saw Emery's shoulders relax now that some experienced muscle had arrived to back them up.

Wendy certainly looked well-muscled, curvy and solid and dark—like Emery. No wonder Connor thought she was sexy.

"I'm well known." Alec leaned into Emery with his answer that wasn't an answer.

Had they really come to terms with this guy before? Because Connor sort of wanted to punch him half the time.

"I've been investigating for a few days," Wendy said, keeping the distance between them. "In the spirit of transparency, I'll admit that I was nearby when the Leonards were killed, tracking another vampire. At least…I believe it to be *another* vampire. When Mallory Leonard was killed, I thought perhaps I was mistaken and that she was the culprit, and another hunter had beat me to the punch. But nothing seems to be adding up. Before I could gather any evidence against her, or William, he was dead and there was…you, Emery," she looked to him steadily, "coming out of that house unscathed.

"Perhaps my fellows in town, who I have not been in contact with and do not know personally, are the ones in the wrong. Perhaps they too were following the vampire I've been tracking and made a mistake. Of course, that wouldn't explain killing again unless they are still following false leads. Or, of course…unless I'm missing something that would suggest the Leonards weren't as good as they appeared to be."

"No way!" Emery jerked forward, fists clenched. Connor had the urge to hold him back, but Alec stood there watching in apparent amusement. "There have never been any murders around here, not until the hunters came. The Leonards never did anything wrong. They were good people."

Wendy remained perfectly composed and calm as she kept her gaze centered on him. "But William turned you. With your permission?"

"Uh, he…" Emery faltered back a step.

"I thought not. And as you've become accustomed to your abilities, I'm sure you realize how easy it would be to travel to nearby communities to feed and leave your lair far removed from your hunting grounds. So in truth, with so many small towns nearby, and the larger Twin Cities only a few hours away, you can't really say you know whether or not they ever killed anyone. Can you?"

Connor felt sick, because he'd been the one to defend the Leonards initially, and now this woman was making so much sense that he hadn't considered. He'd just assumed. But the truth was they didn't know anything. They didn't know much about Alec either. Connor eyed the vampire on the other side of Emery warily, who noticed and tossed him a raised eyebrow as if he could read his mind—and maybe he could. He wasn't exactly jumping to the Leonards' defense.

"However," Wendy said grandly, loudly, to recapture their attentions, "I would be terrible at my job if I didn't investigate thoroughly, and there is always proof whether or not a vampire is killing unwarranted. As I've said, so far I've found nothing to suggest the Leonards are at fault. So while I'd ask that you not jump to defend someone without evidence, please understand that I don't condemn without evidence either. You certainly don't seem to have any ill intent, Emery. Your friend there is human, after all, and he's still breathing."

Connor shivered under her stare as her dark eyes drifted to him.

"Are you offering your services then, Wendy, darling?" Alec asked, crossing his arms with a twisted smirk, no doubt because of the play on her name to match Connor's own train of thought.

She met Alec like a worthy challenge, the humor gone from her expression as she said, "The pact means something to me," and inclined her head like a subtle bow, which seemed strangely formal, Connor thought, given the rest of this odd exchange.

She turned to Emery once more. "Be careful. The vampire I've been tracking is still active. She killed last night, here in this town. It won't be in the papers, maybe barely even noticed. He was a drifter, an easy mark to keep things under the radar. She's… dangerous, erratic, but keeps to a weekly schedule as if she were otherwise following the rules. She won't hunt again for another week, which might buy us some time. Hopefully, the other hunters will be busy following her trail, assuming it's yours. But I know my mark, and you were busy at play practice and then headed straight home last night."

"You've been following me?" Emery scowled at her.

"That much I said already."

"Yeah, but…everywhere? Night and day? So much for my police babysitter…"

Connor opened his mouth to second that, before realizing the guy was probably looking for them in the woods about now if he'd come upon an empty car.

"He's not inept," Wendy said, and then grinned, "just not as good as I am. But the other hunters in town are my equals to be sure, as I haven't caught any sight of them. They don't know your identity yet, Emery, or where you live, but they may very well know your face, which is more than enough. If I found you, it won't be long before they do as well. You must be vigilant any time you're out in the open. They won't always wait for nightfall to strike.

"For now, I wanted you to be aware of my presence, and to know that as long as I have no reason to suspect you of breaking the pact, I am here to help." She looked right at Connor, right at him with a twist of her lips, which made him gulp at how penetrating her stare was. "Hunters aren't like the movies, love. We aren't mindless killers, assuming all vampires or other supernatural creatures are evil. Some monsters aren't monsters at all, just like people. There is a strict code we follow, in line with a pact made in the late 1600s when the current vampire king took over. He didn't like wayward vampires giving others a bad name, and made a pact with the hunters of the time to keep things in line. If vampires kill, they are killed in return. If they don't, they are left alone. Quite simple, really. If these other hunters here are doing otherwise, it's murder like any other situation. We square on that?"

Connor and Emery both looked to Alec, who nodded on their behalf. A pact between vampires and hunters? Alec hadn't mentioned that before. Maybe he hadn't wanted them to know. After all, even if this was all a misunderstanding, these hunters still killed Alec's children. Maybe he didn't feel like being forgiving.

Wendy reached into her jacket pocket, and Connor tensed, wondering for a split second if she was going for a weapon, but while Emery went rigid beside him, Alec remained stoic. She pulled out what looked like a simple white business card and walked cautiously forward. Alec moved to meet her.

"My information, should you need to contact me. Though I will be keeping a close eye on Emery," she said as she handed Alec the card.

"How diplomatic," he said. There was an air between them as though neither fully trusted the other. Connor felt the same way about both of them, and shifter closer to Emery until their arms bumped.

"Until then…stay safe," she said with a glance at Emery and Connor, and then turned to head into the trees behind her like a creature of the night herself, disappearing into the shadows.

"Wait!" Connor called before he fully realized he was intervening. The others all turned to look at him, and he scrambled to think of what he'd meant to say. "This is all vaguely daunting and very 'the night is dark and full of terrors' and all, but…how can human hunters take on vampires so easily? I mean, should we assume there are dozens of these guys, because, no offense, but with the things Em can do, and with Alec on our side too," he decided not to bring up that he was a little distrustful of the vampire right now, "just how much could someone like you do?"

Alec gave an over-exaggerated eye roll in response while pocketing the business card, and took two measured steps back, perpendicular to them, to give Wendy a clear line of sight, which seemed…terrifying. Wendy and Alec shared a glance that looked suspiciously like he was giving her permission.

"Simple rule, love," Wendy said as she stalked back toward them. "There is always someone bigger and stronger than you. It isn't about power. It isn't about numbers. It's about timing, planning, and skill. And sometimes…" she reached swiftly into her jacket again, "misdirection."

The flash instantly blinded Connor, but before he could cry out, he heard Emery shout instead—his senses had to make the light much worse. Connor stiffened, blindly groping with both hands to find Emery, only to come up empty. He was incapable of preventing whatever hit him and sent him crashing to the ground, landing on his back with a thud and puff of air.

When his vision cleared, Emery was above him, with Wendy positioned behind him, holding a large machete to his throat—and where had she even been keeping something like that?

"If I had really wanted to attack, I simply would have staked you from behind about now," she whispered beside Emery's ear, who looked as though he was still blinking spots from his eyes, and snarled at her with a glint of fangs to prove his discomfort. She stepped back and released him, hands raised in surrender. "Of course, beheading works too."

Emery blinked rapidly, wearing a deep grimace as he spun around to glare at her, before noticing Connor on the ground and reaching down to help him up.

Alec's laughter filtered over to them, having known to shield his eyes and stay out of her way. "Shall we cover potential hunter tricks to be aware of next training session?" he said with a humored tone.

Emery huffed.

"Fangs," Connor whispered. They were still out from reacting to Wendy.

Emery covered his mouth, then closed his eyes to help will them away. They were gone and his eyes less bright and intense when he nodded to Connor in gratitude. He had to work on that.

"Goodnight, boys," Wendy said as she crossed the small clearing in the direction she'd initially headed toward. The machete was conspicuously missing again, hidden somewhere unknown. "Do work on your reflexes," she added, and smiled dangerously over her shoulder before disappearing into the trees.

CHAPTER 12

I finally got to meet my police escort when Connor and I trudged out of the trees. He was shining a flashlight into the park after checking over Connor's abandoned car. Thankfully, Connor had a lie ready, spewing off something about kids throwing a rock at his window, and him darting out of the car after them. He said that I'd followed in concern—making me out to be the responsible one—and repeated how sorry he was for doing something so foolish.

"Em knocked some sense into me, Officer. It won't happen again," he said.

Somehow we convinced him not to report the incident to Tim or our parents, since we swore it was just middle schoolers out in the park, and yes, he should totally check that out. He followed us in his cruiser first at a visible distance as we made our way home, but nothing else eventful happened.

Most of the tension in my chest lifted after meeting Wendy. At least now I knew who had really been watching me all this time, and that—as far as I could tell—none of the other hunters had gotten as close. Connor didn't trust her, or Alec really, but I couldn't believe either of them meant us harm. Alec had obviously kept things from us, but maybe they just hadn't come up yet. He was sort of flighty and weird anyway. Besides, if it was all because he intended to kill the hunters when he found them, I wasn't sure I could blame him.

I plodded down the stairs the next morning feeling like I hadn't slept a wink. Unfortunately, vampirism does not beat out insomnia.

"There you are, honey," my mom's cheery voice greeted me, along with the smell of her signature French toast—which was odd. She usually only did something larger for breakfast on the weekend, since she left for work before Dad.

Mom worked at the local radio station, one of the regular on-air personalities in the mornings, and Dad did design for a sign workshop. A couple of times, when Connor had to get something really crazy built, he'd ask for my dad's help, like with the completely unnecessary neon 'Man Cave' sign in Connor's prosthetics workshop. Dad had also helped put LED lights in several of Connor's first arm designs, but Connor had grown out of that lately.

"Why didn't you tell us Mr. Leonards' brother gave you a job?" Dad said.

"What?" I stuttered in the doorway to the kitchen, blinking away the remaining blurriness of having just woken up and getting dressed on autopilot.

The familiar sight of Dad digging into a helping of French toast while Mom worked on another batch at the stove was overshadowed by Alec sitting at the table with his own plate. He twirled his fingers at me in a semblance of a wave.

"Alec!" I said more accusingly than in greeting, which I hoped was the name he had given my parents for whatever ruse this was, since I did not have a working filter yet this morning.

"Good morning, Emery," he said in a near flawless American accent. "Given the nature of everything that happened with my brother's passing, I wanted to be sure your parents were aware I was in town. It really meant something running into you the other day and that you agreed to help me go through the house, but I didn't want anyone worrying about you spending time with a stranger. I was just telling them how we met several times while I was in town visiting Will and Mallory before, and that I've decided to stay for as long as I can until I sort things out with their estate."

I took a moment to process all of that. It would make things easier if my parents expected Alec to be around rather than trying to hide him, or hide going to see him. But wait. At the house? He was staying at the Leonards' place?

I spoke up quickly when I realized everyone was staring at me. "Right, yeah, sorry, I'm still half asleep. I met Alec way back when I started working for the Leonards. He made me call him by his first name then, said it would be too confusing if there were two Mr. Leonards." I managed a laugh and smiled as genuinely as I could as I took a seat at the table and accepted the plate of French toast my mom handed me. "Sorry I didn't mention anything. I wanted to wait and make sure Tim was okay with it. I was afraid the police would think you had something to do with the murders." I looked to Alec leadingly.

"Not to worry, Emery, my alibi is airtight against anything sordid having happened, including phone records of when Will called me right before..." He trailed off, the look of anguish on his face very real before my mom touched his shoulder and he pulled on a smile. "Well...I spoke with Chief Ashby as soon as I got into town, and didn't want to bother you, of course, Emery, but when you offered to help go through Will and Mallory's things, I just couldn't turn you away. I'd rather not be in that house alone. I won't be any bother or interrupt his school or extracurriculars," he said to my parents, "and of course he mentioned his police detail, and I am all for that. I'll be sure he's never out at the house without his escort present."

It amazed me that Alec had covered all of the bases that Tim or my parents might bring up, though it would have been nice if he'd warned me about this first. I looked to my parents hopefully.

Mom turned from flipping the newest set of toast on the stove, one hand on her hip while the other waved the spatula. "As long as you're sure you're okay with this, honey. I'm serious about you always keeping us in the know about where you are for a while."

For the rest of the school year, she meant—or maybe the rest of my life. "Of course," I said, and shoveled in a mouthful of French toast. I was so glad right then that it tasted as good as I remembered, even if everything I ate was useless calories now.

"Shall I see you after school today, then, Emery, before you're off to practice?" Alec asked, pushing away from the table, signaling his intent to leave. He couldn't quite alter the strange way he smiled, or the ethereal way he moved, or the glint in his eyes, but his eccentricities were dulled enough by his acting that my parents seemed blissfully unaware he was actually a slightly cracked vampire.

"Sure thing," I said, wondering for perhaps the millionth time how this was my life now. "Happy to help."

~

Connor

The next few days were so hum-drum normal—other than Mr. Leonard's funeral—that Connor nearly forgot Emery was a vampire, and that they had a dark goddess version of Buffy the vampire slayer on their side and a way to see Alec without raising suspicion.

Mr. Leonard was cremated like his wife, which Connor thought fitting for a pair of vampires, but the urns were buried side by side in the local Catholic cemetery. Neither Emery nor Alec burst into flames standing on hallowed ground during the burial. A good portion of the town was in attendance, and the ladies of the church had made enough 'funeral sandwiches'—as Connor called them—to feed everyone and half the state of Minnesota, which were buttered buns with slabs of ham or turkey and cheese, as well as the usual copious amounts of casseroles and desserts, like lemon bars, Special K bars, and too many other bars to name.

"Is it like *I am Legend*, where vampires are only affected by religious symbolism they believe in?" Connor asked Emery after the funeral, feeling it inappropriate to pose the question to Alec just now.

"How should I know?" Emery said. "My parents raised me agnostic."

Connor decided to let that one go.

As of late, he had to help out backstage before Emery joined him for practice, so Alec had taken to picking Emery up after school and driving him in for practice later. Connor found ways of getting out of his duties whenever possible so he could join them. It wasn't as if they really needed him every day to help backstage; it depended on the scene! Of course, Aurora wasn't too happy about that, but he just had to drop one word about wanting to keep an eye on Emery at the Leonards' place—alone with some distant 'brother'—and that seemed to be more than enough to get her grudging approval.

Apparently stakes and machetes weren't the only things Emery had to worry about, or the flash bomb Wendy had used on them. Being set on fire would likely kill a young vampire, and while bullets to vital organs wouldn't kill him, they could still slow Emery down until he healed. Over time, his resistance to everything would increase.

"Even beheading?" Connor had chuckled.

Alec just shrugged.

They also went through the Leonards' house; that hadn't been a complete ploy. It turned out that there were official records claiming Alec as William Leonard's brother, and the house legally belonged to him now, though Connor didn't believe for a second that any of their surnames were actually Leonard.

Most of their belongings were going to be donated, but Alec kept a few things. When he asked if Emery wanted anything for himself, he requested one of Mrs. Leonard's paintings. Cloak and Dagger looked badass behind Emery's computer desk.

Possible ambush by hunters, or a crazed homicidal vampire hiding around town, barely registered when they attended class and play practice like normal. Once the weekend rolled around, Connor's pulse thrummed at the thought of Emery feeding from him again. Every time they were alone, a little thrill shot up from his gut, and he waited for Emery to ask permission, and then entrance him as he leaned down toward his neck.

Only it didn't happen. It was Monday now, the lack of blood leaving Emery scowly and short-tempered.

Connor had Advanced Placement Literature and Composition after Jazz Band, one of the few classes he had with Emery, and also with Jules. Jules spent most of the period working on creative writing projects instead of class work since the college she was aiming for only accepted one AP English credit and she'd already gotten that by acing their AP Language and Composition test last year.

As the three of them left the music alcove together, Connor noticed that Emery wore a frown and kept scratching the back of his neck as if his skin felt too tight. Part of it had to be the need to feed, but it had also been almost a week since they first met Wendy—when she'd told them that they had about a week before the vampire she believed to actually be causing trouble killed again and drew the hunters back out. They hadn't learned anything new from Wendy.

Connor opened his mouth to say something to Emery, but after glancing at Jules, he merely knocked elbows with his friend and shot him an encouraging smile as they traipsed down the hallway.

"I am so twitterpated lately. Why am I not dating anyone?" Jules said to no one in particular. "Why are none of us dating right now?"

Connor's stomach lurched. He tore his gaze away from Emery, but couldn't help saying, "You mean each other? Coz sorry, Jules, you're not really my type."

She smirked at him.

"And wait, did you say twitterpated?" Connor said with a scrunch of his brow. "Like *Bambi*? Is that some girl way of saying you're horny?"

"Yes," she said simply. "Haven't you learned girl code by now?"

Connor knew a few things—he had way too many girl friends to not know a few things—but this one was new. "Nice. I am so stealing that."

They entered the Lit and Comp room to catch Mr. Krall already starting his aged cassette player for their morning ritual of listening to five to ten minutes of an episode of *A Prairie Home Companion*, and took their usual seats: Jules in front of Connor, while Emery sat at Connor's left by the window, two rows from the front. The early morning sun streamed in perfectly, almost fully bathing Emery in its rays, and his face pinched in annoyance. One glance at Mr. Krall, who never failed to remind them that he'd been their age in the 60s and could care less about something as benign as a baseball cap or sunglasses in the classroom, Emery slid the aviators from his pocket to place over his eyes.

"Em," Connor whispered, receiving a mild head tilt in reply like his friend could barely keep his chin up, "you okay? I was thinking we should probably, um…take Alec's suggestion sometime soon, you know? Like tonight."

Emery's grimace spread to his eyebrows. "I'm fine."

"Yeah, well, you look half dead."

"Maybe because I'm *undead*."

Wow. If vampires could be hypoglycemic, that was definitely a sign, no matter how quiet Emery was keeping his voice. "Dude…" Connor started, but was cut off as Mr. Krall turned up the volume on *A Prairie Home Companion* to get everyone to quiet down, clashing with the beeping intercom that signaled classes had begun.

The News from Lake Wobegon began, where "all the women are strong, all the men are good looking, and all the children are above average," and Connor sat back with a huff.

He should have brought up Emery's resistance to picking a set feeding time to Alec. Asking his best friend to suck on his neck was one of the harder things to request off the cuff when they got home from play practice.

Connor snuck his cell phone out of his pocket, one of the things Mr. Krall was not groovy about, and was about to shoot off a text to Alec when he noticed a recent missed message from Wendy. She finally had a viable lead on the other vampire one town over, and might be able to take care of their problem tonight before anyone else died.

Hoping the good news would ease Emery enough that Connor could convince his friend to finally feed later tonight, he glanced over only to notice a tense crinkle of Emery's brow, eyes closed beneath the aviators, and a white-knuckled grip on the edges of his desk. The long sleeves of Emery's shirt were tugged up from his forearms, revealing tan skin that looked strangely pink, and irritated, and…smoking!

Connor jolted in his seat.

As the truth of what was happening caught up with Emery as well, he pulled his arms under the desk and covered them quickly, but his seat meant that the sun still struck the side of his face and neck.

He met Connor's gaze, and despite the dark shades, Connor could see Emery's eyes faintly glowing a brighter green behind the glass, with the edges of his fangs peeking out over his lips, and an expression of silent pleading on his face as the skin currently in the path of the sun started to sizzle.

CHAPTER 13

I couldn't move. The pain was intense, like grabbing a pan right out of the oven without protection and hanging on tight, only this was as if someone had pressed a piece of scalding glass to my face. I was going to scream. I was going to bolt out of the classroom at super speed and give myself away. The panic built in my chest as fight or flight vied for control, and there was no way to fight without burning.

"Mr. Krall!" Connor shot his hand into the air, then turned and grabbed my hand, yanking me up out of the chair and away from the beams of sunlight.

Instant relief washed over me, but it didn't last; the burns were already bad and not healing, I could feel it. I ducked my head, trying to keep the side of my face from being too visible to the rest of the class, who were all staring at us as Connor dragged me toward the door.

"Em's going to be sick, I need to get him to the bathroom!" Connor said in explanation, not even waiting for permission as we raced from the room.

"O-Okay, but don't dawdle out there!" Mr. Krall called after us.

Our school didn't use hall passes, and Mr. Krall always told us to just ask and go if we needed to use the bathroom, no need to suffer if we hadn't had time between classes. And this was an emergency. It didn't matter if the type of emergency was a lie.

I sucked air through my teeth like a hiss, the pain steadily increasing. I'd never burned myself like this before, but I'd watched my mother go through a second degree burn once on her forearm. The pain lingered long into the next day, the worst she'd ever experienced, she said. She wasn't wrong.

How much I needed to feed struck like a gong in my head, a throbbing between my ears, making my vision and thoughts equally blurry. I barely noticed anyone we might have passed as Connor hauled me into the nearest bathroom and closed us inside the handicap stall. No one else was in here. I registered how Connor intended to help me and lurched away from him, going for the lock on the door.

"Em!" Connor grabbed my shoulder. My vision was too tunneled to put up a fight, my body shifting from burning in the sun to chills rippling through me, my face still stinging. "Dude, I get that you've been avoiding feeding. I can understand it's weird and maybe freaking you out, but it's been over a week and you are burning in the sun from stalling. You won't heal if you don't get some blood in you. You won't be able to pass any windows or leave school at the end of the day either. We have to do this."

I shivered and grabbed my arms, running my hands over the fabric covering the fainter burns beneath. At least they weren't as bad as my face, but Connor was right—none of it was healing. I'd waited too long. But I couldn't help it. Everything had seemed better, brighter, entirely doable, even if I was a monster—until I imagined sinking my fangs into Connor's throat.

"I thought I could get over it, but it's the *one* thing…" I said, voice low as I stared at the stall door, keeping Connor behind me, his hand still gripping my shoulder. "I know it scares you. You shouldn't have to do this."

"What?" Connor said, tightening his hold on me. "Em…"

"I saw the way you were with Alec last week. The glamouring makes you think it's not so bad, but then after…the look on your face." I shook my head. "And sometimes the way you look at me now…I know you're thinking about it. You shouldn't have to do this," I said again.

Connor's hand dropped away. My shoulders tensed as pain pulsed through me, a haze entering my vision as though it was going red with hunger and the need to heal. I envisioned myself turning on Connor and tearing into his throat, not gently, not something I could fix later, and then throwing up all of the blood into the toilet once I stopped and realized I'd killed him. The irony was that the only way to prevent that from happening was to do as Connor asked.

"Look at me, Em," he said. His voice rarely sounded that soft, and slow—patient. He had an energy in everything he did, the way he moved, and talked, and animatedly gestured. Soft and slow were rarely part of that vocabulary.

I turned, keeping my eyes closed, still shivering. If I could quiet my pulse for a moment, maybe I would regain some of the control I'd lost. When I opened my eyes, his smile was too understanding, his eyebrows downturned like I was the biggest idiot in the world but he put up with me anyway, every day. He reached up and pulled the sunglasses from my face, tucking them into the pocket of the dark flannel over his T-shirt.

"I'm not afraid. Believe me, Em, it's not fear. I could never be afraid of you. Honestly, the reason I got a little weirded out with Alec was because...well," he shoved his hands into his pockets, "it feels kind of...good, in the glamour, and even after it heals, and... it was creepy coming from him, because I don't really trust him, you know?

"Here I was, thinking you'd get some weird idea about me having the hots for the guy, and instead you thought I was scared? Of you? If I'm scared of anything it's of you thinking I'm some kind of a masochist for kinda looking forward to this." He shrugged, eyes darting away from me, his smile twisted in distaste—at himself. Then his eyes flicked back to me, open and honest.

Why do we always put our insecurities on other people? If I'd just told him why I kept putting off feeding, if he'd just told me how it actually made him feel, we could have avoided this. I was more at fault though. As long as I'm honest, Connor is always honest back to me.

A fresh wave of pain overtook the burns on my face and I cringed, stumbling forward a step like I might face plant right into the tiled floor. Connor caught me, both hands braced on my shoulders.

"You have better control now than when you first bit me," he said. "It doesn't matter that you're hurt this time, and need it more. If you were able to be cautious about things and stop yourself before, you can again. So have some faith in yourself, Em. I do. Just remember what Alec taught you. The guy's nuts, but he's at least good for that."

I lifted my head, my blurred vision focusing on Connor's renewed smirk. I couldn't laugh, couldn't smile in kind, but I nodded. "Okay."

If I'd gotten over my reservations sooner, we could have done this in my bedroom again, somewhere safer and more comfortable, instead of me backing Connor up against the wall of a dirty bathroom stall in school, the toilet two feet to our left, and the chance of someone coming in and wondering why two sets of feet were in one stall.

I took a few deep, controlled breaths, staring at Connor's neck, but not yet descending. The smell of Connor so close to me overpowered anything coming from the bathroom. The mint, the sawdust, and something rich and earthy that I knew must be the blood in his veins calling to me more directly with how much I needed it now, wanted it.

I recalled what Alec had taught me about glamouring someone effectively, and pulled back, my hands on Connor's shoulders now as his dropped to his sides. I looked deep into Connor's honey eyes, focusing on the way the colors intensified and sharpened, until I could make out all of the brown and bronze and gold flecks that individually came together to create his unique color.

There was a thread between us now, Alec had explained, and I could feel it. I pictured it as an actual, visible thread unwinding from my hands on his shoulders and coiling up around his neck, ears, and forehead like a patchwork crown. I willed a message into the thread that he feel nothing but peace, pleasure, joy. I saw the moment when he sagged back into the wall behind him, his expression blank, mesmerized by the power in the thread connecting us.

Only then did I bend toward his neck, pushing the pain of my burns away from the forefront of my mind, thinking only of Connor enjoying this as much as he said he did, and for me to only take the amount I needed. I didn't have to will my fangs to appear, that happened naturally, and they were already mostly unleashed just from instinct when I'd started to burn.

The salt of Connor's skin. The way my fangs sank smooth and easy into the veins there, drawing blood at a slow pace, as Alec had taught me. Going slow made it gentler for Connor and easier for me to keep control. My hands slid down until I pressed lightly on his collarbone and chest to steady him against the wall—to steady myself.

Any sense of time drifted, any sounds from the bathroom faded out, just me and Connor and the taste I couldn't describe as his blood filled me. There was nothing coppery about blood now. It touched every taste bud—salty, sour, bitter, and sweet—but mostly savory. Alec said it tasted like life. I'd thought he was being overly poetic, but I saw now how right he was.

A tingling sensation crawled across my skin, everywhere the sun had burned, as the damage knit itself back together and the pain subsided.

Connor whimpered, his hands moving to my waist, both skin and plastic cool to the touch as his fingers found the line of skin where my jeans and shirt met. He couldn't help himself while enthralled, especially with the emotions I forced on him, to feel like this was something he wanted and enjoyed. But if he really did enjoy it, did it matter if part of the pleasure came from swindling him? Was it still swindling if he was aware of it?

The taste of him, the subtle feel of his fingers on my skin, being so close to him and that intoxicating smell that was his alone, filled me with more than nourishment. I wanted to press closer, sink my teeth deeper, feel his hands slide up my back underneath my shirt and cool my overheated skin—

I broke away, a shaky breath leaving me as I stared at the puncture marks left behind. Connor might not be afraid, but I still feared myself and what I might do. That had to have been something like bloodlust I'd just felt, and part of me wanted to sprint the other direction. I might have given in and hurt him. Why would I feel something like that if I didn't want to hurt him?

I waited for my pulse to still before biting down on my tongue to draw a small trace of blood, and licked along Connor's wound to heal the marks. The taste didn't leave me feeling like I wanted to bite him again, as the power from feeding filled my veins, healing my burns fully and leaving me satisfied and more alert than I'd been in days. But the nerves in my stomach felt alive with fierce fluttering I didn't understand—didn't trust.

Once Connor's wounds were gone, the blood lapped away, and I felt like myself again, I pulled back, looked into his eyes—I didn't need to keep contact to hold a glamour, or to break one, but it made it easier—and released Connor. He sighed, leaning more heavily into the wall and tightening his grip along my waist, until he realized what he was doing and jerked his hands away.

"Okay…I just need to down that power bar in my backpack when we get back to class, and I'll be fine," he said, huffing a few times to catch his breath.

Only a few minutes had passed since we left class. I could tell everyone something just hadn't agreed with me from breakfast, if anyone asked, no harm done, no additional questions. Mr. Krall would continue his lessons undeterred. It was almost too easy.

I stared at Connor and pressed a hand to my own neck, feeling how warm the skin was, hotter than my hand, like I was burning up, but like it was something nice instead of a fever.

"I'm so warm now," I said. A pleasant surge of Connor's blood raced through me. It felt so good—too good. I wanted to claw it out from under my skin. If it increased each time, this want, and the enjoyment of it, would I become something Wendy needed to hunt? I hadn't asked Alec what reasons vampires had for killing people. I'd just assumed it was the same reasons humans did.

Because they could. Because sometimes people did bad things just because they wanted to. Because not everything had an answer. I wanted an answer to this though. There had to be an answer…

"Dude, are you having hot flashes?" Connor said, a chuckle in his voice as he pushed from the wall. He didn't look overly pale, or unsteady on his feet, though as soon as we moved to leave the bathroom, he leaned heavily into my side.

"Feeding makes me warm," I said, keeping a hand at his back so it wouldn't be too obvious that I was ready to catch him if he stumbled. We headed back to class without running into anyone. "Sunlight makes me hot. Lack of either and I'm freezing. So… yeah, I guess I am having hot flashes."

Connor elbowed me when I didn't smile, so I tried to will one onto my face, but it got stuck somewhere between a grimace and a twitch of fear. Connor narrowed his eyes at me; he could always read my expressions.

"I'm not afraid of you, Em," he said, hushed and serious.

"I know." I did. I was afraid enough for both of us.

What else could that feeling have been, wanting to press closer to Connor and envelope him while I fed, if not something terrible?

CHAPTER 14

Wendy

The sun had almost set. Vampires weren't limited by nightfall as long as they fed regularly, but Wendy had been watching this particular mark for weeks. The vampire would wait to feed until tomorrow night, but once darkness fell, she would be on the move.

Wendy had finally tracked the vampire to a neighboring town, only twenty minutes by car—or motorbike in her case—from where Emery Mavus lived. The other hunters were likely pursuing the same vampire now, but Wendy hadn't seen any sign of them.

She parked her bike behind an Arby's at the edge of town. Rain had recently stopped after mostly sunny skies all day, and now the temperature was dropping low enough for the damp grass to freeze. The Minnesota weather was almost as temperamental as Wendy was used to in Devon, where she had completed the Commando course at Lympstone. Hunting vampires was ever so much easier than training to be a Marine. Less people to deal with. Even less grueling physical exertion usually, though she kept in shape easily enough when half the time she was sent sprinting after creatures that could scale the span of a ballpark in moments.

She was almost certain she had seen movement behind the petrol station a few paces further down the main highway. It was a familiar setup for any town's outskirts in the Midwest: fast food, rest stop, motel. A fruitful place for a vampire to hunt, looking for transients passing through. Maybe the vampire was planning to break protocol tonight and feed after all.

Wendy's various tools and weapons were hidden around her person in pockets, strapped to her limbs, and tucked inside her jacket. Anyone passing would assume she was a biker taking a break from the road, deciding between food and filling up. Most people left a striking and strong looking woman alone, and the type of people looking for trouble would regret it if they tried anything.

Her eyes trained on a trail of smoke coming from the back of the petrol station. Some kid on his break. She shifted her attention to the front of the station as she walked up. A couple of young women chatted as they left from the main entrance, carrying sodas and a bag of snacks to their car before taking off. Two other cars remained parked, while a truck finished filling up and the owner headed inside to pay.

When Wendy's eyes went back to the smoking attendant... he was gone. But she was certain she hadn't heard the door, or any telling signs of movement.

She broke into a run for the back of the station, coming around the dumpster to find the attendant sprawled on the ground, not moving, his burnt out cigarette smudged out into the concrete. In less than thirty seconds she assessed the damage. The young teenage boy was out cold, unconscious but not bitten, not seriously injured.

"Hey, that's my truck!" a yell preceded a screech of tires.

Wendy darted around the side of the building in time to see the newly refilled truck peeling out of the parking lot onto the main road. She'd been made. Worse: she'd been outsmarted. By the same vampire. Again.

Knowing the attendant would rouse soon enough and recover, Wendy headed back to her bike, keeping a steady pace rather than running. It wouldn't do her any good to hurry. The vampire would keep the headlights off, not needing them to see in the dark, even with the near pitch blackness of rural Minnesota roads, and would likely ditch the truck before reaching her destination. Wendy's infrared had helped spot the vampire more than once, but the night vision setting wasn't useful on the road when another vehicle's headlights could blind her at any moment.

She was being played with, that much she knew, because the vampire was headed out of town in the same direction they'd come from—back toward Emery Mavus.

~

Connor

Connor snuck a peek at his phone again, being careful to hide it in his large cargo pockets and only look when he knew the Robotics teacher, Mrs. Swanson, was looking elsewhere. She would not look as kindly on distractions in class as Mr. Krall, not when power tools were involved.

Connor respected her though. Learning how to build robots in a virtual environment, and then building the real thing with physical parts, was the best compromise. Plus, Mrs. Swanson let him bring in his own LEGO sets for added 'efficiency' with his robot models. Design was half the battle.

He was still a little disappointed their team hadn't gone to Nationals for the FIRST(For Inspiration and Recognition of Science and Technology) Robotics Competition, but they'd made a decent showing at their initial competition and at Regionals. They'd had six weeks from January into February to design and build a robot to solve a specific problem, this year being to traverse a set obstacle course and climb a pyramid of blocks, which sounded easy enough—the challenges always did—until they reminded themselves that they had to program the robot to actually do all of the things necessary to accomplish that. They'd killed the competition in their first tournament, being maybe the slowest robot, but the only one to get all the way to the top of the pyramid.

The Championships would be in a few weeks, but when Connor considered that he would have had to travel out of state with so much going on, he wasn't as heartbroken anymore as he'd been initially.

Mrs. Swanson had an ever-changing curriculum for them depending on how FIRST went each year, so with less than two months of school left, they were working on end of the year projects, and given a little more leeway since they were seniors. Everyone was given the choice between a solo project or breaking into groups. While Connor had appreciated Nick's offer to join his group that was trying to redesign a better floor cleaning robot to actually get into corners effectively, Connor wanted to focus on prosthetic designs.

He was working on creating a standard template for mass production, something that would appeal to larger audiences. He hoped to finish both an arm and leg design before the end of the year. Ever since he first worked on a leg for Michael, Connor had wanted to start a company to offer free prosthetics to people who couldn't afford them. Of course he also wanted to make custom designs, though he figured those he could sell, maybe even sell costume pieces and prosthetics to movie sets to help fund the free designs.

At first it had been a pet project, a fun dream, but over the years, he and Emery had both taken the idea more seriously. The plan was for Emery to go into business school so they could run the company together. It certainly took away the threat of never seeing each other after high school.

Connor hadn't thought to ask Emery if his plans would change now that he was a vampire, but why should they? Although, if they became an overnight sensation, or ended up on the cover of TIME someday for their efforts, it might put a lot of attention on someone who should probably stay under the radar from mainstream media.

Connor sighed and fired off a quick text to Emery in Psych. Wendy's news the previous night had been daunting, to say the least, especially when they'd already been on edge with Emery almost bursting into flames in AP Lit & Comp. The vampire who was the real threat had turned tail and headed back to town—their town—when someone new was scheduled to be eaten *tonight*.

They couldn't exactly ditch play practice to help Wendy hunt the vampire down, so it had been decided that Wendy would cover one side of town while Alec watched the other, and Connor and

Emery would stay at play practice, on guard in case something happened that actually required Emery to dash out into the night. Hardly likely, Alec had texted them. We'll keep watch, love, Wendy added.

Connor was struck by how weird it was to be on a group text with Buffy the vampire slayer and an actual vampire. Well...two vampires, technically.

"That's strike one, Mr. Daniels," Mrs. Swanson's voice jolted him from his attention on his phone. "Don't make me take that for myself for the rest of the day."

Connor quickly shoved the phone back into his cargos. "Sorry, Swanny. I'm...preoccupied. Having trouble simplifying this arm design. I always go all out for mine, you know? But so far this is way too complicated for mass production."

"You know how to think simple, Connor: lowest common denominator," she said, leaning over his desk to look at the mock up designs and partially created palm he'd done so far in a neutral grey color.

"Eliminate anything not necessary for function. Fun comes later," Connor said, reciting one of her first lessons to the class. "There are too many individual pieces, right? I like intricacy, but if I'm honest, I can get the same amount of dexterity in the fingers with probably half the parts."

"That a boy," Mrs. Swanson smiled, then dropped the expression with a fiercely raised eyebrow. "Now don't let me catch that phone out again or it's mine."

"Yes, Ma'am."

She moved on through the class and Connor sighed again—deeply. Her advice was helpful in regards to his arm design, but he still couldn't think about anything other than Emery and the horror show that was currently their lives.

"When you finish this in the next couple weeks and my group's still scrambling to get our cleaner bot to work, you'll help out, right?" Nick bumped his shoulder as he sidled up.

Nick had grouped with the Kenosha twins. They were wicked smart, but tended to get on each other's nerves and argue. Only Nick with his calm demeanor and who was slow to anger could have partnered with them. They'd always set the group on edge when they were working on their FIRST project, but they had also been the ones to jointly come up with how the arms of their entry robot swiveled to lift up over each block of the pyramid.

"You bet, man," Connor said. "And flattery will get you everywhere, but I still don't think I'll have this and a leg design finished in a couple weeks. Maybe three."

Nick snorted. "Heard something went down in AP Lit yesterday. Mavus isn't sick again, is he? Opening night's only a few weeks away."

Connor smothered the panic that lurched in his chest and pulled on a smile; no one had any reason to suspect the truth. "Nah, more like food poisoning. Would have spoiled our morning *Lake Wobegon* with projectile vomiting if I hadn't yanked him out of there in time. He's fine now. You saw him yesterday."

"Sure," Nick nodded, ever the straight face with his calculating dark eyes. He paused to brush a coil of hair from his face. "Something's been up though. He having mood swings after breaking up with Liz? Wouldn't think so. Never thought they were a good fit."

Given the usual trajectory of these conversations, Connor anticipated an ambush. "I'm working up the nerve to confess before prom, okay? Can everyone just give my love life a rest?"

Nick shrugged. "I was asking about Mavus's love life, not yours."

"What about your love life, huh?" Connor said, scowling. "Who are you taking to prom?"

"Dude, I've been dating J. J. for a week now."

Connor's eyes nearly bugged out. "What? Jason Jeffrey and you? Since…last week?" Everything with Emery had clearly warped his perception. That kind of news would have definitely been high-end gossip and he couldn't remember hearing a word. "Hey, that's awesome, man. I mean, he mentioned having a thing for you once, I just didn't realize you were interested. Who asked who?"

"I asked," Nick shrugged again, this little half gesture with one shoulder that seemed to be his default movement for everything, no matter how mundane or exciting. "It's this thing where you just do it. And then it's over. Not all that hard, as it turns out."

"Yeah, when they say yes..." Connor grumbled.

Nick just shrugged again, though an eye roll accompanied the shoulder roll this time. "Whatever, dude. You know Jules and Aurora are going stag together—"

"Is it still stag if it's girls—"

"So if we need to force you and Mavus to go as friends, that's fine, man, but no one's missing prom."

Connor huffed. "Michael put you up to this, didn't he?"

Again, Nick shrugged. Connor kind of wanted to smack him if he did that one more time.

"Back to work, Mr. McPherson. Don't leave your partners hanging," Mrs. Swanson called over to them.

Nick nodded, raised an eyebrow Connor's direction as if that summed up anything else he might have said, and headed back to the Kenoshas.

Connor looked at his half-made prosthetic and sighed a third time in defeat. Everyone was against him. *For* him, but against him nonetheless.

~

I felt like I was going to be sick, but I knew it was just nerves, not any real nausea. Vampires couldn't get nauseous, could they? Vampires shouldn't even be able to get sick. At least that meant I was finally free from chronic sinus infections. But I still felt queasy. Feeding was bad enough, and whatever this new yearning was when I looked at Connor—my *retainer*—which made my gut twist even tighter. Maybe it was because I was a new vampire, and the hunger would get easier. I hoped so, but I didn't know if I trusted myself to feed from strangers any better than I fed from Connor.

We were working on Act II for the night with the entire set flipped around so that from the audience's perspective, they were seeing what happened backstage for the play within a play. We basically all had to mime an entire Act while also going out 'on stage' to perform the normal roles.

We had started from the point when the actors first start doing the play they'd been rehearsing in Act I, after some drama backstage, and the drama continued while they tried to do their opening night. As Frederick, I was sort of the bubbling idiot who just wanted everyone to get along, and who got a nose bleed at the slightest sign of violence. Over the top was necessary when we didn't technically have any normal dialogue during this portion of the play. Everything had to be obvious gestures and manic stage whispers.

Connor gave me a thumbs up from the sidelines as I dashed off stage holding my nose after having my foot stomped on—mimed, never actually stomped on; at least not on purpose—and I tried to forget that someone might be dying somewhere tonight.

I found little comfort in my would-be mentor and semi-bodyguard both being out hunting the rogue vampire, who may or may not be the true cause of all of my strife lately. If we could just get the rest of the hunters off my tail, at least I could return my focus to existing like a normal person again—a normal person who also had to drink the blood of his best friend once a week. And star in the school play. And get through the next two months of school until graduation.

I was so distracted I almost bumped into Nick during his cameo. He was a stagehand, not one of the actors, but since there had to be a few pretend stage hands 'backstage', we'd worked it out for him to sit on set during Act II, usually eating. At one point, he walked the whole length of the set and snagged a bag of chips from behind the fake prop table. He'd come up with the eating idea on his own. The first few weeks of practicing this Act, I'd had trouble keeping a straight face every time I saw him.

Now I skidded to a stop as I nearly bowled him over. I tried to make it look over the top, like I'd done it on purpose as some last second physical adlib. The next time I was out 'on stage', I risked checking my phone, which would have infuriated Mark if he caught me, and definitely caused Aurora to shoot me a glare. I shrugged apologetically, as I read the latest group messages.

```
Connor: Any news?
Wendy: Tracked her to the park and lost her.
Rounding toward the school now.
Connor: The middle school?!
Alec: On my way.
Wendy: She doesn't appear to be hunting.
Just leading me on a wild goose chase.
Alec: Odd…
```

Odd?! Why was she heading toward the school? A harsh hiss from Aurora alerted me that I'd missed a line. I fumbled to remember where we were, stuttering before I picked up on where I'd left off and shoved my phone back into my pocket. I cast a furtive glance at Connor before racing back onto the real stage. There wasn't much of the Act left, and it was already past ten o'clock. As soon as we finished, Mark would let us go home.

I sprinted up the stairs to the second floor of the set where I was meant to get tangled up in bedsheets. When Jules finally joined me as her character Brooke so we could get tangled together, she shot me a subtly raised eyebrow and a smirk, like she was impressed with my portrayal tonight. Apparently, looking flustered for this role was coming easier and easier, since all I felt were nerves calcifying in my stomach.

Through the next several minutes, I thought I saw Connor trying to get my attention from offstage, but there was no time for me to really look, not with the way my character was yanked around set. By the end of the Act, I was untangled from Jules but basically pushed back on stage with a sheet covering my face, while I blindly hoped I didn't actually stumble over anyone else—at least in a way that wasn't intentional comic relief—and waited for the final lines to be said. As one of the characters exclaimed she was pregnant, everything hushed, and Act II ended in a jumble as the curtains closed.

Before I could even hope to rip the sheet from my face, I felt someone's hand on my wrist, tugging me across stage. I stumbled, shuffling my feet to keep from falling, demanding to know who had hold of me and what was going on, but the grip just squeezed tighter. I took a deep breath through my nose, trying to ignore the sheet, focusing instead on the person with me and pushing everything else away. I smelled sawdust, plastic, paint—nothing helpful—until I caught a whiff of mint. Connor!

"What is going—?" I started to say as I finally caught my bearings enough to tear the sheet from my head. Connor had dragged me deep into the bowels of backstage, behind the flats and prop table where stagehands rarely treaded unless they were racing across set to tend to a curtain that had been forgotten.

I blinked as I saw Mandy a few feet in front of me, the prop master and my very brief sophomore girlfriend, looking dazed like she'd hit her head or was half asleep. Then I saw someone's long fingernails snake up over the curve of her shoulder, another hand sliding around her waist, and then the full figure of a person standing behind her, some woman I'd never seen before who looked crazed and wild even before I saw the glint of fangs.

Connor still had hold of my wrist. He must have seen the vampire first, must have realized, and grabbed me before anything worse could happen. Anything worse than the vampire Alec and Wendy were supposed to be hunting having found her way on stage—to kill the cast.

CHAPTER 15

I'd never been afraid of vampires in fiction. Not even when they were written to be scary, messy and brutal. Thinking back on Mr. and Mrs. Leonard, knowing Alec now, and being a vampire myself, I wanted to believe vampires didn't have to be bad, that I didn't have to be some dark, evil thing just because of what I was. But the vampire in front of me made my heartbeat stutter, and I couldn't move.

Her nails were long like claws, clutching around Mandy's waist and throat. She might have looked like anyone else from our town in a dark blue blouse, jeans, and a tan jacket. She wasn't dirty or unkempt. She was just a woman, a few years older than me maybe, her skin darker like mine, not pale like Alec's or the Leonards', her brown eyes fierce and glowing, her dark hair in tight curls all down her back. If her expression had been neutral or smiling, she would have been pretty, nice looking, normal.

She dug her nails into the side of Mandy's throat. I could hear Mark calling everyone together at the front of the stage, not yet noticing that I was missing as he went through his notes.

"Aren't you a pretty young thing?" she said in a near hiss, sizing me up with eyes that seemed too wide, bulging. "Hadn't seen you this close yet."

Yet?

I saw Connor dig for his phone out of the corner of my eye, subtle, controlled movements, but if I noticed, I knew the vampire would too. She did, and tightened her hold on Mandy. I saw Mandy choke slightly, though her gaze remained glassy and distant.

"No back up, boys, or we're going to take this quartet down to a trio," she said. She was slightly shorter than Mandy, or maybe purposely hunching, so that much of her was hidden, using Mandy as a shield. "Do you know her, care about her? Or are you just sweet boys who don't like to see any poor innocents get hurt?" The nails on Mandy's neck dug in deep enough to draw blood, just a slight trickle that made my stomach lurch. "Stop it!" Connor said, though not loud enough to alert anyone else. We couldn't risk them coming back here and getting involved. "What do you even want? I didn't realize vampires played with their food this much." His bravado wasn't as strong as I was used to; his voice shook at the end of each sentence, a small quaver and yelp in his voice like it was breaking.

I reached out and gripped his wrist as he'd grabbed mine to lead me here, and felt the tremor in it.

The vampire began a low, tittering giggle, as crazed as her expression. "Mmm, I am hungry, that's true. But you're more my prey tonight, dear," she said to me. "See, they can't sense you like I can. Smell you. They don't know which one you are, but I knew the moment I got close. They think I'm crazy, stupid, that they can cast me aside when I'm done. That's why I won't lead them to you, not just yet. Not until I've had some fun."

"Now isn't that interesting," Wendy's rhythmic accent sounded from around the curtain. She appeared a moment later, elegant and calm in her strides, in her same leather jacket, her hair twisted up into a hasty bun, like she'd done it just before revealing herself, knowing she was in for a fight.

Connor shifted the hold I had on his wrist into a tight squeeze of my hand, lacing our fingers together as he backed up a step to let Wendy take his place, and tried to pull me along with him. I looked back at him and shook my head. Wendy was still only human, and I...I wasn't. I let Connor's hand go.

"Aren't you a resourceful hunter," the vampire said, sneering over Mandy's shoulder. "I thought I lost you back in that town, but you followed me here again. No fair...no fair..."

"Who sent you to track down the boy?" Wendy asked. She didn't look armed, but I knew the appearance of that was on purpose. "Did they also lead you here to hunt and rouse suspicion against the Leonards? Why?" Her words were clipped, precise, like leading an official interrogation.

"Wait...someone was setting up the Leonards to bring in hunters?" I said as what Wendy had implied clicked into place. "And now they're trying to set up me? Why?" I shot at the vampire, louder than I intended to.

She didn't respond, just giggled again and continued to run her nails up and down Mandy's bleeding neck.

"Emery, I need you to get her out of the school," Wendy said.

"What?" My eyes darted to her, my heart trip-hammering.

Wendy remained trained on the vampire. "Your police escort is out front. Use the back exit out of the school. You're stronger than you think, stronger and faster than she is, given your lineage. When the opportunity presents itself, *get her out of the school.*"

"Oho," the vampire said, amused by our discussion. "What's this game now?"

"Emery…" Wendy said again to make sure I was ready.

I whirled to face Connor by the curtain. "Tell Mark I had to leave. Then get yourself home. I'll call you."

"What?!" Connor nearly shouted.

"Emery? Connor?" Mark's voice called out.

"Please," I said, holding Connor's gaze for just a moment more, willing him to at least nod and acknowledge what I'd said. Once he did, I turned back to face the vampire. "Okay," I breathed. Wendy had a plan; all I had to do was follow it.

But I didn't expect her attack to hit Mandy. I knew it wasn't an accident when a gadget like a tiny, portable Taser flung toward Mandy and latched onto her shirt, shocking her with sparks of electricity. Her body went limp, dropped, fell from the surprised vampire's arms, who titled her head in wonder and grinned at me in the split second I had to react.

I vaulted over Mandy's body, summoning the speed Connor and I had practiced, and pushed myself to run as fast as I could. I grabbed the vampire by the scruff of her jacket and raced out the stage back door, through the halls, and out the school to the bank of a ditch just down from the football field. It was hidden from view of most traffic with a spattering of nearby trees. I only just started to feel the vampire struggling, fighting against me, when I pushed her away and she toppled over into the ditch.

Skidding to a halt, I paused to catch my breath, before realizing I wasn't even winded, just anxious and trembling from adrenaline. Wendy had a plan...I just didn't know the next part. When the vampire got to her feet, I squared my shoulders and clenched my fists. She dusted herself off and cracked her neck from side to side as if it was all in good fun. I could only guess that Wendy thought my 'lineage'—Alec—was older than this vampire. Whether or not that meant I was faster and stronger, I'd soon find out.

"Who told you to find me? Who set up the Leonards?"

The vampire laughed and shook out her dark curls. "He doesn't like our kind very much. He'd prefer chaos, disorder to shake up the masses and give him leave to do as he pleases. I don't mind a little chaos, you see. Of course, he thinks he can do away with me when he's done, but I'm not concerned. I can have my fun, give him what he wants, and be on my way..."

"Stop talking in riddles!" I yelled. "What's his name? Why did he do this?"

"She isn't going to tell you that, Emery," Alec said, melting out of the shadows into moonlight. I'd forgotten he was on his way, and the tension sagged from my shoulders at his arrival. He looked more like a traditional vampire tonight—well, one who'd been shopping at Express Men; dressed in black slacks, a navy button down, and a longer black jacket than usual.

The vampire tripped back a step, her expression losing its glee for the first time as she hissed, "You..."

My new mentor's notoriety with everyone we met was starting to nag at me.

Alec waved at her with a twirl of his fingers. "Me," he said. "You are a difficult one to catch up with, aren't you, my dear? And who are you, exactly? You've been causing so much trouble lately, and it seems you also had a hand in my children's demise." His eyes flashed with something darker than a predator, like I had seen only briefly before, reminding me that vampires were—or at least could be—killers.

"*Your* children...?" she said, her bug-eyes even wider as she hunched low, warring with whether or not to fight or flee, and which would least likely lead to her getting torn apart. Just how powerful was Alec?

"Mine," Alec said succinctly. He tugged at his jacket, one sleeve at a time. "You weren't going to play nice with Emery, but you'll give me a name, won't you?" he grinned and then immediately dropped the expression for something chillingly blank. "Who hired you? What are they after? Is their current ploy only to lead the hunters to kill Emery and do away with any witnesses to their crimes against William and Mallory, or do they have loftier goals? Tell me!"

The vampire flinched. She glanced at me. At Alec. Then up the hill I'd brought us down, where I turned to see Wendy moving swiftly across the grass.

"Mandy—"

"She's fine," Wendy cut me off. She slowed as she reached me, not seeming any more winded than I was. She nodded to Alec then turned to me fully. "My apologies for the shock, Emery. The voltage she received was the lowest possible setting, not damaging. My motivation is and always will be to make certain the right people are protected." She inclined her head at me, including me in those she felt needed protection.

She wasn't just a hunter, I realized; she was a soldier.

Wendy shifted until she was parallel with me, Alec bookending the other vampire between us on the other side of the ditch. The vampire tried to back away, but I moved to intercept, and Alec and Wendy moved to match me, until we made a circle around her, blocking any escape.

"I didn't know they belonged to you," the vampire said to Alec, hands clenching and unclenching at her sides.

"Pity," he said, "but not the point at the moment. You still haven't answered my questions."

"Why bother?" she shot back. "You'll kill me anyway once I give you what you want. Maybe I'll take these secrets to the grave, and watch on from the afterlife as you squirm for the truth. They're coming for you...*Emery*," she said with a roll of her head toward me, knowing my name now and using it with a twisted curl of her lips, "and they won't be nearly as nice as all of us." She gestured outward to indicate Alec, Wendy, and herself.

"You'll just kill more people if we let you go," I said as that dawned on me. There was no vampire prison, and nothing could stop her from taking her next victim, which she planned to feed from tonight. It was why Wendy existed.

My stomach bottomed out as I imagined the night playing out like some gory horror movie. Mr. Leonard was the first time I'd seen someone dead, but I'd never watched someone die.

I looked to Wendy, to Alec, but they were focused on the vampire, preparing to take her down. And she just laughed. She knew she couldn't get out alive, and wouldn't tell us anything if there was nothing in it for her. She was going to die for nothing.

"Please," I said, stepping forward as I saw the vampire ready to launch herself at Wendy, like she thought it the smarter choice for a last ditch effort. "Tell us something, anything."

She paused, looked at me, frowned and shook her head. "No one is more dangerous than someone living a lie, kid. But who's to say you'll know the difference when the time comes."

Her crazed grin returned, and the hunch to her form, low to the ground. Then Wendy called out, "Emery!" as she darted toward me.

The vampire didn't train her sights on me though. She started to, then pivoted at the last second and launched herself at Wendy, catching the hunter off guard. They tumbled to the ground, and when the vampire jumped to her feet, she had a stake in her hand that I hadn't even seen on Wendy's person. She headed for me again.

I froze. Why do they say fight or flight when the third option is so much worse? When you can't do anything but stand there and wait for the inevitable because you can't imagine running? You know it wouldn't do you any good, but you can't stomach fighting for your life either if it means killing someone else.

"Emery!" Alec called, and I snapped alert, doing the only thing I could think of—I charged.

I charged the vampire as she gunned for me, and bowled her over like sacking a quarterback. She hit the ground hard, the stake thudding into the grass as her hand snapped to the side. I rolled away from her, grabbing the stake as I went, and held it up in defense, tried to imagine stabbing it into her heart like I'd seen in a dozen movies, but my hand shook, her face furious as she snarled at me. I couldn't think or breathe as she rose up to come at me again.

Alec swooped in like a rolling wave of smoke. I couldn't be sure if what I saw was reality or a mirage from him moving so fast, but he seemed like mist one moment and then was whole the next, falling upon the vampire and sinking his fangs into her throat. She flailed as he pinned her to the ground, drinking greedily, his eyes blazing blue and then…red, I thought, like some terrible demon. The vampire shuddered and convulsed as he drained her of every last drop. When he was done, minutes later, the other vampire looked ashen, eyes wide but unseeing now, while I stared from sitting half on my hip in the grass, holding a useless stake. And then, as Alec released her, she crumbled into dust like she had never existed.

I choked and scrambled away. Mr. Leonard hadn't crumbled like that. Or his wife. A stake had killed them both, but had still left bodies. The myth of vampires falling to ash was from something much worse, I knew now—from being drained until they were nothing but a husk of their former self.

I threw the stake away from me. I wanted to go home. I wanted to crawl under the covers and hide in the dark. I wanted to throw up. I wanted, more than anything, to be human again and to have never seen these things or felt this awful ache. But that was the one thing I couldn't do. And when none of the other options seemed possible either, I pulled my knees to my chest and cried.

CHAPTER 16

Connor

Connor resisted the urge to race to Emery's side when he saw his friend hide his face in his knees and sob. He was supposed to head straight home, not shout a hasty, "Em had to dash, Mark, hit with the stomach flu he's been fighting. See you tomorrow!" before zipping out of the middle school and following after Wendy's retreating form. He'd managed to stay out of sight and hide behind a collection of trees as he watched the fight.

Mandy had awoken with a shiver, suffering aftershocks from whatever Wendy zapped her with, a device the hunter had quickly snatched back before darting out into the night after Emery. Connor was left to pick up the pieces from their encounter, but thankfully, Mandy didn't remember anything. Connor told her she'd tripped, hit her head and cut her neck on part of the set, and must be disoriented. She bought right into it in the aftermath of the vampire's glamour, and headed around the curtains to the front of the stage without a second thought.

Then Connor was off, where he watched the fight unfold from the safety of a large tree. Alec moved so much faster than Emery; he seemed to dissolve and then reform in a completely different location. He drank the other vampire until she was nothing but dust, and Connor pumped a fist into the air from where he hid in celebration.

But the sight of Emery in tears reminded him of how real this was. It wasn't a game or a movie; Emery had just played a role in ending someone's life. The vampire, however twisted, cruel and murderous, was dead. The weight of that caused Connor to sway against the tree.

"Em..."

"Emery," Wendy said, going to him swiftly after tucking the thrown away stake back into her jacket, "it had to be done. You will be safer now. It's all right to be shaken, but do not be burdened by her loss. You were only protecting yourself."

Connor nodded along, wanting to comfort Emery as well, but he knew he'd only upset his friend if he revealed that he had seen it all.

Wendy tried to place a hand on Emery's shoulder, but he brushed her off, burying his head further into his knees. Alec stepped over to them, appearing so normal now, not wicked and fierce as he had while draining the other vampire. His expression was neutral, no common manic grin, no witty retort to rouse Emery. He swooped in, knelt down, and with a strength that awed Connor, pulled Emery up from his fallen position until both of them were on their knees. Alec crushed Emery against his chest and held him, *hugged* him.

"It's never easy the first time, dear boy," Alec said so softly that Connor barely heard him. "I hope there never has to be a second. Whoever sent her here will pay, but by my hand, not yours. I won't let them take you as they took William and Mallory..." His voice hissed, hollow and haunting without any humor in it.

Connor heard truth in the words he hadn't yet known from Alec. He had always suspected the elder vampire was merely playing the fool, wearing an impressive mask that held something else beneath. And as those thoughts played in his mind, watching Emery sob against Alec's shoulder, the vampire tilted his head up, pale blue eyes centering right on Connor's hiding spot.

If it hadn't honestly felt like the temperature dropped around him, he might have offered a cheeky wave, but that stare felt like a warning. He nodded. Alec and Wendy had this one; Connor should have gone home. He'd do that now, give them the appropriate amount of time to head off, then leave in his Thunderbird.

Hiding more fully behind the tree when Emery finally pulled away from Alec, Connor couldn't see what happened next for fear of being caught, but he heard murmurs of thanks from Emery, more comforting words from the others, and then their voices began to fade as they herded Emery away. Wendy would give Emery a ride home on her bike, while Alec glamoured the police escort not to take notice. Connor would have to hurry to beat them home, though he could always tell Emery he'd been detained by Mark for notes.

He had to see Emery when they got home, even if it was a school night. Connor could count on one hand the amount of times he'd seen his friend cry. Teary-eyed was one thing, but full on bawling dug in so much deeper. They'd been blessed with lives that rarely touched on trauma. Up until the murders, the worst thing that had ever happened in their small town was Michael losing his leg. And while that had been terrible, at least he'd lived, come out of it even more insufferably popular and cocksure, especially with Connor around to make legs for him.

Facing death week after week wasn't good for anyone. Connor wanted to hug Emery as Alec had and never let him go. The world outside each other's arms was getting scarier by the day.

Connor leaned back against the tree and checked his phone. 10:17. He'd give it three more minutes, then run to his car and take a shortcut home.

"You're his friend, aren't you?"

The phone shot up into the air and Connor fumbled to reclaim it, his heartrate skyrocketing. "Who the hell—?" he started before he'd even looked up, but then cut off.

He didn't know the man who materialized from the more distant trees. He might have looked normal enough for these parts, like a deer hunter in matching dark green jacket and trousers, combat boots, and a hat pulled down over shaggy dirty blond hair, if not for the crossbow in his arms. Deer hunters didn't load their bows with wooden bolts.

Connor tried to step back before remembering the tree was still behind him. A vampire hunter. His mind raced, jumbled, searching for the proper reaction. His friend? Yes, he was Emery's friend. Was that a bad thing?

"I can't track them directly from here," the man said, stalking toward Connor assuredly, crossbow at the ready, brown eyes narrowed and face stern, "not with the older one tailing, and the other hunter with him. She'll make me for sure, if the vampire doesn't pick me off first. So you're going to tell me where they went—where he lives."

A few more misfires in his brain went off before Connor computed what was happening. He clutched his phone to his chest. "Didn't you hear? Didn't you see?" He pushed off from the tree to meet the hunter halfway. "They killed the other vampire. She was the real baddie. Em's being set up!"

Barely a few feet remained between them as the hunter stopped... and grinned. "I saw. Who do you think hired the bitch?"

The ground fell out from under Connor, seemed to almost literally fall away as his stomach plummeted. "But...why? Em's never done anything. He's never hurt anyone!"

"But he was there. Leonard turned him to spite us, the clever bastard. Your friend was there. We can't have any witnesses or loose ends."

Connor backed away again, this time angling slightly left, hoping to bypass the tree. "We?" he said, and clutched his phone tighter, wondering how much he could risk before the hunter made to take it.

The school wasn't far. They were out the back exit, where no cars were parked, but there were still a couple dozen kids inside, and Emery, Wendy, and Alec were still close. If only Connor could just sneakily call one of them, but he'd have to look down at his phone to swipe the pattern correctly on his lock screen.

"Oh, I'm not alone," the hunter said, grinning wider as if to say he didn't mind giving up that information, like it didn't matter what he told Connor—that couldn't be good. "There are several of us in town, and you'll never tell us apart from another tourist or passerby, kid. That's what makes us so good at what we do."

Connor's elbow hit the tree and he corrected further left, still moving, slow and steady, while the hunter pursued him at a matching pace. "I thought you had a pact. You only kill if they kill, and vice versa. Why setup the Leonards?"

"Some of the others with us care about all that," he said, one hand running along the curves of his crossbow. With the speed at which something like that could shoot, it wouldn't matter if it was

wood; it would still feel like a bullet to Connor. "Me and the boss…
we just like to kill monsters. Figure there are a few too many around
now. Things have gotten too friendly. But make it look like the good
ones are just as bad as the killers, and hey, every hunter around
takes up the call." His eyes were cold as he trained the crossbow
forward. "We just got a little more cleanup to take care of before
we're out of this town and on to the next. So you're going to tell
me—"

Connor cleared the tree and took off running in the opposite
direction, punching at his phone to pull up someone, anyone, and
thanking every deity that might be listening that he had Alec in his
phone. The older, bizarre, and sometimes terrifying vampire was at
the top of his contacts.

He raced for the ditch where Emery had been fighting moments
ago, but an overlarge bolt sunk into the ground just ahead of him,
narrowly missing his foot. A warning shot, but the jolt of it, of jerking
back and trying to avoid tumbling over the protruding projectile, only
unbalanced Connor worse than if he'd tripped over it.

His ankle caught in the thick grass and bumps of the hill
leading out of the ditch. He hit the ground hard on his shoulder and
rolled twice, winded as he came to a stop on his back. His phone
slipped from his hand but he could see it blinking, dialing. A photo
from *Nosferatu* pulled up.

"Alec!" Connor cried just before a foot came down and
crushed it, silencing his only lifeline.

His left hand remained outstretched toward it, exposing the
silver, hard plastic fingers of his Terminator prosthetic. The hunter
hovered over him, eyes drawn to the hand. He huffed a taunting
laugh and bent down on one knee. One hand still held the crossbow
while the other yanked back the sleeve of Connor's long-sleeved
shirt to his elbow, where his prosthetic connected.

"Convenient," the hunter said. He dropped Connor's arm back
to the ground and stood. "See, kid, now I can do this—" he said as
he stepped onto Connor's hand with a crunch.

"Hey!"

"—and not even hurt you. But I bet you'd rather I didn't
destroy this thing, wouldn't you, since it seems you need it. Be a

little hard to grapple with only one arm." He pressed more weight onto Connor's hand, and there was a loud snap amidst the continuing crunch of plastic.

"You should try it with only one testicle, asshole," Connor spat, and swung his free fist up between the guy's legs as hard as he could.

The hunter gasped and hunched over, surprised enough that Connor was able to reach over and release his prosthetic at the elbow. He slipped free, leaving it and his phone behind. He rolled to his feet, but didn't get more than a step before the man had him by the ankle, and he fell right back to the ground face first.

Connor kicked and kicked and fought with every fiber in him, but the man's strength was like a vice in his fury. He flipped Connor over onto his back again and planted a knee in his chest to hold him still.

"You little brat," the hunter growled, still panting from the punch. "I might have let you go if you'd just given up the monster's location."

Connor readied every insult he could think of, because Emery was not a monster, never, never would be, but his struggling ceased when the hunter brought the crossbow up to point between his eyes.

A blur zoomed past Connor's vision and the hunter was gone. His breath caught, gasped out of him, as he shook and shook and tried to tell himself to just pull it together, stay calm and get up, *get up!* He rolled to his feet once more, scrambling up from the ground, and darted his eyes around the ditch until he saw the bowled over hunter several yards away, still shaking his head from whatever had hit him.

Alec stood nearby, reaching down to retrieve Connor's crushed prosthetic. He looked at the arm, one finger dangling that had snapped beyond repair, and tossed it back to the ground with a snarl. "Some men have no sense of decorum," he muttered. He whirled on Connor then and grabbed onto him at lightning speed. "We have to go. I can't guarantee your protection if there are others."

Connor saw the hunter stir over Alec's shoulder and start to get up.

"Wait—" Connor protested, when the world lurched like a punch to the gut, a whirlwind of sounds and wind and dizziness. When it finally stopped, Connor blinked at his surroundings to find himself standing in his bedroom.

"No!" he turned on Alec, who was already on his phone, dialing Emery. "You have to go back! The hunters, some of them are in on it! He knows everything! You have to stop him!"

Alec held up a hand as he spoke into the phone, "Emery, Connor is with me in his room. Come when you can," and ended the call just as swiftly, though Connor was certain he'd heard a muffled cry before the call ceased.

He barreled into Alec, pushing him toward the window. "I'm fine! Go! You have to go!"

"Connor—"

"He wants to kill him!"

"Connor!" Alec grabbed Connor by the shoulders and pulled him in like he had done to Emery, squeezing almost too tightly to still Connor and force him to calm down. It only served to choke something like a sob from Connor's throat, and screw that! He didn't have time to cry; someone had to be the strong one.

"Please," Connor said, clinging to Alec, because he was still shaking, and not really breathing, and he could feel his heartbeat thrumming in his ears.

"Connor? What happened?" Emery's voice was tight with panic as it called from the window. Vampire powers sucked at times like these; Wendy had to have already gotten Emery most of the way home, and he'd gone all Flash speed for the remainder.

Connor pushed Alec away from him, which seemed ineffectual because he was so used to wearing his prosthetic. His misshapen elbow didn't reach far enough to touch Alec's chest in sync with his right hand, the sleeve dangling uselessly. Alec allowed him to dislodge from his arms, and Connor looked up at the vampire with a pinched expression.

"You have to go back," Connor said, ignoring Emery.

Alec nodded.

"Wendy's making a perimeter search around the neighborhood," Emery offered when Alec moved to take his place at the window.

Connor didn't miss the way his friend's eyes trained on his empty sleeve. "What happened?" he asked again.

"I'll be back," Alec said, and disappeared into the night.

Left alone with Emery, while his long-sleeved shirt, without his prosthetic to fill it out, flopped at his side in the way he most hated, Connor felt incomplete, like he was broken. But he couldn't afford to be broken, not now. He turned away from Emery to find another shirt.

CHAPTER 17

Connor wasn't wearing his prosthetic. I glanced around the room, remembering he'd had the Terminator one on today, but I couldn't see any sign of it. Alec had looked too stoic before he left, the same way he'd been with me outside the school. The echo of what happened was too fresh in my mind, like a gurgling of acid in my gut.

Connor turning away from me, rummaging through his dresser with only the use of his right hand, made it so much worse, and I didn't even know what had happened.

I walked to the bed and sat down. Our parents would be wondering where we were, and with the cop on my tail diverted for the rest of the night, and both me and Connor up in his room without having used the door, we didn't have much time. I wanted to sit and not think for a while, because whenever I thought about what happened—chanting inside my head that it had to be done, Wendy and Alec were right, there was no other way—I'd hear my mother's voice.

"If it feels wrong, honey, it probably is."

I looked at Connor, who'd changed out of his long-sleeved shirt into a T-shirt, his left arm ending just below the elbow. I'd seen it plenty of times like this, but he never seemed to meet my eyes when he wasn't wearing a prosthetic. He looked around his room searching for a replacement, before sputtering a stream of curses.

"They're all in the workshop," he bit out, running his right hand back over his buzzed hair, eyes trained on the floor.

"Connor…"

"It was stupid," he interrupted, and proceeded into a tirade about what had happened, how he'd followed us, watched the fight, and been caught by one of the hunters—a hunter who was part of the setup, working against the other hunters and me, and he wasn't the only one.

It wasn't stupid; it was terrifying.

Both of us, me on the bed, feeling sick and small; Connor pacing, not looking at me, fidgeting with where his arm should be. We both felt wrong. We should have found some solidarity in that, but Connor finished his rant with a huff and turned away, like he wanted me to leave. Then he spun around, arms crossed, hiding his elbow behind his good arm, and his expression cracked.

"I'm sorry, Em. You shouldn't have to deal with my freak out when you're having your own."

"What?" I gave a humorless laugh as I stood. "You said he had a crossbow on you. He broke your arm. He might have killed you if Alec hadn't found you. Your freak out's more justified than mine."

"Em—"

"Connor?" Georgia's voice made us both jump as she opened the door, carrying a basket of laundry. Her eyes narrowed behind her glasses. "How did you get up here? I didn't see either of you come in. Emery, it's a little late to be over, don't you think, considering everything? Should I call your parents—"

"No!" I didn't want to make them worry any worse than they already were. I wanted to stay, to talk to Connor about this, but adolescence and overprotective parents were against us. "Sorry, George," I said, mustering a smile I also cast on Connor. "It was just a long day and we had something to talk about. We'll catch up tomorrow. Right?" I eyed Connor hopefully.

His eyes danced with dread, and the way he tightened the hold on his elbow made my stomach twist. He didn't have to hide his arm from me.

"Sure, Em. First thing. Nothing to lose any sleep over." Which translated to him being certain he'd have nightmares about this, but that he, in no way, wanted to bring it up on the ride to school tomorrow. I planned to convince him anyway.

"Sorry, George," I said again. "I'll get right home. Night, Connor."

"Night, Em."

Georgia smiled and shifted the laundry to one arm so she could grab my shoulder when I walked past, kissing my cheek, so much like my own mom.

As I headed down the stairs, I heard her ask Connor, "Sweetheart, what happened to your arm?"

I just wished tomorrow would come quickly.

~

Connor

Connor managed to convince his mother that he'd messed up his Terminator arm at play practice. He told her not to worry, that he didn't feel like replacing it when he just wanted to sleep. She dug out a pair of his jeans and a couple shirts from the laundry basket and set them on the bed before kissing him goodnight.

"I'm just bummed about the arm," he said when she gave him that 'if you want to talk, I'm here' expression. "It was my favorite, ya know?"

"Okay, honey. Get some sleep and don't beat yourself up over it. It's an excuse to finish a new design, right?"

"Yeah."

Connor lay back on his bed on top of the covers, having kicked his laundry to the floor. His mom would scold him if she saw, but he didn't want to deal with anything right now. He glanced at the walkie talkie on his dresser, wondering if Emery would try to talk to him, hoping he wouldn't. He felt sticky with sweat from the mad dash and subsequent fight with the hunter, the pulse of adrenaline fading and making his joints stiffen. The room felt stifling around him, and the silence of being alone closed in, making him feel like he couldn't breathe.

He jumped off the bed and tore over to his window, throwing it open to gulp in some of the cooler, spring air. It helped—marginally. Then he heard a stuttered breath. A whimper.

"Em?" he whispered, even though he knew the voice didn't sound like Emery, but who else would be out on Connor's roof?

His bedroom window opened up onto an overhang, offering access to the upward slant that led to the main roof. He'd been chastised more times than he could count when he was younger for climbing out there, but in recent years his parents had given up thinking he didn't sneak out on occasion. Sometimes he and Emery would lie up there under the stars, usually on summer nights with nothing else to do but keep each other company.

Connor climbed out onto the overhang and started the careful shuffle up the slant, recognizing the voice, but not truly believing it until he saw Alec sitting there, legs dangling from the top of the roof. Connor sat beside him silently. Alec didn't even turn his head. His sobs had stopped but his cheeks looked wet when Connor glanced at him.

The sight of this elder vampire in tears, hundreds of years old likely, who Connor had seen move faster than his eyes could follow and kill another vampire with barely any effort, eased some of the tension in his chest. He dug deep inside of himself for an edge of snark, as he rocked sideways until his shoulder bumped Alec's.

"All talk, huh? Thought so. Mr. and Mrs. Leonard were like your kids. You joke about it, but it's the truth. I heard what you said to Em after you offed the other vampire. He's your legacy now, huh? You ever turn anyone else?"

Alec shifted beside him. "No. And neither had William or Mallory."

"Wow. So Em's really…"

"All I have. Yes."

"I'm sorry." Connor looked at him again, and this time he waited for Alec to look back at him before continuing. "You should tell him. You don't need to play the eccentric psycho bit. Everything's messed up anyway, and Em is not doing okay. He almost burst into flames at school yesterday because he kept avoiding feeding."

"He *what*? Youth," Alec said with a sigh and dramatic roll of his eyes. He used the gesture of turning away to more easily wipe the tears from his cheeks. "I'll talk to him. But you're rather bold, aren't you? Eccentric psycho bit? What makes you think it's an act? Either way, I am completely in control of my faculties, thank you, and eccentricities are a virtue."

Connor snorted. "Pretty sure you made that up, but whatever." They sat in companionable silence for some time. Worry concerning the hunters that might be lurking in the night, seeking them out at that very moment, became a distant echo sitting beside Alec, powerful and ancient and on their side, like a well-trained lion. Connor reminded himself that even domesticated lions killed their masters on occasion, but tonight he felt safe with Alec, sitting on his roof.

He hugged his arms against the chill in the air. A T-shirt wasn't nearly enough to keep him warm, and Alec did not produce much body heat—no surprise there. Connor brushed his hand over his stumped elbow.

"So, just out of curiosity," he said, thankful Alec's eyes didn't linger when he caught the vampire looking at his missing arm, "if I became a vampire…"

"No. Your arm would not grow back," Alec answered before Connor could finish. "You were born without it, correct? If you had a disease, your vampiric cells would heal you as your human cells were replaced. If you lost an arm after being a vampire, your cells would regenerate. But you can't regenerate cells that were never there."

"Right. Had to ask."

"Mmm. My apologies again about the prosthetic. It was a work of art." Alec produced the crushed Terminator arm from his other side, handing it to Connor. "The hunter was gone when I arrived back at the school. I tracked his movements into the trees but lost him. They are very talented indeed to escape my senses in so short a time. I'll keep a closer watch."

Connor nodded, toying with the broken finger as he held the prosthetic in his lap. He could reprint it with some modifications, a few new ideas he had to make it better. It wasn't a total loss, no disaster. It just felt like one. He set the arm aside.

"There's one other vampire question we never asked," Connor said.

"Yes?"

"Does a vampire have to be a certain age to turn someone? Like…could Em turn someone now if he wanted to?"

"Of course," Alec said, "but it wouldn't be allowed. There are rules. Vampires must be granted permission to turn others, or there would be an epidemic of young vampires turning their friends and family."

"But, as his mentor or whatever, wouldn't he just need to ask permission from you?"

"Yes, I could grant him that. But I won't. He comes from a strong line, powerful blood, but being so young dilutes what would be passed on. We usually don't allow for a vampire to turn others until they are at least a century."

"Oh…" The pit in Connor's stomach deepened. He'd tried to avoid thinking these things, about how Emery wouldn't age but *he* would. How eventually there would be years between them and no more chances to be more than friends.

Connor tipped to the side as Alec leaned into him. He scowled at the vampire only to find a wry, knowing smile.

"I should not be so cruel," Alec said. "Old habits and all. Of course I understand what you are really asking, Connor, so let me be blunt. No, I will not give Emery permission to turn you. But if it was something you both wanted, I would be happy to turn you myself. I get the impression you haven't actually asked Emery about this yet."

"Of course not, that would be…" Awesome if Emery wanted to be with him; devastating if he didn't. "I mean, sure, we've been friends our whole lives, but 'let's spend the rest of eternity together' is a little much."

"Is it? That's what William and Mallory did."

"Really?" Connor looked at him with more eagerness than he'd meant to reveal. Alec smirked, knowingly again—he knew. Of course he knew. Everyone freaking knew.

"A little later in life, granted," Alec said, "and it is a shame Emery was turned so young. Living out eternity with your best friend isn't so bad though. You saw how happy they were…" His voice trailed, his pale eyes growing distant, darker.

"I'm really sorry, Alec."

Alec closed his eyes, and when they opened again, the darkness was gone. "So am I."

"Do you have any friends like that? I mean, besides…" Connor didn't want to bring up the Leonards again, but the conversation inevitably drifted back to them.

Alec's expression turned wistful. "I'm afraid I haven't been so lucky. Oh, I've had companions, lovers. Good friends, certainly. But not someone to share eternity with. I am always ready to try again though." He chuckled with a devious, playful edge, and Connor couldn't help laughing with him. "You should get to bed now. I'll keep a close eye on both of you tonight, rest assured, while Wendy surveys the neighborhood. Tomorrow, Emery's police escort will be back to his duties."

"Yeah, I guess you're right."

Connor sat a moment more, looking across the yard at Emery's house, wondering what his friend was thinking, if he was okay, if he would ever be able to look at Connor the way the Leonards looked at each other. Connor tried to be selfless with Emery; he could be his friend for a lifetime, never knowing him more intimately or having his love returned, but not for eternity. He couldn't live at Emery's side forever never having what he really wanted.

Slowly, he stood, scooping his Terminator arm up and making the slow, careful descent down the slant toward his window. His balance was a little off without a prosthetic on, but he didn't waver. As he climbed into his window, he turned back to Alec.

"Thanks. You're not so bad, ya know? Downright tolerable sometimes."

The smile Alec offered him was genuine, joyful, and contained decades of secrets—no, centuries, maybe longer—of all the reasons why Alec being 'not so bad' might not be entirely true. Connor didn't mind.

"Goodnight, Connor."

"Later, *Fright Night*."

CHAPTER 18

I texted Connor to meet up in his backyard before we headed to school. That way the returned police babysitter could see me arrive at the house, but not get a clear shot of us until we left through the gate again and got into Connor's car.

As soon as Connor slipped out the sliding glass doors to meet me inside the fence, I hugged him, holding tight but careful not to crush him, or his red prosthetic that I'd only caught a glimpse of before pulling him in.

"Em—"

"We both almost died last night," I said, speaking against his neck, not allowing myself to think of how I'd sunk my teeth there. "It's easy not to think of it that way because it turned out differently, but it's true. I never want to think about what life would be like without you. I don't know what I'd…how I'd…" My voice caught and I tried to think of what else I'd meant to say.

"Em, dude, calm down, it's okay," Connor said, flesh and plastic arms encircling my back. "It'll be okay. This is all freaky and intense, sure, and maybe my near-death experience with a crossbow haunted my dreams a little, but Wendy and Alec got our backs."

I snuffled a laugh into his skin, but it wasn't funny to me, not really, how I'd gotten my best friend caught up in my nightmare.

After another brief squeeze, I let him go, and the way he lingered, his hands dropping more slowly than mine, consoled me that he wasn't afraid of me, even if he should be. "You trust Alec now?" I scrunched my nose as I took in what he'd said.

"Eh," Connor shrugged, "he's growing on me." He nodded toward the gate and we turned to leave the backyard, both of us retrieving our bags that had ended up on the ground. When we exited onto the driveway to get into the Thunderbird, he said, "By the way, you had the stomach flu, that's why you left before notes last night, so groan a little today but swear you're feeling better if anyone asks."

We tossed our bags in the backseat and climbed into our respective places in the car. He started the engine, his red fingers on the steering wheel standing out to me more than usual after seeing him without an arm last night. He tilted his head at me before pulling out of the driveway. His gaze was tight, strained despite his grin.

"Then promise, promise me no more bullshit, holding off feeding. We do this like clockwork. Imploding during AP Lit is not the way you want to be remembered."

I huffed an even less believable laugh than the one I'd released while we hugged. It was stupid how long I'd gone without feeding, thinking I could avoid it, that if I just waited long enough, somehow all this insanity would go away.

Sometimes, singing in choir, doing my homework, answering a question in class, or enacting one of the scenes from the play, it did all go away, and for a moment I forgot about Mr. and Mrs. Leonard and what had happened to me. But I couldn't just live and pretend everything was normal. Last night had proved that. The vampire was dead, but those hunters, however many of them were in on this plot, wanted me dead too. One of them knew what Connor looked like. What I looked like. Maybe they all knew now.

"Em," Connor said, insistent, still waiting for an answer.

"Yeah," I said, plastering on a smile. "No more bullshit."

As we headed to school, a vision of Alec moving like mist to attack the other vampire, drinking her down viciously and leaving her as nothing but dust, tightened a knot in my chest. But as much as the thought of being brutal like that unnerved me—especially if I hurt someone I cared about—I looked at Connor and knew I was too selfish to do this without him.

~

Connor

Connor had a free period after lunch with Aurora, which often translated into a really long lunch, but also gave them the opportunity to do nothing for a while. He'd had Zero Hour for years with Jazz Band, which earned him an extra period that he could fill with fun bonus classes, like Personal Finance—more practical than fun, but his mother had sure been proud. Now that it was senior year, he wanted that free period free. Aurora shared the sentiment.

They sat on a tabletop in the cafeteria where the Juniors were having lunch, taking up a whole table that could have gone to someone actually eating. Though technically Aurora was still picking at her fries, dipping them in ketchup and then into the shredded cheese on her tray. Connor had dumped his food fifteen minutes ago.

"What about *Lucky Number Sleven*," he said. "Lucy Liu is totally the romantic lead in that one."

"Correct," Aurora nodded, "but that's first and foremost an action move, not rom-com."

"Why does it have to be romantic comedy?"

"Because that is the tried and true genre for romance, Con-Man. Admit it, without looking it up or doing an impressive online search, you can't think of any mainstream American romance movies with Asian leads. It doesn't happen! I am forever shunned to the stereotyped role or cute Asian best friend."

"Well, you are cute," Connor said thoughtfully. "And one of my best friends."

She mimed shoving a ketchup and cheese covered fry in his face, but he took advantage of the gesture to snap his jaws and swipe it from her fingers. She snorted and shook her head. "If this is your romantic comedy, Connor, you are doing something terribly wrong. Your leading man is completely unaware of the plotline."

The memory of Emery's warm hug that morning sent a shiver through him. "You think *you* have it bad never being cast in leading roles? Where's the gay romance box office hit I've been waiting for all my life? And if you say *Brokeback Mountain* to me, I will punch you in the boob."

Aurora responded by punching *him* in the boob, which—*ouch*—really hurt. She was freakishly strong for someone so tiny. "Anyway, that isn't even what we were talking about. I said I hate how half the time female roles are only written in to be romantic interests. No substance. No purpose. Just a tight ass and a pretty face to dress up the movie poster and give the guy some arm candy. Where's the action film with the girl as the kickass sidekick or partner—or hey, as the hero herself—without needing to make it about sex? Why does there have to be romance in everything? Girls are just shoved into the supporting role, Asian girls even more so."

Connor stole one of the fries from her plate while he tapped his feet on the seat he should have been sitting in. They were seniors; if they wanted to sit on the tables, they were allowed. Unless a teacher walked by. "It's kind of funny, right?"

"What's funny?"

"I'd give anything to be typecast as the love interest. Frankly, I'd trade spots with any girl in this school to have some of those stereotypes instead of my own."

Aurora cocked her head at him, another fry suspended between them, having come dangerously close to getting ketchup in the long braid over her shoulder as she gestured. "You want to be an object?"

"I want to be an option." The humor drained from his face as he said it, leaving the conversation quiet and stilted. He stared off into the throng of the cafeteria, not really looking at anyone or seeing anything but blurs of color.

Aurora surprised him with a fry in front of his eyes, and he had to accept it, eat it out of her fingers, or risk her actually smashing it into his face. "Imagine if you were gay and Asian. Then you'd really be screwed."

Connor laughed as he chewed. "How about an Asian lesbian?"

"You wish," she giggled. She pushed her tray away from her finally and sighed. "One thing does not solely define someone as a person, but being half Korean is all anyone would care about at a casting call."

"Good thing you can't act worth shit."

She smacked him with a backhand to the chest.

"Ow, geez! That's why you're queen of backstage! No one can compete with your managerial skills."

"Damn right. And it's *empress*, peon."

"Hey, gimp!"

Connor pivoted on the table to look behind him at where Michael Fergus and his thousand-watt politician's smile was swaggering toward them. He hopped up onto the table beside Connor and leaned forward to acknowledge Aurora.

"Hey, Frank," he said.

She smiled sweetly—a little too sweetly, in Connor's opinion. "Hey, Michael."

"Good thing I caught both of you, actually," Michael said as he leaned back. "As you know, Prom is less than three weeks away—"

"Oh god," Connor groaned.

"—and I need some advance opinions on the theme Student Council is unveiling on Friday. Ready?"

"What is it?" Aurora peered around Connor expectantly.

Michael kept his voice low so none of the Juniors would overhear, but spread his hands out in front of him like a magician doing a magic trick. "Elements."

Connor scrunched his face in confusion. "Like sun and rain and snowstorms?" They already called the winter dance Snow Ball; the last thing Minnesota schools needed was to call more attention to the elements.

"No, dude," Michael scoffed, dropping his hands to his lap with a smack, "like fire and wind and lightning."

"Oh. So can I come as Captain Planet?" Connor brightened. It would almost be worth it to attend Prom if he could paint himself blue for the night.

"How about Captain Cold, smart-ass? You and Mavus can revive your couple's costumes from Halloween."

"For the last time," Connor jumped on the defensive, the usual swirl of nerves and discomfort filling his belly at the mention of his feelings for Emery, "that was not a couple's costume! Cold and The Flash are nemeses!"

Michael shrugged. "Whatever you need to tell yourself, man."

Aurora giggled, and not the way she giggled around Connor with a snort of derision mixed in, but overtly melodic and adorable. She even flipped her braid over her shoulder. "I think that theme sounds amazing, Michael. Did you come up with it?"

"All me," Michael crossed his hands over his heart. "I figured that way we can cover anyone who prefers simple designs, like just doing a color scheme, and the more creative. Meagan and I are going as fire. She has this idea for comets—"

"Isn't it weird going to Prom with your ex?" Connor broke in.

"Why? We're still friends. We already made plans. Plus, we're King and Queen—"

"Still haven't voted yet, and Liz—"

"—so it's not weird. She's dating Skylar now, but he was already going with Shawna, and—"

"Our lives are a soap opera, that's what this is," Connor muttered, turning aside to look at Aurora, who seemed rapt with attention on Michael's animated gossiping.

Rapt with attention. Giggling. *Sweet.*

The hypocrite!

She shrunk in on herself when she caught Connor scowling.

"Well, I gotta get ready for class," Michael said, dropping to his feet and spinning on his heels to elegantly walk backwards away from them. He tossed them a small salute and a wink. "You guys have been super helpful. Elements will be a hit."

"Hey, she's the only one who actually—" Connor tried, thrusting a thumb at Aurora.

"Later, gimp!"

"Urg." Connor sagged, watching Michael walk away, not even missing a step as he spun forward. At least he handled his prosthetic like a champ, even if he didn't upkeep it very well. "And you," Connor knocked Aurora with his shoulder as hard as he could, nearly toppling her off the table, "what was all that, huh? Have I just never seen you around Michael before, because that… that was shameless."

The blush to Aurora's face completely undermined anything she attempted to say. "I don't know what you're talking about."

"You were sweet to him!"

"I can be sweet!"

"You're never sweet. On your best days you're cynical."

"Being cynical around you is a sign of lasting friendship," she said, coiling her long braid over her shoulder again and staring at the floor. "Sweet is for the uninitiated."

"You like him," Connor hissed at her, a whisper but still an accusation.

Her shoulders visibly tensed. "Please, that is so cliché. He's captain of the football team."

Connor opened his mouth for a comeback but thought of something better. "That doesn't solely define him as a person," he mocked.

Aurora bristled, lips pursed in indignation. She snatched up the fork from her tray and pointed it at him threateningly. "If you say one word…"

"Please," Connor huffed, "you'll what?"

"Tell Mavus every single way you've ever waxed poetic about his ass."

"I've never—"

"Connor," she growled dangerously.

Scare tactics clearly weren't going to work; she was already terrified, he could tell. He knew that look only too intimately. "Truce," he said, holding up his hands. "Neither of us says a thing."

Slowly, she lowered the fork.

"But…if you're really harboring a crush on Fergus, and you expect me to come clean about liking Em, then this is a pact. We confess before the end of the year. Me…before Prom. No matter what happens." After all, nothing could be worse than accidental vampirism and hunters on their tail.

Aurora squinted at him. "Consequences?"

"Just a promise. No consequences if we back out other than our own missed chances."

She slammed the fork down onto her tray. "You're on."

CHAPTER 19

Sunday came too quickly, with no news on the hunters. If they knew where Connor and I lived, they hadn't acted on it. Maybe it was because Wendy or Alec were always on watch, as well as the police officer still following me around, but I knew they'd dismiss him soon, even without any leads on the Leonards' murders. Eventually, with no activity, they wouldn't waste police resources on me. We had to find the hunters and take care of them, but they were smart. They were lying low after the incident at the middle school. If only I could talk to the ones who weren't in on this crazy plot, explain the truth. We didn't even know how many of them were out there.

I felt the hunger long before a week passed, but subtle at first, dismissed somewhat if I ate normal food, but that never really satisfied me. The week before, when I'd tried to wait it out—tried to avoid Connor's help—it had started as a pain, an ache low in my gut. It grew much worse by Monday right before I started to burn in the sunlight. I'd promised Connor I wouldn't do that again.

So that next Sunday, he came up to my room. Alec had tried to talk to me earlier in the week, but once I realized what he was about to say, I stopped him. I didn't want to start on fire in the middle of the school, or out on a walk someday. I was just scared. I didn't trust myself with Connor, with anyone, but I knew I had to feed.

"Do you honestly feel a desire to hurt him? To drink more than you should?" Alec asked me.

"No? I mean, not really, but there's this feeling when I have him close, like I just want to…" I trailed because I didn't know what I wanted, but there was hunger there; I couldn't describe it as anything else. "I'm afraid one day I won't be able to stop," I said before I could censor myself.

Alec grabbed my chin, made me look at him, but his hold and expression were gentle. "Focus on how you always do stop. And if you ever start to feel differently, truly as though you cannot stop yourself or that you want to hurt Connor or anyone else, come to me. But what you are feeling now when you feed from him…" he let me go, smiling in amusement, "…it's not bloodlust, dear boy. You have nothing to fear."

That didn't make it any less awkward when Connor came over and we tried to small talk, like the purpose of getting together wasn't so I could hold him down, bite his neck, and drink a pint of his blood.

During one particularly awkward silence, Connor finally said, "It doesn't have to be weird, Em. It's okay, you know? I don't mind. I even kind of like it, remember, so…take what you need."

The sight of him sitting there on my bed, tilting his head back and to the side, exposing his neck for me, brought that hunger surging to the surface. I shook when I first gripped his shoulders, my senses overrun. They heightened out of control, holding Connor close like that, smelling him—the mint and cedar, the blood thrumming under his skin.

I almost forgot to glamour him. I didn't trust myself yet to do it without eye contact, even though Alec swore it was possible, so I pulled back to look at Connor, deep into his eyes, and saw them dilate. Like before, I willed it to feel good for him, to feel nice, not painful. He gasped when I bit down, but more like a sigh, like relief. Relief filled me too with the first rush of blood over my tongue.

When I was younger, this was how I imagined wine would taste, fruity and full and exhilarating. But as good as the blood was, as much as I craved it and feared I might lose control someday, the feeling of Connor in my arms grounded me. We were here, we were safe, we'd survived so much already. This I had control over, even if I couldn't control anything else.

Something still plagued me though, buzzed at the back of my mind as I fed from Connor, holding him tight against me. Alec was right, it wasn't bloodlust, but I couldn't pin it down. I focused instead on how, once again, I pulled away when I was supposed to, stopped without any trouble, healed the wound, and brought Connor out of the glamour to receive a smile from my friend, no sign of fear.

It wasn't bloodlust, but there was something here I hungered for, something new...

Then it was Monday again, and life went on. Maybe life as a teenage vampire could be normal. Normal enough. The beeping over the intercoms sounding ten minutes into Honor Choir certainly was familiar.

The principal announced another bomb threat and everyone groaned. I'd lost count now of how many times we'd evacuated over to Trinity. A couple more times, maybe even only one, and they'd add on days to the end of the year for sure. I slipped my sunglasses onto my face before we left the choir room, anticipating the sunny skies outside. The familiarity eased the knot in my chest. At least this kind of crazy I understood.

Connor beamed brightly at me as we shuffled in our Honor Choir and Jazz Band lines to walk together. No fear. No judgement. No weirdness even. Just my friend.

"Got cards for us again, Aurora?" I asked.

She patted her shoulder bag proudly.

~

Eli

His spot on the roof was well hidden, secure, with an immediate escape route planned to avoid detection after he took the shot. A security officer patrolled the grounds at all times, but it was expected that anyone who came into the school would report directly to the office to sign in. No one paid much mind to an adult walking confidently into the school as if he knew exactly where he was going. Confidence, purpose. Act like you belong, and no one second guesses you.

Eli Bane had learned that well over the almost thirty years since he'd begun his training, taught to blend in, play the right roles, make the right calls to take homicidal vampires out of the equation. People's lives were at stake; there was no room for error.

Slipping into the girls' bathroom long enough to write the bomb threat—copying the handwriting of whatever girl had started the false threats in the first place—that was easy. Walking right back out of the school without the security officer even giving him a passing glance—child's play. Setting up the shot now from where he perched on the roof, well, that was just his duty.

His dark hands steadied around the crossbow. Gamble had been adamant after his encounter with the vampire kid and his friend the week before—this teenager, turned by William Leonard, was worse than most experienced vampires they'd come across in recent years. He'd forced his friend into being a retainer, made threats against his family to keep Connor Daniels quiet about what was going on, and still had plans to kill to feed even with a willing blood source. He had to be stopped.

Eli wished there was another way. He mourned every vampire, especially those turned young who couldn't handle the change. Maybe Emery Mavus had been a monster all along, and being turned merely revealed his darkness on the outside.

The rush of students from the doors carried a din of noise up to Eli. He looked through his scope, this particular crossbow setup for covert shots like a sniper rifle. He'd take the shot, the kid would fall, die, and Eli would be gone before anyone else had to get hurt or know what had really happened in this small, infected town.

The morning sun beat down on his back, warmer than previous days, a tease of summer in the midst of Minnesota spring. None of the trees swayed; no wind to disrupt the shot. Mavus wore sunglasses against the brightness of the day, but several other students donned shades of their own as they headed across the large parking lot, spilling onto sidewalks for their trek to Trinity church. They were escaping a bomb threat; no one expected a sniper on the roof.

Mavus and his friends had yet to pass the halfway point of the parking lot along their journey, walking in loose, jumbled lines, which occasionally blocked Eli's view, making him wait for the perfect moment to take the shot.

In his scope, he saw others—the retainer, Connor Daniels. They only knew the identity of these boys because of Gamble's efforts. Tracking down their addresses would be easy now, but this was a safer bet than making a raid on a residential area. The Leonards' home had been secluded, ideal. But this, too, taking advantage of the chaos that would ensue, was all Eli needed.

Mavus and Daniels chatted with their friends like normal teenagers, nothing seeming amiss, other than those sunglasses that Eli knew the real purpose behind. He waited for a moment when Daniels would slip, drop his mask, prove with a brief glance to the side that he feared his friend who had threatened him, fed on him, as Gamble had informed them. Instead, each moment that Eli watched where Daniels was unobserved by others, his expression never changed, save the twitch of wider, lingering smiles directed at Mavus when no one else was looking.

Eli's finger faltered on the trigger. He had to take the shot now, before the distance grew too great. Gamble swore Mavus was a monster, that Daniels was a prisoner. One shot and the hunters' time in this town would be over. They might hunt the elder vampire that had been spotted, they might not. For now, the elder hadn't done anything but kill another vampire that had trespassed on his territory. Once Mavus was dead, this awful business would end.

Eli took a breath, focused on the farthest point to the right of the white star decorating Mavus' T-shirt, like a perfect bullseye painted just for him…and fired.

~

Connor

Connor's eyes kept straying to the aviators he'd given Emery, and to the perfectly fit Captain America T-shirt he wore. His pact with Aurora didn't seem so desperate anymore. The way Emery's mouth on his neck had felt last night, and with no word from the hunters, only spurred on his confidence. He could do this. He could tell Emery. He could finally confess the truth. If Emery felt nothing, then why did he hold him tenderly and shiver against him while he fed? How could Emery look into his eyes so affectionately when he released Connor from the glamour?

The theme for Prom had been announced Friday afternoon, just as Michael had said: Elements. Everyone buzzed with ideas— every senior and junior, and the few sophomores who would attend on the arm of an upper classman. Some people talked about LED lights to signify lightning in their looks. Others planned to be windblown fairies. Connor still liked his Captain Planet idea.

"Come on, we could do a group thing, me as Captain Planet, all of you as Planeteers. Earth," he pointed at Nick, "Fire," at Emery, which he'd swear was in no way a jab at him almost bursting into flames in class, "Wind," at Jules, "Water," at Aurora, "And...hey, Nick, think J. J. would be our Heart?"

"Give it up, Con-Man, you are not painting yourself blue for Prom," jeered Aurora, spoiling his fun.

"But it's such a good idea!"

"Then *you* be water," she said, "and I can be Gaia, goddess and Mother Earth. Way more fitting."

"I'm telling you," Michael Fergus jumped in—and where did he even come from? He wasn't in Jazz Band or Honor Choir. Connor noticed Aurora stand up straighter and hold her bag against her more tightly at his arrival.

"You and Mavus should be ice and lightning," Michael went on. "Reinvent your Flash and Captain Cold couples' costume."

"Anyone else noticing the 'Captain' theme?" Jules said with a nod at Emery's T-shirt.

Connor shot the devilishly handsome and very much smirking Michael a death glare for once again calling their Halloween outfits a couples' costume, as well as implying that he and Emery would be going to prom together. They had made no such plans.

But Emery laughed. "Hey, that's not such a bad idea. I don't want to wear a full body suit for Prom, but maybe we could tweak it, get red and blue tuxes or something."

Connor nearly tripped over his feet. He snapped his gaping mouth shut when he saw all of their friends—every last conniving one of them—toss him a smirk or wink or encouraging nod.

"I mean, if you want to go. I wasn't really planning on it after Liz…" Emery trailed but easily shrugged off any lingering resentment about the breakup, "but if you wanted to do the stag thing together like Jules and Aurora, I'd be up for Flash and Cold."

"Really?"

"Unless you were going with someone else?"

"No! I, uhh…probably would have crashed the girls' walk and earned myself a black eye for ruining their photo ops. You should totally come—I mean, we should totally go together, you know, so…you can keep me out of trouble."

Emery's blinding white smile stretched wider Connor's direction, the shades in place as he turned to face him, walking backwards across the parking lot. His dark hair and mocha colored skin gleamed golden in the sunlight, and there was a flush to his cheeks, probably from feeding on Connor's blood the night before.

"Tell you what," he said, "you come up with a good idea for what to wear, maybe you can convince me."

A zip sounded like something being swung sharply through the air, and Emery's smile dropped as if it had been struck from his face. He stopped, expression blank, the color draining from his cheeks. Only for color to resurface over his heart, staining the white star of Captain America's shield a dark, seeping red.

Gunfire filled the air as Connor dove forward to catch Emery before he could drop dead weight to the concrete.

CHAPTER 20

I felt myself sinking, the world darkening, the worst possible pain in my chest. Then Connor's arms were around me.

"Em!"

Shots fired all around us, but didn't seem to hit anyone, as if maybe someone was firing into the air rather than at any targets. This wasn't a shooter. Alec said bullets would sting but easily heal. This felt like fire. This was a wooden bolt meant to kill me.

"C-Connor…" I tried to talk, but my vision grew hazier. I couldn't feel my limbs, could barely feel his arms holding me, trying to keep me upright.

"I got you, Em. Come on, come on!" he shouted at someone else. "You'll be fine, Em, you'll be okay, just trust me."

"H-How do you…kn-know…?"

"Because if you'd been hit directly in the heart, you'd be dead by now." His voice didn't catch, didn't stutter, just stated it matter-of-factly. Connor was always better than me in a crisis, even if he'd lament his very existence if someone drank the last Dr Pepper during an all-nighter.

I closed my eyes, took a breath, trusted him to fix this. But I couldn't move my legs. "I c-can't…"

"I know. I got you."

Connor's prosthetic was far from bionic; it couldn't lift more than a flesh and blood arm. I weighed more than him, more muscle mass, the tiniest bit taller. Adrenaline was the only answer I had for how I found myself lifted, carried, whisked across the parking lot as more gunfire sounded and screams filled the air around us.

There were closer, hushed voices with us, voices I only made out once we stopped moving—Jules and Aurora. The others must have scattered elsewhere.

I blinked to see that we'd ducked into the side choir room entrance we normally weren't allowed to use unless it was an emergency. I figured this counted.

"Connor, we have to get him to the nurse. Call 911," Aurora said, steady and to the point.

Jules muttered nearby, less collected but not as hysterical as those outside. "Oh my god...oh my god..."

"911 is already on the way from the bomb threat," Connor said, "and the nurse can't help him. Em, I need you to look at me. I need you to focus on me."

The pain in my chest had gone numb, cold as if someone had pressed an icepack to it. My vision swam but I saw Connor's face above me. He had me laid back on the choir room floor, just inside the door, huddled and hidden behind rows of risers and chairs. His eyes looked even more honey-colored this close, wide with determination.

"It went right through, Em, but it didn't get your heart. It was close though...too close. You need to feed. Now."

"What are you talking about?" Jules said, shriller than before, pacing. "We have to help him!"

"Connor..." Aurora tried.

I shook my head. The girls were with us, they were here, they'd see...

"It doesn't matter, Em. We don't have time to wait and hope you'll be fine on your own, or that Alec or Wendy will show up to help. We need to do this now. It's the only thing we *can* do." He lifted me up into a sitting position, and a pulse of renewed pain ratcheted through my body. The bolt might have gone straight through, but it felt like it was lodged deep in my chest.

I smelled blood—mine. It clashed with the sweeter smell of Connor, the now familiar smell of him and the reminder of how rich his blood tasted. My arms hung limp, but my mouth drew closer to his neck, exposed as he tilted his head and pulled me in.

The consistent beeping from the bomb threat still sounded over the intercom. The gunfire outside had stopped, but not the screaming. The jumbled protests and exclamations from Aurora and Jules, tripping over each other to understand what we were doing, rose in volume, as my fangs extended. I needed blood so badly, I couldn't stop to look Connor in the eyes, but I still thought with every fiber in me that he please, please not feel any pain, as I bit down and pressed my lips to his pulse point.

There was a gasp—my own, Connor's, one of the girls, I didn't know—before all sound drowned out in the din that roared through my ears as I fed.

Just as the wound in my chest had begun to feel like ice, now it burned, like a match ignited on my skin, chasing the cold away. The heat spread…and spread…but didn't intensify, evening out through my body as Connor's blood filled me and healed the damage. When my arms could move again, they pressed to his chest, feeling the softness of his T-shirt.

His arms were still around me, plastic around my back, the warmth of his real hand holding my head. He whimpered as he held me tighter, not pained, I knew—at least I'd succeeded in that much. What I didn't expect was what remained when the heat left me just as the cold had left, and in its wake was longing.

I could feel Connor's heartbeat through my palms on his shirt, beating wild. I loved that rhythm. The thrum of it on my lips, drinking down his blood, mouthing his skin. I clutched his T-shirt as he clutched me equally closer, and all I wanted was to move my mouth from feeding up along his neck, to his jawline, and kiss my way to his lips.

I gasped away from him, thrown by this new desire, finally understanding what it was, hovering beneath the surface whenever I had Connor close like this. Becoming a vampire had made me lose my mind. I couldn't lust after my best friend. He never looked at me that way. We'd known each other our whole lives. I didn't want to be that kind of predator, taking advantage of having to be this intimate each week, not with him. He'd never trust me again if he knew I felt this way when I fed.

"The Leonards were vampires!" Jules gave a sudden cry, as if victorious in some hard-won endeavor. "So many things make more sense now…"

I brought a hand to my mouth to wipe away any traces of blood, though I hadn't yet healed Connor's wound. He hissed as the glamour faded, and I could have kicked myself for being so careless. But my eyes were drawn to where the others stood over us, looking curious and discerning, but not afraid—somehow not afraid.

"They do?" I said, because I couldn't fathom how seeing me feed on Connor made other things 'make more sense', even though I'd been through all of this from the beginning and knew how it connected.

"Freaky sense," Aurora said with a shrug, "but sense. The murders. How weird you've been acting lately. The new shades."

"Oh my god, are there vampire hunters after you? Was this a hit?" Jules exclaimed.

I pressed a hand to where the bolt had punctured me, felt the hole in my shirt, the smooth skin beneath, already healed. "I think it was…" I dragged my eyes back to Connor, who stared at me with a curious half-grimace as he reached for the bite marks on his neck. "Wait!" I stopped him, snatching up his wrist. "Let me heal it."

Our eyes locked, his pupils large and black, as he nodded, licked his lips, and—no, no, no—what was I going to do about this? For now, all I could do was what I'd said I would.

I bent toward his neck again, biting my tongue to draw blood. I licked the wound smooth, feeling Connor's prosthetic hand grab my waist. A sharp intake of breath from him and it was over, the wound gone as if it had never existed, but I knew better than to think something hadn't changed, shifted between us, at least for me.

"You gonna glamour these two to forget what they saw?" Connor said, grasping my hand so we could help each other stand.

"What?" Jules pouted her glossy lips, large blue eyes wide with accusation.

"You want to run that by us again?" Aurora folded her arms more tightly.

"Urg," I groaned. Alec would not be happy about more people knowing my secret, but I couldn't glamour my friends. They weren't even freaking out despite having plenty of reason to. "You guys have to promise me—"

"Please," Aurora interrupted with a jut of her chin, "do either of us look like some wilting violent who's going to faint at the sight of blood, or suddenly think you're evil just because you have fangs? But you better tell us exactly what is going on."

So I did—the abridged version, though with several interjections from Connor. Yes, the Leonards were vampires, but good people, who'd been murdered by crazy hunters, only some of the hunters might be good and just thought I was evil. They'd clearly discovered my identity, and knew Connor's face too. This attempt on my life today would not be the end of it.

Jules looked appropriately ruffled and fidgety, but Aurora just tapped her fingers on her arm, lips tight. I knew her well enough to see a shimmer of fear in her eyes, but she stood like a wall of confidence.

We moved out from behind the risers. The beeping had finally ceased over the intercom. Connor leaned into me, dizzy from the feeding, but I hadn't taken as much as I normally did. He steadied himself and waved away my concerned expression.

Before the girls could ask too many questions outside the narrative I'd given them, police officers burst into the room. I recognized the officer assigned to watch me—Officer Nustad. He radioed to Tim that he'd found me, before rushing over to us.

"Are you hurt, son? Some of the students mentioned they'd seen you fall, thought you'd been hit. You're bleeding."

"Uhh…"

"Just got nicked, Officer," Connor came to my rescue—again—poking his plastic finger through the bloody hole in my shirt. "Looks worse than it is, just a graze, but we dove for cover as soon as we realized Em was the target. Please tell me you guys caught the shooter."

"Working on that now," Nustad said, while the others with him moved on to the next room. "Found an unregistered rifle on the roof and we're tracking where we think the perp went. We'll let you know as soon as we're able to go public. For now, I'm going to stay with you until we've cleared the building and deem it safe to walk you from the premises."

The hunter had left behind a rifle. Made sense, if only to keep the cops from guessing the truth. It wasn't a bullet that had hit me though. The real weapon and the owner of it were long gone.

"Everyone else okay?" Nustad asked.

"Nothing we can't handle," Aurora said. She shot me a protective once-over like she was my newly appointed bodyguard and would stop at nothing to protect my secret. Likewise, Jules smiled sweetly at the officer and nodded.

I'd always known Connor would see me through this mess; I never should have doubted that our friends would do the same.

Nustad turned away to answer his radio, and Connor and Aurora shared a secretive glance as Connor whispered, "Called it."

"What?" I whispered back.

"Bomb threat diversion," Aurora said, pointing to the ceiling. "Real threat on the roof."

"And no one takes us seriously." Connor shook his head.

Jules and I just scowled.

~

Connor

Aurora nudged Connor with her elbow once they were finally escorted from the choir room. Connor readied himself for a smirk, a teasing comment, gentle but insistent prodding, but there was no mockery in her expression. She'd seen. She knew now how deep into unrequited love he'd fallen. Connor might have been able to hide his feelings from Emery when they were intimately connected while he fed, but from the outside it had to look different. There was apology in Aurora's eyes, sympathy for Connor having to be that close to what he wanted without possessing it.

She elbowed him again, let the smirk sneak onto her face, and said, "All the more reason," vague enough so it wouldn't matter if Emery overheard.

All the more reason to confess. Maybe. Maybe…

They joined the rest of the school outside as the last students to be rounded up. Nick, Michael, and several others rushed Emery as soon as they saw him. Connor even noticed Liz hovering nearby, the rumors that Emery had been shot, maybe killed, having circulated quickly. No one had been hurt, not a single shot connecting with a student. The police were hard-pressed not to chalk it up to a prank, especially with the weapon left behind for them to find, but the fact that Emery had been targeted couldn't be ignored.

Tim shouted loudly from within his cruiser when Connor, Emery, and the girls were ushered over to him to give their statements. Connor had never seen the police chief so red in the face. He slammed his radio into place when he hung up.

"This never should have happened," he said to Emery directly. "I'm not blaming Nustad. He stayed at his post, keeping an eye on you, and nothing seemed out of the ordinary. But getting past school security was a joke, it turns out, so we'll be posting actual officers at all exits for the remainder of the week, and make sure Nustad stays on you like glue. This was no prank, and I don't think it had anything to do with the previous bomb threats. We're going to do everything we can to catch this guy."

He didn't say 'killer', didn't comment on how Emery was at risk of being hunted down and killed, but the threat was real.

"No play practice tonight," Tim said. "I've already talked to Mark."

"But—" Aurora tried to speak up.

"I know the show's this weekend, and how much all of you have invested in it. We won't make you cancel, but you'll have to do without tonight's rehearsal. It's too soon after what happened today. We need to make a more thorough sweep of the area, be sure they won't take advantage of any panic or confusion to try again. There'll also be a curfew in effect for all students until further notice—11PM, no exceptions, including on play nights."

Jules and Aurora huddled together, their faces much more drawn at this news than at discovering Emery's secret.

"What about cast parties?" Aurora challenged.

Tim gave her a withering look. "You get an accommodating parent to let all of you spend the night; you can do as you like, so long as no one is out and about after 11PM."

Aurora nodded, a glint in her eyes that said she'd make sure that happened. As seniors, they'd been looking forward to their last hurrahs with cast parties all year.

"We expect you to police yourselves and go straight home—to your own homes—between school and play practice every day."

"We do that anyway," Connor said, "and this guy still got into the school."

"I'm aware," Tim said, fists clenched, though none of his anger was directed at Connor, just at the world at large. "Your parents are all on their way. Tell me what happened, in the best detail you can, then you can join your friends until you're picked up. School's cancelled for the rest of the day."

Connor had never been so disappointed to hear those words. Getting an occasional snow day, which during some winters in Minnesota was more than occasional, was a blessing, a treat. This felt like punishment, like they were prisoners with no control over their lives, more than being snowed in had ever felt.

When the on-hand paramedic checked over Emery, he had to slice himself open briefly with a fingernail to explain the blood, since his wound had healed, and which healed again by the time it was covered with bandages. Once they'd explained what had happened a dozen different times between Tim and several of their friends, it was a relief to see their parents pull up.

Alec and Wendy had both checked in through text, deciding to hang back once they knew everyone was safe, since extra bodies hanging around the school would only raise suspicion. They would look for the hunter too, but with police all around, finding the right trail would be difficult.

Connor hesitated before getting into his car. Emery's parents had driven his dad there so he wouldn't have to leave the Thunderbird behind. He and Emery would only be a yard apart once they were home, but it was still early morning. He couldn't spend the rest of the day sequestered from his friend.

"Come on, kiddo," his father said. "We'll all meet up at our place, huh? Let you boys stick together for the day?"

Connor and Emery both perked up.

"I'm sure otherwise someone would end up climbing the trellis again," Kay said with a pointed look at Connor.

He denied nothing.

They tried to find Jules and Aurora in the crowd before they were ushered from the school, but both girls had already gone. They'd Skype them later, they decided. There was much to discuss, with Wendy and Alec too, difficult as that might be when all of their parents—save Connor's mother, who hadn't been able to get away from the hospital—had taken the rest of the day off. Tim and his officers could only handle so much though. Connor didn't know what had caused the hunter to miss Emery's heart, close as it had been, but he didn't believe they'd luck out a second time.

The few minutes Emery was out of his sightline, after seeing him shot, and bleeding, slurring his words and going limp, were the longest of Connor's life.

CHAPTER 21

Being in Connor's house felt more secure than the school, or anywhere really, other than my own home. I no longer believed the hunters might tear into our neighborhood and cause a scene. Plus, Officer Nustad was right outside. We were safe—for now.

It was lunch time before we knew it, after all the fuss at school, explaining things to our parents, messaging Aurora, Jules, Wendy, and Alec that we needed to talk, the sooner the better, though we didn't mention to Wendy and Alec that the girls knew my secret. That felt like an in-person sort of admission.

We ended up in the living room, talking, debating guilty pleasure movies we could watch to pass the time—to distract us all, more like, though no one said that. We hadn't thought about my torn, bloody shirt until we were sitting there, which gave me and Connor a few minutes to escape as he helped me pick something from his closet. He grabbed his *Hitchhiker's Guide to the Galaxy* 'DON'T PANIC' T-shirt. He snickered as he handed it to me, and we fell into helpless giggles.

It's funny sometimes how much you laugh when the emotion you're feeling is more like helplessness, but it did make me feel marginally better. Until I started to change, and Connor made a concerted effort not to look at me. Changing my shirt in front of my friend, something I'd done countless times over the years, should not make my skin heat up. I lost my train of thought, fumbled my words trying to remember what we were talking about, and headed out of his room while still pulling the shirt over my head.

Paul had grabbed the first three *Die Hard* movies. That small semblance of normal made it easy to sink into the sofa next to Connor.

Georgia came home from work in time to join us for the end of *Die Hard 2*. Everyone being over didn't disrupt her plans for dinner in the slightest; she always cooked enough for a small army, product of growing up in a large family and only knowing recipes that served close to eight people, which ended up being just enough when the doorbell rang…and Alec and Wendy both stood there.

"So sorry to interrupt," Alec said, donning his American accent. The pair was dressed as if they had just moved in next door— suburban casual; Wendy in dark jeans and an emerald blouse; Alec with a violet button down beneath his customary black jacket.

"We heard about the incident at the school, and wanted to check that everyone was all right," Wendy said, a softness to her tone that caught me off guard, though at least her accent remained intact. Not that Wendy wasn't nice, but soft wasn't the first word that came to mind.

"When we realized your car was in the driveway, we decided to stop over. My wife recently arrived from Norwich, visiting family," Alec gestured to Wendy, nearly causing me and Connor to choke. "She had a death in the family as well, and thus we were separated for the respective funerals, sadly. Wendy, this is John and Kay Mavus, and…"

"Georgia and Paul Daniels," Georgia said, having answered the door. The entryway had a clear view into the living room. She ushered them inside after shaking both their hands. "You're Will's brother, aren't you? Kay mentioned something."

To his credit, Alec never faltered when talking about the Leonards, even when fielding lies. "Indeed. Emery has been so kind as to help me sort through things at the house. Of course I understand now if that might be put on hold after today's events. I really am so very sorry." He passed his cool, blue gaze around the room.

"We were pleased to hear no one had been seriously hurt, though it does unnerve us that no perpetrator has been caught yet," Wendy said, catching our eyes with a brief glint of steel, as if to say, no, they hadn't caught him either.

"George just took lasagna out of the oven," Paul said, as he rose from the couch and moved to shake their hands as well. He had a standing belief that 'the more the merrier' was always true, and often turned simple get-togethers into full-blown shindigs. "Join us for dinner?"

The table was large enough to accommodate all of us, and somehow, maybe because Alec and Wendy were both eerily good at playing roles outside the truth, it never felt awkward—eating lasagna with my parents, my best friend's family, and my mentor and vampire hunter bodyguards.

Once dinner was over, conversation flowing naturally, we ended up in the living room with Wendy while Alec kept our parents busy in the kitchen.

"We're not fully empty-handed. I spotted the shooter."

"You did?" I nearly shouted, before remembering not to draw attention to us.

"Saw him, and he saw me," she confirmed, "heading into a motel. He dodged me and will not return to that same location, but I know his face. He's memorable. 5'10", mid-30s, solid build, African-American, blue eyes." She rattled it all off like an interrogation recap.

That didn't fit anyone I knew. The warmer the weather got, the more outsiders came through town, taking time to go out on the lakes, like everywhere in Minnesota. But with fewer tourists this time of year, he wouldn't be able to blend in easily.

"Another thing—he missed." She poked me in the chest where the bolt had struck, right over my heart. "These hunters are skilled, love; he wouldn't have missed unless he had doubts. We can use that. If I can find him again, he might be willing to talk."

"There's something else," Connor said, nudging me with his shoulder.

"Right, uhh…see, when I fed from Connor, we weren't exactly…alone."

"Someone saw you?"

"Our friends, Aurora and Jules. They're cool with it—crazy cool actually, they won't freak out or tell anyone—but we figured you should know."

Wendy nodded, her calm expression masking her opinion on this development. "I'll inform Alec if you aren't afforded the opportunity to speak with him tonight. He may want to glamour them."

"No!" Connor protested. "They're not a threat. Seriously."

"It isn't my call to make," she said.

I squeezed Connor's arm. "It's okay. I can talk to Alec later. I just wanted to thank you," I said to Wendy. "All of this...you hardly even know us and you've done so much. I know it's your duty, the whole code thing, but I really appreciate it. All this danger and chaos, someone out there actually trying to kill me..." I didn't know how to finish that sentence, so I let the silence say the rest for me.

"Are you like former MI6 or something, with all these covert ops skills?" Connor asked, his jovial curiosity helping to break the tension.

A sly, teasing smile spread across her face. "Too many Bond films, Mr. Daniels? I'm not special ops, though I did serve."

"I guess I just figured, the whole vampire hunter, mysterious badass thing had to mean you either did some serious *Mission Impossible* stuff at some point, or...ya know," he shrugged, but his eyes betrayed a look I knew well, one that promised he was going to push someone's buttons and hope it didn't blow up in his face, "... survived a vampire massacre and lost your entire family?"

"*Connor*," I hissed.

Wendy surprised us both by laughing. "Too many movies is right. No, boys, no tragic backstory quite like the one you're thinking. Quite the opposite in some respects. I was a member of The Royal Marines, spent some time in the Middle East. Imagine my surprise encountering vampires for the first time in the desert."

"Vampires in the desert?" Connor repeated. "That's gotta suck."

"Not as much as you might think, when you work out the details. You're expected to be bundled up against sun and sand out there. One day, a pair of them helped me save a family from a collapsed building. I wouldn't have believed what they were if I hadn't seen their speed, their strength. The situation didn't allow for subterfuge on their part, but they took the risk to do the right thing. So I backed them. Kept their secret.

"Another town over I made the mistake of approaching the next vampire I found, assuming he'd be the same—gentle, not a monster. I was wrong. He killed several civilians and a few soldiers before I took him down. There are good vampires, and there are bad, just like people.

"You're familiar with the phenomenon where once something is brought to your attention, you see it everywhere?" she asked.

We both nodded.

"Once I knew what to look for, vampires were easy to spot, good and bad, everywhere I went. How could I rightly ignore something so few people had any knowledge of? Seemed more fitting to put my military skills to use on a more personal front. So I left the Marines."

"Why come to the States, though?" I asked. "Do we have more vampires than other places?"

"Not more. The answer is actually much simpler. My family lives here now."

"You have family?" Connor asked incredulously.

She folded her arms with a humored eyebrow raise, more relaxed than I'd yet seen her—maybe the blouse helped. "No tragic backstory, remember? I've seen death, like many soldiers, and some at the hands of vampires, yes, but my family is doing quite well. My parents live in Florida. My brother attended university at Grinnell in Iowa. He married an American. She's lovely. Makes it easy to traverse the countryside, visiting them when I can. They think I run private security. Though if it ever seemed necessary to tell them the truth, I wouldn't hesitate.

"I do what I do, Emery," she focused on me, "because I don't like to see the wrong people die, or anyone die for the wrong reasons. Human or vampire, that doesn't matter. People are people."

The Leonards being murdered, meeting that other vampire who seemed so psychotic and uncaring about anyone she hurt, getting shot at and nearly killed today; all of it made it difficult to remember that there were good things in my life too, good people.

"Thanks," I said, though it seemed an inadequate response to someone trying to save my life.

"I suppose we should be heading home and stop imposing on these fine folks, right, dear?" Alec exited the kitchen with our parents following.

I hated lying to them all, but I thought Wendy had it right. If it was ever necessary, I wouldn't hesitate to tell them the truth. I knew they'd understand, be accepting, especially if Aurora and Jules could be, but for now, I didn't want them to worry any more than they had to.

My parents and I headed home when Alec and Wendy left. As soon as I got up to my room, I turned on my computer and Skyped in Connor, Jules, and Aurora. Alec texted me the moment Wendy told him about the girls discovering I was a vampire, and Skyped in as well. Jules made an appreciative comment about modern vampires having Skype on their phones, and Aurora mentioned having seen Alec near the school.

"Might want to tone down the creepy vibe if you don't want the cops picking you up."

"Creepy?" Alec scoffed.

"Insulting you already? She must like you, *Fright Night*," Connor said.

"What lovely friends you have, Emery," Alec oozed sarcasm, though he promised not to glamour the girls to forget.

Aurora insisted on being kept in the loop about the hunters, and as payment for being part of The Scooby Gang—Connor's word choice, because he could not stop with the Buffy references after Wendy's arrival—she and Jules promised to let us know if they noticed anything strange, anyone out of the ordinary, especially anyone meeting the description of the hunter Connor encountered or the one Wendy had seen.

The problem was, all we could do, once again, was wait. We had to go to school, follow curfew, keep tabs on each other, while only Wendy and Alec could search for the hunters and keep an eye on things at a distance. The cops had kicked things up a notch, but as much respect as I had for Tim and his officers, the hunters had already proven they were better.

We signed off and I rose from my computer desk, only for the walkie talkie on the charger to crackle. Everything I'd felt at the school, the surge of longing, of wanting more from Connor than just blood, suddenly came back to me like a repressed memory. This was Connor. He didn't even date. Maybe didn't want to. I couldn't spring something like this on him with everything else going on. I didn't understand it myself. Of course I loved Connor. He was my best friend, like a brother—well, obviously not too much like a brother if I was thinking about how nice it felt to have him in my arms. But what if it was only the blood, and I was tricking myself into thinking I wanted more? I needed to sort through how I felt before I told him anything.

"Em? You there?"

"Yeah, man. What's up? Something you didn't want to say with the others listening in?"

"No, just...well. Sort of? Are you okay? With everything that happened, I barely even got to ask. That bolt had to hurt."

I smiled into the walkie. Where was the line drawn between loving someone so much you never wanted to spend a day without them, and having those same thoughts while also wanting to kiss them? "I'm fine, Connor. It hurt, yeah, a lot. Maybe the worst pain I've ever felt, including Swine Flu, and you remember how much that sucked."

"Misery," Connor agreed.

"But you fixed it. You...saved me." Somehow he'd carried me into the choir room, and I still didn't know how he'd found the strength. "It's a good thing you enjoy being bitten, or I'd feel bad," I laughed, trying to shrug it off and gauge how he responded.

He laughed too—nervously? Embarrassed that that was true? "Fine, fine, call me a masochist. But if you need it, and I enjoy offering, seems we have the perfect symbiotic relationship."

My stomach fluttered. I could move faster than light, punch through a wall if I wanted, and tear open someone's throat with my teeth, but I still got butterflies. Over Connor.

Shit.

"Lucky me," I said, trying to laugh again, to not let any telling emotion into my words. "Thanks. Really. I couldn't do this without you." And I didn't want to. Ever.

"Yeah, Em, any time. Always."

I scratched my neck, searching for something to change the subject to. "How does Alec act so normal around our parents anyway? It's weird, right?"

"Who says that's the acting part?" Connor chuckled. "He's got layers, dude. I bet we'd never guess some of the things we don't know about him."

Or each other, I thought, which was silly because there wasn't anything we didn't know about each other, nothing we'd ever kept from each other, other than this. Me. Right now. Not knowing how to tell him that being close, physically, in ways we'd never been before, had shifted my entire perception of him.

"Emery!" my mother's voice called from the hallway.

"I uhh...I need to go, Connor. See you bright and early?"

"Sure, Em. Later."

Mom entered my room just as I replaced the walkie on the charger.

"Everything okay?" I turned to her.

"I was just heading to bed. I'm opening tomorrow at the station again, so I need to get a good night's sleep." She pulled me in, hugging me tighter than usual, and kissed my cheek when she pulled away. "I love you."

"I love you too, Mom."

"You know why I tell you that every night before bed?"

I tilted my head at her. "Because it's true?"

She chuckled and playfully smacked my shoulder with the back of her hand. "Because when I was a little girl, I realized I didn't say it nearly enough to your grandparents. And one night, and I don't even remember what I was watching on TV or if it was a movie, but some character had this speech, this beautiful speech about how if you love someone, you should tell them at every opportunity you get because you never know when you might lose them."

"Mom..." She shouldn't have to worry about losing me, not yet.

Her smile was like a photo negative; the same image as what it should be, but distorted, wrong. "That night when I went to bed, I kissed them both, told them both 'I love you', and hearing each of them say it back, well…you can't compare anything else to that feeling, and it never gets old, never boring."

Her green eyes glistened. If it had been weeks ago, before this mess started, I would have rolled my eyes at her and laughed, called her sentimental. Now the tears were infectious, and I didn't want her to know how scared I was.

I hugged her again. "I love you."

"I know, honey. Just be safe, okay? Whoever these people, this person…whoever they are, don't give them any openings to take you away from us."

I struggled not to squeeze her too tightly, swallowing back the thickness in my throat. "I won't. I'll be careful. Nothing bad's gonna happen, I promise."

After she left, part of me believed those words, believed that Alec and Wendy could protect me, that I could defend myself if need be. But I wasn't as focused on the danger of the hunters as I should have been. After what Mom had said, all I could think about, lying in bed that night, was Connor.

CHAPTER 22

The next day, school was worse than it had been the morning after Mr. Leonard's murder. Now there was confirmation I was a target; I'd been shot at. It was like having celebrity status for all the wrong reasons. I didn't want to talk to anyone about this. I didn't want to answer questions. I couldn't tell anyone the truth! I longed for everyone to forget, to go back to talking about the murders, or the bomb threats, instead of how someone out there wanted Emery Mavus dead.

Michael broke up the largest gathering of rubberneckers when a couple Sophomores tried weaseling information out of me. His charisma could command any crowd, at least long enough for me to duck to my next class. He must have spread the word to leave me alone, because it toned down after that, but not completely.

I had Connor, Aurora, Jules, Nick, someone around me at all times to run interference, but my mind wasn't attentive for a single lecture or assignment. I might as well have been asleep all day. I didn't think they'd rescind any of my college acceptance letters if my GPA took a nosedive after constant threat of death and personal trauma—or so I hoped. Though life wasn't generally that forgiving, and college was the least of my worries.

It didn't help that I was unconsciously—and also consciously—avoiding Connor.

Practice was better. These people knew me. They also knew that we had lost an entire practice and had to skip straight to tech rehearsal so we could still get in two full dress rehearsals before opening night. Michael commanded the school with his smile and status as Student Council President; Aurora commanded backstage with sheer intimidation tactics.

We started tech at 6PM, hoping to be done by 9:30 so everyone could get home early and have some time to relax before curfew. On show nights, we wouldn't start until 7:30.

It was during Act I, waiting outside my door to enter in a few minutes with my pants down, that a strong hand gripped my arm and pulled me between a pair of flats. I spun toward my attacker, fangs bared.

"Did you just hiss at me?"

"Alec?"

"Interesting ensemble for a high school play," he said, eyeing my plaid boxers and the pants around my ankles with a quirk to his smile. "Also, while it's lovely you're on high alert, dear boy, you might want to avoid showing off the goods to anyone who drags you into a dark corner."

For a split second I thought he was still talking about my pants being down when he mentioned 'the goods' before I remembered to reel in my fangs. "Sorry."

"I realize you don't have much time, so apologies for doing this here, but even someone who can move as silently and as fast as I can should avoid drawing unwanted attention from the police. So listen closely. Things are going to move very quickly from this point on. Two of the hunters have been seen, we have their descriptions, and a failed attempt on your life has the town in hysterics. The hunters can't risk being found out. They'll attack within the week, by next week for sure, and when they do, it will be in full force."

I craned my ear toward the stage. I had maybe two pages before my entrance. Why was Alec explaining this to me in person when we'd already discussed most of this last night and anything new could be sent to me over text?

"I will do everything in my power to protect you, Emery, but it has come to my attention that you are dragging your heels. When facing potential death, as well as graduation, which some might argue is far worse—not that I can speak from personal experience, mind you; education in my time was quite diff—"

"*Alec*," I said, twisting my face in frustration.

"Right." The T-shirt beneath his jacket caught my attention— *Bill & Ted's Excellent Adventure* with the words 'Be Excellent to

Each Other'—but my eyes snapped up to his when he said, "Your infatuation with Connor isn't going to handle itself. You could be dead next week."

"I..." The flush to my face made my cheeks feel heavy, so all I managed after that was, "What?"

Half a page left before my cue; I had to get back into position. "Desire for him outside of blood. Friends for years, finish each other's sentences types. All the mopey, dopey, doe-eyed nonsense, 'oh I might hurt him', can't go anywhere without him—goodness. Anyone could tell. If you're waiting for your libido to catch up with your heart, dear boy, he's not bad looking. Not my type obviously—"

I wasn't sure I wanted to know his type. "Alec—"

"Yes, yes, time to go on stage," he said, gripping my shoulders and spinning me around with a swift shove that nearly toppled me over into the flat partially blocking my path. Then his voice was right at the side of my face, whispering near my ear, devoid of any humor, just like the night he killed the other vampire. "Try not to think about what you've become, what's after you, or what comes next. Think about now and how you feel, and if that all points to the same person, only a fool would sit back and do nothing. Off you go now!" he finished brightly, and shoved me forward again.

I tripped over to the door, since I still had to hobble with pants at my ankles. When I glanced back before making my entrance, Alec was gone.

~

Connor

Connor watched from his curtain cocoon as Emery played out the remainder of Act I. Emery seemed flustered when he reentered with his pants down, but then, that was part of the role, maybe he was just really into his character tonight. Personal issues didn't usually affect Emery's stage performance; he immersed himself when acting. But Connor knew him better than anyone, and something was definitely off.

It made sense he would be distracted, distant. He had been bombarded by everyone at school. But he also kept shying away from the simplest act of even looking Connor in the eyes. Maybe he had given himself away when Emery fed from him after the attack. Maybe he'd seemed too eager, admitted too readily how much he enjoyed the give and take of being Emery's retainer. He wanted to confess his feelings, but first he wanted to be sure things could still be normal between them. Having known and loved Emery all his life, he should never doubt that his friend would always be there for him, but he needed a reminder, something simple to prove that despite everything, the two of them, friends forever, would never change.

After getting off the walkie talkies with Emery the night before, Connor had stayed up well into the wee hours searching every online shopping site he could find. He knew just how to put a real smile back on his friend's face.

During the ride home, he asked if Emery would come over, assuming their parents agreed, since it was barely 10PM.

"What's up?" Emery asked once they were safely alone in Connor's room. He scratched the back of his neck, glancing away. This was worse than Connor had thought. "Did Wendy or Alec send you a message or something?"

"Sit," Connor said, shoving Emery onto the edge of his bed, which made Emery laugh with an unfamiliar awkwardness that Connor did not understand but didn't think meant his friend had grown to hate him. "Dude, we have plans to make. Check this out." He sat himself at his desk, close enough to the bed for Emery to see his computer screen as he pulled up the windows with all of the items he had found for Prom.

"Whoa, that burgundy suit is perfect," Emery leapt up to hover over Connor instead, one hand on his shoulder as if no uncomfortable strangeness had ever existed.

"Wait 'til you see the ties. This is going to be epic."

To pull off their outfits for Prom's theme of Elements, portraying The Flash and Captain Cold from DC Comics, Connor had found Emery a burgundy suit, dark red button down shirt, yellow tie, and a red vest with yellow lightning bolts. For himself, he'd found a navy suit, black button down, and an ice blue tie and matching vest with snowflakes.

"Ice and Lighting, baby—geek edition," Connor announced after showing off his finds, which all in all didn't amount to too much coming out of their respective bank accounts. "We have to order like pronto to get everything in time, but it's doable if you're in."

"Send me the links," Emery said, and dropped back onto the bed. "You so need to turn the Rocket-Punch arm into a fake cold gun. It's already blue! Can you imagine? I mean, I know we're short on time…"

"I can make it work. Doctor it up with some icicles and snowflakes, get the hand to unhinge open—yes please. I can even make it fire, like a water gun or something! I don't even care that Aurora will kill me if she sees it near her dress."

Emery laughed, full out like Connor hadn't seen in days, maybe weeks. "And you need some sweet shades for his goggles! Or were you going to wear regular goggles?"

"I considered it, but then I'd get that line around my eyes. Shades it is. So…we'll do the whole walk and pictures and everything?" He turned back to his computer, punching in a search for blue tinged sunglasses, though he mostly turned away so his hopeful expression wouldn't make him look too eager.

"Of course. Why wouldn't we?"

Something happy and light blossomed in Connor's chest, and he grinned at the computer screen wider than he would ever let Emery see. "Oh, check out these!" he said as he enlarged a photo of a pair of silver-framed sunglasses with blue lenses that looked like a costume prop out of *RoboCop*.

"Yes. Those."

"We have a winner." Connor spun back around in his chair, fully prepared to make the full purchase for every single item for his outfit later that night. He spun away from his desk, pushing off with such force that he moved the roller chair slightly across the carpet and accidentally knocked his knees into Emery's.

Emery's hands shot forward to grip his thighs and stop any further forward momentum. Connor chuckled, choked off into a strangled cough, and held the edges of his chair to keep from instinctually reaching for Emery's hands instead. Emery's eyes looked so, so green this close. They'd grown brighter since he became a vampire, and not only when he vamped out.

Slowly, Emery withdrew his hands and his right jerked up to scratch at his neck again. "I didn't think you cared about going to Prom."

"I didn't, it's just—" he hadn't had a reason to go until he had the chance to go with Emery, "—the theme. It's pretty cool, right? We'll knock everyone dead. And Michael will finally get off my back for wanting to ditch. 'Every high school experience should include Prom'," he rattled off, trying to impersonate some winning speech Michael had made at some point. "And, ya know, everyone else will be there. Might have to hijack someone's house if we want any after party shenanigans, but it should be fun. Just promise me that, if at any point, you see my dateless-wonder-ass sitting on the sidelines like some lame wallflower, you'll drag me back onto the dance floor."

Emery's hand dropped, and he looked up to meet Connor's eyes with the warmest, brightest, white-toothed smile. His dimples stretched whenever he smiled like that, eyes crinkling like his dad's. Connor melted in the wake of it like facing down the heat of a blazing summer day.

"Of course, Connor. Wouldn't want to leave my date without a dance partner."

All rational thought flew from Connor's brain. Because Emery was kidding, teasing, he had to be, but then his cheeks flushed with color like he hadn't realized what he'd said until it left him.

"I just mean—"

"Right. Platonic dates, I know—"

"Unless…"

"Unless?"

The air sucked out of the room. Connor didn't dare blink and lose the connection of their eyes on each other at risk of imploding.

176 | AMANDA MEUWISSEN

"Sweetie, did you boys want anything?" Connor's mother called as she entered the room, still in her scrubs from that day. He would have chucked the nearest object from his desk at her if he'd been able to do more than gape in horror.

"Uh, we're fine, George. Actually, I…I should probably head home."

"Wait," Connor stood up in a panic, reaching for Emery's arm, and then flinching back, not wanting to push. "Everything…I mean, it isn't…I didn't mean…"

"It's fine, Connor," Emery said, looking back at him with that smile again, and maybe more of that flush to his face that—shit, was Emery blushing? At him? "I have to order my outfit for Prom, right? See you tomorrow."

"Uh…y-yeah. Tomorrow. Night, Em."

His mom raised an eyebrow at him after Emery breezed past her.

"Night, Mom," he said pointedly, in his best 'so not telling you right now' voice.

She shrugged and shut the door behind her.

Connor dropped back onto his bed, arms spread, legs dangling off at the knees. He had no idea what the hell had just happened, but it was a good thing, a definite good thing. He had over a week before Prom. Plenty of time to confess.

Tomorrow. He'd tell him tomorrow.

CHAPTER 23

Connor

Connor did not confess his feelings to Emery that morning during their carpool. He choked the second he saw him, that smile, the way Emery avoided looking at Connor for an entirely different reason now—maybe this had always been the reason. At least he thought so, hoped so.

Connor felt like he was living in one of his fantasies, sharing these little moments, furtive glances, not quite obvious flirtations, but then the occasional, very blatant one that tripped one or both of them up, and wow, they were terrible at this, only it was also kind of fun.

He didn't fear the rejection he'd always been prepared for. Nothing was guaranteed, they were still going to Prom as friends, but they were going to Prom. Together. In complimentary outfits. And whatever Emery had been about to say last night, it hung around them like a wonderful cloud, keeping everything else at bay. Even the random passerby at school still trying to pester Emery about the shooting was dismissed without any of the tension from yesterday.

Connor was still grinning to himself when he and Jules finished their AP Calculus test early and were given leave to hit up the Home-Ec class for cookies. Every day, without fail, the students in Home-Ec baked the meltiest, gooiest chocolate chip and monster cookies imaginable, sold in pairs for only twenty-five cents. Jules insisted she had a constant extra five pounds to her figure during the school year because she couldn't go a day without them.

They found a corner in the hallway that connected Home-Ec to the gym and weight rooms—the worst/best idea the school ever had, considering anyone taking part in weightlifting warm-ups had to walk past and suppress the temptation to buy cookies. Connor had seen more than a few people shoveling chocolate chip delights into their mouths before returning to class.

Sitting with their bought and treasured treats, Jules pulled out her DS. "Pokémon? I owe your Vileplume a rematch."

"Bring it," Connor said.

It took six turns before his Pokémon fainted, and he blamed his almost laughable concentration on wondering what Emery might be doing at that moment.

"Ha! Pwned," Jules mocked him. If he was being honest, he could probably count on one hand the amount of times he'd actually beaten her in a match, yet he never got tired of trying. "So…Mavus is, like, invincible now, huh?"

Connor glanced up from his screen to see her eyeing him as they brought out other characters to battle. "We explained the other night—all the usual vampire tropes apply. Except he can be in the sun, as long as—"

"He feeds regularly," she finished, "which he's been doing on you?"

"Uh…yeah."

"And that's not weird for you?"

"Weird how? Weird…scary? No. Painful? Not at all. He can do this whole thing where he makes it—makes me think, anyway—that it feels good."

Jules made a sound like scoffing a laugh. "Aha. That explains the even more love-struck than usual expression you were wearing while he sucked on your neck."

Connor nearly dropped his DS to the floor, which wouldn't have hurt it too badly, since they were sitting cross-legged. "That obvious, huh?"

"Even to him eventually, if you're not careful."

"Yeah, actually…I think he knows."

Jules stopped playing mid-fight and dramatically set her DS on the floor between them. "Mavus has been Captain Oblivious since all eternity, Connor. Explain."

He did, as best as he could, though saying it all out loud made the sequence of events and his subsequent conclusion sound completely moronic, like he was reading way too much into simple glances and fumbling sentences between them.

"Oh god, I'm way off base. He doesn't know. I just want him to know and be interested back so badly, I'm hallucinating."

"Connor," Jules rolled her eyes at him, though it never carried the same bite as when Aurora did it, "first of all, you're nutso, he clearly has been acting funny around you, and not just 'I'm a vampire and recently nearly died' funny. And second? Who freaking cares?" she said loudly, leaning forward right into his face.

Connor leaned back from the sheer momentum.

"He knows, you know he knows, you both maybe sorta feel the same way. Oh my god, it is all so middle school! Can you just confess already that you want to go to Prom as dates, real romantic make-out on the dance floor dates, and stop guessing at implied meaning? You need to get this over with. Right now."

"Right…now?" Connor nearly dropped his DS again, and had a momentary surge in his limbs of fight or flight.

"He's coming out of Psych next, right? You can sideline him in the social sciences hallway before everyone meets up for lunch."

"What? I can't. Not now, not like…during school." Not that he'd considered when he would do the confessing, only that he should, though he'd already psyched himself out not to.

"Connor…"

"Jules!" Anne Bitker rushed at them from the direction of the weight room, clad in her gym clothes and looking several shades of panicked. "Thank god, do you…" she glanced at Connor, dropping her voice to a whisper, "…do you have any werewolf repellent?"

Jules nodded stoically, reaching into her backpack. "Gotcha covered." She produced a small pocket book in bright red with a zipper, and cross-stitched on the front were an assortment of colored flowers and the actual words 'Werewolf Repellent'.

"Thank you! I'll give it back during 5ᵗʰ period. You are a life saver," Anne gushed, and raced back in the direction she had come from.

Connor blinked dumbly down the hall after her, then at Jules. "What just happened?"

"Werewolf repellent."

"Which is?"

Jules cocked an eyebrow at him. "Something you only need during a certain time of the month."

Connor opened his mouth, closed it. "Clever," he nodded in approval.

"No derailing, Connor. Don't make me get all Aurora-esque tough with you. She might hit harder, but I hold grudges longer."

"You're going to hold a grudge over me if I don't confess my undying love to Em this second?" He was indeed stalling for time, but his stomach felt so tight, he didn't think he could stand.

"I am going to Prom with my best friend because of lacking viable options," Jules said slowly, deliberately. "You have the chance to go with your best friend as actual *boyfriends*. Do not interfere with my ability to live vicariously through you."

The tension in Connor's stomach twisted to snapping point. He fought for something to say as the bell beeped over the intercom to signal it was time to switch classes. "So you wish you and Aurora were going as girlfriends?" he said lamely—he knew that wasn't the case.

Jules didn't have an angry expression so much as a dumbfounded one, that made him feel supremely inadequate. She scooped up her DS and stood. "Like a Band-Aid, Connor. One motion and it'll be done. That awful feeling in the pit of your stomach? That's not going away, in fact, it'll only get worse every day until you finally do something about it or drive yourself crazy. Do you really want to start feeling this way every time you see him? Because I guarantee you, seeing him in his tux for Prom, walking in together, taking pictures, that isn't going to be fun with this confession hanging over your head, it's going to royally suck. Okay?"

She touched him gently on the shoulder, then pushed as hard as she could, nearly toppling him down the single step that led further down the hall toward the main commons and the labyrinth of other hallways to the Psych room. If he hurried now, he might still catch Emery before they got corralled and surrounded by the rest of their friends for lunch.

"I seriously love you," Connor said before turning fully and starting a light sprint down the hallway.

Students began pouring out of nearby classroom doors, blocking his way more and more as he expertly navigated them, dodging and weaving around bodies. The social sciences hallway would be emptying, and if Emery was part of the main throng, then Connor would simply tug him back into the hallway so they could do this in private.

That fight or flight sensation returned, and he fueled it into adrenaline to keep his legs pumping, running faster and faster as he passed more and more people who weren't Emery. Maybe he was dragging his feet, as nervous to see Connor as Connor was to see him, and for the very same reason. That was the vibe Connor had been getting since last night, and after so long swearing he felt nothing even remotely romantic from his friend, Connor would know when things shifted, wouldn't he? He'd know if this was something else, if it was just more of the same, instead of Emery finally coming to his senses. He'd have to.

Fewer and fewer people blocked his path, most ignoring him, paying no mind to a senior full out sprinting through the halls, but if Connor stopped now, he knew he'd turn on his heels and run the other direction. He just had to reach the end of the hall, turn the corner toward the Psych room. He could already picture it—Emery standing there, having come out of class late for whatever imagined reason, looking up just as Connor dashed into view, that blinding smile breaking across his face.

Maybe Connor would just kiss him. Throw all his insecurities aside and kiss him like some cheesy rom-com movie, and everything would fall into place without having to say a word. He'd kiss Emery, Emery would kiss him back, and the confessions would pour forth from both of them when the kiss ended, Emery having finally realized that he'd felt the same way all along and just never knew it.

Fireworks, music swell, magic. If this was Connor's story, he deserved that kind of ending. Wasn't that what everyone had been telling him? That if he didn't reach out and pen in the ending to his own story himself, it would never happen? This was it, he was finally going to come clean, finally going to tell Emery everything he'd been terrified to say for so many years—*years*—and grasp his happily ever after, despite any roadblock or stumbling mistake that might come after.

He felt foolish for waiting for so long, felt that awful twist in his stomach unwind and lighten and transform into blind excitement. He could do this. He wanted to do this. He'd just needed a final push, and if nothing else, Emery's smile the night before, and the pleasant, nervous tension between them this morning was all the encouragement he needed to believe his feelings were returned.

Connor crested the corner, a faint squeak of his sneakers sounding when he pivoted, all bystanders gone, behind him now, heading for the cafeteria or other classrooms, as the social sciences hallway came into view.

And everything stopped. Dulled. Dimmed. At the sight of Emery almost like Connor had envisioned. But in the arms of his ex-girlfriend.

Fuck.

CHAPTER 24

"Emery, can I talk to you?"

I spun around as I made to leave the Psych room for lunch to see Liz following closely at my heels. I slowed, throat suddenly tight. "Uh, sure. What…what about?"

She gestured ahead and we continued out of the room. Sometimes I forgot we had this class together, since we sat on opposite ends of the room and hadn't really talked since the breakup.

Her brunette ponytail sat high on her head, gently curled. She didn't wear makeup other than lip-gloss and eyeliner, but she looked especially pale today, like she might be coming down with something. Then I realized—she was nervous.

She pulled me a step further down the hall, away from the door so we could be alone, as everyone else headed in the other direction. Anticipation flared inside me. She had a date to Prom, I'd heard, this wasn't some last ditch effort 'let's go together since we would have if we hadn't broken up' thing. But then what?

"Yeah?"

Her arms tightened around her books; she didn't like to carry a bag. The way she smiled, like all of her attention was on me, reminded me why I'd liked her in the first place, even if the smile didn't reach her eyes with anything but gloom. "We've been avoiding each other."

Oh god. What if it *was* a last ditch effort 'let's go to Prom'?

"And that's silly, we were friends for so long before we dated. I know it's because of how I broke things off, which was awful. Immature. I should have explained in person, talked things out with you instead of…" She looked at the floor.

"Breaking up with me through a note?" That had stung, especially since she'd handed it to me herself like we were in junior high and incapable of adult conversations.

"Yeah," she said, slowly raising her eyes to mine. "You deserve to know why. The truth is, I like you, Emery. Who wouldn't? You have all the qualities I thought I'd want in a boyfriend—smart, driven, cute." A corner of her mouth twitched up.

For a moment I felt dread, but something in her expression said this wasn't leading to her begging me to take her back.

"You're a wonderful guy, Emery, but despite everything that went right, everything that's so great about you, I never felt that spark. I would have broken things off sooner, but it's senior year and…I know how stupid this is going to sound, but what I dreaded most was the thought of having to start over."

I wasn't sure if I should feel relief or shame that we'd been thinking the same thing. "That isn't stupid."

"It's not fair though. Staying together because we should have made the perfect couple, without actually feeling like we were. Not that it was any fairer to shove a note in your hands and run off," she hugged her books tighter to her chest like a stuffed animal, "but that's why I wanted you to know. I want to be with someone who makes my heart race. Who makes me smile just by walking into the room. Maybe that's cheesy or too romantic. Maybe I'm setting myself up for failure, wanting some fairytale ending. But I don't think it's too much to ask to have all the right things fall into place and also feel a spark that shakes you right to the core of who you are, every time you see them."

Her eyes glossed over as she said it, imagining that dream coming true, someone I could never be for her. It was cheesy. And romantic. But it was too nice a thought to want to tell her she was wrong. I wanted that too. I'd always wanted that. I don't know what had made me think it was ever right to settle. Because only one person always made me smile just by walking into the room.

"It's not too much to ask," I said, feeling an ease and warmth ebb through me, the last bit of tightness that had existed wondering if I could ever pass Liz in the hallways again without flinching, falling away. "Do you think…" I trailed, but bolstered myself to ask, "Do you think that spark is something you only ever feel at first sight? Or is it something that can grow over time?"

Tension filled her shoulders as she looked away.

"I'm not saying—" I shook my head, feeling too dense for my own good. "I don't mean us. I know we're not right for each other, Liz, you did the right thing, even if it wasn't the best way. I agree with everything you've said, but do you think it's possible? That a spark could be there but you keep missing it or misinterpreting it, and suddenly, one day, it's just…there?"

The warm brown of her eyes searched my face, and finally the smile she offered me touched every part of her expression. "Sounds like you already know the answer to that question."

I laughed, used my free hand to scratch my neck, while the other readjusted the backpack over my shoulder. "Yeah…maybe. Hey," I met her gaze again, earnestly as I could, "thanks for this. For telling me. I like being friends. We should be friends. I'm not mad at you. I think it all happened the way it was supposed to."

"Me too. And I am sorry, Emery. Lesson learned. Breaking up with a note is a total dick move," she nodded resolutely.

We shared a laugh, loudly and all too familiar. I reached forward with my right hand and pulled her against me, hugging her, feeling her snuggle and chuckle into my chest, arms encumbered with her books but still able to lean into my body. For today, closure for this one lingering part of my messed up teenage life felt like everything I needed.

I couldn't wait to see Connor again. I felt like I finally knew what to say to him.

And then there he was. Standing at the mouth of the hallway. Mouth open, limbs tense, eyes betrayed. I pulled away from Liz, but Connor was already backing out of the hallway, sending me this little salute and strained smile like he was ready to be a good friend and leave me in peace.

"Liz, I, uhh…" I snapped my attention back to her, "I have to catch up with someone. But thank you. Really."

She nodded, might have said something more, but I didn't hear her. Connor was out of sight by the time I dashed after him, but I had to find him. I might have even used my vampire speed, regardless of who might see, but once I cleared the opening and turned to head down the next hallway, he was already gone.

~

Connor

Connor considered feigning illness to get out of classes the rest of the day. He felt nauseous enough. But when he arrived back in the main commons area, having taken back hallways to be alone for a few minutes, Aurora had him by the arm before he could dart off to the nurse's office.

"Jules said you were going to confess to Mavus. So?" She eyed him hopefully.

Connor gasped, out of breath from sprinting. He couldn't say it, couldn't explain, just shook his head.

Emery joined the group, eyes trained on Connor, but Jules and Nick were there too, and a handful of others, so whatever Emery might have said got drowned out by the bustle of the cafeteria. Connor grabbed Aurora's hand when she tried to pull away, keeping her at his side as they moved to the front of the group to keep Emery behind them.

At the lunch table they talked around each other, participating in conversations but never directly to one another. Connor glanced away if he ever caught Emery's eyes on him. The thought of Emery getting him alone made the nausea worse, explaining the situation like he owed him, like he knew and pitied him because he was going to be happy with Liz again, obviously, get back together and forget whatever nonsense Connor had invented was happening between them.

They didn't have any classes together after lunch. It was easy to nod as everyone parted, mutter a simple, "Later, Em," like everything was normal.

Emery hadn't mentioned anything to anyone about what happened with Liz. Maybe they were still working things out, didn't want to be public. Maybe Emery wanted to get Connor alone first to tell him they wouldn't be going to Prom together after all. After the last bell, Connor dashed into the bathroom and dry heaved for five minutes but nothing came up. He felt as helpless as he had when he first realized he loved Emery. There had been no joy in the revelation, only panic and fear.

He knew that eventually they'd have to talk this out, at least about Liz, but he wanted to avoid it for as long as possible. If Emery did know and gave him some 'we'll always be friends' speech, Connor would never recover. He didn't want to feel that kind of pain, which he knew would somehow be worse than what he felt now.

He plastered on a smile, glad that Aurora and Jules rode with them to the middle school. He stared at Aurora pleadingly to pull her usual move of claiming the front seat, even though Emery attempted to go for it, and sighed relief when Emery had to climb into the back instead.

Connor's grip on the steering wheel was knuckle-white the entire way despite the jokes he made, the way he laughed, and listened to what the girls said. Emery remained quiet, not joining in as he had at lunch. The rift between them felt ten miles long.

Emery expected honesty from him and he had lied and hid things from him for years. He might not even be remotely attracted to guys, let alone Connor, and that was no one's fault. Connor just needed to cool off, put some distance between himself and what had happened so that eventually the distance between them lessened.

He couldn't be with Emery forever as just his friend, but he could be his friend for his entire, short-lived, human life and take some solace in that. Even if one-day Emery turned someone else to spend eternity with.

Connor went through the motions backstage, direct and deliberate in everything he did. When it was time to prep Emery's pants, there was no teasing banter, no flush to his cheeks, just the nausea. Feeling the warmth of Emery's skin beneath his fingers when he undid the button, slid down the zipper, dropped it belt and all to the floor, made him tremble.

"Connor," Emery whispered, staring right at him. Connor could feel the heat of his gaze even while trying to avoid it. "Can we talk? After practice? I really need to talk to you."

He stepped back, his chest tight and breaths labored from being so close to Emery, hidden from everyone else in this part of the set. He glanced up, Emery's eyes looking dark in the shadows but still green, always so green. Emery had a plate of sardines taped to his hand, a piece of paper taped to the other, his pants down around his ankles, and it should have been hilarious, ridiculous. But he looked beautiful to Connor, no matter what he wore, or said, or did, just by standing there.

Connor's eyes felt hot, budding with tears he refused to let Emery see. "Sorry, Em, I'm not feeling so good right now, and I have this, uh…test tomorrow, so I should get in some last minute studying. I think I might head home early. I'll ask Nick to give you a ride, yeah? I'll make sure he can before I go. Must have caught that bogus flu bug of yours." He tried to smile, to joke, to brush the whole thing off.

Emery's eyes and lips downturned all at once like he was melting. "Okay. But we'll talk tomorrow, right?"

Connor nodded, backing away, not looking at Emery or anything really as he nearly clipped a flat with his arm. "Yeah, Em, 'course."

"Feel better."

"Sure. Knock 'em dead." He cleared the set pieces, turned around and waited for the moment when he knew Emery could no longer see him. Then he was running.

CHAPTER 25

Connor

"Hey, kiddo, what's up?" Connor's dad asked when he walked in the door at 8:30. "Can't be done with practice early, it's your first full dress rehearsal, right?"

Connor sighed and dropped his bag onto the bench by the entryway. He toed off his shoes and lugged his way into the living room. His dad had an old episode of *Kitchen Nightmares* on, Gordon Ramsay's English-accented voice yelling dimly in the background. His dad turned it down a couple notches as Connor came in and slumped down onto the sofa next to him. His mother had 3rd shift tonight at the hospital.

"Gonna share, or do I have to pry it outtaya?" his father nudged him. He was skinny like Connor but all muscle. With the way Connor was sagged into the cushions, he nearly fell over from the firm push.

"Not feeling well."

"Liar. What's the real answer?"

"Urg." Connor dropped his head back against the cushions, watching some blond chef yell about Yelp scores ruining her business instead of her terrible cooking.

"I'd guess girl trouble, but I know I'm not that lucky."

Connor groaned again.

"Only teasing." He reached over and scrubbed his hand over Connor's shorn head. "I'll just never get past not being able to bond over the wonders of boobs with my son."

"Hey," Connor sat up straighter, "we've had this discussion. I agree on the wonders of boobs. Boobs are awesome, I love boobs, I just prefer them at a distance." He gestured out toward the television and the rather busty waitresses as he collapsed back into the cushions. He didn't feel the same anxiety he used to talking about this sort of thing with his dad, not like after he'd first come out. He knew his father meant well, he just didn't handle unexpected change with much grace.

There was laughter in his father's voice as he said, "Okay, okay, you're a boobiphile who doesn't want a girlfriend, I can dig it. But no boyfriend either, huh?"

"Dad..."

"Hey, I can inquire. It's my right as parental figure here. It's just weird, I don't know," he said, crossing his arms and lounging back to mirror Connor. "I feel the same way about you dating some boy as I do your sister."

"Really? I thought dads were supposed to be protective of their baby girls, but secretly hope their son is a sex god." Connor snorted. If his father did want that of him, he was going to be sorely disappointed.

"I think it's different than that, actually," his father said.

"Yeah?"

"Yeah. Coz see, imagining you with some girl..." he sighed, looking off past the TV, "I think, if you could be half as lucky as I was winning over your mom, well, there you go, how could I not be happy? But thinking of you and Ryn both bringing home some guy... that just makes me think of myself, and how I still don't deserve your mother. I guess it's more projection than sexism? Maybe not with all fathers, but you know, for decent, enlightened men like me." He brought one hand to his chest and patted it dramatically.

Connor laughed.

"Just make sure he's a good guy, whoever he ends up being, okay?" He reached over and grabbed Connor's head again, shaking him playfully.

Connor batted him away. "My tastes are way too discerning for anything less, Dad."

"Ah, so it is guy trouble."

When Connor didn't answer, his father shrugged and turned back to the television.

"Okay, none of my business. But when you're ready to spill, I'm all ears. And quite a bit of nose too, but your mother seems to love me anyway." He tapped his nose and grinned at Connor. Connor had lucked out and not inherited quite as prominent a schnoz as his father.

"Thanks, Dad."

He watched the rest of the episode before heading up to his room. Connor had already ordered everything for Prom the night before. He wondered if he should cancel now, and sat staring at his computer screen until it was almost 10 o'clock.

He should have expected the muffled static that came over the walkie talkie, signaling that Emery was home.

"Connor, you there? Can we talk? I know you're not really sick."

Shit. Connor had to work on his lying skills. He considered for maybe two seconds ignoring Emery and turning the walkie off before plucking it from his charger. "Yeah, Em, I'm here. And I don't know what you're talking about, I am totally laid up and miserable."

"If that's true, it's not because you're sick." Static sounded over the line before Emery pushed on, "You saw me and Liz. What do you think happened? Do you think I'm suddenly back together with her and going to ditch you to take her to Prom instead?"

Yes. "Em..."

"Because I'm not. That isn't what happened. Just...let me explain."

"...okay. So explain," Connor said, and held his breath waiting to find out that it was somehow even worse that what he'd imagined.

"She was just apologizing to me for how things ended. We talked about what a good thing it was that we'd called it quits, how we're both better off, how we both want more than what we had, to be with someone who..." Emery trailed, taking a few breaths that came across the walkie as crackles. "Someone who makes our hearts race. And faces flush. Who makes everything better every day. I never had that with her. I hugged her because we'd finally put all of it behind us, so we could be friends again. That's all."

"Oh," Connor said, as the sick feeling in the pit of his stomach dissipated into nervous flutters.

"Yeah. *Oh.* But then you ran off and wouldn't talk to me."

"I know." Connor closed his eyes, squeezing the walkie tighter. "I'm sorry. I thought you'd done something stupid after all of our hard work setting that bear on fire," he laughed miserably. "That was some primo bonding time, man, I could not stomach you going back to her after that."

"So you did think we'd gotten back together," Emery said, smile clear in his voice, even through the shoddy reception.

"I plead the fifth. So...how'd practice go the rest of the night? Mark isn't pissed at me, is he?"

"No. Aurora is though."

For more than just leaving early, Connor figured. But he couldn't turn this reconciliation into something more. Not now. He couldn't confess over walkies. They needed to shake this off, rediscover whatever it was they'd found the night before. Then Connor would tell Emery. If something was there, building between them, it would still be there tomorrow, or next week, or whenever he was finally ready to confess.

Besides, Emery didn't lead the conversation there either. They just talked, like they usually would—friends who could discuss anything and nothing, and always make each other feel better. They talked for almost an hour that night before they said goodbye.

~

The next morning felt like déjà vu, what happened with Liz just an unfair detour that had made me anxious all the rest of the day and during practice, fearing that I'd screwed everything up for good, especially when Connor ran away from me for a second time. Whatever I was starting to feel for him, he felt it too, it couldn't just be him being a good friend and not wanting to see me with the wrong person, not with the way he acted.

I sort of wanted to pull my hair out. At times we'd ease into our usual pattern, like nothing was different, but those typical silent moments that hit every conversation eventually, they stretched longer, both of us struggling to fill the void with something that wasn't...well, I didn't know what it might be if we let it go on too long.

It was strange wanting Connor, and being fairly certain he wanted me back, neither of us having a damn clue how to move from point A to point B. How did people do that? How did anyone do that? It wasn't like this with me and Liz. We hadn't been as close of friends, but Connor and I knew everything about each other, the most embarrassing stories, the most depressing and frightening.

He could list off every celebrity crush I'd ever had, including Chun-Li, which probably didn't count to some people as a celebrity, but it did when Ming-Na Wen played her in the movie—first crush I ever had, and Connor still smirked at me whenever we saw the actress in something.

Maybe it should have been a hint when we watched the *Mortal Kombat* movie that, for once, I wasn't thinking about *Street Fighter* and how badass Chun-Li was in comparison to Sonia Blade, but how attractive Linden Ashby was as Johnny Cage, and how much he reminded me of Connor. If Connor had some serious martial arts skills.

It wasn't the first time my celebrity crush had switched sides on me, but I never told Connor when that happened. I always thought he'd think I was teasing him, like I was joking around or belittling that he liked guys if I mentioned that, sometimes, I did too. Usually, I did prefer girls. It was just starting to dawn on me that maybe, more than anything else, I preferred Connor.

Alec was no help. After lunch, he messaged me an emoji of two smiley faces kissing and a question mark. I deleted the message and texted back,

```
Any word on the hunters?
Spoilsport. No.
Let me know if there is. How's Wendy?
Deep in the trenches following leads. Be
sure and feed earlier this week.
```

Why? What for?
You had a close call, dear boy, you'll need
it. Make it a Saturday night date. You'll
be busy with set strike Sunday, won't you?

That was true, I hadn't given it much thought, but we had to
strike the set right after the matinee performance Sunday afternoon.
That wouldn't give us much time Sunday night.

Fine.

Alec sent the kissing emoji again. I deleted it—again. There
had to be an easier way to shift from being best friends to wanting
more than that. Preferably without vampire mentors getting
involved.

The energy once we arrived at the auditorium that night for
our final dress rehearsal should have tipped me off right away that,
despite everything that had happened—maybe because of it—we
were headed into Joke Night. It happened every year, every show;
at some point, one of the dress rehearsals became a competition
to see who could ad-lib the most or try to trip each other up. The
idea was to have fun and be silly to make sure we didn't peak too
early during the run of the real show. Mark usually encouraged it,
though he had warned us against doing anything too crazy with this
show, given the odd nature of a play-within-a-play and having a
completely rotating set.

Once the mood of all of the actors and stagehands became
clear, the first thing we considered doing was switching what was
usually water for our shared bottle of 'whiskey' with pickle juice.
Then we thought of Sophie Thorp, who played Dottie. She didn't
take well to pranks.

"Ew, no you can't swap the water in the whiskey bottle for
pickle juice. Even if I know it's there and avoid drinking it, it'll still
smell awful. No one would fall for that."

So that was out. I didn't care for food related pranks anyway,
like the year we did *Dracula* and swapped out some of the plastic
garlic for the real thing, and some of the corn syrup blood for
ketchup. The stage smelled like bad Italian cooking all night.

For this year's joke night, Amos, who played Selsdon, handed me a new pair of boxers so we could match. He also lost his pants at one point during the show, and he had two pairs of white boxers with hearts on them.

Most of the night was just all of us being more relaxed, knowing the show well enough that we could throw each other for an occasional loop and carry on regardless. A joke here, an exaggerated delivery there, and the nerves of opening night looming tomorrow faded into the background. The very idea that there had been a shooting at the school Monday, that I had been shot, was forgotten in lieu of goofing off.

Of course, someone always pushed Joke Night too far. Sophie might have escaped pickle juice in the whiskey, but Danny Fenton felt like he owed her one for her getting to smash a piece of pizza in his face during our Freshman play and wanted revenge. At one point in the show, he got to dump a plate of sardines all over her head. She wore a bandana to protect her hair, so she could slough off most of the sardines afterward and replace it with a fresh bandana.

Tonight, Danny glopped as many sardines as possible onto that plate, and had Connor cover it in goop. That plate was teaming when Danny snuck up the stairs with it, nearly dropping it in the process and ruining the whole effect, and then dumping it on Sophie's head with an audible plop. She bit back a screech as the extra goop rolled down her neck, and proceeded to deliver her best performance for the part, since she was honestly ready to strangle him. Of course it only made the scene go more smoothly.

But the problem wasn't Danny. Sophie would get over it, laugh it off, since she still kept most of the gunk out of her hair. Connor was the one who pushed the envelope. He made up a plate of his own sardines, just as messy and piled high as Danny's had been. After the set was turned back around, just before Act III started, he ambushed Aurora and got her right in the face.

Even Mark gasped.

Aurora clenched her fists, looked at Connor all red in the face, and stormed offstage to begin ordering everyone into places for the final act. Connor looked to me for help backstage, but I just shrugged. Silent cold-shoulder Aurora was way scarier than her screaming. He was on his own.

He should have seen it coming too, because she was more diabolical than all of our friends put together. The show ended with all of us running through the various doors on and off the set, chasing each other with props, and then stopping when we got out front to pause, bow, and continue on, all to the *Benny Hill* theme.

After we'd taken our final group bow together, music still playing, all of us laughing and panting backstage, Mandy pushed Connor onto the leftover tarp from the fall musical *Singing in the Rain*. Aurora waited up high on the set piece above him, and poured the entire remainder of the bucket of sardines on his head. She'd made sure he wasn't wearing his headset, but his buzzed hair, and black shirt and jeans, were soon covered in the sticky mess.

He stood there sopping wet in goo, mouth agape. Then he raised his hands in surrender. "Never mess with the empress!" he called.

"Damn right!" Aurora yelled back.

Connor laughed, wiping goo from his face. I couldn't help falling over myself laughing with everyone else. He didn't have to worry about Aurora's wrath any more than this, it had been enacted, but he was still in no condition to walk across stage.

Mark came back and saw us when he heard the commotion. He bit back a laugh of his own, but couldn't keep from smiling. "Will somebody hose him off before he wrecks the set? And clean up every spot of dropped sardine goop you can find. Come on, get moving! Gotta get you kids home before curfew!" He clapped his hands.

Mandy ran back to hook up the hose.

"I got it!" I said when she brought the hose forward, then went back to turn it on while I aimed. I let the nozzle pour water into the trench first to make sure the pressure was okay, then yelled, "Gun it!" and as soon as Mandy had it on full tilt, I turned it toward Connor, nearly toppling him over backwards.

"Dude, you so suck!" he cried through the barrage. It got all of the goop off of him at least, but left him even more sopping wet.

Mandy turned the water off and I let the hose drip into the trench. My eyes hadn't left Connor's body since I started spraying him. With the goop, I hadn't noticed, but soaked from head to toe in water now, Connor's T-shirt clung to him like a second skin. He always wore baggier T-shirts, button downs over them or a hoodie, and changed facing away from other people, especially if he wasn't wearing his arm. He complained about being too skinny, too scrawny, but he'd been hiding a toned physique like his dad under all those layers. I didn't understand how I'd never noticed before.

Connor wiped the water from his face, still laughing, lifted his T-shirt up and out from his body so he could squeeze some of the excess water, and I watched droplets dribble down the toned muscles of his abs to disappear inside the soaked denim of his jeans. The smile dropped from his face when he caught me staring, but he froze there, shirt still lifted, eyes on me.

"It's decided!" Aurora called, gathering the actors and crew to her only a few feet from Connor in the trench. We both turned, finally tearing our eyes from each other. "Cast party is after Saturday's show, at my place. Everyone who comes either has to leave by 11PM—and remember we probably won't even arrive by then—or stay over. The basement and two bedrooms are all ours, so bring your sleeping bags, kids."

"Hey, umm…" I walked up to Connor while he remained dripping in the trench, waiting for at least some of the water to dissipate before he trudged across stage. His honey eyes made me lose my words for a full ten awkward seconds. "I mean, uhh… Alec said it might be a good idea to feed a little early, after the whole shooting thing. Maybe Aurora will let us take one of the bedrooms so we can do that after the show Saturday. We'll be so busy Sunday…"

"Bedroom," Connor repeated, flushing despite the chill of the water, and finally dropping his shirt to slap against his skin, still clinging tightly to him as he shivered. "Totally, good idea. I'll ask her. Then we can relax Sunday. You know, after all the manual labor." He gestured around at the set.

Relax. Right. If that was possible. I knew I wouldn't be relaxing any time between now and then. "Awesome. Thanks. Yeah, let me find you a towel so you don't soak the Thunderbird too badly on the way home."

Another ten seconds passed. No words. Just us. Staring.

"I'll, uhh…go do that," I said, and dashed off to find a towel.

We'd been finding time for me to feed from Connor for weeks now. He bounced back quickly, even though this time I'd taken more in a single week than seemed healthy. My vampire blood over his wounds helped with that, but still. I should have worried more like I used to about hurting him. Should have worried about the hunters. About so many things. But all I could think about was how this time it didn't feel like setting up a feeding schedule.

It felt like we'd just made a date.

CHAPTER 26

Alec

Alec watched the man like a predator on the prowl, though he had no intention of hunting him. His keen eyes always surveyed people like prey. It was how he had survived for so long.

The man was just as Wendy had described—5'10", African American, blue eyes—beautiful. In truth, Alec had tracked him the moment Wendy first found and then lost the hunter, though he hadn't told her that or anyone else. The other hunters eluded Alec, careful and meticulous in their subterfuge. This one doubted, and made mistakes because of his doubt. But he hadn't missed Emery's heart by chance or lacking skill. Wendy was right about that. He'd missed because of a final changing judgment call. Alec could use that, but he needed to know why.

At first he'd hoped the man would lead him to the others, but despite Alec never once allowing himself to be seen, he sensed that the hunter guessed at his presence. The way he looked over his shoulder, feeling Alec's eyes on him, but didn't attempt to lose him with any of the hunter tricks Alec was used to, spoke volumes—decibels. He wanted Alec to watch him. So for now Alec would remain in the shadows and keep this tidbit of information to himself. If he had spotted the other hunter, the one who had attacked Connor, he might not have been able to contain himself, but this hunter was different. This hunter had promise.

Alec faded into mist, invisible in the light of day, moving ever closer to peer inside the window of the new motel the hunter had moved to, on the other side of town from the one where Wendy had spotted him. He had photos of Emery and Connor spread out on the table in front of him. And one, Alec saw, of Wendy. This photo, the man plucked away from the rest and tucked into his jacket. Alec assumed that while the other hunters knew all of their faces now, they knew very little about Wendy, and this hunter wasn't sharing anything he had discovered. He meant to bide his time, learn what he could, and keep it from the others until he was ready. A detective at heart seeking answers, not following the lies of those in charge leading him astray.

Good boy, Alec thought. *I'll keep your secret just a little longer if you prove useful.*

~

I only had about a half hour between school ending and needing to get to the middle school for hair and makeup before the show. Mom would bring me dinner around 6PM. Most of the cast and crew scarfed down food in the makeup and hair room, as long as we were careful not to go near any costumes or eat while we were wearing them.

Connor had wanted to stop home too, change into black clothes for backstage since the ones that had been gooped and soaked last night were still in the laundry. He and the girls were over at his place while I was at mine, dropping off my bag and grabbing up a pair of comfy clothes to change into after the show. No cast party Friday night—at least not this year. Getting one parent to agree to have everyone stay over the whole night was lucky enough.

"Hey, Dad," I said, breezing past the kitchen to bring my backpack up to my room. I stopped before I got to the stairs, swung back around, gaping. Dad was at the kitchen table, cleaning a gun. "What are you doing? Is that Paul's?"

Dad set the solvent and brush aside, and rose to wash his hands at the sink. "Nope. Your mom and I decided to finally, haha, well, bite the bullet and buy one of our own."

My stomach sank. Not because I minded. Going shooting with the Daniels and Franks was a family activity we'd done for years. Mom and Dad had insisted it was one of those important life skills everyone should have, like swimming, "You know, in case of zombie apocalypse," Mom had joked. But we'd never owned one. Never needed to. Connor's family was stocked and lived right across the street.

I knew exactly why things had changed now. And everything pointed to me.

I dropped my bag to the floor in the corner and walked slowly into the kitchen. A gun wouldn't do anything against vampires, but it would work against hunters. The thought of Mom or Dad having to shoot one of them churned my stomach.

"Hey, cheer up, it's just a precaution," Dad said, all smiles as he started to put everything away, leaving just the gun, a 9MM, on the table.

I sat and stared at it with a sigh. A gun wouldn't help me. My abilities as a vampire far exceeded what a gun could do. Somehow that made it all feel worse, that I was a more dangerous weapon than something many people feared.

For the first time, I felt a surge of wanting to tell my father the truth—everything. The girls had found out on accident, and they had been amazing ever since, not treating me any different, or acting like anything had changed, other than occasionally offering a report of someone weird they'd seen around school. I couldn't live my whole life never telling them. Eventually they'd notice when I hadn't aged after a decade or three.

My dad sat back down at the table across from me, the gun between us. He slid over a Tupperware container of cookies that Aurora's mom had brought over yesterday. They still smelled amazing.

"This isn't your fault," Dad said.

It is though, I thought. All of it.

"Something else bothering you?"

I stared at the cookies. At the gun. At Dad. The combination made me think of Mrs. Leonard, that first day they let me into their home. "What if I have something sort of big to tell you?"

Dad rested his elbows on the table and smiled. "Then I guess you better tell me."

"It's big, Dad. Like life changing."

"More than murder and mayhem?"

"Yeah."

His expression shifted more serious. "Emery, you can tell me and your mother anything. Life changing events are what we're here for. I can't imagine what you've been going through after seeing Will like that, and having the shooting at the school. It's too much for someone your age, any age. All I know is how much your mother and I are worrying, so I know it's ten times worse for you. I don't want you blaming yourself though, thinking you're doing anything wrong. Unless you're going to tell me you had something to do with the murders—"

"What?" I looked up from having dropped my gaze to the table, and saw the grin quirking on Dad's face again. "That's not funny, Dad."

"I didn't think it was, but you're acting like it's the end of the world. If you're scared, I get that. Unless it's something else? Feeling like…maybe you wish you had been shot?"

My eyes widened at the way his crinkled, because this finally was an honest question, and the last thing I wanted him to think was that I was suicidal. "No, Dad. I don't want that, or think I deserve what's been happening. It's nothing like that."

"Then is it a new girlfriend you're planning to run away and elope with," he smiled again, "because there isn't much that would change the way I see you. Nothing could ever make us love you any differently or less."

"It wouldn't be a girl, Dad, not now," I said before I realized how that sounded. When his eyebrows rose over his dark, dark eyes, I recognized the different turn this conversation had taken. "I just mean, uhh…" I couldn't back out now, but Connor had become a more prominent life changing factor in my life than vampirism, and every other thought vacated my brain.

I stared at the tabletop again. These were different nerves eating at my insides than before, stronger ones, with sharper teeth.

"I think I might be bi," I said, half expecting the words 'and I'm a vampire' to follow this sudden outpouring of honesty. "Or, you know…that I like another boy." I peeked up slowly to see Dad's reaction.

He blinked at me. "That's it?"

"Uhh…yeah?" Other than the vampire thing.

After a moment of silence, he reached over and slid the bowl of cookies closer to me. "Want a cookie?"

"Dad! I'm being serious."

"And I'm being 'Dad'," he laughed. "Did you expect me to freak out? You know your mom is bi."

"Well, yeah, but…" that had seemed less important considering she married my dad.

"But what? You better not let her hear you acting like it doesn't matter. She'd jump into her whole tirade about how sexuality has nothing to do with commitment, and you do not want to be on the receiving end of that. She didn't suddenly stop finding both men and women attractive after meeting me and deciding to be monogamous, not any more than I stopped enjoying the sight of a beautiful woman. It's just that now when I see one, I tend to think…boy, my wife would look good in that outfit."

"Dad," I groaned, though I couldn't stop the smile from filling my face.

"I'm just saying. I never had any problem with who she is, the only thing that matters to me is that she chose me and we're happy together. If you like this boy, the only thing that matters is whether or not he likes you back, and that you're both honest about what you want from each other."

"You make it sound so easy." I slumped further in the chair, leaning back, then decided I did want a cookie and snagged one. Dad did too. "I guess I didn't know what to expect, telling you about this. I thought you'd react more like…"

"Like Paul did with Connor?" His voice dropped lower, softer.

"Yeah."

Not that Paul had been awful in quite the way most people fear about coming out to their parents; I'd never expect that from Paul or Georgia, but he'd still been shocked, maybe even disappointed, and asked a few too many times if Connor was sure. It weighed on

Connor for a long time, that question. I felt the same weight now, but Dad didn't ask.

Instead, he said, "You gonna tell me who it is? Or is that a bigger secret?"

I finished the rest of my cookie rather than answer.

"Fair enough," Dad nodded.

"It's still kinda new," I said. "And weird. And I haven't technically told him. We keep dancing around it, but I'm pretty sure he knows, and that he feels something for me back. The whole thing took me by surprise. Ever since the Leonards, I don't, we've just... we've found ourselves in more and more intimate situations. Which has never happened before. Not like this. And I'm around him every day, like all the time, and..." I looked up to find Dad smiling at me again, "...and I am so giving away who it is, aren't I?"

Dad chuckled, dimples showing. "I can play ignorant if you want."

I had to laugh too. This was a complete mess from what I'd expected to tell him.

The clock on the wall reminded me that I had limited time to get what I needed and rejoin Connor and the others across the street. "Thanks, Dad. We're figuring it out. Or we will. I have to head to the middle school. This...I mean," I gestured at the bowl as I stood from the table, "the cookies helped."

"They are a cure-all. I think I'll have two more," he said, and did take two cookies before replacing the cover, "before your mom gets home and hides them on me again."

I considered confessing my other secret, but now wasn't the time. Dad pulled me in for a hug before I could leave the kitchen, kissed the side of my hair, squeezed too tightly on purpose until a gasped and laughed, and smacked his back to be let go. And with the release of pressure as his arms loosened, some of the other pressures on me dissolved with it.

CHAPTER 27

Connor

Opening night went off without a hitch. Connor made sure to stay out of Auroroa's way and to do all of his prop work in a timely manner, never where he shouldn't be, no repeats from Joke Night on an actual show night. She would not be forgiving if someone slipped up.

Everyone was so exhausted from getting through the first night, no one even complained about having to hurry along with greeting the audience after the show so they could get home before curfew, even if it was a bit of a rush. Mark and the other adults would stick around afterward to make sure anything left unfinished was completed or placed back where it should be for tomorrow night.

Connor slept like the dead—or maybe undead; he hadn't thought to ask Emery if his sleep patterns were messed up from being a vampire. They didn't have any plans to see each other until makeup and hair call the next night, which technically was when Connor should be making sure his Mom's newest batch of sardine goop was stocked and ready. The actual Styrofoam sardines they could reuse; the goop, not so much. But after dedicating all of Saturday during the day to getting ahead on homework so he wouldn't have to think about anything the rest of the weekend, he snuck up to the makeup room as soon as he had the chance to see Emery.

"Dude, you seriously killed it last night," Connor said, leaning back against the makeup counter while Emery added powder to his face to counter the bright lights of being on stage. "Alec and Wendy coming tonight?"

"Yeah. Actually in the audience this time too, not just lookout. They don't think the hunters will attempt another public attack, not with all the cops they have watching the place. Officer Nustad is even going to tail us to Aurora's and stakeout until morning, just to be safe."

"It's like you have your own secret service watching over you."

"With none of the perks of being president."

"There are perks?"

Emery flicked some of the excess powder on the end of his brush in Connor's direction, filling the air with tan-colored dust.

"Hey! My pasty complexion would look awful that shade. Save the brown and beautiful for yourself."

Emery laughed and turned away with that brilliant smile again, eyes diverting and then flicking back to Connor at a side angle, as if to make sure he wasn't teasing. Oh, Connor thought Emery was beautiful, that was never in question, so he forced himself to meet Emery eye to eye and not flinch away, answering his questions with silent certainty.

Either that, or Connor was totally missing all of Emery's cues and making a complete jackass out of himself, but he preferred to believe the former.

They were interrupted by the flurry that was Jules getting her blond curls fluffed, and painting her lips red for the show. Before long, Connor and Emery were on opposite ends of the auditorium, actor and stagehand, playing their parts.

Aside from them being off center when they rotated the set between Acts I and II, enough that Aurora literally dangled over the pit for a moment since the end of the set lengthwise was just shy of being too long for rotation on a good day, night two went as perfectly as night one. The 'whiskey' leaked, and Amos nearly tripped during one of the comedic handoffs of the bottle between characters, but nothing noticeable or catastrophic happened.

Alec and Wendy, playing the parts of husband and wife, even hovered after the show to congratulate Emery on a wonderful performance.

"And you as well, Connor," they stopped when they caught sight of him, back a ways from the actual talent most people wanted to see after the show, "I know these things don't run themselves. What was your role as stagehand?" Alec asked.

The American accent threw Connor, but other people were within earshot for him to offer a snappy comment. "Sardine manager. And pants prepper for Emery."

"Is that an official title?"

Wendy elbowed him hard enough in the ribs that he actually gasped. "Be nice, dear," she said sweetly, in an 'or I'll murder you' sort of way. Connor loved having a pseudo aunt who could kill a man fifteen different ways in his retinue.

"Have fun tonight at any rate. It's when the chaos dies down that you'll want to be watchful." Alec leveled a serious stare on Connor before grinning with a touch of his manic side and whisking Wendy away.

Connor really needed to ask them what they did all day. Did they meet up? Discuss Connor and Emery and their annoying, teenage ways? Get Mexican for lunch at Miguel's and compare notes? How did one *be* part of a thrown together but highly effective hunter-vampire duo?

Connor's thoughts were interrupted as Aurora grabbed his arm and yanked him back down the hallway to the auditorium. "Party time, Con-Man. Let's get a move on already."

A whirlwind of minutes later, everything was as in place as it needed to be for tomorrow's matinee, all of the actors out of their costumes, everything packed away neatly, as the whole collection of students involved in the show—and a handful of others tagging along for fun—headed to Aurora's for the cast party in one long procession of vehicles.

Emery used one of Aurora's handy makeup wipes to remove the gunk from his face by the time they pulled into her driveway. It wasn't only Officer Nustad keeping watch on the house with dozens of kids piling in to claim the large split level as their own for the night, but two other squad cars strategically placed around the neighborhood as well. It almost would have put a damper on the night's festivities, but Aurora was having none of that.

Music blared from upstairs, where various finger foods, soda, and punch had been setup in the kitchen, and the furniture had been rearranged downstairs to accommodate as many sleeping bags as possible. A few people claimed couches, though Aurora had first pick as hostess.

She'd graciously offered her bedroom to Emery and Connor for later, which Connor did not need to think of like *that* if he didn't want to give himself a heart attack, and the way Aurora had looked at him when he explained why they wanted the room had not helped.

"Mavus is going to suck on your neck at the party? If you two just want an excuse to make out, the room is all yours. No need to invent reasons."

"We're not—"

"Oh please, you better be, or I will be highly disappointed."

Aurora looked like her mother—practically a carbon copy—despite her father's white-blond hair and pale blue eyes. Her parents were only there when they arrived though, electing to stay over at Aurora's grandmother's a few blocks down.

Her mother had put a hand on her hip and said, "You'd have to be the biggest dumbasses on the planet to pull anything stupid with three cops hanging around the neighborhood, so behave yourselves."

Other adults moved in and out during the cast party, like Mark. Although, once he left, and it was only the remaining kids who'd be staying through the night, the nature of the games they played shifted.

"Who's up for 'Honey, if you love me'?" Sophie shouted above the din of people talking and lounging in various chairs and spots on the floor.

Connor groaned. Whoever was 'it' had to pick someone in the room to approach, say 'Honey, if you love me, won't you please, please smile' and get the other person to laugh before they finished the phrase. Connor could get other people to laugh fine, but he hated how he always cracked when someone went for him.

If adults were present, there were generally rules about no touching, or no *inappropriate* touching anyway. Without any adults left in the house, all rules promptly went out the window. There were many creative ways to draw out saying that simple phrase. If the person laughed, they were the next one 'it'. If they didn't, their attacker had to move on to the next person.

The various attempts and people who cracked, or didn't crack, had everyone roaring with laughter before long. Hopped up on too much adrenaline and sugary food and drink, curfew and the cops outside became a distant memory.

The color drained from Connor's face when Nick ended up 'it' after several rounds and headed his direction. Nick was collected, stoic in most situations, which meant people expected him to be dull or at the very least respectful of boundaries.

He was not. At all. He was like a polite time bomb that could do something completely out of character at a moment's notice.

He snatched up Mandy's plate of strawberries and whipped cream that she'd only eaten a handful of, eliciting a mild protest, and set it down beside Connor as he knelt in front of him.

"Honey, if you love me…" he started, and damn it, Connor's cheeks were already twitching. Nick grabbed Connor's right hand and dipped his pointer finger in the whipped cream, "Won't you please, please…" and opened his mouth to suck off the sweet substance in one long, smooth motion.

"Oh my god!" Connor burst out laughing, wiping his finger on his jeans after his initial shock, and pushing Nick away from him, "I hate you so much right now! But clearly J. J. is a very lucky man."

Nick's deeper laughter rumbled, though his expression remained more of a quirked smile on only one side of his face.

"You're up, Con-Man," Aurora announced.

"Yeah, yeah." Connor stood and pushed the plate of strawberries and whipped cream back toward Mandy, who held up her hands and shook her head now that someone's finger had been in it. Connor shrugged and looked around the room.

His first thought was to go for one of the easy targets. Jules hadn't been singled out yet, and she was always quick to smile, maybe one of the quickest, other than him. She had scooted away from everyone to try to hide from plain view.

Emery sat in front of her, still smiling wide and chuckling with the others around him over Nick's antics. Jules pointed a jutting finger down at Emery over his head when Connor's eyes landed on her.

Emery was the absolute king of 'Honey, if you love me'. Ever since they were Freshman, even before that back in 7th grade doing chorus parts in the Fall Musical, no one had ever been able to get Emery to smile. He'd only ever been 'it' for the game if he volunteered to start.

Emery glanced down at the carpet, then flicked his eyes up again to meet Connor's, his smile settling into something blank but patiently waiting for Connor to move toward him, like he expected him to, wanted him to. A bundle of nerves spread out from the depths of Connor's stomach. It was the perfect chance to be bold without anyone having to know it meant something more. Even if literally everyone in the room knew anyway.

Connor mustered his most over the top grin, intent on making a real show of this, as he sauntered toward Emery. There were a few snickers, a few comments about there being no way Connor could get Emery to smile, not a chance, and then Connor was on him. Emery sat with his knees drawn up, but dropped them open to let Connor come closer, which was nearly enough to call Connor's bluff at being able to do this.

He straddled Emery boldly, a knee dropping to either side of him, as a chorus of oohs and aahs sounded loudly around them. "Honey, if you love me," he said, scooting closer, and practically shaking from how intimately connected they were. He placed his hands on Emery's chest who, as rules usually dictated, did not touch Connor back, but kept his hands planted on the floor. Connor leaned forward, as if going for Emery's lips, only to duck to the side at the last moment and whisper, "Won't you please, please smi—"

They toppled back with a crash, and as Connor clung and tried to right himself, he saw that Jules, who Emery had been half leaning against, had scooted back, holding a hand to her face to keep from laughing too loudly.

Connor was draped all over Emery, on top of him, in front of most of the people they knew. He froze within the din of laughter and louder oohs and aahs that accompanied their topple as he lifted up and saw the stunned, blushing expression on Emery's face.

"Mavus totally smiled!" someone yelled.

All at once the moment broke.

"No way, it was a grimace from landing on my back!" Emery said, as Connor scrambled off of him and they righted themselves on the carpet.

"Whatever, man, he totally got you."

"I swear," Emery defended and turned pleading eyes on Connor. "Back me up."

If it had been any other cast party over the years, Connor might have played mischievous, 'Oh, I don't know about that, Em, maybe you're just trying to get out of admitting I finally bested you', but this time, tonight, Connor was drowning, and he wasn't sure he wanted to be saved.

"Must have been a grimace," he said. "Too bad. Guess I'll have to get you next time."

The naysayer groaned, along with a few others, while most of the crowd cheered that Emery was still king. It didn't matter to Connor. His eyes and focus were only on Emery.

Aurora stood and announced that it was high time they moved onto something else, since Emery retaining his crown all the way to Senior year was a definite sign the game was over. A volley of ideas for what to do next went up around the room, but settled on putting in the DVD of their Freshmen year spring play to reminisce and laugh at old times.

As people moved about to change positions for the best spots around the TV while Aurora set everything up, and a few headed upstairs to refresh their food and drinks, Emery took hold of Connor and dragged him down the hallway toward Aurora's bedroom.

"Come on, while no one's looking. Wouldn't want to make it too obvious we're headed to one of the bedrooms," he said quietly. "Someone might get the wrong idea."

"Right..."

But Emery's smile was wide again, beaming, which further made it impressive that he could get through round after round of 'Honey, if you love me' without cracking. They slipped inside the room and closed and locked the door behind them.

"You sure you're okay with this?" Emery asked when they moved to sit on the bed.

"Yeah, Em, it makes sense for you to feed now instead of tomorrow, when we'll be even more exhausted. I've told you I don't mind."

"I know. You enjoy it, right?" he said with a twist to his smile.

"You think I'm a freak, don't you?"

"No! I just…I don't know how to…I mean, I don't really remember much about what it felt like when Mr. Leonard turned me, so I can't relate. But as long as it doesn't hurt you. As long as I'm not…a burden."

"You could never be a burden to me, Em." Connor turned to better face him.

"Okay. Do you wanna…lie back maybe? Be more comfortable?" Emery gestured at the full sized bed. That they were sitting on. Together. Alone in a bedroom during a party. And wow, Connor hadn't realized what a cliché this was until just now. Other than the about to be fed on by a vampire part.

"Sure."

It felt so unfairly awkward, scooting up the bed, weirder than any time they'd done this before, because that strange new something between them was like some giant pink elephant in the room that they were trying to climb over to reach each other—obvious, ridiculous, and way too big a hurdle to move past without stumbling. Actually picturing a pink elephant in the room did help Connor relax though, difficult as it was not to laugh out loud.

He laid back on the pillow, on top of Aurora's dark purple comforter, and let Emery lie beside him, propped up, one hand by his head, the other reaching over to box Connor in and support his hovering weight. He didn't radiate much body heat, but that was probably why he needed to feed sooner. It had gotten used up healing the damage from the wooden bolt. But there was an intimacy in his presence, right there along Connor's side.

Their eyes met, honey on green, and the light in the room dimmed, all the ambient sounds of the rest of the cast and crew out in the living room fading as Connor succumbed to Emery's glamour. His nerves left him just as readily, even if it would only last as long as the glamour held. He floated on a cloud with Emery snuggled beside him, tucking into his neck because he wanted to be there, wanted to be close, not only because he needed the nourishment Connor provided.

Even in the glamour, Connor felt the prick of fangs, but it wasn't painful, not there on his cloud, content and safe. It made him shiver, shudder, cling to Emery with both hands. There was no dizziness as the blood drained, drawn away down Emery's throat and over his tongue, just bliss.

Mmm, Em's tongue, Connor thought. He wanted to feel it. He felt it on his neck, but he wanted it against his own, wished he was bold enough to ask for that, to take a chance, turn his head, and pull Emery to him. But the moment was already over, the feeding complete all too quickly. Connor felt a rush of disappointment as the glamour faded.

And then froze when the strokes of Emery's tongue over his wound became a firm press of lips. Then again, a little higher, closer to the dip behind his ear. *Again…*

"Em…" he gasped, more like moaned at the feeling of his friend kissing his neck—*kissing his neck*, not biting him or healing him or something else that could be construed as anything other than kissing.

Emery pulled away, as startled as Connor had been, his eyes trained on the pillow. "Sorry. I didn't—"

"No, I…I liked it," Connor said, breathless, a little dizzy from the feeding, but not enough to want this to end.

Slowly, Emery's eyes, pupils blown and looking so dark, so black, drifted over Connor's face. "You're not still glamoured, right?"

"I'm talking, aren't I?"

"Can I kiss you again?"

The blossom of nerves in Connor's stomach expanded so large, he could only nod, unable to form words or think how else to respond.

Emery's face disappeared into the crook of his neck, another press of lips to where the wound had been. And another. Like trying to make up for every time he had fed from Connor, apology and gratitude combined. Chaste, warm kisses moved higher along the tendon, until he reached Connor's ear again, just beneath it, and Connor shuddered all down his body from the way it tingled through him.

His right hand reached up, finding the edge of Emery's T-shirt hanging away from his body. When he pushed past it, he found the skin of his friend's stomach, so warm now, pulsing with power and blood because of him. His other hand reached for Emery's head, plastic fingers tangling in his hair, but he didn't want to hold Emery there. He wanted more than the feather light touches up his neck.

"Em…" He tugged lightly on the thick strands, just enough to get Emery to lift up. With one hand on Emery's warm skin, the other being as gentle as he could at his head, Connor's breath hitched at all the possibilities before him. Those dark green eyes shimmered with apprehension, but Connor had no intention of telling Emery to stop.

He tightened his prosthetic's grip on Emery's hair, nodded once to make it clear to his friend that, yes, this was everything he wanted, and pulled Emery down until their mouths met.

CHAPTER 28

Connor's tongue—*god*, I never knew how much I'd wanted to feel it. And his mouth. And his skin. All my weight rested on my hands on either side of him, unable to touch him back, but his flesh and blood fingers slid up my chest beneath the shirt, his prosthetic behind my head, holding me as we kissed—*kissed*. Me and Connor.

All the anxiety I'd been fighting off for days, weeks, drained out of me. I felt awake and alive from the fresh blood, blood he'd offered, that he enjoyed giving me, and channeled it into kissing him deeper. Before suddenly wondering if he tasted blood in my mouth.

"Oh god, is it gross? Do I taste like…?" I brought my hand to my mouth when I pulled back, hoping I hadn't ruined this.

"Huh?" He blinked at me, a tired and dopey smile in place, and no traces of smeared red on his lips. "What? No. You taste amazing. I think your body absorbs it right away."

"Oh."

"Come here." He pulled me down again, licking into my mouth, plastic hand tangled in my hair, maybe even a little caught, but I didn't care. He felt so warm, and I was on fire, the blood making my face flush, even as so much of it surged down into my belly.

His other hand got trapped at my collarbone, unable to push any higher in the confines of my shirt. I pulled back and tore it over my head. Connor made a strangled noise at the sight of me, and slid his hand down the faint trail of dark hair below my belly button. Being a vampire didn't make me any less ticklish; I sucked in a breath.

"I love your pudge…and your treasure trail…and your skin."
He flushed almost immediately after the words left him, and I know
I must have too. I wanted him to understand that he did the same
thing to me.

"The way you looked all soaking wet, *god,*" I said. I moved
my hands from pressing into the mattress to slide his shirt up,
revealing the concave of his stomach, the firm muscles he didn't
realize he had. "Why do you hide all this?"

"Wouldn't want to blind anyone when I reflect the sun," he
said matter-of-factly, so wholly Connor, I fell forward into him
laughing. He laughed too, and coiled his arms around me to hug
me to his chest.

Other people couldn't possibly understand how right it felt to
have both flesh and plastic fingers at my back, touching my bare
skin. I pushed my hands up to his shoulders, stretching his T-shirt
more than I should, and nuzzled my face against his neck where
I'd bitten. Not even a faint line or hint of reddened skin remained. I
pressed another kiss there.

Connor whined and pushed at me. When I lifted up, he arched
his neck to reconnect our kiss. Most of my weight was on top of
him now, my upper half fully covering him while my legs lay to the
side. As we kissed, hurried and wet, I shifted, lifted one leg over
him until I straddled him and our hips aligned.

I tugged at his T-shirt until he stopped kissing me long enough
to pull it over his head. My hands returned to his chest, smoothed
down his shoulders and arms. I rocked into him. Gasped. Rocked
again.

"W-Wait, Em. Are we going too fast?"

I froze as I lifted up to look down at him. His cheeks were
rosy, his lips pink, his eyes hazy and impossibly dark beneath
me.

"Only because it's us, and this is all weirdly awesome," he
said. "Or is skipping to the good part sort of mandatory, because
it's…us, and this is all weirdly awesome?"

I ran one hand over the closely cropped edges of his hair. "Do
you want to stop?"

"Not even a little. I've wanted this for so long."

I almost let our lips touch again before that registered. "How long?"

Some of the apprehension I'd been seeing from him the past several days wavered in his gaze. "Way longer than I'm comfortable admitting."

I kissed him. I hadn't imagined it. He did want me, had for a long time. My nerves dwindled with each new press of our lips, leaving behind raw, buzzing want.

If I hadn't fed, I think I would have wanted to bite him, but as much as that passing realization worried me, it was gone a moment later. I wanted to taste him with my tongue not my teeth. Because it was Connor. And he was wonderful. Knew every crevice and dark corner of me and still wanted to be my friend. He'd been there during the worst and best of my life, both of which seemed to have found me in only the past month. We slotted together like it had always been this way, like maybe we'd done it all before in another life and just hadn't known it until now.

"Do you think Aurora will kill us for doing this on her bed?" I said, grinning.

"I think she'll throw us a party," Connor said. "Then kill us. So worth it."

We kissed, pawed at each other's bare chests, and rocked through our jeans. I felt overheated in the best way. I reached between us to pull down Connor's zipper.

He tensed and grabbed my hands with both of his. "Um, wait, I, uhh…I lied."

"You don't want to—"

"I do! I don't mean that. But, uhh…remember when I told you I lost my virginity to Andy Grayson?"

I relaxed my hands against his stomach. "You lost it to someone else?"

"No…we maybe got about as far as him attempting to steal third base and I chickened out. I've fooled around with others, you know, but nothing really substantial. I've always been too hung up on you." He paused, his eyes going wide like he thought I'd be shocked to hear that. I was—Connor had been hung up on me? For how long, how many months, years? But it didn't change anything about what I wanted now. "I just don't want you expecting much," he said quietly, "since I'm a little more inexperienced than I let on."

"And you think Liz and Mandy means I'm any different?" I'd told him every time I had sex, which wasn't any grand number—my two high school girlfriends was plenty, sometimes felt like too much when it hadn't worked out with either of them.

Now I felt awful for having told him, if he'd secretly wanted me all that time. Not that I'd ever gone into detail, that never seemed right, but when I thought back on it now, his groans of 'ew, dude!' from just admitting I'd slept with them probably held more meaning than I'd realized.

I reached one hand for his face. It was soft, barely any fuzz. His father, despite his bald head, could grow a beard almost as thick as my dad's, but Connor had inherited his mother's finer hair. His cheek felt smooth beneath my hand, and he shuddered at the touch.

"This is new territory—period," I said. "We don't have to do anything else. I want to, I do, but I only just realized how much I was missing. We can wait. Whatever you want. I'm just glad I can finally tell you, I was so scared to, but…" I didn't know how to explain that it had taken becoming a vampire to wake me up.

"Me too, Em," he said, his human fingers curling around mine that still rested at his beltline, and drawing them back to the zipper. "It's always been you. I've always only wanted you. I've waited long enough."

His kiss was searing, biting. I even felt his teeth a little, insistent and fierce. Connor was goofy on his best days, jittery and animated. I didn't expect the way he could be slow, and deliberate, and focused all on me. I was so blind. He'd been focused on me all this time.

I don't remember hearing anything else from the peanut gallery out in the living room. Maybe an occasional louder cheer as they laughed watching our Freshman Spring Play, but the words didn't reach us.

Aurora's clock showed that at least an hour had passed when I finally looked at it, lying beside Connor. Only I wasn't tired like I might have been when I was human. I still felt invigorated from the blood. Adrenaline pumping from everything else. But sweaty and breathless and content.

I looked at Connor. His eyes were closed, but his mouth stretched in a wide grin.

"It really sucks how hungry I am right now, because I do not want to leave this bed," he said, stretching his arms above his head at odd angles like a yawning cat. With his shirt off I could see where his prosthetic connected to his elbow. It looked so red next to his white skin.

I touched my fingers to it and traced down to his wrist. "I could do my whole Flash routine, and zip out and up the stairs without anyone seeing me."

His eyes sparkled as he opened them. "Seriously? Coz that would be amazing."

I leaned forward to kiss him before rolling out of the bed and pulling my shorts back on. I hadn't actually tried to use my speed like that before, but I figured everyone still awake and restless in the living room would be too focused on whatever they were watching and talking about to notice a blur of motion.

In just my underwear, I stood at the door, looked back to see Connor's wide, hopeful eyes, then flashed out the door and up the stairs. No one was there, so I slowed down once I arrived to take more care in what I grabbed for Connor. Once I had a plate loaded with meat, cheese, and crackers, I held one hand to the food to keep it from flying off. I was back in Aurora's bedroom in moments, and closed the door behind me.

I listened to hear if anyone outside the door made any distressing noises. Nothing seemed out of place.

"Ta da," I said, handing the plate to Connor as I moved back to the bed. He'd slipped his underwear back on as well and sat up cross-legged to dive into the spoils.

"I see that this arrangement is going to continue to have awesome perks," he said, shoving a cracker sandwich loaded with meat and cheese into his mouth. I'd forgotten that it was best if he ate something after I drank from him.

I settled in next to him, sitting cross-legged as he was. Some of that awkward silence filtered in, since he couldn't contribute much to conversation while stuffing his face. I just watched him, waiting to wake up. Waiting for the last several weeks—the Leonards, becoming a vampire, being shot and hunted, and now... what had just happened with Connor—to have been a strange but still pleasant dream.

"Something on my face?" Connor grinned.

"Huh? No, I...well, yes, actually." I laughed and pointed at the cracker crumbs in the corner of his mouth. He brushed them away. "But no, I just...I don't know. It's all so crazy. It should be weirder. Becoming a vampire should not be what makes everything in my life clearer, but here we are."

Connor finished chewing his most recent cracker sandwich and set the plate on the nightstand. The way his eyes darted told me he had several things to say, but couldn't decide where to begin. "I think we're doing this wrong," he finally said.

"All of that seemed pretty right to me."

I laughed when Connor rolled his eyes and jolted forward to push me off the bed. Thankfully, the carpet prevented my thud from being too loud and alerting anyone in the living room. "Ow," I looked up at him from my sprawled position.

"You're a vampire; that didn't hurt."

"I guess you're right." I shot forward faster than he could counter, and yanked him down on top of me, careful to break the fall so he didn't land too hard. He groaned anyway, biting back a yelp and struggling away until he was lying next to me.

"Cheater."

"You started it."

"I did."

"Why do you think we're doing this wrong? What should be different?"

He rolled onto his back, but tangled his legs with mine, his head on my shoulder and right hand pressed to my chest. I don't think I realized how tentatively he used to touch me before, now that he knew he had permission to touch me as much as he wanted.

"Nothing needs to change, you know. Between us," I said. "I don't want things to change. You're my best friend. You'll always be my best friend."

"So we can be that, me and you, just with added kissing and sexy times?" He ducked his head. "Coz that deal sounds way too perfect to not have a catch."

We slotted together just like before, like we always did, only now I got to hold him. Only now there were no more secrets, nothing left unsaid. "No catch. Who says it can't be like this all the time?"

"Skeptics, mostly. I prefer to be a romantic."

"And a giant dork."

"And that." He grinned as his eyes lifted to meet mine. "Can we go back on the bed though? Aurora's carpet might be thick, but my bony ass does not appreciate the lack of padding. Plus her Spock plushie is so judging me for my illogical existence."

I looked up to see said plushie staring down at us from the dresser. This was why I loved Connor. This was why it was meant to be him. Because he was my best friend *and* he made my heart race.

I laughed so hard getting up from the floor, my eyes watered.

CHAPTER 29

Connor

Connor sat on the edge of the stage, eating out of one of the many boxes of pizzas that Mark had provided them for set strike. The matinee show had started at 3PM, finishing right at dinner time. They'd be taking down the set and cleaning up their several weeks' long mess of the spring play right up until curfew. Connor needed the extra calories. Especially after last night.

He grinned to himself around another mouthful, lulled by the din of power tools and chattering voices behind him. A few others were scattered on the stage or in the auditorium seats eating while they took a break. He and Emery had fallen asleep in Aurora's bed, woke before most of the others, and dressed before anyone noticed them leaving the room together. The police escort was there waiting to drive with them home, though nothing seemed to have happened during the night.

Connor kicked his legs, humming as he ate. He'd kissed Emery. He'd done significantly more than just kiss him. Everything he'd fantasized about for years had finally played out in real life. Well, not *everything*, Connor snickered. But enough. So much.

"What are you grinning about, slacker?" Aurora said, plopping down beside him and snagging a slice of pepperoni, which she proceeded to remove of all pepperoni since she liked the flavor but not the actual meat on her pizza. At least Connor got the castoffs.

Connor considered keeping what had happened in her bedroom last night a secret right up until he looked at her and remembered their pact. "How mad would you be if I maybe lost my virginity in your bed?"

Aurora froze, mouth open around her first bite of pizza. Slowly, utterly calm and collected, she took a bite, chewed, swallowed. "Less mad that you told me in time to change my bedding before I slept in it tonight. But what does 'maybe' mean?"

"I don't know if it counts. We didn't...you know." He set his own half-eaten slice down and made a sort of twisting motion with his hands as if he were holding a ball, which he realized only as he did it in no way conveyed what he meant.

"I don't even know how to respond to that," Aurora said, taking another bite.

"It's easy for you. Girls have built in anatomy that breaks to signal you're no longer a virgin."

"Hey, that's not fair. First of all, not technically true. Plus, that assumes penetration decides virginity. And sure, that can work with a guy and girl, or two guys, but what about two women?"

Connor inclined his head closer to her. "I'm pretty sure there are many ways that can work with two women."

Aurora smacked his shoulder with greasy fingers, which in turn caused Connor to grimace. "I have an easier answer for you, Con-Man. Did you achieve orgasm with the assistance of another person?"

Connor glanced around to make sure no one was close enough to have overheard that, but even those who were couldn't hear them over the power tools. Still, he whispered when he answered, "Yes."

"Mazel tov!" Aurora raised what remained of her pizza slice.

"Huh," Connor said, leaning back on his hands, "I agree with your assessment."

"So who was it? Or am I stupid for asking?"

"Uhh...we didn't actually discuss if we're going to be all public yet, so..." But before Connor could finish his embarrassed rambling, Emery appeared from behind him and leaned down over his shoulder, kissing him soundly as Connor looked up in surprise, and then settled onto the floor between him and Aurora.

Aurora raised a curious eyebrow, valiantly keeping her grin in check.

Connor blinked. Blushed. Leaned into Emery's side. "It was Em."

"Nice."

"Huh?" Emery looked at each of them, as if just then realizing he had kissed Connor in public for the first time. "Was I not supposed to do that?"

Connor scooted closer to him, "You're good," and kissed him right back.

"Oh my god, is this a thing?" Jules' voiced shrilled from close by, suddenly right behind their heads. "Did I just see that? Did you two finally get your heads out of your asses?"

Connor looked up to see Jules already on the floor, pushing in between Emery and Aurora to get as close to them as humanly possible.

"How many people were rooting for this?" Emery asked.

A few others working on various cleaning or set dismantling had looked their way as well, and were talking or snickering while not hiding at all who they were talking and snickering about, including Nick.

Aurora and Jules shared a look and said in perfect harmony, "Everyone."

Jules snagged a slice of pizza, but she'd only taken a few bites before Mandy tried to take her power drill.

"What, you're on break," said Mandy, "I need it."

"Nah uh. Get your own. I'll break when I'm dead." Jules dumped her half chewed slice in the box. "I do not get enough opportunity to use power tools." She raced off to finish the set piece she had been helping take apart.

They ate, chatted, eventually got back to work, and when Connor passed Aurora in the halls later, carrying out loads of costume pieces that had been on loan, he whispered to her, "Your turn."

She frowned at him, only for her dark eyes to widen in dread once she realized he meant: *you have to ask out Michael.* It was so worth the harsh punch she delivered to his tricep. "You said no consequences!"

"Ow!" Connor struggled between hanging onto the box he carried and dropping it to the floor to rub his assaulted arm.

"Yeah, other than our own missed opportunities, and now that I can speak from experience, trust me, you do not want to miss out on opportunities this awesome."

Aurora tossed her head as if to whip her hair over her shoulder, but it was in a bun again today so she just ended up looking incredibly dramatic. "The difference being that Michael doesn't know I'm alive."

They shuffled over to the corner, and Connor did set the box on the floor, when a couple of other students carrying loads out to Mark's car passed through the door to outside.

"That's ridiculous," Connor hissed.

"I'm peripheral, Con-Man, purely background noise to his high school life. He knows I exist, okay, but he wouldn't even know to think of me that way."

"Exactly. So work on getting him to start."

Aurora pouted her full lips at him in extreme exaggeration. If Michael participated in the spring play, Connor would have pushed her in the direction of the Student Council President that second.

"One dance at Prom," he bargained.

"He has a date."

"They're going as friends."

"But—"

"No buts. One dance. I'll even ask him for you. We can make it a whole ruse where I beg him to dance with you so you stop stealing Em away from me as the way better dance partner."

She opened her mouth again then paused. "Okay. But if I make a fool of myself, I'm taking you down with me."

"Deal."

With his mind thoroughly distracted now to thoughts of Prom, it dawned on Connor that he and Emery hadn't actually discussed things at length about this new arrangement between them. He sought his friend out after unloading the last box of costumes, finding him in the choir room that they used as their Green Room, vacuuming.

"That is so cheap, Em. Vacuuming is the easiest job for set strike."

"Why do you think I volunteer to do it every show?" Emery grinned. He unplugged the cord and started winding it around the handle to transport to the next room.

Connor sat down in one of the choir room chairs. "So…we're going to Prom, right?"

"Didn't we already decide that? I bought a burgundy suit for you."

Confirmation of eBay transactions should not offer quite as much relief as what surged through Connor to hear that. "Right, sure, but now we'll actually be…dates?"

Emery rolled the vacuum cleaner out of the way so he could sit next to Connor. "Guess so. That okay? Because if you don't want to label anything yet—"

"I love labels," Connor said hastily, bumping his knee against Emery's. "I will go down in history as the one-armed gay kid with pyromaniac tendencies if it means I can also be your boyfriend." He would have cringed if Emery hadn't immediately laughed at his rambling.

"Boyfriend," Emery nodded, and leaned just a little bit closer. Side by side in the chairs, nearly identical in height, Connor's eyes were drawn to Emery's approaching lips. "Sounds good to me." He kissed him. Light. Simple. Then pulled away.

Connor shivered down to his toes.

He inwardly cursed when a group of stagehands cut through the choir room to reach the catwalks, but only because he wished he and Emery had more time alone. After school tomorrow, though, and every day after, they were free with the play behind them now. There was a whole week ahead of them to spend time together.

And, after that, Prom. Connor had a date to Prom. With Emery. Not a friend date, but the real thing.

That night, after dropping Emery off at home, Connor couldn't wipe the smile from his face.

~

Bane

Douglas Bane gathered the hunters under his charge to him. He'd led this particular group of men and women for nearly a decade. They had moved from the small town in which Emery Mavus lived to one to the south, keeping under the radar from the rogue hunter and elder vampire they had spotted guarding the young teen.

Eli's failure at the school had cost them. The police were on higher alert than ever, watching roadways, eyeing tourists and any unfamiliar faces, and chaperoning Mavus everywhere he went. Even without the police, the elder vampire and hunter were enough trouble. Taking Mavus out at the school had been the ideal scenario. Quick. Clean. Eli had never made such a glaring error before.

It grated on Bane, and confirmed that he was right not to bring his nephew in on the crux of their mission just yet. Eli was young, experienced but still soft; he pitied these creatures when they wore pleasant faces and feigned living normal lives. Bane knew better. They were monsters, pure and simple, a plague on mankind that had long since overstayed its welcome. The pact between vampires and hunters was a joke. Eli would come to realize that in time.

They were six hunters in total for this mission—over a dozen when they met up with others the next state over. Bane had considered calling in those reinforcements, but the problem wasn't being outnumbered or outgunned. So far they had been tripped up by timing, lack of information, and mistakes. Now the only part that mattered was time—planning everything to perfection and moving at the exact right moment.

Prom the following weekend gave them that opportunity.

"I know many of you are restless. So much time spent in this tiny town, all for one vampire and his mentor. But consider the evidence before us. They have a hunter under their thrall, blind to their evil. A poor teen boy forced into blood-letting as a retainer. Who knows how they might spread after the example of William and Mallory Leonard?"

The others all murmured agreement, crowded into his motel room, Gamble among them, including another man and two women. Eli remained near the door, arms crossed—silent.

He'd taken the risk of staying in the town longer, he said to keep the hunter and elder vampire on his tail to deviate them from catching wind of the others.

"Any additional information to share, Eli?" Bane asked his nephew.

"Nothing, no evidence to suggest Mavus or his mentor is clean."

Bane held back from smirking, but only just.

"There's also no evidence to suggest they're not," Eli said louder. "Or that Daniels is under any duress, or that the hunter has been glamoured. You keep telling us they're dirty, Uncle," he centered his gaze on Bane. "But what do we have to believe that other than your word?"

Silence settled over the others as they eyed Eli, each other, and finally Bane.

Gamble spoke up. "And my word's not enough together with your own family's? They're a virus in this community, and we're the only thing that can prevent it from spreading. These vampires are so low, they glamoured Daniels to attack me. I almost had to maim the poor kid. I'm lucky I got away before they came back to collect him, or I'd be the next victim lying in a ditch somewhere."

"Only there haven't been any victims recently," Eli said. "How do you account for that?"

"Bane already said. They got Daniels as retainer."

"He couldn't feed both of them and still be standing, and you know it."

"So maybe they're hunting smarter," Gamble spread his arms wide, leaning back against the lone table in the room while the others all perched on the beds, "keeping a lower profile, waiting for us to show our faces again. Maybe they glamoured more retainers out of those other friends of theirs. You saw the bodies the Leonards left behind, and the ones we know had to be Mavus and his mentor."

Of course, Eli and the others didn't know that those victims had been planted by the vampire Bane hired. It slowed things down with her killed, made it difficult to keep up the ruse, but the bodies left in her wake had been enough to bring them here, slaughtering a trail of vampires along the way that made the few humans sacrificed more than worth it.

Bane stared into his nephew's familiar blue eyes, so like his own, and like his sister's, long dead now. How Eli could have sympathy for the creatures that killed his mother, Bane would never know. His own blond hair was scattered with white in his older age. He knew he looked older than he was, after the life he'd lived, practically raising Eli from the age of fourteen, but by then the kid already had so many ideals in his head.

"If the only evidence we have for now points more toward them as heartless killers than not, you know what we have to do," Bane said to Eli directly.

He nodded to Gamble in thanks, then looked to the others. Each of them was a good enough hunter on their own; together they were a force. In time, Bane knew he would be able to sway all of them to the true cause, as he had swayed Gamble. It was time the pact crumbled and all vampires were eradicated. Until he believed the others were ready to hear that, he'd play the game, manipulate the situation, until there was no more doubt that all of these creatures were better off in the ground.

"I don't like the thought of going after the cops," Eli said. "They don't deserve to get caught up in this."

"That's why you're the one playing bait, and Gamble's taking point while the rest of us hold the perimeter and close in," Bane said. "If you're so worried about civilians then you be responsible for keeping them safe. The police are only doing their jobs, I agree. And so are we."

Each of the hunters with him slowly began to nod, starting with Gamble, until only Eli was left. Eventually, he nodded too.

Bane kept his grin in check a second time. "Good. We go over the plan until it's solid. Come Saturday night, this ends."

CHAPTER 30

Everyone in school knew Connor was into me. Everyone. How had I been so blind for so long?

Okay, maybe not everyone—Liz seemed fairly surprised, though happy for us, especially if her talk with me in any way influenced us to get together, which I told her it had. I couldn't call what Connor and I had discovered a fairytale, that might still be a ways off, but he did make my heart race. And as initially awkward as our attempts at flirting had been, or the first few hours trying to navigate around what was and wasn't okay now that we were dating, by the end of the day Monday, everything had gone back to normal.

It felt easy, almost too easy, just being us, being friends, laughing about the same things we always would. Only now, when we wanted to, one of us could lean over to the other and kiss them. I think I was more likely to fail tests that week than any I had after first becoming a vampire.

We didn't get to relax Monday night though. We had visitors. The play was over, and the hunters hadn't made any moves, no sign of them at all. Alec and Wendy had been watching us and the town even more hawk-like than the police, and Tim still had all of them on high alert. No suspects. No leads. Two murders and a school shooting later, they had nothing. Tim looked stiff and straight-lipped every time I saw him, usually only in passing.

"Neither of you have seen any sign of the hunters?" Connor pressed, up in my room that night with Alec and Wendy—snuck in, not by invitation as Mr. Leonard's brother and his lovely wife. That way we had longer to talk, and Alec could zip Wendy out of the house fairly easy without anyone seeing.

"I picked up a minor trail leading out of town," Wendy said, "but it isn't enough to know which direction they went. It's my belief they're holed up in a neighboring town, biding their time and planning, before they make a larger, last ditch effort against us."

"Agreed," Alec said. He smiled widely. "And I'm afraid I haven't caught sight of anyone."

Connor crossed his arms and scowled. "You know, you're pretty useless for some ancient vampire. You're actually only like a couple hundred years old, aren't you, and the crazy act is just to make yourself feel special?"

Alec laughed. The banter between them had a rhythm now. It probably helped that I no longer feared that Alec was some terrible, dark force that might kill Connor if he overstepped his bounds. Alec always smiled more genuinely when Connor called him out or teased him.

"Never ask a gentleman his age, dear boy."

"I thought that was ladies."

"Some gentlemen *are* ladies."

"Are you two quite finished?" Wendy said, hiding a smile that softened her usually tough exterior. "I realize this is a special time for you boys. Graduation coming, your play over and done with, Prom looming. I remember how important those things were at your age. But do not take the hunters' silence to mean surrender. They made a spectacle to take you out, Emery, and failed. That they are biding their time this long means they are putting a detailed plan in place. We must be ready."

"Goodness, my dear, must you spoil their good mood?" Alec said, tossing his hands into the air dramatically. "Such daunting theatrics."

She raised an eyebrow at him. "You realize it isn't necessary to call me 'my dear' when we aren't playing the part of husband and wife."

"But you are such a dear, Wendy, darling, even if I would never be so bold as to call you mine."

"Yet you just did."

"Oh god, are you two flirting?" Connor groaned. "Please don't be flirting. I don't think I could stomach that."

Wendy's smile was dismissive, flustered by all of us, but not by Alec directly, not the way Connor meant. It was more like the way Connor and Aurora interacted. And I could tell what Alec was doing, despite Wendy's best efforts to be serious. Getting us to laugh, and forget ourselves, and not feel quite as much like the world could end at any moment.

"Not to worry, dear boy, we'll leave the flirting to you two," Alec winked.

Connor spun and gaped at me. "You told him?"

"He had not," Alec said in seeming victory, "but that confirms it. Did you need The Talk? Have your parents and lacking sex education in today's system failed you? It's not usually my jurisdiction as a mentor, but if I must…"

"Please don't," Connor held up his hands.

Wendy crossed her arms and turned her head to keep from grinning too obviously, but Alec continued on undeterred.

"The birds and the bees can get quite complicated, you know. You see, sometimes bees like other bees. Sometimes birds like birds. Sometimes bees like birds *and* bees."

"You are the weirdest vampire ever!" Connor burst out laughing.

We laughed so hard, all of us, that I was lucky I caught the faint sound of footsteps coming up the stairs. Mom probably thought we were up here alone, joking around—she looked more relaxed each day she caught us joking rather than wallowing or having just survived some awful hardship. The last thing I needed was for her to find Alec and Wendy up here and start asking real questions. I hadn't even told my parents about dating Connor yet, though they knew we were going to Prom together.

We quieted as I shushed everyone and motioned toward the door, listening. Mom's footsteps passed by and continued down the hallway to her room.

"In all seriousness, there are more pleasant things I wish we could discuss," Alec said, his animated and extravagant figure mellowing as he spoke more softly. "So many over the centuries have called what we are a curse, Emery. That doesn't have to be true. With good friends, and support, a careful handle on your abilities and your needs, the world is open before you with a myriad of possibilities. You don't have to be stunted because of what you are. Clearly, you have not allowed your fate to interfere with claiming a few new horizons," he gestured at Connor.

Connor's pale skin flushed around his jawline. "You did not just call me a horizon."

"But," Alec's smile slowly dropped as he raised his voice and looked at me, "Wendy is not wrong. The hunters will act, and it will be soon. Be vigilant. We will be as well. Keep your police escort ever in sight. It's possible the hunters are waiting for another false sense of security to take hold, and for the police to remove your escort before they attack with less resistance. But if they have another plan in place, we must be ready. If you trust your friends, inform them to be more watchful as well."

Connor and I looked to each other and nodded. Aurora and Jules hadn't brought up my vampirism much, barely at all, especially not at school with others around, but I trusted them to help if we needed them.

Wendy said they should go, get back to patrolling the streets in case the hunters surprised us. I'd thanked her so many times for sticking around, when really, she didn't owe us anything. She always had the same response, that it was her duty, her pleasure and privilege to help. This time I just offered her a grateful nod as she headed for the window.

Alec paused to admire the Cloak and Dagger painting he'd given me. "A light in the darkness is important, but that doesn't mean there is anything inherently bad about the dark. If one existed without the other, well," he looked at me, smiled that more rarely seen, genuine expression, "life would get rather boring, wouldn't it?"

"You are such a sap," Connor said.

"I'm sorry," Alec touched a hand to his chest with an instant shift in countenance, "have I given my blessing on this relationship? If I have, I may have to rescind it."

Connor pushed him, shoving him toward Wendy waiting at the window, and Alec chuckled at him, Wendy all the while shaking her head.

Somehow, these people and the situation in which I'd come to know them, no longer carried only ill-omen. I didn't know quite when it had happened, but I had new friends in Wendy and Alec, not to replace the presence that Mr. and Mrs. Leonard had been in my life, but to build from it, remind me of it, and feel like some of this tragedy came with a blessing too.

~

Connor

Connor tapped the screwdriver on his desk, staring at the somewhat mangled amalgamation before him. He'd finished his base models for an arm and leg early so he could focus on Prom as an extra project. He'd taken parts from both the Rocket-Punch arm and his gun arm prototype, swearing to his mom up and down that, when he brought them to school, he wasn't going to wear either of them, just work on a new design in class. Of course, he hadn't mentioned his plans to turn those arms into a Frankenstein's monster of a prosthetic. That would've definitely garnered more disapproving looks from her.

He still had to figure out how to adequately switch the projecting hand from the Rocket-Punch mechanics to a hinged release. He had to have everything done and ready to receive a new coat of paint by Friday or it would never dry in time for Saturday night.

"Looking good, Connor," Mrs. Swanson said in passing. "Need a hand with anything? You look stumped."

Connor couldn't resist plucking his arm from the desk and waving it at her. "Plenty of hands over here at the moment, Swanny. But A+ on the puns today." The hinged hand flopped backward.

Mrs. Swanson smiled, crossing her arms and inspecting the arm after he set it back on the desk. "What's the hinge for?"

"It's supposed to pop open on command."

"For what? Water gun effect?"

"Something like that. I have everything figured out for the internal workings to get it to fire, but I need a trigger. I don't want to have to use my other hand. Should be able to get it to release in a single motion from the prosthetic itself. But without accidentally triggering it when I don't want to."

"And you of all people haven't taken Spider-Man for inspiration yet?" She grinned at Connor, waiting for her implications to sink in.

Connor's eyes widened when they did. "Swanny, you are an evil genius."

She laughed. "Just don't get me in trouble with whatever it is you're going to have this thing do. If you wear it to school, no super villainy in the hallways."

"Yes, Ma'am."

In the gym during Prom, or maybe outside the school at some point, was an entirely different story.

"I can't wait for you to see it," Connor told Emery that night over their walkie talkies. He was getting ready for bed, and set the walkie down on his dresser so he could change his shirt and remove his prosthetic. Falling asleep with it on risked damaging it during the night, or caused weird sleep lines on his body.

"I'm glad going to Prom as Captain Cold inspired you," Emery crackled back at him. "You sure you can get it completed for this weekend?"

Connor finished tugging his T-shirt over his head and set his prosthetic on the dresser before snatching up the walkie again. "Totally. Wish I could have brought it home to work on tonight, but I had too much other homework. The rest of the week I should be able to though. All of this coming together is totally fate, Em." He meant the arm, but he blushed a little as he realized it also applied to them going to Prom, and actually, finally dating.

"It doesn't really shoot, right?"

"Not bullets, obviously, it's supposed to be my cold gun. Plus, Swanny never would have gone for that, or the school board for that matter. I just wanted a gun arm at some point, I don't care what kind."

"So what's it shoot? Ice cubes."

"Real funny. Halon 1301."

"Uh, what?"

"It'll basically be a fire extinguisher. I should be able to get it to fire off once, whenever we're ready to try and get it on video, assuming we're outside so I don't get in serious trouble. Nick's going to help me with the chemistry part since, well, you know me and chemistry." He chuckled as he recalled the botched exploding teddy bear, the moment he could pinpoint when all of this started, the morning before Emery became a vampire.

He lay down on top of his covers, holding the walkie close to his mouth.

"Well, you couldn't inherit only your dad's good qualities," Emery said.

"As long as I keep my hair. And these dashing good looks, of course."

"You joke, but your looks are pretty dashing. And you got your dad's body."

"Oh my god, you are not implying you think my dad has a hot body."

Emery's laughter cut off halfway, indicating he had released the talk button during his chuckles. "I think *you* have a hot body," he said eventually. "The fact that it came from your dad is beside the point."

Connor grinned, but couldn't help the way the expression started to drop. "Is it weird?"

"Your body?"

"Liking me?"

"What do you mean?"

Connor shifted nervously on the bed. "You've never liked any other guys before."

"Actually…I have. I just never told you about it."

"Seriously?" Connor propped himself up on his elbow. "Why not? And who?"

"No one at school or anything. Just…people. Actors, mostly. Hot guys at the mall. It wasn't very often though, usually I like girls. It's different with you. You're not some sexy stranger I can only look at from a distance," he said with a smile in his voice.

Connor couldn't mirror the expression that he imagined on his friend. "Right."

A brief silence responded before Emery asked, "Does it bother you?"

"What?"

"That I'm not gay."

"No. Of course not. I mean..." Connor let himself flop back onto his pillow, thankful Emery wasn't in the room with him. He doubted he could look him in the eye right now. "Bother isn't the word, it's just..."

"Tell me."

"You said it yourself, Em. Usually you like girls. And it helps knowing there have been other guys, even if just passing crushes, but I can't help feeling sometimes like..." He sighed audibly, taking his hand off the talk button so it wouldn't come across as loud static. Then he said, "Like I have twice as much competition to keep you."

Silence responded. Fifteen seconds felt like a full minute when no one said anything.

"Em?" Connor asked quietly.

A knock at his window made him jump. Emery crouched outside, balanced on the overhang of roof. Connor nearly tumbled off the bed in his haste to respond. He set the walkie on his nightstand as he moved to open the window, though it was a little awkward with only one arm.

"Dude, what if Officer Nustad saw you?"

"He can't see this spot from where he parks," Emery said, climbing in with one smooth, graceful motion, like a cat with his perfect balance and control ever since becoming a vampire. He closed the window behind him.

Connor shuffled back a step. He tried to cross his arms then remembered he couldn't, his good arm eventually flopping back to his side. "I didn't mean anything by that, okay? I'm being stupid."

"Yeah, you are," Emery said, smiling as he crossed to Connor. "You don't have twice as much competition. You don't have any competition."

Heat crept up the back of Connor's neck. Emery was dressed for bed too. T-shirt. Soft, flannel sleep pants. Socks. He'd used his vampire speed to flash across their lawns in socks. There wasn't even any chill coming off of him from being out in the cooler night air, not with how fast he'd gotten there.

Connor was barefoot, in a shirt and boxers. They'd jumped straight to intimate when they confessed their feelings, but that time, he'd kept his arm on. He felt far more naked now without it, even fully dressed.

Emery reached for him, and Connor sagged into the hand that cupped his cheek. A press of lips, just their lips, neither pushing for anything deeper, still made Connor shiver and feel his blush rise further up his face.

"No one else I've ever kissed made me feel the way you do," Emery whispered.

"Ditto," Connor said, pressing his forehead to Emery's, eyes still closed. They leaned forward for another kiss and Emery's other hand found the curve of Connor's missing arm.

He flinched. He didn't mean to, it just felt different when he had one of his prosthetics on. He felt incomplete without it. He was incomplete without it.

"What's wrong?" Emery asked, his dark brows scrunched in concern. "I get why you acted weird the night that hunter broke your arm, but now too? It's just me, Connor. Just us. I've seen you without your arm before. When we were little, there were several years there before you even had a prosthetic."

"I know that." Connor cringed, turned away from Emery. His hand came up to clutch at his stump before he could stop himself. "But now it's been years that I've had one. Sometimes I forget I don't have a normal arm. And seeing it and touching it are totally different."

"Are you saying you wish I was creeped out?" Emery asked incredulously.

"No, god, it's just…I don't know why, but it's different when we're all close and—" Connor flinched again at the feel of Emery at his back, fingers snaking across his arm to cover the hand trying to hide his stump.

"I'm not going to think it's weird now, just because we touch more. There's nothing weird about it. Maybe you can be a little weird with how mad scientist you get with your arm creations, but that's just part of your charm," he chuckled. He pried Connor's fingers away until it was just his hand curled around the smooth, rounded limb. "Besides, you hit me over the head with it all the time. You think I'm suddenly going to start thinking of you as handicapped?"

Connor huffed out a laugh, leaning back against Emery and letting himself relax into the feeling of him touching the one spot Connor sometimes resented about himself. "I hate that word. I'm hardly...handy," he said, wiggling his elbow.

Emery's breath stuttered against the back of his neck. "Jerk. Your prosthetics are awesome. And we can help so many people making a non-profit out of your designs, but you're still you when you're not wearing one."

"You still want to do the non-profit thing?" Connor turned in Emery's hold, breaking the connection of his touch, but wanting to look him in the eyes again.

"Of course. Why would that change?"

The fact that Emery's once again scrunched brow proved that the thought of not following through with their crazy after high school plans had never once crossed his mind, made it impossible for Connor to do anything but kiss him. This time, when Emery reached for the curve of skin at the end of his missing arm, Connor didn't flinch away.

EPISODE 31

Connor

The night Emery snuck in through Connor's window was so branded into his mind, every day afterward he expected for the other shoe to drop—more than he had after their night in Aurora's bedroom. Eventually, Emery would realize his mistake. Like someone else. Like some girl again. Grow annoyed and overwhelmed by Connor's insecurities. Or the hunters would just bomb their houses.

None of those things happened.

There were tests and activities, the usual humdrum of high school life. Some nights Connor had homework. Most nights he worked on his prosthetic for Prom. He didn't get to spend much time with friends outside of classes, including Emery, but by Friday the paint job on his new arm was drying. Once Saturday came around, he couldn't wait to show Emery how his outfit had all come together, especially the arm.

Jules and Aurora had elected to get ready at Connor's house. "It's not any fun alone," Jules had said, "plus I want some male opinions on this dress!"

Aurora had followed through with her Gaia idea, Mother Earth, goddess of all things, decked out in deep blues, and purple, and shimmering browns like some glorious field of flowers. It flowed around her, sleeveless and willowy. Jules, however, had gone with a more Norse goddess look, mostly white with gold trim, and some of her Renaissance Festival leather armor pieces for greaves and vambraces. She'd made a faux lightning bolt out of Styrofoam she could use as a staff—and throw at people.

Connor and Emery both sat back and watched the girls model their outfits, fuss over each other's hair, get their makeup just right, before Emery excused himself into the bathroom to put on his outfit. Connor hid behind the door of his closet to do the same.

He switched out his prosthetic first. It was heavier than he was used to, but nothing like an actual fire extinguisher, since he didn't want nearly that amount of foam or pressure going off. It had just enough Halon 1301 to give a small burst once, mimicking the cold gun effect Connor was going for. After tonight, though, he'd remove that portion and consider this a seasonal arm. It was perfect for the holidays, painted in various shades of blue and silver, with sparkling snowflakes all down the forearm. He'd even pulled out some of his old blue LED lights so that every crevice glowed.

It was basically the equivalent of having bedazzled himself, Aurora said. He didn't mind. The arm had turned out bad-ass.

He just hoped the rest of the outfit didn't look too absurd. He wasn't exactly the suit and tie type. He could wear a T-shirt with a flannel or hoodie over it for the rest of his life. Emery was the one who pulled off high-collared sweaters or Henley's with natural GQ poise.

Connor tugged at his tie, picked at a snowflake on the vest, and rolled his shoulders in the confines of the blue tux. He had the left sleeve rolled up somewhat to better show off his arm. He looked a little unbalanced like that, but the arm was so cool, it was worth it. Everything fit immaculately—his mother had made sure of that, having hemmed and fitted both boys' suits during the week. Connor felt like James Bond, but even when he bit his lip and observed himself in the full length mirror along his closet, he wondered if he looked even remotely that good. He imagined Aurora laughing. He imagined everyone laughing.

"Connor Daniels, stop fixing your guy liner, and come out from behind that door!" Aurora said. She and Jules waited patiently on his bed—as patiently as Aurora did anything.

Connor steeled himself to just present the finished product to the room with one swift motion, when he heard his bedroom door open.

"Ready?" Emery called.

"Connor's holding out," Jules said.

"But you, Flash, look good enough to eat," Aurora added. "Very snazzy, Mavus. Come out here already and get a look at your boyfriend, Captain Cold! Before Lady Thor and I claim him for ourselves!"

Those old butterflies were back, like a swarm of hornets in Connor's stomach. He smoothed his hands down over his ice blue vest one last time, before taking a deep breath, and stepping out into the open. He spread his arms wide as he came into view of the girls on the bed and Emery standing beside it. He also flourished his blinged out arm a little. He'd never been so proud of one of his prosthetics.

"Well?" The hornets buzzed and churned in Connor's gut when none of them said anything.

Emery looked tailored to perfection. Connor had seen him in suits before because of the many plays and musicals. This one held much more character than any of those. Burgundies and reds were a great color on him, with his dark complexion and green eyes. The little yellow lightning bolt accents on the vest and the yellow tie solidified the character he was personifying, but the snug fit, his gelled and tousled hair, the way one of his hands clenched as he looked at Connor...

"What?" Connor said, darting his eyes to the carpet.

Aurora twirled her finger in a vague motion at his body. "I'm just cataloging this for later."

Jules snorted and smacked her arm.

"So it's good?" Connor asked, trying and failing to not glance up too expectantly at Emery.

"It's good," Jules nodded.

"Really? You're not just messing with me? You swear I don't look ridiculous?" Connor shifted and tugged at the bottom of the vest.

Emery stepped forward, and his blank expression blossomed into a grin. His clenched fist loosed as he reached for Connor's prosthetic and inspected the design, the paint job, the smattering of snowflakes. "This is amazing. You look amazing."

"You should totally clean up more often, Con-Man," Aurora said.

If it got Emery to look at him like that, Connor might take that advice. He felt heat in his cheeks, he always did whenever Emery's eyes lingered on him, but it felt highly inappropriate when he was portraying Captain Cold.

He tugged his hand away and pointed it palm out at Emery with a smirk. "Hands off the goods, Flash, or I might have to ice you."

The girls giggled.

Emery squared his stance, settling into the act as well. "You'll have to be faster than me first, Cold," he said, and zipped forward using his vampiric speed, not having to hide it from Jules and Aurora.

They giggled harder as Connor's prosthetic froze around Emery, caught up in his arms before he could act or even blink, and felt soft lips press lightly to his.

"Save it for the after party, boys!" Aurora said. "Let's go. Jules convinced my dad to let her drive his Charger. Screw limos. Did you see that baby in the driveway?"

Connor had. It was black with a red stripe down the hood. But at the moment, he cared more about the way Emery's hand pressed to the silky material of his vest before he pulled away, licking his lips after their brief kiss.

"Driving the T-bird, Con-Man?" Aurora asked once they were headed downstairs.

"Nope. Dad's letting me take the motorcycle. Screw limos indeed." He curled in the fingers of his plastic hand and offered it to her for a fist bump.

Connor's mom stopped them for a few photos before they could escape. The official photos weren't enough, she said, and also told them to be sure to take plenty of candids with their phones. Soon the girls had driven off in the Charger, cheering loudly out their open windows as they sped away, and Connor handed the extra motorcycle helmet to Emery.

Normally, he would have worn his dad's, but since his mother's was blue and his father's red, it made more sense to match their outfits. Connor's mom got a couple quick shots of them on the bike before his dad waved them off and pulled her back into the house. Officer Nustad followed at a respectable distance once they pulled out of the driveway.

Alec lay in wait for them at the school, watching the exterior with the other officers, but planning to go inside later and act as a sort of invisible chaperone. "Someone needs to make sure you young people aren't doing drugs or grinding on the dance floor," he'd said.

Wendy would act as a secondary escort on the way there. Emery had texted her just as they were leaving, so she knew to follow on a corresponding path one block over.

What worried Connor was the thought of the hunters holding out until after graduation. The police would surely back off then, figure it must be safe enough to leave the boys alone, and then— BAM. Maybe the hunters would follow them to college, attack on campus, away from their tiny town.

But tonight, with Connor's mind focused on Prom, on him and Emery decked to the nines for as public a date as they had yet had, he never saw the ambush coming.

"Connor!" Emery called over the roar of the bike as they drove down the mostly empty street along the edge of the park.

"What is it!?"

"It's Nustad! He's not..." Emery's voice drowned out a moment as he turned to look over his shoulder, "...he's not behind us anymore!"

"What do you—"

A clatter and blur of something tumbling out onto the road was the only warning Connor received before the bike jerked forward and flipped, end over end. Time slowed as Connor sailed through the air, not breathing, not able to concentrate on what was happening, other than anticipating the moment when he would land and crack his helmet or break several bones. He hadn't been going fast enough to kill them in a fiery crash but there were worse things.

Connor huffed as he landed, his shoulder jolting from the sudden stop, but no other pain assaulted him. His helmet was secure and in place. Nothing felt broken. He looked up and saw the black tint of Emery's visor on the fittingly red helmet, equally intact, and finally felt the warmth of Emery's arms around him, holding him in a crouched bridal carry. He'd caught Connor, saved him, while the bike skittered and rolled several feet away from them.

Emery set Connor down and pulled the helmet from his head. "Are you okay?" His eyes glowed bright green and frantic.

Connor shucked his own helmet off. "Barely banged up, thanks to you. What happened? Where's Nustad?"

"I don't know." Emery looked around the dark, empty street. It shouldn't be this empty, not even with their police escort mysteriously missing. They'd landed just off the curb leading into the trees of the park, the denser woods where they'd first met Wendy. "I noticed it was darker, that his lights were gone, and when I looked back…nothing. Look at that stuff." He pointed to something like plastic netting with hard protruding triangles sticking up in the road. No wonder they had flipped.

"We better get out of here before whoever threw that makes another move." Connor could feel eyes on him from every direction, but he didn't know if it was legit or just paranoia. That thing in the road looked like hunter gear.

"We'll have to leave the bike. I'll run us to the school, as fast as I can."

Connor nodded, readying himself for Emery to scoop him up and take off at max speed.

Just before he saw movement in the trees behind them.

"Look out!" he called, trying to shove Emery out of the way. But the next thing thrown at them wasn't a weapon.

Emery spun around to face the trees just as Connor recognized what had rolled toward their feet and closed his eyes before the bright white of the flash bomb could blind them both.

~

I couldn't see. The explosion of light was like the device Wendy had used on me, but so much worse. My eyes stung, and I groaned as I reached out for Connor.

"Come on!" he called to me, gripping my arm. He yanked me behind him at a run. "It's okay, I can see! Just keep moving!"

I obeyed, trusting him to lead me through the woods. I only knew he had dragged us into the trees because I felt the occasional brush of leaves against my legs or the top of my hair. If only I hadn't looked and been blinded, I could have gotten us out of there in seconds, safely to the school where Alec could have intervened. I just had to hope that Wendy was on our tail as planned.

"Call Wendy!" I said.

"Already dialing!" Connor's fingers clung tighter to my wrist. We moved at a constant, forward momentum, until I heard his breath increasing to the point that he'd soon need to slow down or stop, his heartrate as loud to my senses in my blind state as my own, thrumming in my ears.

The blurry dark blobs of trees started to materialize, spots dancing in front of my eyes. I still needed Connor's direction, but I guessed where he was headed. If we could get to the hill in the center of this part of the park, where kids often sledded down in winter, the school wasn't much farther beyond that, and it provided plenty of cover.

"Wendy!" Connor cried in relief into his phone. "Thank god. Yes, we're okay. In the woods, in the park. Right, where we first—ah!" He cried out as a loud crack sounded as if his phone had exploded. "Shit!" He tugged me along faster, and I distinctly felt something crunch beneath my feet.

"What happened?!"

"Arrow! Keep moving!"

Little by little my vision cleared. I could see the hill now, only a few yards in front of us. Then, in my periphery, I saw movement darting on a parallel path off to our right. The large shape of a crossbow lifted with a fresh bolt aimed right at us.

I gripped Connor around the waist and zipped us several yards forward out of the line of fire, where we tripped at the base of the hill and nearly tumbled. I could almost see again, but not clearly enough to take off for the school. I needed thirty more seconds—just thirty more seconds.

When we righted ourselves to turn and face the approaching hunter, I ushered Connor behind me, but he pushed back against my nudging and stayed at my side.

"You," Connor growled. I couldn't make out the details of the hunter, but I guessed this was the same one who had attacked Connor before, maybe the one who shot me at the school.

"Clever boys, but we've outmaneuvered you," the hunter said, voice low and cold. "Your escort's on a wild goose chase. Your hunter friend? Too far away. And the perimeter of this place is surrounded. We've set traps along every conceivable way out. And you're not getting back the way you came in without going through me. Doubt you're fast enough for that." He centered the crossbow on my heart.

"Wait—" I tried, raising one hand, hoping that somehow I could talk him down, because I didn't trust my sight or my speed to race toward him before that bolt released.

"Not interested," he said—and fired.

The sound of air being cut made my breath catch. I froze, waiting for the same awful pain I'd felt at the school, only worse, because this bolt wouldn't miss. I only realized why there was no pain when the last of the spots in my vision faded and I saw the back of Connor's buzzed head.

"Shit," the hunter hissed.

"Connor...?"

He slumped. I caught him under the arms, slowly lowering him to the ground as his body went limp. I had to rest him on his side, because his back—his back had four inches of the end of a crossbow bolt sticking out of it, and nearly as much sticking out the front. Crimson was already seeping from the point of impact, staining his vest and button down.

My arms shook as I looked up at the hunter only feet from us, frantically trying to reload his crossbow. It was a repeating model, but that had been his last bolt—the bolt sticking out of Connor's chest.

A roar erupted from me before I registered forming the sound. As my fangs lengthened in my mouth, and fire surged through my gut, I leapt over Connor. Rich, heady blood poured over my tongue as I sank my teeth into the hunter's neck, cutting off his cry for help. The crossbow clattered to the ground. The prey in my arms seized.

All I saw was red.

EPISODE 32

Feeding from Connor had never felt like this—no limits, no reason to hold back. I felt filled, warmth spreading to every part of me as I drank without care of how much I took. I clenched my teeth down tighter, willing him to feel pain, worse than just what was on the surface, but terrible, bone-deep through the glamour.

He screamed, then gurgled, then fell silent as I drank, and drank, and drank...

"Emery, stop!"

No. He needed to pay. He had to pay for what he did to Connor. Connor...lying in the grass with a bolt through his chest because of this man. And others too. There were others to blame. I'd kill them all when I found them.

"Emery, please!" A gloved hand gripped by shoulder, but I whipped my arm back, shoving the owner several feet away from me.

The hunter's heart was slowing, I could feel it. His body not even able to hold itself up, spasming as he lost blood faster and faster.

"Emery..." the voice softened, pleading. No hand accompanied it this time but it grew closer as it spoke. "You don't want this. Connor is alive. You can still help him. Don't prove them right for what they've done tonight. Please. Don't be the monster they were looking for."

I howled as I pulled my fangs from the hunter's neck. Only then did I feel the tears on my cheeks. Only then did I feel how I was shaking as hard as the man in my arms.

I dropped him, the blur of red fading from my vision as I looked down and saw him seize slightly before going still, eyes closed, wound not bleeding freely but smeared with scarlet. His chest rose faintly as he breathed, shallow but steady. I hadn't killed him. But I'd almost…almost…

"Emery," Wendy's voice came more solidly now, her gloved hand back on my shoulder. This time, I didn't push her away. I blinked tear-filled eyes at her. Her expression was neutral, but I saw in her dark eyes the relief and sympathy. "Connor is conscious. Stay with him. I discovered the hunter's vehicle nearby. I'll drive it right to you so we can bring him to the hospital."

"But what if I—"

"You can't speed him there in his condition. Stay with him. Keep him awake. And don't remove the bolt."

I nodded, and darted around Wendy toward Connor's fallen form as she moved to the hunter. I jerked my head back to her when I heard the flip of a switchblade, and watched her slice the hunter's neck to hide the puncture wound. Then the jingling of keys as she raided his pockets.

My eyes returned to the blue tuxedo. To the two feet of crossbow bolt through Connor's torso. "Connor…" I said, crouching by him and placing my hand on his arm.

His honey colored eyes lifted toward me, but seemed to look through me, unfocused. "Em…" He groped forward with his flesh and blood hand, his prosthetic trapped beneath him. I took it, lacing our fingers together. "Don't kill him…please don't kill him…"

"I didn't. He's…" I glanced back, torn between wanting the hunter to pull through and not knowing if I truly cared. "He's alive. But he did this to you, and I…I couldn't think. I didn't know what else to do."

"I know…" he said, smiling faintly. "But it's n-not so bad. Doesn't even…hurt. Which…probably isn't a good thing," he cringed.

I looked at where the bolt had entered, between one of his ribcages, I'd guess, under the lungs but above the organs. Or so I hoped. If I was right, he could survive this, but Connor was skinny, compactly built. That bolt might have hit anything on the way through.

The rumble of a van alerted me to our surroundings again, and I looked up to see Wendy navigating through the trees. I had no idea what she'd done with her bike. It didn't matter. If the hunters had really surrounded this place, waiting for that other hunter to make his move, backup could be coming any moment.

"You'll be fine," I said to Connor, squeezing his hand. "Your mom's the best nurse in town."

"She's not on...call tonight."

"I think they'll let her take an extra shift."

He snorted. "Hope it makes a nice...battle scar."

Wendy ran up to us, the van parked as close as she could get, back doors wide open with an empty backend, no seats, and plenty of space. "Get the hunter in first. Then Connor, as carefully as you can."

"The hunter?" I frowned at her.

"Do you want to leave him to die? We could leave him, hope his fellows find him and take the risk to bring him to the hospital themselves, so we can catch them. But you'll put his life at risk. Is that what you want?"

I did. I really did. But I knew it wasn't the right answer.

Connor's hand shifted in my hold, squeezed my fingers as I'd squeezed his. His eyes couldn't quite focus on my face. "It's okay, Em," he said.

I clenched my eyes shut, because it wasn't. It really wasn't.

I pulled away, patted his hand, then dashed to grab the hunter as fast as I could and deposited him in the van, pushed over to one side to leave more room for Connor. I wasn't as gentle as I could be; the one piece of revenge I allowed myself, besides what I'd already done to him. Then I returned for Connor. At first I moved to lift him carefully, slowly, but he hissed, and Wendy placed a hand on my back.

"Quick as you can," she said. "Careful, but quick. He'll feel less pain, and it isn't far enough to aggravate the wound as much."

I nodded, and darted with Connor to the van as swiftly as I had the hunter, though I laid him down more softly, still on his side, facing the wall of the van, so he wouldn't have to see the hunter with him. I crouched into the corner by his head, as Wendy shut the doors behind us and got into the driver's side door.

"Keep him talking, Emery, the hospital's not far," she said.

"T-Tell me," he said, groping for my hand again. I let him have it. "Does she know…Nustad…what happened?"

"They cut him off at an intersection, rammed him after you turned the corner," Wendy said, barreling back through the trees. Every bump and jerk of the vehicle had me clinging to Connor tighter. "Then from what I could tell before I continued after you, they sped off, luring him to the chase. With one of them in each vehicle, and our friend back there, I'm guessing they had three hunters stationed at the various sides of the park, one intended to move in and be backup. Though why backup didn't show, I don't know. It isn't like a hunter group this organized to leave the final kill to one man. Even if some of them are lying to the others, someone else should have been there to finish you off."

"Cheery…isn't she?" Connor laughed. Then coughed. Then cringed and shivered, as his eyelids fluttered.

I put my other hand to his cheek. "Eyes on me. You'll be fine. This is nothing. Straight through. They'll fix it. They'll fix it…"

"It would be pretty…mean…if my love story w-was a tragedy."

"Don't say that. It won't be. It's not."

"It's okay," he said again—he kept saying that, even though his eyes looked through me. "S'okay, because…I got to have you…" He pulled his hand from mine and reached for my face the same way I was holding his. He missed at first, so I used my other hand to help him.

Then it hit me. "Did you just steal that from *Starship Troopers?*"

"D-Dude…I keep telling you…best movie ever," Connor said, smiling.

I couldn't help it—I laughed. And Connor laughed. Before he coughed again. A sniffle came next, from me. I could feel the tears building even through our laughter.

Connor's eyelids fluttered again.

"Stay with me…please…"

"We're here."

I looked up to see the bright lights of the hospital as we pulled in. Wendy practically dove out the door, running inside to alert someone to bring a stretcher.

"Him first," I said, when two large EMTs arrived to lift Connor out of the van. One of them was Doug. His full lips weren't smiling this time when his eyes met mine. They wheeled Connor out, and I followed close behind them, not caring what happened to the hunter, though I knew they'd be back for him, someone would be back for him.

I wasn't family. I couldn't go back with Connor. But Wendy was there, to sit with me in the waiting room. Our parents arrived in stages. First Connor's, his mother in her scrubs, having changed at home to be ready, bursting into the emergency room to help however she could. Then mine. All of them hugged me, held too tight but not tight enough, talking at me. I knew I talked back, explained as best I could, though Wendy stepped in.

She'd been out for a ride. Saw our accident. Saw the man they'd brought in when he attacked us. She came to our aid, and together she and I took him down, cutting his neck, which seemed to have caused significant blood loss. Then we'd brought everyone here in the perpetrator's own vehicle.

"So this is the shooter? The murderer?" Paul asked, eyes frantic despite the calm way he sat, hands folded between his legs.

"Lord only knows," Wendy said. "Hopefully it's over now."

They thanked her. It was easier that they knew her, or thought they did, as Alec's wife. It made a convenient truth, but it didn't matter when Wendy and I both knew more hunters were out there, and nothing was really over.

I felt like a weight lifted from pressing down on my chest when Georgia came running out, crying but smiling, to tell us that Connor would be okay. The bolt really had missed everything vital, right between his ribs, too low to nick his lungs. He'd recover fast. He was young, resilient, and the shot had been everything one could hope for in a wound like that.

"Who uses a crossbow? On kids!" My dad shook his head.

The hunter would live as well, but his blood loss meant he was still unconscious.

My parents went to the cafeteria to get Paul some coffee. I stayed behind, watching them finish up on Connor through the glass. I could only barely see into where he was, since the curtains were drawn, but Georgia had tugged them aside just enough to give me piece of mind, catching my gaze with a warm smile. Her confidence made me feel confident. Connor would be fine.

I still stood at the glass feeling helpless. And tense. And guilty.

"I would have killed him," I said, when Wendy walked up beside me.

Alec had joined us after we learned Connor would pull through, having tried to catch the hunters in action taking Officer Nustad around town, but by the time he'd discovered the police cruiser, the hunters were long gone.

"If you hadn't been there to stop me…"

"But I was, Emery. And he'll be fine, much as he doesn't deserve it," she said.

"All this time, I just didn't want to be a killer. Didn't want to hurt Connor, or anyone I care about. But it still happened. It wasn't me, but it's because of me. And then I turned right around and proved I am a killer…one moment of losing control away from being a killer like them."

"Emery," Alec said, the pair of them bookending me as we stared through the glass. They were finishing dressing Connor's wound. He was unconscious now, put to sleep while they worked. "Control is something that must be honed. Nurtured. You're no different than anyone who's ever reacted when a loved one was put at risk, maybe a little more brutally than you would normally, but it doesn't make you a killer. Or a monster. Just human, ironically enough."

Wendy's hand came up to rest on my shoulder. "Do you know the difference between a predator and a killer, Emery? A predator hunts to survive. A killer does so because they enjoy it. Don't confuse the two. You are better if you choose to be better. I've known that only too well over the years. Good and bad exists on both sides. And you are not the latter."

I knew their worldviews were broader than mine, their combined experiences dwarfing anything I could have thrown back at them, but it didn't make me feel any better. Because when it came down to it, I was more upset that Connor had been hurt than the hunter. And I cared more that he might think of me as a killer than I cared that I'd almost killed the man who hurt him.

Georgia caught my gaze through the glass again. She gripped the curtain; she had to close it now. I nodded, focusing one last time on his unmoving form before it was closed off from me, and the way he looked stripped down to his navy suit pants, even his arm removed and set aside.

"He looks so breakable like that," I said. "Not just because he's hurt, but...without his arm. He feels vulnerable without it, I know he does. But it's stupid of me to think he is. He's not. He isn't handicapped. He doesn't need me to protect him. He's the one who protected me..." My voice cracked, choked off, and all the wetness came pouring from my eyes again.

"Now, now, Emery," Alec said, "without one of those fantastic prosthetics of his, I doubt he considers himself at all *handy*."

I stared at him, because...really? How was he my mentor when he was so much more like Connor? I laughed in response to his crazed grin. Wiped my face. Took a breath. He patted my shoulder as Wendy's hand finally released the other. We turned from the glass to find seats again in the waiting room. It helped that they didn't need to leave, that their presence just made mine and Connor's parents like them both more as kindly 'neighbors'.

"What do we do now?" I asked whichever one of them would reply.

"Keep on as before," Alec said.

"And track down the remaining hunters," Wendy added. "The one you spared might yet yield some answers."

"Doubtful, but I might be able to assist with that."

I jerked to my feet the moment Wendy did, because while I hadn't seen this hunter before, I recognized Wendy's description of him.

Dark skin. Blue eyes.

He walked toward us from around the corner of the hallway into the waiting room, hands raised. His tightly coiled hair was close to his head, though not buzzed like Connor's. His face scruffy. Wearing jeans, a T-shirt, button down, and leather jacket. His eyes were hypnotic against his darker skin.

"And why, dear boy," Alec said, rising as well, but slowly, not having jerked upright with me and Wendy, "would we trust you?"

The man lowered his arms as he reached us, and turned his attention directly on me. "Because I'm the one who shot you at the school. And missed—on purpose."

EPISODE 33

Eli Bane. He sounded like someone out of a comic book—Connor would have approved. He was a lifelong hunter, part of a family of hunters. He had the story Connor had expected of Wendy. His family killed by vampires, raised afterward by his uncle, who had orchestrated the attack tonight.

Eli was supposed to be the driver of one of the cars distracting Officer Nustad, but he'd convinced another hunter to trade with him, putting him as Gamble's backup. Gamble, the hunter who'd attacked Connor once before, and who had almost killed him tonight.

Eli didn't believe that his uncle had planned all this knowing I wasn't evil, didn't believe the story the vampire we killed told us, unless she meant only Gamble had hired her. It had to be Gamble; not his uncle; his uncle would never do such things.

"But he'll see now," he said to me. "You brought Gamble here to be saved when you could have killed him. You had every right to defend yourself, to attack when he shot your friend, but you resisted. My uncle will understand that, he'll see the truth, and we can call all of this off. The others will listen too."

"You sound fairly certain," Alec said. "Everyone is certain when it comes to the fealty of family. What if you're wrong?"

"I'm not."

"Alrighty then. Why don't you run along and arrange a meeting with your uncle? We'll sort this out together."

"Alec," Wendy spoke up.

"What?" He turned to her. To me. "Don't you trust him? It's really your call, Emery. Would you prefer we take a different path? Or shall we hear the hunters out?"

The anger in me thinking about Connor, how easily he might have died tonight, swirled in my stomach. But this hunter wasn't to blame. If he was anywhere near as skilled as Gamble, or Wendy, then he had to be telling the truth when he said he'd missed the shot he took at me on purpose. I didn't want more bloodshed, more enemies, if we could find another way.

My parents would be back soon. Paul too. Georgia could come out of that room any minute. So I looked at Eli steadily.

"Mr. and Mrs. Leonard never hurt anyone. Mr. Leonard turned me because he panicked. Because you forced him into a corner and he couldn't see any other way out. I know that doesn't excuse it, but neither of them deserved to die. I don't. Connor sure as hell doesn't. So if you're serious about making this right, then talk to your uncle. Wendy's different than what I'd expect of hunters. Maybe you are too. So prove it. I'll give you my number, and once you have a time and a place, we'll meet. I just want this to be over."

"So do I, Emery." He smiled, one side of his face a little more animated than the other, a little more dimpled, as if the other half was designated for regret. "So do I."

~

Connor

Connor opened his eyes slowly, feeling numb and fuzzy around the edges from forced sleep. He didn't usually take sleeping pills, but this felt like waking from a Nyquil binge. His chest ached, right at the center groove between the sides of his ribcage. His right hand lifted from the bed automatically when he remembered why. It barely rose two inches, connected with tubes at the crease in his elbow.

"Connor!"

Thank god. "Em." Connor breathed relief when he turned his head and saw his friend—his boyfriend—rise from a chair in the corner of the room and approach the bed. "They let you in?"

"They moved you out of the ER. Your mom said it was okay. It's been hours." He still wore his burgundy suit pants, but only the red button down shirt remained of the rest of his outfit.

It was then that Connor remembered how ruined his own Prom outfit was now, the tie sporting an impressive hole, not to mention the likely stain of crimson over the tie, vest, and shirt. "Those hunters better reimburse me," he grumbled, even as Emery placed a hand on his upper arm. His prosthetic was missing from his left side.

"They had to remove it," Emery said, reading Connor's mind like always. "It's fine. It's right over there." He gestured to the corner of the room where Connor's clothes and his Captain Cold arm were neatly stacked.

"Oh god," Connor realized, "it's been hours? How many hours? Those bastards made us miss Prom! Our senior year! When I finally had the chance to go with you…" He trailed, succumbing to a smile with the way Emery smiled back at him.

"I'm sure it's still going. It's only 10PM. Aurora was ready to head right over once word spread about what happened, but I told everyone to enjoy themselves, since the hospital probably wouldn't like a bunch of high schoolers in formalwear showing up all at once. She said she and a few others are still planning to try to sneak in to see you once Prom ends at 11PM. I guess she's going to convince Tim to be their personal chaperone since there's still technically a curfew. Of course, everyone thinks it's safe now that the murderer was caught."

"Caught? Not dead?" Connor cringed as soon as he said it.

Emery cast his eyes down at the side of the hospital bed. "It was close. If Wendy hadn't… He'll make it. They have an officer posted with him, but he's still unconscious after so much…blood loss."

"Hey," Connor prodded until Emery looked up at him again. "Don't guilt trip yourself over him. You stopped. Like you always stop. And honestly, if our positions were reversed, even with Wendy showing up to play Buffy and save the day, I don't know if I would have been as altruistic. When he had that thing pointed at you, and I knew he was going to fire, that he didn't care, wouldn't listen, I just…"

Emery chuckled. "Imagine that."

"What?"

He stroked his thumb across the top of Connor's hand. Met his gaze directly. "Here we were playing at hero and villain, and instead, tonight? Captain Cold saved The Flash."

Laughter bubbled out of Connor. "Well they are a special brand of nemeses, you know. So what else did I miss?"

Emery disentangled his hand gently and stood up straight. He explained about Eli, about meeting up with the hunters, with Alec and Wendy as back up. "But he hasn't called yet. I still think it will be tonight. I have to go. We have to make sure they won't try anything. If the rest of the people are as bad as Gamble, they might come after you again too. I can't risk that."

"So instead you'll risk meeting them on their terms? I don't like this, Em. How do you know you can trust this Eli guy?"

"I don't. But we have to try something."

"Wish I could go with you."

"You just worry about recovering. I'm actually impressed. You seem pretty okay for someone who was impaled earlier tonight."

Connor shifted in the bed, staring down at the IV in his arm. "Whatever pain meds Mom's got me hooked up with sure do help. Plus, if nothing vital was hit, I'll be back on my feet in a week."

"Right," Emery huffed.

"It's true. Ten days max if I take it slow. I bet I can walk myself to the bathroom already. You know, once I yank this annoying business out of my arm." He shook his arm slightly. He didn't like feeling constricted and confined to the bed.

"I should find your mom and dad," Emery said, "let them know you woke up. I think they were going to call Ryn."

"Oh God no, she better not come home early from college just for this. Although, if it cons a better graduation present out of her…" He tilted his head thoughtfully.

Emery laughed, grinned wide, and leaned over the bed, hands resting where Connor's missing arm left space. "I really don't know what I'd do without you."

"Me either. But I know it'd be boring." His mouth, relaxed into a smile, went slack as Emery descended toward him.

The first press of lips forced a short intake of breath. It was all still so new, no matter how many times they'd kissed since the first one. Connor would never take the thrill of the sensation for granted. The soft press, the faint flick of Emery's tongue as their mouths opened just enough to connect more deeply. He sighed into the feeling, maybe more tingly than usual thanks to the pain meds and whatever else was coursing through his veins, but he knew that the brunt of what he felt was still all because of Emery.

"Guess that confirms that theory."

Connor gasped as Emery jerked upright out of the kiss. They both turned toward the open door to see John and Kay looking in on them—a half bewildered, half pleased grin on Emery's mother's face.

"You two say you're going to Prom as friends, and then this?" She planted her hands on her hips. "Why the big secret? How long has this been going on?"

Connor doubted she'd accept the truth that they honestly had been too busy to think about sitting their parents down and explaining that their friendship had progressed another direction over the weekend.

Emery still tried. "We forgot? It seriously just happened, Mom, we didn't think to tell you."

"Just happened as in tonight? Because otherwise you have no excuses." Her words didn't carry any bite or accusation though. They couldn't, not with the way she was smiling.

"It's that whole you and my mom always wanted to share grandchildren thing, isn't it?" Connor said, completely straight-faced.

Kay mimed the expression and tone right back at him. "That, and you two have been pretty obvious the last few weeks. Did you really think we wouldn't figure it out?"

"I will bodily remove her if you two need a moment," John offered.

Kay elbowed him in the side. "Except *your* parents are on their way back to the room, Connor, and they will be harder to remove."

"It's okay," Connor said, turning from the pair just inside the door to look at Emery—at Emery in just a red button down and burgundy dress pants like deep, rich blood. Connor didn't mind though, the fitting color, in the strangest year of his life where his best friend had to become something out of his favorite horror movies before they finally hooked up. "We're good. Right, Em?"

Emery's brilliant white smile answered him. "We're good. I'll keep you updated."

"Do. Like, seriously, dude, text me, I don't care how late. I…have my phone, right?" Connor looked around frantically, remembering that he was stripped down to just his own suit pants and confined to a bed.

Kay walked over to Connor's clothes and produced his cell phone from out of the pile. "I'll set it on the table next to the bed, but sound off. What could you two possibly have to talk about yet later tonight that can't wait until morning? You should be getting rest, Mister."

Emery and Connor both paused the exact same brief beat of time before answering in unison, "Prom."

"Yeah," Connor said, "we missed Senior Prom, Kay! I need juicy details, and Em's the only one who can grill everyone for some. It'll help make the night feel more normal. Though it doesn't make up for missing out on showing off those awesome outfits…" he pouted, not needing to feign his disappointment; that part was real.

"Your mom got several wonderful photos at least," Kay said. "I already saw them. Well, even before the accident. She posted them on Facebook pretty much immediately."

"Of course she did." John rolled his eyes.

Emery's phone beeped to indicate a text message. He pulled it out and managed to keep his eyes from widening too obviously, but Connor noticed, Connor understood. "You know, Mom, Dad, I hate for all of us to leave, but since Connor's awake, Tim sort of wants us to congregate at home. There's an officer waiting to tail us."

Connor knew it was more than that. An officer likely was waiting for them, but as soon as Emery was home, he'd use his abilities to sneak out of the house and meet up with Wendy and Alec.

Connor gestured for Emery to lean down toward him, kissed him again, but used the proximity to whisper, "Text me every half hour. If you forget or something happens, I'm coming after you."

"It'll be fine," Emery assured him, amusement in his eyes more than worry. "See you soon, Connor."

"Yeah, Em. Be safe."

Connor had the sinking feeling that even his best wishes wouldn't be enough.

EPISODE 34

Eli told us to meet him behind the middle school where we'd killed the other vampire, and where Connor had first encountered Gamble. The hills and trees around the area hid it from surrounding roads and neighborhood windows. We wouldn't attract attention, but that could also be bad if we needed help.

I told my parents I would just be up in my room on the phone for a bit and then crash to get some rest. I hoped neither of them came in to check on me. Within five minutes, I was out my window. I messaged Connor once the first half hour had passed.

    It'll be fine. Heading to the meetup now.
    You don't know how many there are.
    I have Alec and Wendy.
    Just be careful, Em.

Wendy stayed with me as we approached slowly from the school. Alec did a swift pass around the perimeter before returning to us.

"Five of them in total, including our dear Eli," he said, matching our pace once he materialized out of the shadows. "No hidden sniper I can see. They're well-armed."

"That merely means they are cautious," Wendy said.

"Yeah." I nodded, trying to keep the nerves in my gut under control.

These people had tried to kill me. Eli had tried to kill me. And now I'd nearly killed one of them. What if the others didn't see it the way Eli did, and saw me as more of a threat than as someone who brought an injured enemy into the ER?

Eli and who I assumed to be his uncle stood in the center as we approached, the other three hunters forming a semi-circle behind them, two women and one man. Eli's uncle was Caucasian, but their eyes were the same. Bane's mostly white hair and fine lines over his face made him look grizzled and hard, while Eli still had some softness. Unless it was all an act.

"That's close enough," Bane spoke once we were about three yards away.

The other hunters all readied their weapons, keeping them trained on us, me and Alec in particular. Bane's canvas jacket and mostly earth toned clothing wasn't at all grimy or torn. He took pride in his appearance for someone who spent most of his time out in the elements.

"So you put Gamble in the hospital and then ask for a parley," Bane said.

"Uncle…"

"No, Eli, I'd like an explanation from the boy. You want to be left in peace, for us to believe you aren't a danger to those in this town and elsewhere, but how can we be sure? How can we trust you?"

My fists clenched as I took a step forward. "Gamble shot my friend."

"I'm guessing he was aiming for you," Bane said.

"He was," I faltered slightly, my fists loosening, "but that doesn't excuse it."

"So your friend jumped in front to save you, got caught in the crossfire. How do we know you didn't glamour him to protect you? That you aren't forcing him to be your retainer?"

"I—"

"How do you know he *is*?" Alec moved up to be parallel with me again. "Or are we throwing out the idea of innocent until proven guilty? You know it only leads to chaos, allowing supposed victims the only say with no burden of proof."

"Sounds rather righteous coming from a monster who might be the guilty party," Bane growled.

"Might be. *Might*. What a concept?" Alec spread his arms wide, his more manic side starting to show, which set the three hunters behind Eli and Bane on edge, twitching with their weapons. "The pact requires proof."

"Yes," Bane nodded, "before a hunter can take a life or before a vampire can take out a hunter. Yet your...charge here, nearly killed our companion—"

"For trying to kill him, if we're being technical," Wendy said. "We're talking in circles. What is it you want, Bane? Here I stand, one of you, clearly not glamoured, defending these people. I have watched them, been with them these many weeks, and can attest to their good natures. So if you aren't here to provide any proof that there is reason to hunt Emery, or William and Mallory Leonard's sire..."

It seemed the other hunters weren't aware of Alec's identity, because Eli and the three with guns on us all flinched. Bane remained steady.

"...then what do you want? Because the senseless violence and attacks disrupting this town must stop."

"I agree," Bane said, and slowly, he began to move forward to meet us. "Eli seems quite certain we have nothing to fear from you. Our man lives, though it will be difficult to remove him from the situation you've left him in, since he is under police guard for attempted murder—"

"And actual murder," Alec said, an edge to his tone when talking about his children.

"For that we did have evidence," Bane said.

"Did you? The vampire woman had another story."

"So Eli said."

"And do you have a response to that?"

Bane stood in front of us, in front of me, while Wendy and Alec flanked me. He looked to each of them before settling his gaze on me. "I'd prefer we ended this here, now, before anymore needless lives are lost. We're at an impasse, Mr. Mavus. We can extract Gamble once he's well enough. We can administer any punishment that might be necessary. And your friend is recovering quite well, I hear. Why don't we leave it at that," he extended his hand toward me, "and call it a night?"

I stared at the offered hand. I knew this man from nothing. I'd only known Eli the few moments we spoke. He seemed decent, eager and hopeful back by the other hunters, nodding for me to accept this olive branch. Gamble could be an outlier. Even if Bane had been in on the plot, maybe he was ready to cut his losses.

So I reached forward. "Okay. I just want this to be—"

A jolt shot up my arm and tensed every muscle in my body. I couldn't breathe, couldn't move. I could barely shift my eyes to see that as Bane's hand clasped mine, something had shot out from his sleeve and attached itself to my wrist, sparking with electricity as it dug into my skin.

I heard gunfire and saw both Wendy and Alec drop. My heart seized from more than the shocks running through me, but it hadn't been normal bullets or wooden ones. They were both shaking on the ground, arcs of blue lightning dancing over them.

"Uncle, what are you doing?!" Eli called.

"Electricity is a wonderful thing, Mr. Mavus," Bane said to me. "You can take something bigger than you, stronger, faster, more powerful in every sense, but affect their nervous system and they still drop. This isn't over, boy, not yet. I still have use for you."

He ripped his hand away from mine but the clamp around my wrist remained, shooting electricity through me so I couldn't move. I couldn't hold myself up either, so once Bane released me, I dropped, spasming on the ground beside Wendy and Alec, and feeling the fight drain from my body.

I thought I heard Eli still arguing, still calling out, trying to understand, not having been part of this trap, but he was just one man. The others followed Bane, all reason or evidence aside, and we'd walked right into their hands.

I thought of Connor as the world around me dimmed, hoping he didn't do anything stupid when he didn't hear from me, and get himself caught up in this too.

～

Connor

Connor checked his phone again. Fifteen minutes late. It was 11:15 and still no word from Emery like he's promised to check in every half hour. Connor had promised his parents he would only stay up until midnight, giving him a few more checks from Emery to sooth his mind before sleep. But Emery had only checked in once, already out of communication.

It was possible their meeting with the hunters was going long, and Emery didn't want to be rude by sending a text in the middle of discussions, but how long did it take to say no, I'm not a killer, please stop trying to murder me and my friends?

Connor clutched his phone tighter and dropped his head back onto his pillow. His mother was staying the night there, but had taken on an extra shift to get some work done instead of just fretting all night. His father had gone home, since Connor wasn't in any danger. He actually felt strangely fine, all things considered, even enough to lower his IV meds so he didn't feel as fuzzy. The ache wasn't too bad. He preferred that to having so many drugs in his system that he felt numb. But there was no way he could get out of the hospital on his own.

"Psst, hey, Con-Man, you alive?"

Aurora pushed open his door, sneaking inside the room, still decked out in her Prom dress, though her hair had lost a bit of its curl from hours of dancing and revelry. Jules came in behind her, in much the same state, following by Nick and Michael, neither of whom had their dates accompanying them. Michael had a crown on his head—of course.

"What are you guys doing here?" Connor hissed.

"I told Mavus I'd be stopping by," Aurora said. Only the dart of her eyes around the room, at his prosthetic on the table, the machines attached to him, displayed some level of discomfort.

"I didn't think you'd actually be able to pull it off. How'd you get them to let you in? It's nowhere near visiting hours and none of you are family."

Michael stepped forward. His suit was burnt orange with gold, the jacket buttoning more on one side with three clasps that looked like the heads of comets. "Meagan was the tail," he said, catching Connor's once-over of his outfit and gesturing down his legs to indicate the skirt Meagan had likely worn. "And we got in because I can be very persuasive. Do you know how many nurses I had swooning over me when I was here for my leg?"

"I can only imagine," Connor droned.

Nick had gone more Jules's god route and looked like Poseidon, not in a traditional suit but with a long vest that reached his ankles in various water themed shades of blue. Connor had seen the trident he planned to use as an accessory earlier in the week, which had probably been left in the car.

"No JJ?" Connor said to him, then turned to Michael. "Or Meagan? You ditched your dates for me?"

"They wanted to hit the after party," Nick shrugged. "It's at JJ's house anyway. We'll meet up later. Were you seriously shot with a crossbow by the murderer?"

Connor gestured down at his bandaged midsection, the covers of the hospital bed down by his waist. "Something like that. What about Tim?"

"He gave us a free pass to stop and see you as long as we head straight for the after party once they kick us out," Jules said. "He's got everyone patrolling for the cars that distracted Officer Nustad."

"They won't find them. And if they do, the hunters won't be with them anymore."

"Hunters?" Nick questioned.

Aurora and Jules exchanged a glance.

Connor looked around the room at his friends, Michael and Aurora on one side, Jules and Nick on the other. He couldn't get out of the hospital without help, but with four extra bodies, who'd already managed to get into the hospital and ditch their police guard...

He snatched up his phone from the bed. Nothing. Still no new messages. Emery was in trouble, and Connor's only hope of helping him were the people in this room.

"What if you didn't go to the after party?" he asked, gipping the IV and ripping it free from the catheter in his arm. Then came the catheter itself. That stung a little more.

"What are you doing?" Aurora dashed closer to the bed.

"Em's in trouble. The only people who could have given him backup were with him, and it wasn't enough. I haven't heard from him in twenty minutes. The only chance he's got is us." Thankfully, they'd already removed the heart monitor since he was stable. Connor tossed the covers aside and cringed as he sat up, shifting his legs over the side of the bed.

"Whoa, Connor." Michael moved forward as if to stop him, nearly pressed against Aurora's back. Her cheeks colored and she fought to keep her eyes facing forward. She definitely hadn't danced with him during Prom, or taken advantage of him tagging along for this visit. "You were impaled. And what are you talking about? What's going on with Mavus? They caught the killer. Right?"

Connor looked back at Jules and Nick, Jules' eyes wide with an almost imperceptible shake of her head, but Connor didn't have a choice. "They caught one of them," he said, "but Em went to meet with the others. And if we're going to save him then I have to tell you two what Jules and Aurora already know. And then you're going to bring me to my house to load up."

"Load up with what?" Michael asked, taking Connor's good arm as Aurora took the other, and helped him down from the bed. He ached, especially with the IV no longer pumping drugs into him, but he could manage, as long as he took it slow.

"Guns. Weapons," he said to Michael steadily. "Tonight, boys and girls, we're dealing with vampire hunters."

EPISODE 35

Connor

Helping Connor into his button down, shoes, and prosthetic should have been the easy part, but sneaking out of the hospital didn't prove a challenge either. Connor spotted his mom down the hallway, but she continued on down another corridor. She'd be back to check on him eventually. This wasn't a situation where Connor could get back into his hospital bed with no one having been aware. They'd get caught. They'd get in trouble. They just had to hope it was after they saved Emery's life, assuming the hunters hadn't killed them on the spot.

Connor refused to believe that was the case.

They snuck past the reception desk in full view. Connor mixed in with the others, but just chatting, and walking, with Michael thanking the woman at the desk for letting them say a brief hello to their friend, and the nurse barely even looked up to acknowledge them. Gamble and his police watchdog were in another wing. They were outside and in Jules' Charger in a matter of minutes.

Nick was unsurprisingly silent during the ride, but Michael couldn't stop saying things like, "Mavus is a vampire? A vampire?! And we're going after vampire hunters? With guns?"

"Just go with the flow, Fergus," Connor said when they pulled into his driveway.

"How are you all handling this so calmly?"

Jules shrugged from the front seat. "It's surprisingly less earth-shattering than you'd think. I actually totally forget Mavus is a vampire half the time."

"So he can't do anything cool?" Nick asked.

"Oh, he can do plenty of cool," Connor said, "but he's still Em. Come on."

The street was quiet. Connor just had to hope his father was in bed.

He wasn't. The TV being on alerted him of that as soon as he slipped in through the backyard sliding glass door with the others, but when no other sounds gave away that they'd been detected, Connor tiptoed into the living room and found his father passed out on the couch. He was a deep sleeper, and they only needed a couple minutes.

Connor gestured them into the guest room, where they kept the gun cabinet. Connor had a key for it on his keychain and unlocked it without hesitation. There weren't enough guns for everyone, but he didn't expect most of them to try target practice for the first time on a bunch of living breathing human beings.

He claimed his mom's .22 rifle and handed Aurora the 9mm. She nodded, looking far more poised than she had with Michael Fergus leaning against her back. Connor reached down to grab extra bullets, but when the motion caused him to wince and worry about pulling his internal and external stitches, Aurora grabbed the bullets for him, and he stuffed them into his pockets.

"Your parents gave you a key to their gun cabinet?" Michael asked incredulously.

Connor didn't even turn to him as he worked on loading the rifle, and Aurora did the same with the 9mm. "I'm 18, and not stupid."

"But you are stealing guns out of the cabinet right now," Nick pointed out.

"That is true," Connor admitted, "I also know how to safely handle one and am doing so because someone is threatening my best friend's life. Want me to put them back?" He looked at Nick and Michael pointedly.

"No," Michael said.

Nick shook his head.

"Good."

"But what are you going to do?" Jules asked.

They had guns, bullets, and as Connor watched Aurora, he gaped a moment at how she unhooked her flowing skirt, revealing shorts underneath with a shrug. Jules didn't have that luxury, but they'd manage.

"Aurora and I don't have competitions over who can hit the bullseye the most times for nothing," Connor said. "The point will be to NOT hit anyone, unless we have no other choice, but if we can distract them, give Em and the others a chance to get away, anything, then we have to try."

"You're assuming the hunters are still at the place they told Mavus to meet him," Nick said. "What if they're not?"

What if they had already killed Emery and headed out of town, he meant, but didn't want to say it. But no, not with how much Tim had his officers scouring the town and blocking the ways in and out. Getting out of town with bodies wasn't an option. The hunters had to lie low, somewhere no one would look for them, and the patch of woods down from the middle school was just out of sightlines, not near any major roadways, with the perfect amount of space to keep prisoners. Or bodies. Or to bury bodies…

But no. *No*. Connor still had a chance to save Emery.

"What about us?" Michael asked when they turned to leave the guest room. "I'm not saying I want a gun. None of us have the skills you two do, but then what? Won't we get in the way?"

"You want to leave?" Connor asked.

"No," Michael said firmly, "but I don't want to be the reason something goes wrong either. I'm fine with playing distraction, keeping lookout, just being extra bodies to help however we can, but what can we use to defend ourselves?"

Jules offered a thoughtful grin and gestured them all back out to the Charger. Connor's dad never once stirred, and when they reached the car in the driveway, Jules popped open the trunk to reveal a collection of old baseball bats, and the wooden axe from the spring play.

"I may have claimed this baby as my own," she said, touching her fingers to the silver and red painted prop. "Senior's prerogative. So this is mine. But when we get there, boys, the bats are all yours."

Connor and Aurora carefully stowed their guns in the trunk with the rest. Michael threw his crown in there as well. They were silent as they drove toward the middle school, waiting at any moment for one of Tim's patrols to appear and stop them.

When they reached their destination without incident, Connor only felt more nervous, but he pushed all hesitation aside and had Jules park at the front of the school so they could move around to the back on foot and hopefully take the hunters by surprise. Every footfall reminded Connor that he was far from 100%, and a single wrong twist of his midsection could put him in serious peril again, but nothing was keeping him from saving Emery.

~

My body ached from the shockwaves of the device Bane had used to subdue me. If I was coming to, I should have felt better than this, healed, restored. Then I stretched my arms forward and saw that the wrist cuff remained, sparking with little shocks of blue lightning. A course of electricity still ran through me, making it difficult to do anything more than sit up. I cringed, and reached with the other hand for the cuff on my right.

"Try to take it off and you'll be hit with a worst blast than the one that first knocked you out," Bane said, stepping into view only a yard in front of me.

As my vision finished clearing, I took in my surroundings. We were still in the copse of trees behind the middle school, more hidden and tucked away than out in the dip of the field down the hill, but still within view of the buildings. Alec sat in the grass beside me, also conscious and wearing a similar cuff on his wrist that sparked and made him grit his teeth. He nodded to me, then over at Wendy tied up on the ground surrounded by the other three hunters. Eli was tied up with her.

"I assume this is an easy situation to understand," Bane said. "Try anything, and I'll shock you. And don't think you can use your typical speed in your current condition. At the moment, I assure you, I am faster." He held a device in his hand, like a remote.

Eli called out, "This is insanity, Uncle! You have no evidence to suggest they've done anything but protect themselves! Please, Prosser, Mitchell, Gatch," he looked at his fellow hunters above him. "You believe in the pact. I know you do. You can't side with him just because he's the one leading, just because you've trusted him in the past as someone who uses his authority with honor. This? There is nothing honorable about holding either of these vampires captive."

All three of the other hunters shifted on their feet, furrowed brows or frowns making it clear that they questioned Bane's motivations. They could be swayed. But I'd learned only too recently in school how easy it can be to follow along with what someone in a position of power tells you to do.

"So why don't I clear things up?" Bane said, turning back to face the hunters, while keeping his stance squared with us still visible in his periphery. He looked back at me. "I'm sure you're curious. I'm sure there is a very specific question rolling around in your head, Mr. Mavus. Care to share it?"

There was one question, the only question left to ask. "Why haven't you killed us yet?"

Bane grinned and backed up a step to gesture grandly at Alec for the other hunters to see. "Because we can't seem to figure out just exactly who you are. Alec, is it? *Alec*. But who are you really?"

"You killed my children," Alec said through grinding teeth, one knee up with the arm without the wrist cuff resting on it, as if he were ready to spring to his feet at any moment, "and you have repeatedly threatened a child of theirs. Your people are the reason Emery's good friend, an innocent bystander, is in hospital. Isn't all of that enough to tell you who I am and why I am on his side?"

"You think I'm so blind," Bane sneered, oldest amongst everyone around us, but the age in Alec's eyes was showing, the coldness that still tripped me up sometimes. "I know who you are. Alec? Just Alec, sire to the Leonards and patriarch to young Mavus? Please. I'm sure you've had more names than I can count. Maybe even something like…Judas? Or Cain?"

The hunters with Wendy and Eli all stood up straighter, held their weapons tighter. Eli's eyes widened and his mouth fell slack. Wendy alone remained unmoved. Her wrists were bound behind her, tied to Eli's, hidden from view.

Alec, for his part, merely smiled, but it was sinister and dark, with no light reaching his eyes. "Now you're just flattering me."

Bane huffed and stalked closer to Alec, but held back just out of arm's reach. "I don't care which legends are true, but one thing I do know is that you are him. You are the king. The beginning of all the rest. Even with six of us against one, catching the wife alone, she put up an incredible fight, the kind of power you don't see in vampires so young, only a few hundred years old. The husband was the same. A fighter, powerful, the kind of power that could only come from a direct line to the source."

I heard what Bane said, but it didn't compute. The source? The source of all vampires? The king who had struck the bargain with hunters in the first place? That was Alec? He'd be the oldest, most powerful thing on the planet.

I looked again at Wendy, and realized she'd known all along.

"You've never created other children. Not since the beginning. And all of those initial children who spread the disease—"

"Who stole their power, it was not granted to them," Alec spat.

"That's one version," Bane said. "Either way, all those children are long dead, but their creations continue to plague the world, for thousands upon thousands of years. Maybe longer. There's no way to know for how long, how old you really are, which tales are true, which historical figures you've been. How you've shaped history."

"You flatter me again," Alec said. "I merely live to live. My hands have been in nothing but the quest for a peaceful existence and the lives of my children. Children, I'll remind you, that you killed without provoca—" He cringed and fell back to the ground after making to stand, stronger electricity shooting up his arm.

"You're the reason for every death any of your children, direct or otherwise, ever caused," Bane said, using his device once more until Alec growled and nearly fell back prone. "That's provocation enough. No matter how you want to look at it, my sister and countless others are dead because you exist."

"The king…" Eli said, shaking his head as if to dismiss that this was true. I didn't know if I felt safer knowing this, or betrayed that he hadn't told me.

"Do you understand now, Eli," Bane said, "why the ruse was worth it?"

"So you admit, freely and under your own will," Wendy spoke up, "that this was all a ruse? That you had no evidence of William or Mallory Leonard defying the pact, or of Emery having committed any crimes? You killed them and planned to kill Emery initially just because you wanted to. You continued in the charade, knowing you were in the wrong, once you realized you had a chance to catch the king. The very man who created the pact you swore to uphold."

"Man," Bane sneered, jabbing a finger back toward Wendy. "You are a fool if you think he is anything other than a monster. That any of them are!"

"Is this really the man you want to follow?" Wendy ignored him and looked up at her jailers, who as shocked as they seemed to be to discover the vampire king in their midst, looked wary of carrying through with orders from an authority they were no longer sure they trusted.

"Enough talk!" Bane shouted at her.

Eli looked distant as he leaned against her back, the other hunters faltering, unsure, but not willing to act in our favor either.

Bane turned back to Alec. "If we kill you…they'll all know. Every vampire would feel it. Some believe your death would cause them all to die, but if that's only another myth, and instead they're alerted to your demise, they'll all come after us, and we won't be able to hide."

"Fascinating that you think you can hide now," Alec said. That icy tone was low and controlled. He didn't seem afraid, even though Bane had the upper hand, but I knew he was angry.

It was just like my dad, the way anger, even though he rarely showed it or had reason to explode, would build at the corners of his eyes. Alec just needed a reason, a chance to act. What he might do, could do, likely would do to Bane played out in my imagination like a swath of carnage.

"Better we kill Mavus, and keep you around," Bane said, using his device again when Alec jerked at the mention of harming me. "Yes...we could keep you alive just enough that no supernatural shockwaves would filter to the others. They'd never know. Not until we kill them all too."

Finally, Alec fell back, the electricity shocking him again and again as Bane continued to use it on him. I growled before I realized I was poised to jump to his defense, and Bane switched the frequency to me. It hurt as much as it had the first time, and I couldn't move to do anything about it. I gasped when he released me.

"I've heard tales...that you could be burnt to a crisp and rise from the ashes." Bane stood over Alec, who blinked as if barely conscious. "Beheaded and still laugh at those who lopped it from your shoulders. Even staked you could potentially come back. But I don't need you dead. I don't want you dead."

He pulled a wooden stake from his jacket. He didn't hold it over Alec. He took two steps closer to me and yanked me up from the ground, holding me against his back with the stake pressed to my chest while we stood facing Alec on the ground. The consistent shocks made every move I attempted feel sluggish. All my heightened strength had fled me.

The look in Alec's eyes as he sat up again made me shiver, even though he wasn't looking at me, but past me, at Bane.

"I'll let you live until the last of your precious children are wiped from the earth," Bane swore to Alec, "and then...if one of the ways we usually kill you monsters isn't enough, we'll try them all, over and over again until—"

The crack of a rifle shattered the stillness of the trees around us, one particular tree, just behind the gathering of hunters, exploding out from the center of its trunk as the shot hit home.

All three of the hunters with Wendy and Eli turned at the sound, one of the women immediately backpedaling away and training her gun on their surroundings. But the other two didn't react fast enough. The shot was all Wendy and Eli needed to reveal that they had been slowly working themselves out of their bonds.

Together, they leapt from the ground, each of them taking down a hunter and wrestling their weapon away. Wendy succeeded in moments and had her hunter on the ground. Eli struggled enough with his that the hunter who had backpedaled returned and aimed her gun at his back.

Another rifle shot fired, hitting a different tree, and sent everything into a new surge of chaos as Bane threw me to the ground and whirled around to discover just who it was that had started attacking them.

I already knew. And it thrilled as much as terrified me. I just hoped Connor knew what he was doing.

EPISODE 36

Connor

Connor had ten rounds before he'd need to reload. He had enough extra rounds in his pockets, but hoped he didn't fire so much that it came to that. So far he'd fired twice, all exactly where he intended, with mostly the intended results. He had eight shots left. He resisted the urge to aim the next one at Bane's head.

"We need to distract them," he heard Aurora hiss over his cell phone. She'd hooked them all into a conference call before they left the Charger.

"I'll go right," Jules said, "make as much noise as I can to get the far hunter to come after me. Nick, cover Wendy."

"Cover how—"

"Just stay in the trees behind her and watch in case you need to tackle the hunter she downed. He might try to go for his gun again, or another weapon. Michael, stay with Aurora so she can get a clear shot around Bane from the other side. That way they won't be able to pinpoint where Connor's shots are coming from."

"Okay," Michael said, his voice wavering only slightly.

Aurora might be empress of backstage, but Jules knew strategy. Hours upon hours of running raids in MMO RPGs had its advantages.

Connor stayed where he was, the most hidden location possible with a tree for cover and a bush blending him into the scenery on his left. He could see everyone in play from his position, except for his friends hiding in the trees, making a perimeter around the hunters.

A loud pattering noise came from the right. The hunter who had been going to rescue her comrades on the ground turned instead toward the nearby trees. Once she reached them, the silver and red of the prop axe flew into view, and the next thing Connor saw was the hunter on the ground, dazed. Jules snatched up the woman's gun and hid back behind the trees.

Wendy had the gun she'd taken from one hunter, while Eli mirrored her, aiming the gun he'd taken at the last of the three, leaving only Bane, armed with a stake and the device he'd been using to send shocks through Emery and Alec.

"You continue to defy me?" Bane roared at Eli.

"Yes, because this is wrong, Uncle."

"Even knowing who he is?" Bane pointed at Alec.

"Especially knowing that."

Alec, looking barely conscious, tilted his head at the hunter who had switched sides for them.

Bane snarled and pointed the device in his hand at Alec, who arched in pain off the ground, then at Emery, who cried out. Connor made an abortive jerk forward, his stomach muscles clenching as he flinched, but held back, sending ripples of pain up his chest where he was still healing, and really, really should be in a bed right now with more high quality drugs pumping through his system.

He fired again, the bullet zipping past Bane's ear into the distant trees.

Bane glared his direction. "You think I can't tell where you're coming from? If I know where you are then you have very few bargaining chips, while I—" He raised the device again, but cut off as a bullet lodged into the tree behind him, coming from Aurora. He whirled around, unsure how to keep the new shooter, where he believed Connor to be, and Wendy and Eli in his sights all at once.

The hunter Jules had downed was shaking her head as she crawled to her feet, looking over the ground for her lost weapon. When she couldn't find it, she stood slowly, raising her hands in appeal to Wendy and Eli, who still had guns trained on the others.

"You better be willing to kill me," Bane said, eyes darting everywhere around him that presented danger. He pressed the device again, keeping Emery's body seizing as he snatched him from the ground, the device and stake clumsily held in his hands until he had a hold of Emery like before.

Connor didn't dare take a shot with Emery in Bane's arms. Emery could survive a bullet, but how injured was he with those shocks ripping through him? Aurora didn't risk it either. Wendy and Eli stood at a standstill with the hunters, though none of them looked ready to leap to Bane's aid.

"Connor, if you get a shot, take it," Jules whispered over the phones. "I'll make sure the chick by me stays out of it. Nick, move around so you can grab the device Bane's carrying if he drops it. Aurora, back up anyone who needs it."

"Wait, where did Alec go?" Aurora asked.

That was a stupid question, Alec was right—

Connor gaped. He'd been so focused on Bane and Emery, he hadn't been paying attention, but right there on the ground where Alec should have been was just the wrist cuff, sparking all on its own in the grass.

"Do you think either of them would show mercy if—" Bane grandstanded, but cut off abruptly when he saw the empty space on the ground. "How…?"

The air was tense, charged like the electric current running through Emery, as the small clearing within the trees stilled, everything quiet, and Connor gasped in a breath. He had a shot. Bane stood still facing just where he needed him, too shocked at finding Alec gone to react fast enough. Connor slid his finger onto the trigger.

"*Now,*" a voice whispered near him, and he fired, spurred on by the sound.

Connor jerked his head behind him, expecting to see Alec, but there was only a rustle of the bushes. When he looked back, he saw Bane on the ground, having released Emery and the stake and device, as he gripped his calf where Connor had shot clean through. He'd have aimed higher for his thigh—or his head—but then he'd just be like Bane and Gamble, and both Connor and Emery were better than that.

Jules revealed herself from behind her tree and tripped the female hunter back to the ground, gun tucked into her belt as she held the heavy wooden axe over the hunter in warning. Aurora and Michael came out of hiding on the other side, Aurora keeping her gun on Bane, while Michael stood by imposingly with one of Jules' baseball bats, looking to each of the hunters as if daring them to make a move.

Just as swiftly, Nick appeared from the trees to kick the stake away from Bane and pluck the device from the ground. He found the off switch immediately, and Emery sagged to his knees in relief when the last of blue sparks faded from traveling over his body.

Connor was the last to step into the clearing, since he'd been poised the furthest back. He held his rifle pointed at the ground, since Aurora had Bane covered.

Bane didn't seem surprised that they were all teenagers. He was from a family of hunters; well-armed teens was likely old hat for him. But he sneered up at Connor as he laid out on the ground defenseless.

"You missed," he growled.

"Take that from the super-villain handbook?" Connor said, sharing a smile with Emery as he climbed to his feet. "Try this response then," he turned back to Bane. "I didn't."

Aurora and Michael moved to help surround Bane, while Wendy, Eli, and Jules ushered the remaining hunters together to keep a better collective eye on them.

It was when they were all together, clearly the victors, with Emery recovered now as he tore the cuff from his wrist, that Alec appeared, clapping.

"Well done, children. Truly inspired. I didn't even break a sweat."

Connor wasn't sure if he was impressed or annoyed, which pretty much summed up his general feelings toward Alec.

Bane rested his head on the ground as Alec approached him. "You could have gotten away at any time."

"Indeed," Alec said. "But where would the fun have been in that?"

"The shocks didn't affect you?" Emery gaped at him.

"Oh, they smarted just fine, dear boy, but not enough to incapacitate my level of power." He grinned his manic grin, but it soon dropped, and that familiar sadness that proved his age showed through—an age Connor now knew was much higher than he'd ever guessed. "My sincerest apologies for the pain you had to endure tonight, Emery. Had it been necessary, I would have stepped in, but you see, I had faith that we would not be fighting alone tonight. I didn't realize quite so many would come to our aid," he gestured at Michael and raised an eyebrow at Nick, who shrugged back at him, "but all the better. If I'd intervened sooner, you see, this man would no longer have his head." He looked down on Bane coldly. "I didn't think you wanted tonight's events to end that way, Emery."

Connor shivered just from the chill in Alec's gaze. Bane stared up at him with equal hatred.

"Besides, you hardly needed my assistance," Alec brightened, slapping his hands together once more as he looked around at everyone involved in the rescue and finally rested his gaze on Connor.

"You're really the king?" Connor asked. They'd arrived just in time to hear that reveal, if it was true. "Just how old are you?"

"Now, Connor," Alec pointed a playfully accusing finger in Connor's face, "what did we say about asking a lady his age?"

Connor snorted.

"Wow," Emery said, "I can't believe it. Any of this. You're…" he pointed, flabbergasted at Alec, "and you guys…" he looked around at his friends, "I don't know what to say." He finally settled on, "Thank you."

"Now you know why your bloodline is so powerful, Emery," Alec said, placing a solid hand on Emery's shoulder. "So, as my successor, should such a time ever arise that I am…gone, the role of leader, as the closest to the source, would fall to you. So I ask you now," he glanced down at Bane then turned his attention to the three hunters held in place by Wendy, Eli, and Jules with her axe, "what should we do with these hunters?"

～

Me? The weight of Alec's hand on my shoulder felt ten times heavier as I looked at Bane's followers. Eli had sided with us, but what about them? They hadn't been given much chance to hear our argument, but I could tell they had doubts. None of them looked at us—at me and Alec, or the humans on our side—with disdain the way Bane did, only curiosity, and maybe disbelief.

I still couldn't believe Jules had downed one of the hunters with a prop axe. But then, yes, I could, just as much as it didn't surprise me to see Aurora pointing a 9mm at Bane on the ground, her aim never wavering.

I looked back at the group of hunters. "Who of you actually buys his bullshit?" I gestured down at Bane. "If we really were like he thinks, we could kill all of you. Glamour my friends. But that's not who we are. Mr. and Mrs. Leonard weren't like that either. You heard the truth. Bane wants to kill people like me without discrimination. He wants Alec for some twisted plan to wipe us all out. But I'm still just me. I'm no different than I was before this happened to me, and suddenly I was under attack. By you.

"Wendy told me about the pact. It's supposed to mean something, right? That you want to help people, to protect them, not hunt down someone who never meant harm to anyone. Alec clearly doesn't have to play nice here—whoever he really is or was in the past."

I had to eye him because I didn't know if Alec was even his real name. Probably not. Bane had dropped names like Judas and Cain. I'm sure Connor would add Dracula or Vlad to his repertoire of *Fright Night* and *Nosferatu* after this. But right now that didn't matter, because Alec was just Alec too.

"So tell me," I said, "if you really believe like he does, or if you're ready to follow Eli instead."

Eli straightened when I mentioned his name. He wasn't the oldest among the other hunters, and I didn't know if his lineage carried any weight to hunter hierarchy, but I could tell he'd be a good leader. He'd gone out of his way to discover the truth, and against all odds, against family and friends, he'd defended us just to defend what was right.

The hunters looked around at each other, each nodding, their faces mostly impassive but resolute. The oldest after Bane, the one Eli had taken down, nodded at me. "We'll uphold the pact," she said.

I sighed before I realized I'd been holding my breath. I didn't know what we would have done with them if they'd said otherwise. I still didn't know what to do with Bane. Turn him over to Tim and the police?

Just as I thought that and looked back at Bane on the ground, I realized that too many eyes had drifted from him to watch the hunters' reactions. Even Aurora was distracted enough that she wasn't ready when Bane slid a knife from a holster on his leg and jammed it into Michael's calf.

Bane leapt up to run, and all of us stepped back from the flurry of movement, assessing how to react. I feared Aurora might fire without thinking, feared Alec might attack, but in the end, neither of them had to do anything.

Connor stepped in Bane's path, dropped his rifle, and aimed with his prosthetic instead. He brought his middle and ring fingers into his palm, otherwise pointing palm outward, and his entire hand dropped down at the wrist with a burst of white foam and smoke striking Bane right in the face. Bane stuttered back and, not even a full foot from where he'd started, Michael tackled him to the ground in true captain of the football team fashion.

"Freeze, asshole," Connor grinned, unable to resist a pun when channeling Captain Cold. I could tell by the way he stared at his arm afterward that he was overjoyed the mechanics had worked out as planned.

"Nice try and all," Michael added, keeping Bane pinned as he sat up with his knees in the man's back and yanked the knife from his leg with one hand while the other kept Bane's arms crossed, "but you got the wrong leg." He knocked on it to the hollow sound of plastic. When Connor stepped up to him, they high-fived—albeit gently, I noticed.

"I suppose this brings us to our next problem," Alec said, all of us, the other hunters included forming a tight circle around Bane, no longer with guns or weapons pointed at anyone. "What of him, Emery?"

Even though Alec had already asked me about the hunters, the question made my breath catch. It shouldn't be my decision. It was Alec's children who'd been killed first. And Eli was Bane's family. The authority shouldn't fall to me.

I looked to Connor. He'd had a clear shot, several clear shots to take Bane out for good. Instead, he'd shot him in the leg, even though he'd been attacked by these people and nearly killed himself. I looked to Wendy and thought of what she'd said when I was looking in on Connor still recovering from surgery.

Then I looked to Alec. "We're vampires. That doesn't make us monsters. Only choice can do that. We don't have to be killers."

Alec smiled, and it wasn't his manic grin. It carried all the age and experience his sadder and darker expressions did, like he was proud of me. "Then we won't be," he said. His expression dropped to neutral as he passed his gaze to Eli. "May I release him into your custody, Eli, and trust that you and your fellows will keep him out of trouble. Rehabilitate him, perhaps. Or enact your own form of judgment for how he and his lapdog in the hospital deceived you. Speaking of…"

"Someone needs to pay—legally—for what happened to the Leonards," Eli said, looking around at his companions. "Unless anyone has any objections, Gamble stays where he is. I'm sure enough evidence can be brought out to close this case. With attempted murder on top of it," he gestured to Connor.

None of the other hunters dissented.

Alec looked Eli over with an appraising nod, and a bit of his hysterical smile slipped in. "You have some promise. I'll be in touch," he said with a wink. "And if anyone gives you any trouble, or decides to change their mind about your uncle…"

I blinked, and Alec was gone from his spot, suddenly behind Eli with a phone that definitely wasn't his own in his hand as he punched in a number. He handed it to Eli, who, while startled, accepted back what was obviously *his* phone without comment.

"Call me," Alec said. "The pact only abides if the next generation passes on the rules."

Eli nodded. He and the others gathered up Bane from where he'd been pinned to the ground, bound his hands, though he couldn't get far on his own if he escaped given his current limp, and led him away, disappearing into the trees.

Nick handed Alec the device Bane had been using, which he crushed with an "Oops," and a shrug, then patted Nick on the shoulder.

I looked at him, at Michael, Aurora, and Jules, amazed that my friends had come to my rescue, some of them not even having known I was a vampire until tonight. Yet here they were, having risked their lives. Knowing Alec was more powerful than he'd let on, that he'd lied—or at least kept some of the truth from me—should have upset me more, but it didn't. He'd wanted to teach me something. Teach the hunters something. And keep the pact strong when everything was over.

"I can't thank all of you enough," I said to each of them, finally resting my eyes on Connor, who held his rifle exhaustedly now that the adrenaline was wearing off, and his body started to remind him that he'd been impaled only hours earlier.

He sauntered closer to me, sluggish but alive. My best friend. My boyfriend. My savior, as it turned out, even when I'd told him not to come.

"I can think of one way you can thank me," he said, the crooked smirk on his face only making me want to kiss him more.

So I did.

EPISODE 37

Getting everyone home that night was the easy part. Aurora, Jules, Michael, and Nick were expected to be out late. Getting Connor back to the hospital, however, almost undid everything. Georgia had already discovered he was missing, and had instigated a search throughout the hospital. Luckily, no one had called out of the hospital yet, not even to alert Paul.

Alec worked his way through everyone, glamouring each one to believe that Connor was safe and sound in bed, while I made sure that was true. I kissed him again before leaving the room, but promised to visit until they sent him home.

"Might even be tomorrow," he said, "unless I pulled some staples or something." He cringed a little as he settled into the bed.

I folded his clothes up the way they'd been—the ruined shirt he'd put back on while coming to save the day with guns that Alec, Wendy, and I still needed to get back to the Daniels' cabinet. Then I set his prosthetic carefully on top.

"You finally got your gun arm," I said.

"Worked like a charm."

"Way cooler than just a Rocket-Punch."

"Totally. It sucks we missed Prom though...*Flash.*" He clung to my fingers before I walked away.

"Next time, *Cold*," I said. "We'll make up for it."

~

Connor

Connor's first day fully back at school was tough, even though he spent most of the week immediately after their harrowing adventures in the hospital and then laid up at home. He hadn't torn any staples, but he hadn't helped the healing process by sneaking out to play vigilante the first night of his recovery either. Wendy offered to feed Emery until Connor was well enough, which he tried not to be jealous over.

They only had a couple weeks left of school before graduation—God willing, and assuming no more bomb threats were called in. Although the actual shootout at the school seemed to have put a stop to whatever freshman had been writing them in the girls' bathroom. There were rumors that the culprit had confessed after seeing what all her troublemaking had amounted to, with real students almost getting hurt by a crazed gunman using the evacuation for cover, but of course, no one knew her identity for the girl's own safety. There were a lot of very angry seniors since it turned out to have been a prank, having threatened to lengthen their final school year.

Connor didn't hold a grudge though, since nothing had come of it in the end, but he still had a good idea for their senior prank as an homage to the year's shenanigans. He'd have to tell Michael about it.

He caught sight of the living Ken doll just outside the school as he was about to pull out of the parking lot that day, with Aurora in his passenger seat and Emery in the back—Aurora had insisted she ride shotgun, as she often did.

"I'm just going to swing by the front to tell Michael something," he said, pulling around to do a full loop of the parking lot before leaving. As he approached Michael at the curb, who was distracted, texting someone on his phone, Connor rolled Aurora's window down so he could call out, only for her to beat him to it.

"Michael!"

Michael looked up. Grinned. "Hey, Frank. What's—"

"I love you," Aurora blurted, causing Connor to gape at the back of her head. "I've been in love with you since middle school. Your green eyes are gorgeous. When you lost your leg, I cried for a week. When Connor started making you new ones, I cried for another week. You're perfect, and wonderful, and it would make my entire remaining high school days worth every insanity, including the one we lived through last weekend, if I could have one date with you before we graduate."

Through the entire tirade, Michael never lost his smile. He held up his cell phone. "You got my number, right? Call me later?"

Aurora nodded, more like bobbed her head several times, then shot out her left hand to smack Connor's thigh as she hastily rolled up her window. "Oh my God, drive away now," she hissed at him.

Connor obeyed. "Um, I'm the one who had something to tell him first."

"You can tell him later! Unless you were about to pour *your* idiotic heart out in similar fashion. Oh my God…"

"That was glorious," Emery chimed in.

Aurora groaned, slouching down in her seat as Connor drove away, Michael waving at them as they went, his charming smile beaming after them pleasantly. "I need to figure out some way to disappear into this seat cushion."

"You need to figure out some way to call him later, is what."

"Oh God, I don't have his number!" She sat up straight again.

"I have it, relax," Connor said.

"Seriously, that was the most amazing thing I've ever seen."

"Shut up, Mavus."

She did manage to call him, which Connor heard all about the next morning. They apparently had a date for that coming Saturday, though she wouldn't go into details no matter how much Connor bugged her. It was also that night when Wendy finally showed up at Emery's house to say goodbye.

"What about Alec?" Emery asked, letting her into the living room, since his parents were still both at work. Connor had gone home with him after school.

"I've informed him I'm moving on," she said, dressed in all leather like they had seen her when they first met, ready to head out on her bike. "He's still sorting through things at the house, since he didn't actually have much time to take care of that before now, being otherwise occupied. I stayed this past week to be certain the other hunters moved on, and that Gamble was safely in custody. He woke up, you know."

"Yeah…" Emery's eyes drifted to the floor.

Connor scooted a step closer to him and bumped his hand gently before lacing their fingers together. Emery squeezed back gratefully.

"Once he's released, he'll go through the system, tried and convicted for the Leonards' murders. It's not full justice, I realize, but sometimes that area gets a bit grey in our line of work. You did the right thing with Bane, in the end, and Eli."

"I hope so," Emery said. "Thank you so much for everything. We really couldn't have survived this without you and Alec here to help."

"Mostly you," Connor put in. "Alec's a bit of a chump."

Emery elbowed him, but Wendy laughed.

"It has been my great honor to meet you both. And don't worry. I'm sure I'll pass through this town again. Or to the Twin Cities perhaps. You're off to university next year, aren't you? Do good things. You'll have a long time to make a difference in the world, love," she said to Emery, mostly, but then included Connor as well when her eyes passed to him. "Don't squander it."

"Later, Buffy," Connor said, pulling her in for a hug. Emery did the same.

Then she was gone.

Before they knew it, it was their last free weekend before graduation, the rest of the week having gone by in a normal, almost monotonous blur. Connor had expected to spend Saturday night watching movies over at Emery's with Jules and a few others, since Aurora and Michael had their date, when there was a sudden knock at Emery's door before they could start the second flick.

Aurora and Michael stood there—dressed in their Prom outfits. Connor gaped at them over Emery's shoulder. Each of them carried a zipped garment bag.

"Special delivery!" Aurora called merrily.

"Time to get dressed, gimp," Michael said. "You too, Mavus."

"What—" Emery tried, but cut off when Aurora pushed her garment bag into his arms.

"Yours just required some cleaning. Con-Man took some tender loving care, and a few replacements." She took Michael's bag from him and pushed it into Connor's chest when he stepped around Emery.

They both stared at the offered bags in their arms, then at the pair at the door, hearing giggling from Jules, and suddenly realized why everyone in the living room behind them had brought along larger bags than one would expect to just crash at Emery's place after a movie marathon.

"Well?" Aurora planted her hands on her ships, long brunette hair curled as perfectly as it had been the night of actual Prom. "Go get changed and get back down here so we can show you your surprise!"

Connor expected the neatly pressed Flash themed suit to be in Emery's garment bag, but he never expected to find his, perfect, clean, the tie, vest, and shirt, having to have been bought anew to look that whole and unstained. He was already wearing the snowflake-covered prosthetic. It had quickly become his new favorite.

"Where are you taking us?" Connor asked when they arrived back downstairs to discover the rest of their guests had unsurprisingly changed into their Prom outfits as well.

Jules stepped forward with a bright grin. "Why do you think we suggested watching the movie at your place, Mavus? Come on."

Still confused, Connor and Emery followed the trail of others from the house, Emery's parents looking on from the kitchen, seemingly having been a part of this ruse. They didn't get into any vehicles though. They merely went next door to Connor's, led to the back fence where Aurora swung the gate door open wide, and Michael gestured them in.

Connor and Emery hadn't seen what Prom looked like in the high school gym. They'd never made it. But they'd seen pictures. Streamers and lights in colors of every element in the spectrum. Art projects adorning certain corners that had some sort of elemental theme. Even a poster of the periodic table, because someone had to make that joke.

The poster was taped to Connor's backyard fence. The lights and streamers hung from the overhang of his roof, and all along the fence. Nick, who'd mysteriously opted out of movie night, was in the far corner of the yard with a full-on DJ setup, playing music that burst forth at the moment of Connor and Emery's arrival, a little louder than the neighborhood would usually allow. But Tim was there, in uniform, arms crossed, looking pleased and as if he had all of this under control. Connor's parents were there too, standing in the sliding glass doorway.

And possibly over half of their graduating class. All dressed for Prom. In Connor's backyard.

Everyone erupted into applause and cheers to join the swell of music. Connor gripped Emery's hand so tight, he was thankful his friend was impervious to most pain or injury. This many people from school could not possibly be this awesome all at once. But he and Emery knew everyone, and everyone honestly looked so happy to have them there, to have done this just for them.

A slight squeal of a microphone alerted them to Michael having moved to join Nick at the DJ table. He smiled at them grandly in his comet suit and addressed the crowd as everyone quieted and Nick turned the music down.

"Prom was great this year, right, guys?" he said, and a smattering of fresh cheers rose up. "But! But..." he waved at them to silence again, "...something was missing. A few someones, to be exact, and for senior year, our Senior Prom, well, we just couldn't let that fly. So, here's to you, Connor Daniels and Emery Mavus, who we are all so happy finally got their acts together and hooked up before graduation!"

Another chorus of cheers—and seriously, Connor was going to kill Michael after he hugged the jerk.

"We just wanted to say!" Michael roared above the crowd, pointing at Connor and Emery. "We just wanted to say...that we're glad you're both okay, that everyone is going to be present next week when we finally leave high school behind for good, and in honor of that, we felt you deserved your own Prom to make up for the one you missed. So this first song especially, but the whole night, is all for you guys. Hit it!" he cried, handing the mic back to Nick, who nodded to the music with a passive smile as he turned up the volume and the song switched to a slow ballad.

Everyone cheered one last time before starting to form up into partners, those closest to Connor and Emery gesturing them out toward the center of the yard. Connor's parents slipped back inside with Tim and closed the sliding glass door, though left the impression that they'd be keeping an eye on everything. Aurora grabbed Emery's free hand, which was still attached to Connor, and started pulling the two of them forward to prevent them from simply standing there stunned like a couple of idiots.

Connor still couldn't believe their friends had done this, even as he and Emery were led into the center of it all, experiencing their own personal Prom.

"If I start crying, punch me," Connor said.

Emery laughed a delirious sound like he was halfway to crying too. He pulled Connor close, and slipped his hands around his waist. Connor lifted his hands up around Emery's neck, flesh and plastic alike. They'd never danced before, Connor realized, as they started to sway. Maybe jokingly, at a cast party or some long night playing video games, music turned up loud suddenly to swing dance and spin each other into furniture. But never like this, closely met and feeling the music, with a full crowd of their peers surrounding them.

Connor caught the sight of Aurora's brilliantly colored skirts in his periphery and turned to look as Michael twirled her and then pulled her back in close. They hadn't completely lied about having a date tonight, the traitors. Connor chuckled and snuggled closer into Emery's body.

"Can you believe this will all be over next week?" Emery said.

"All? Just what exactly are you expecting to end next weekend?"

"You know what I mean. High school. Life as we know it. I'm not complaining about the things I expect to stay the same," he said, leaning forward so that their foreheads touched.

Connor sighed into the connection. "So we're going to move forward like we planned, me with engineering, you with business, both at the U, and start a non-profit together?"

"We accepted early enrollment last November, remember? I love that idea. Doing it together *together* doesn't make me love it any less."

"But we can't pretend like some things aren't different."

Emery pulled back, his green eyes almost glowing amidst the multi-colored lights decorating the backyard. "We don't have to make any big decisions now, but I don't expect you to just be there for me to feed on forever. I'd rather be *with you* forever. I don't exactly know how we'd do that…"

"Alec offered."

"He what?" Emery's feet stuttered, nearly tripping them.

"He offered to turn me, if that's what we wanted, someday. If that's what you want."

"What matters is what you want."

"Em…"

"I want you with me, Connor, but only make that decision if it's really what you want too. And don't make it tonight." Emery grinned as he started to sway again. "We might be on a bit of an endorphin high after this. We have time."

"I know." Connor turned his head to lay it against Emery's shoulder. "But you were the first crush I ever had, Em. I'm never going to stop loving you as strongly as I do now. Besides, you'd get lonely without me in a hundred years or so. And bored. Definitely bored."

"Definitely."

Connor lifted his head, and when their eyes met this time, it was easy to lean forward and press their lips together. The difficult decisions ahead of them could come later.

～

I'll admit, Connor's idea for our Senior prank was pretty inspired. When Connor's sister Ryn graduated, each Senior carried a Lego up to the front and placed it as part of a giant Lego creation they built piece by piece before accepting their diplomas.

We carried squares of toilet paper.

"Get it, coz the bomb threats were always in the girls' bathroom?" Connor laughed jovially about it when he explained to me and Michael.

Michael ate the idea right up. Bomb threats, an almost school shooting, they couldn't keep our class down or sour our dispositions. We took it in stride, and the principal had a pile of toilet paper at his feet by the end of our 250 person walk.

Connor graduated as 2nd in our class behind Nick at number 1, and I came up as 10th, which meant we had a special privilege of being honored as the top 10, and given the option to have one of us give the closing remarks at the graduation ceremony. Michael, as Student Council President, gave the opening remarks, but no one in the top 10 wanted to speak. So I volunteered. There were so many things I wanted to say. I didn't want to bring up the bomb threats—Michael jokingly did that, and referenced the toilet paper. I didn't want to talk about the murders, or how Connor had almost been another one. So instead I told everyone to take a step back and remember one thing.

"We're all angels."

A few snickers flitted through the crowd.

"One winged-angels, anyway," I clarified. "Several of my friends out there know I took this concept from a video game, but that just goes to show how important video games are to a solid education."

More laughs.

"You see, every last one of us is a one-winged angel, proving that it is impossible for anyone to fly alone. Imagine how far a person could go in life if they had 200 wings beating together? We have that power, as long as we never forget what we've shared, and never forget each other."

Several people I didn't usual talk much with came up to me afterward to thank me for what I'd said. Liz even hugged me. But Connor was the one person in the crowd I most wanted to rejoin.

It was the next day that Alec called me and Connor out to the Leonards' house. He'd been at graduation to congratulate us, but didn't stick around with so much family business going on. Connor and I assumed he was asking us over to say goodbye.

He met us at the door and ushered us inside with his usual wide grin. He wore jeans and a 'Han Shot First' shirt, but hadn't bothered with his blazer for once. "My home is your home," he said as we entered and started to take off our shoes.

"Is that how a vampire politely asks us to help him with moving boxes?" Connor said.

We laughed, but gaped a moment later when Alec led us into the living room.

Nothing was packed up. Some things that we had helped him pack up—as part of the ruse when he was still helping with the hunters, and a few times since then—had been unpacked and were back in their old locations. There were even a few pieces of new furniture and pieces of knickknacks and art on the walls.

"I've decided to stay."

Connor and I whirled on him. "Seriously?"

Neither of us tried to hide that we weren't upset to hear this.

"Wait. You realize we're not staying, right?" Connor said. "After this summer, we'll be in the Cities at the U."

"And I'm sure it will be a lovely place to visit from time to time when you need me. I rather like the small town charm of this place. I can see what William and Mallory must have first fallen in love with. You parents are all lovely people. And it's extra incentive to be sure you both visit like good little boys on occasion."

"What if they ask after your wife?" Connor asked.

"They'll just have to forget I had one. And then remember again should Wendy come calling for a visit. I certainly hope you both don't mind." He smiled a little more guarded. You wouldn't think the oldest and most powerful being in the world could look anxious from wanting to please two teenagers like a fretting parent. I kind of loved him for it.

"I kept convincing myself not to beg you to stay so I wouldn't seem like I couldn't take care of myself," I said, and then laughed and scratched the back of my neck, "so thanks for helping us avoid any embarrassing groveling."

"It is pretty cool to have the king of all vampires in our back pockets," Connor nodded with an overly appraising look around the house.

Alec crossed his arms and looked down his nose at Connor. "You think so, do you?"

"Please," Connor pushed at Alec's crossed forearms, not even slightly causing him to sway, "you're a teddy bear and you know it, *Fright Night*. Have you ever even killed anyone before?"

The light mood dropped out of the air the second the words left Connor. His eyes widened and his mouth fell open searching for words to fix what he'd said as Alec's expression turned to cool neutral.

"Wow, that…I didn't mean…I am so sorry, that is—"

"Exactly why the pact means so very much to me, Connor," Alec said in a plain voice. "And also why I've decided to stick around. Youth can be highly motivating. Just think of how much you accomplished with so little intervening on my part. William and Mallory would be proud. Of both of you. Although…" His manic grin returned as he moved swiftly away from us toward an empty space on the wall.

The empty space on the wall where Cloak and Dagger used to hang.

"It's a shame this spot remains so empty. But I believe I may have just the thing to fill it." He reached down and plucked a framed photograph from the floor.

As he lifted it to hang it on the nail still protruding from the wall and then stepped back, we saw that it was a picture taken on the night of our personal Prom, of everyone in attendance who had been able to fit, with Connor and me in the center.

Alec stood back to admire it and grinned. "Aurora is such a dear."

"It would have been her," Connor said, though he was smiling too.

"Did you say something about helping with moving boxes?" Alec clapped his hands together suddenly. "Because I actually could use your help with some unpacking upstairs."

Connor groaned.

I laughed.

Alec turned and called after us to follow him up the stairs. I paused a moment, left in the living room with Connor. The fireplace wasn't going; it was too warm for that now, unlike weeks ago when all of this started.

The rug had been replaced. The coffee table. But the sofa and several other things were still the Leonards' possessions. It might have been sad to stand here after everything that had happened, but Alec understood the better response to living in someone's shadow. It just meant that if you turned around, you'd find yourself looking into the light.

"What?" Connor scrunched his brow as I stared at him.

I reached for the back of his neck and pulled him in for a kiss. Maybe someday soon we'd ask Alec to turn him. Maybe we'd wait a while. Whatever we did, we'd do it together.

THE END

AUTHOR'S NOTE

Everything in this book is true.

Well…based off the truth.

Okay, except for the parts about vampires. But everything else, I swear, is based off of something real that happened to me, my friends, or my family during these young impressionable years of middle and high school.

The first scene? My husband did that. The characters' senior spring play? My senior spring play (I played Dottie). Tim, chief of police, living across the street? Totally happened.

Falling slowly in love with your best friend, and fitting together so well once you finally get your acts together, that it feels like you must have been a couple in a past life? Okay, that didn't happen until college, but still—fact.

I hope you enjoyed this fictional but very personal story filled with memories, shenanigans, and some of my favorite things—like playing dress up as Captain Cold and The Flash.

And vampires.

Made in the USA
Monee, IL
16 April 2023